A GHOST OF A CHANCE AT LOVE

TERRY SPEAR

Discover more about Terry Spear at:

http://www.terryspear.com/

ISBN-13: 978-1-63311-049-6

DEDICATION

To Janice Bolick who follows me everywhere from Goodreads to Facebook, always commenting, and always so sweet. I hope you love the book as much as you enjoy time travels!

CHAPTER 1

In the flickering of the lantern's golden flame, a shadowy solitary figure stood across the room, observing the sleeping occupant. The dim light projected through the amber glass cast eerie shape-shifting characters up and down the burgundy rose-papered walls. In the gloomy darkness, the specter reached out to Lisa Welsh, begging for solace, straining to be felt.

The fragrance of roses permeated the dimness, tea-scented, teasing the senses of the unwitting guest. Except for the rustle of sugar-drained leaves dancing against the windows, the room remained deadly quiet.

Suffocated by the heat of the coverlet, Lisa tossed the quilt aside. Quickly chilled, she tugged it back over her shoulders. The darkness threatened to swallow her whole and drag her into the hellish pit of a nightmare again.

Groggy with sleep, she thought about Barry, the image of him, smug, his eyes blue and cold. "I found someone else," he'd said, and it echoed in her mind like a damn broken record. A girl barely out of high school. *The bastard.* At twenty-one, Lisa was already over the hill? She blinked tears back. She *refused* to give him any more space in her brain.

She attempted to think of something pleasant. And then she had it.

A Trojan warrior's fingers pushed the silky gown up her leg—she, being his Trojan princess hostage. His muscular thigh tensed when he pressed his nude body against hers. She ran her hands over his sculpted back, mesmerized by the smoothness of his skin against her fingertips.

In the flutter of an eyelid, the chills resumed, and the darkness returned. A shudder shook Lisa's body.

Murky figures moved closer. "She can't last long." A man's gruff voice made no attempt to quiet his comment in Lisa's presence.

"We can't wait any longer. The sale—"

"I know, I know, the buyers are getting suspicious. In a town this size, the word will soon get out."

"What do you propose to—"

"You know what we have to do. She'll never be missed."

The heat, the chills, the muscles that ached with every twitch of her body...

Lisa squirmed to free herself of the misery pervading her soul. She twisted and rolled onto her back. She gasped for breath—she couldn't breathe.

In a mournful, strangled voice, she cried out.

The goose down-filled pillow covered her face, pressing tightly against her mouth and nostrils. Her arms felt locked in a vise. She attempted to pull them free from the blanket and comforter.

Were the bedcovers pinning her down? Or something more sinister? Fingers? Gripping her arms, bruising the skin?

Her heart beating pell-mell, Lisa broke free from the paralysis and threw the pillow burying her face onto the floor. Cold, she was so cold. And drained of energy. She rolled over, submerging herself under the covers, trying to push out the chill.

Warmth radiated from the other side of the bed, and she gravitated toward it.

Barry. Sighing, she snuggled against his hard, naked body, his heated skin warming her to the core. She listened to the steady thumping of his heart, the rhythmic drumbeat lulling her back to sleep. Until he stirred. His fingers slipped through her hair, tenderly combing the strands. His simple touch made her crave for more. She nuzzled her mouth against his smooth chest, her fingers tracing his pebbled nipple.

He groaned, leaned down, and kissed the top of her head. Her heart lifting, she raised her face toward him, encouraging more of his kisses. Pressing his mouth against hers, gently at first, the sleeping giant awakened.

She kissed him back, nipping his mouth with teasing bites, touching her tongue to his, making him moan with need. The sound was gratifying after such a long absence. She shifted her body, sliding her thigh over his. But he pressed his hands against her shoulders, moving her onto her back like a man with a calling. Forceful, yet loving.

Yes! This is what she needed to warm her up.

His hands slipped to her breasts, and he caressed,

lifted, and massaged them through her clothes, making her tingle throughout. She stilled her hands on his waist, absorbed in his sensual and needy touch. Then wrapping her in his heat and vigor, he pinned her to the mattress. *Ohmigod, yes!* He hadn't shown her this much ardor in forever.

She ran her hands over the muscles in his back, enjoyed the feel of his satiny skin, the way he pressed against her, his arousal hard against her waist. She wanted him buried deep inside her, passionate, viral, possessive, loving her without hesitation.

With his mouth kissing hers, he swept his hands down her sides and reached for her...*nightgown*? *Not right. Something's not right.*

He lifted it, exposing her, his fingers stroking her naked thighs with a silky caress. But a twinge of panic streaked through her veins.

Not...not her nightgown...too heavy, not long enough...denim...her denim skirt? The illusion shattered. The world as she knew it unraveled, one notion at a time. He was too muscular to be Barry, too tall, and he smelled like leather and a spicy scent not at all like her...her...oh, hell, she was divorced. Barry hadn't lived with her for the last three months.

Her heart and breath on hold, she tried to slip out from under the aroused man who was clearly *not* her ex-husband. He slid his hand higher, toward the apex of her thighs.

Too scared to scream, she squirmed to get free.

"Charlotte," he said, his voice a husky, sexy tenor. "What's wrong, darlin'?"

Ohmigod, had she been out of her mind? Gone to bed with a total stranger and made up an alias?

The cotton sheets scratched her skin, unlike the satin feel of her 600-thread count ones. *Cotton?* She'd put flannel sheets on her bed for the fall as cold-natured as she was. She wasn't even in her own bed. Where was she?

"Get off me!" She tried to shove him aside, but he was like a primed bull ready to mate with his woman, and *she'd* been the one to prime him.

He reached out and touched her arm in a reassuring way. "Honey?" His voice was drenched with lust but sounded concerned, too.

She pushed again, freeing herself from his hot body. She scooted away so fast she fell off the bed. And fell and fell. Finally landing on the unforgiving wooden floor, she smacked her elbow and hip hard. How high was the damned bed?

"Charlotte?" the man asked, but this time his voice was tinged with more than worry.

"Who *are* you?" The covers rustled.

Lisa couldn't see a blamed thing in the dark, and she hoped the naked guy was dressing and leaving the room pronto. At least *she* wasn't naked.

"You're not…she's…" He paused.

Lisa scrambled to her feet, trying to remember where she was and why she was with a naked man in a bedroom that wasn't her own.

"What are you doing in my hotel room?" he finally asked with an accusing tone.

"*Hotel*," she whispered, rubbing her throbbing temple. "Ohmigod, hotel. The Stagecoach Inn." She vaguely remembered leaving Waco last night to come to Salado, to get away after the judge finalized her divorce from Barry, *the worm*.

"Wrong inn," the guy said, matter-of-factly.

"I rented a room here. I'm afraid *you're* the one who's in the wrong place." She attempted to sound sure of herself, not as rattled as she felt. She knew for a fact that she *had* rented the room.

A boot hit the floor, and the bed creaked. "I sure apologize for the mix-up, ma'am. I reckon the clerk made a mistake. I'll be out of here as soon as I can."

"It wasn't your fault." Although she couldn't stop thinking about what she'd nearly done with a total stranger. How could she have thought it was Barry? She guessed after four years of marriage and three months of separation, she still couldn't believe they were finished.

Boots tromped across the wooden floor, then stopped at the door. When the man pulled it open, a hall lamp cast a dim light into the room, illuminating the guy's attire, a cowboy dressed in black. A rodeo type or maybe he was in a country band. Neither of which appealed to her. Although why she was considering it, she hadn't a clue.

He stared at her for a moment, his brows deeply furrowed. A hint of recognition appeared in his dark eyes, his angular face stern, his jaw taut. Her gaze drifted to his lips—a perfectly kissable mouth—if they weren't so grim. He was a much better kisser than Barry had ever been, like he wanted to devour every lovable inch of her—*if* she'd been some woman named Charlotte.

A green cord of envy wrapped around her heart. Why couldn't she garner that much interest from a man who looked like this guy?

The cowboy cleared his throat, ran his hands over

the brim of a black Stetson, and gave her a little nod. "I apologize again, Miss." Then he shut the door, and his footfalls echoed down the hall.

Instantly, she felt bereft. Alone. Unwanted. Discarded. She was a mess and had to pull herself together. Barry wasn't worth the feelings that were churning deep inside her. He was perfectly content, and she was damned if she was going to be unhappy because he'd left her for a teen. Wiping away annoying tears, she vowed not to think about him again tonight. Or tomorrow. Or ever.

Letting out her breath, she inched her way to the door in the dark. She fumbled with the doorknob, searching for a lock. None? She slid her hand up the wall, trying to locate the light switch and a chain for the door. Nothing.

Jeez, wasn't there anything normal about the place?

Tomorrow, if she stayed another day, she was getting a new room.

After locating a chair, she dragged it across the floor and shoved it against the door, hoping it would keep out unwanted guests. She made her way back to the four-poster bed, stumbled on a stepstool, then climbed onto the mattress. Never-ending nightmares, a naked man in her bed, no locks on the door, no light switches, and a bed made for a giant? What next?

She touched her blouse and skirt and wondered why in the world she was wearing them to sleep in. On the other hand, they had saved her from total embarrassment. Too tired to care about anything, she slipped out of her clothes then crawled under the covers. The chill returned to her bones. She shivered, certain she'd never get any more sleep.

Closing her eyes, she considered what she'd done last night. Furious with Barry and his underhanded attempts to get half of her inheritance when he'd been an adulterer, she'd fumed the whole drive down I-35. She barely remembered the forty-five minute trip on the crowded interstate. When she'd arrived at her favorite shopping getaway in the quaint old Texas town of Salado—she'd gotten a room at the Stagecoach Inn.

She took a deep breath. Staying in Salado for the weekend, where she'd always come when she wanted to get away from a rough week at work, was supposed to help her get over the pain. Having a horrible night terror was *some* help and finding a nude hunk in the bed…

She shook her head, wishing the guy had been someone special to her. Then he could have chased away the cold and continued to heat her up.

"It was only a nightmare." Yet, she was unable to shake the sensation that the evildoers who had tried to kill her in the dream were still hiding in the dark, and once they realized she *wasn't* dead, they would attempt to finish her off.

She laid her head on the remaining pillow crumpled in a mass—still warm, the hunk's spicy, rugged scent permeating it. Her heart continued to beat as if she'd run for miles. Her skin covered in chill bumps and the cold seeping into her bones, she untwisted the coverlet and pulled it over her shoulders, intending to have a word with the clerk about her surprise guest first thing in the morning. What if the guy had been bad news?

Her mind wouldn't shut down. Her thoughts still

centered on the way the man's mouth had pressed hard against hers, his large hands reaching up her bare thighs. She no longer needed an imaginary fantasy of the Trojan warrior's seductive embrace while he ravaged her, the scantily clad princess hostage.

Drifting off, she replayed the cowboy's sensual moves, her mind conjuring up a new scenario—the cocky, riverboat gambler, having won her in a keno game, could do with her as he pleased. And he did…until the cold, the rough sheets, and the nightmares faded away.

***

Jack Stanton crawled into bed in the room next to the seductress's, chastising himself for nearly ravishing the woman, who looked too much like Josephine Rogers to be an illusion—the same blond curls, petite features, and prettiest green eyes. The night clerk swore the woman staying there had checked out. Being the good Samaritan or gullible guy he was—depending on who was making the observation—Jack let her have the room. Why in the world he'd thought she was Charlotte or why the woman had kissed him back if she was Josephine, eluded him.

Then his housekeeper's words came back to haunt him. *"You'll find the one for you, Jack. You'll find her at the Shady Villa Inn. She has no one else to look after her. Protect her—keep her safe. Mark my word. She'll be in a twist of trouble before you know it."*

He thought his housekeeper meant one of the college-bound girls who would arrive on the stagecoach in the morning. Bachelors within a fifty-mile radius would be dying to get a word with the women. Hell, as much of a shortage as eligible young women were in the area, as soon as a girl put up her hair, she was snatched up by any fellow looking for a bride. And sometimes the guys could get a bit cantankerous over a new stock of fillies.

So he thought one of the women might need his help. Although that wasn't the only reason he'd come to see if he could get a glimpse of them. But it wasn't his idea. His housekeeper had pushed him out the door, insisting he get on with his life or she'd leave him and his younger brother to cook and clean for themselves. Hell, although she'd been like a surrogate mother since their parents died, he paid the bills. So why he'd allowed himself to even listen to her...

He glanced at the wall separating him from the woman sleeping in his rented room and wondered again who in the world she was. She didn't sound like Josephine, her voice more demure, a strange accent, a little shaky. Josephine would have screamed bloody murder and walloped him good.

A hint of her fragrance lingered, something floral, sweet, and sexy, nothing like he'd ever smelled before. And the clothes she wore, although hard to see in the dark, the skirt didn't reach her ankles, and she showed a hell of a lot of leg.

Cursing himself again, he should have known the woman beneath him wasn't Charlotte. Not the way she kissed him back. Nor the way she positioned her thigh over him in an aggressive way.

He ran his hands through his hair and groaned. Already he was hard and wanting, when he shouldn't have felt anything. Hell, how could he not be aroused when she'd encouraged his attentions? Who had she thought he was? If it was Josephine, he was certain she hadn't gone that far with her beau.

Jack shook his head and closed his eyes. Dawn would come soon enough, and he had a stagecoach to meet. And a woman to rescue, according to his housekeeper.

***

A glimmer of early morning light shimmered through the separation in the burgundy velvet curtains hanging loosely over the window. Shadows flitted across the papered wall in a choreographed dance. Not wanting to rise without turning on some heat, Lisa finally gave up and grabbed her blouse at the end of the bed, then hurriedly put it on. She buttoned the pearls of her lace-trimmed sleeves and slid off the goose-down mattress. After groping around for her skirt, she finally felt the denim and pulled it on. Feeling slightly warmer, she reached over to turn on the lamp but couldn't find it. She slid off the bed and made her way to the door, trying not to stumble over anything in the dark.

Her vision blurred, and her head swam as if a heavy dose of vertigo suddenly infected her. Stumbling back to the bed, she collapsed.

"Why am I so dizzy?" Trying to still the pounding sensation, she massaged her temple.

The last time she'd felt this lightheaded, she'd had heat exhaustion, hiking with Barry in Palo Duro Canyon out west without enough water to chase away dehydration on a hot summer day.

A sickening thought occurred to her—what if she was pregnant? She'd made the horrible mistake of having sex with Barry right before the separation. *Before* she knew he was having an affair and planned to leave her. As irregular as her blasted periods were, she could never be sure.

Not wanting to deal with that scenario, she quickly dismissed the notion.

She lay back down to settle the turmoil in her head and stomach when a hazy light appeared, wavering in the corner of the room. For a second, the dimly lit figure lingered, then vanished.

Groaning, Lisa closed her eyes and rubbed them. "Now, I'm seeing things."

Turning on her side, she saw pale sunlight peeking through the edges of the curtains. She slipped off the bed, went to the window, and pulled the heavy drapes aside. The leaded, opaque glass distorted the view. Admiring the beveling, she ran her finger over the old-time panels. They reminded her of the ones in her mother's sunroom when she was little. A hint of rose wafted to her as if she was in her mother's garden again. A pang of regret washed over her. She'd wished her parents had lived to see her marry. Now she was almost glad they didn't have to see her marriage dissolve in disgrace.

Lisa shoved the window open and took a deep breath of the cool fresh breeze.

Turning her attention to the bedside tables, she noted the lamp sat on the one farthest from where she'd been sleeping, until she'd snuggled with the stranger. She walked around the bed and studied the shiny lantern mirroring her disheveled reflection. When she touched the amber glass, the heat burned the tips of her fingers, and she jerked her hand back.

An oil lamp? She could have sworn she turned on an electric lamp last night. She didn't have any matches to light an oil lamp. Unless the cowboy had lit it while she was dead to the world. But it had to have been hours since then. So why was it still hot?

Another question came to mind. Did the guy come in after she was asleep? She couldn't even remember having gone to bed, let alone much of anything else.

She fingered the necklace hanging about her neck, the deep purple stone shimmering in the sunlight.

Her stomach grumbled. She sighed. It was definitely time to indulge herself in a day spent shopping at the quaint little gift shops, but first things first.

Glancing around the room, she looked for her tapestry bag. Where in the world was it? She was sure she had set it on the floor next to the bed.

Her gaze shifted. No bathroom? She'd never stayed overnight here before. After this, she'd never stay here again. She wasn't into roughing it. When she didn't see her bag anywhere, she peered under the bed's Battenburg lace dust ruffle. No bag, but a copper pot sat near the edge of the bed and, fluttering beyond her reach, a piece of paper beckoned to her.

Curiosity got the best of her. Standing, she looked for something long enough to pull the paper toward her. She spied a cane leaning in the corner of the room, partially obscured by a high-backed, winged chair where the strange light had appeared.

If the previous guest had left it behind, wouldn't he or she have missed it before this?

She crossed the room to the cane and examined the hand-carved ivory handle shaped in the form of a swan's head. Maybe it was part of the nineteenth century look of the room. She returned to the bed, stretched the cane out to the paper, and snagged the floral note.

Dated October 26, 1870, a woman's delicate lacy letters were written on what looked like brand new parchment.

Dearest Bill,

Aunt Polly has brought me here away from the prying eyes of the rest of the family since I have been very ill of late. She has seen to my needs for several days, but she has not come in the last twenty-four hours, and I fear will not return. Although I felt I was recovering, I have been too weak to leave my bed. None of the hotel staff have come near the room. If I do not make it, my darling, know I loved you with all my heart. If not in this lifetime, we will surely be together in the next. Our love for one another can never die.

Yours eternally, Josephine.

CHAPTER 2

Hating unhappy endings since she'd lived through enough of them, Lisa wondered if the woman who had written the letter she'd found beneath the bed had managed to be with Bill again or not.

Examining the other side of the note for clues as to the identity of the author, she found none. Maybe the previous occupant of the hotel room had purchased the letter from one of the antique stores. Maybe a distant relative of theirs wrote it. Odd though. The stationary appeared new, not yellowed with age for having been written in the nineteenth century. However, the style of writing was definitely old world. And of course the date…

She refolded the letter and tucked it into her skirt pocket. Having done lots of genealogy research into her own roots, particularly since she didn't have any close living relatives, the idea of finding out about the woman interested her. Maybe she could ask one of the antique dealers what they thought about the letter before she gave it to the hotel staff. Then she could do more research concerning the woman when she got home.

Home. The marriage was over; she was free. So why did her stomach knot?

She returned the cane to the corner and wondered if she'd been so angry with Barry last night that she'd inadvertently left her bag in the lobby. *Great, just great.* Unable to believe she could remember so little of the previous night, she shook her head. If she'd tied one on, that would be one thing. But she hadn't had a drop of anything harder than a bottle of spring water. At least that she could recall.

She swept through the room one more time and glanced into an oval mirror hanging above a chest of drawers. The cloudy glass offered a gentle and soft reflection. *Ha!* She wished the hotel had a modern mirror for guests. How could she repair her looks when she could barely see herself?

No bathroom was the real kicker. Just a basin of water. She glanced back at the bed, wondering if that copper chamber pot was someone's idea of making the room appear more authentic. She ought to use it.

She felt as though she'd gotten the wrong room and was staying in one reserved for museum tours.

She considered her blurry features again in the wavy mirror. *Good grief.* Movie stars looked like they'd walked out of a beauty salon after falling out of bed. Why couldn't she look like that? Her hair was tangled, looking like she'd been well-loved. Her face heated. She'd nearly been that.

A crease of olive green eye shadow filled the folds of her eyelids. She wiped it away. After digging around in her purse, she found lip gloss and her hairbrush. No foundation, no mascara, no blush, no eye shadow. She looked like a ghost.

She touched up her lips with the clear gloss, giving her naturally red lips a little shine. Then she brushed out her sun-streaked hair flowing over her shoulders in thick curly waves. The strands drifted to her waist.

"I should really cut off this mess," she groused, tugging at a length of it.

But Barry had insisted he liked her long hair. So then what does he do? Hooks up with the new babe sporting a perky, short, curly hairdo, making her look more like a pre-teen.

Lisa grabbed her hair and yanked a navy-blue scrunchy over it to hold the long ponytail in place. As soon as she found a beauty shop, she was having her hair cut. Smoothing out her skirt, she was relieved the wrinkle-free fabric stood up to the manufacturer's guarantee, especially since she hadn't had enough sense to remove her clothes for most of the night.

She studied her blouse for a minute in the smoky mirror and touched the cotton fabric. Her fine lace bra was exposed to the world to see. She groaned, not believing she'd forgotten the camisole she always wore. No matter how much she wanted to shove Barry out of her brain, his actions in divorce court had rattled her.

She yanked on her boots, hurried out of the room, and shut the solid oak door with a clunk. Turning, she ran straight into an unyielding hunk of a man—the same cowboy who had been naked in her bed last night.

The impact threw her against the wall, and she gasped. He grabbed her arm, his expression horrified.

Sturdily built, tall, dark brown hair a little on the longish side, and a hard square jaw making him look ruggedly sexy, he was hot. His dark brown eyes turned black and his lips parted in apparent surprise. "Josephine," he said, under his breath. Glancing at his fingers wound around her arm, he released her and stepped back.

My god, first Charlotte, now he thought she was a woman named Josephine? What was he? A regular ladies' man? No way was she interested in another guy like that.

His searching gaze was so intense, she felt horribly self-conscious, her hands instantly clammy, her heart racing.

"Sorry for, uhm, running into you." Her cheeks felt sunburned and before he could say a word, she hurried down the narrow hall, not wanting any discussion about what had happened in bed between them.

When she entered the hotel lobby, she felt like she'd stepped into a nineteenth-century movie set. A woman wearing a blue dress reaching her ankles pushed a woven wicker buggy toward Lisa. A bustle attached in the back of the woman's dress accentuated her figure from behind, and Lisa wondered how she could sit down in that contraption. A chenille hairnet confined her mousy brown hair beneath an ivory hat dripping with dyed ostrich feathers. She returned Lisa's stare. Her brows lifted slightly.

Lisa smiled, figuring the woman must have been part of the hotel staff, although she hadn't recalled anyone dressing that way the night before. "I love your dress."

"Why, thank you, Miss."

Unable to resist a closer look, Lisa leaned over the buggy, wishing things had worked out with Barry, and she could have had their very own baby to care for in a year or so like they'd so often discussed. A white lacy bonnet covered the baby's brown fuzz-covered head, her face cloaked in sleep.

"She's adorable."

"He's my son," the woman said softly.

Lisa stared at the lace-trimmed gown the baby wore. "Oh, sure." Her skin warmed with embarrassment, but heck, the baby looked like a girl in a gown. "He's really sweet."

Another thought occurred to her. Why would a lady on the hotel staff drag a baby around with her? Maybe an old time arts and crafts fair was scheduled and the woman served as one of the vendors? The Highlander fair was scheduled for next weekend. Maybe this was a Victorian fair.

Lisa glanced around the lobby. High back chairs with wide-winged arms and curved loveseats covered in rich burgundy and green brocades, fit the nineteenth-century décor that looked similar to the antique furniture her grandmother had willed to her.

The cowboy she'd collided with in the hall outside her room entered the lobby. She thought he tried to appear inconspicuous about looking for her, but was doing an awful job of it because as soon as he saw her, his haunted eyes caught her gaze, and he turned away.

A lady seated on a floral sofa in the middle of the lobby, dressed much the same as the woman with the baby buggy, forced Lisa to reconsider the craft show notion. The vendors would be manning their booths, not lounging around the hotel, unless it was too early in the morning. She glanced at her watch. Twelve? No way was it that late in the day.

She put her ear to the face of the watch. Stopped dead. *Just great.* She didn't imagine any of the antique or gift stores in town carried batteries.

Observing the costumes of the patrons and the look of the hotel furnishings, she wondered if she was in the middle of a historical reenactment celebration. She loved medieval renaissance fairs, and the Highlander games in Salado were fun, too. Hmm, or maybe Salado was having a centennial celebration.

She touched her denim skirt and guessed she fit the part. Although most tourists visiting the area wouldn't bother wearing special clothes to fit in. She always did, hating to stand out. Blending in, being unobtrusive, that was her motto.

The woman spoke in hushed tones to a man dressed in a three-piece suit. He pulled a round gold watch from his pocket, glanced at it, then nodded. When they spied Lisa, both turned to gape at her. She guessed she didn't fit in as much as she thought she did.

"The stagecoach leaves in an hour and a half!" the clerk at the check-in counter hollered.

Lisa jumped a little. She had always wondered how much the coach cost, but she imagined it would be expensive, despite the fact it didn't go far.

She crossed the room to the reception desk and caught sight of the cowboy, his gaze following her every move. He smoothed his tussled, sable hair back while he leaned against a timber column and lifted a brow when their gazes met.

Her heartbeat quickening, she attempted to tamp down any interest in the western-dressed stud. She was *not* about to get interested in some other guy.

She turned away and leaned against the now

unmanned check-in counter. Where in the world had the blamed clerk gone?

Tapping her fingers on the well-oiled oak countertop, she glanced back at the stud watching some of the people in the lobby move outside. Dressed in black from the Stetson he cradled in the crook of his arm, to his boots tipped with silver trimmings, he looked like a movie star in a western. His duds appeared new. His silken vest embroidered with swirling designs, reminded her of a gambler. Broad shouldered and tall, he was much more impressive than her ex-husband—the despicable rat.

The way the cowboy had pinned her to the mattress, kissing her and fumbling with her skirt, she wished he'd been more than just a mistake. Her body tingled with fresh awareness, but her reaction to him compelled her to wonder if she'd lost her mind. Why would she be interested in someone new already? A horrible case of *immediate* rebound? Wasn't that supposed to happen later...like a few days, or weeks, or even months? But within twenty-four hours?

The gambler-looking guy glanced in her direction. She focused on the counter, not used to getting caught inspecting a man. Working too many long hours at her auditing firm, not enough sleep, and worrying she didn't have what it took to keep a guy interested in her...

She chastised herself. Barry was a squirrel and so were the other two guys she'd dated before him that she had thought were the real thing. It wasn't her fault she picked up losers—every time.

Unable to quash the uneasy feeling that the gambler dude still watched her, she glanced back. A hint of a smile touched his lips while he stared at the dip in her blouse.

Typical man. Go for the goods first. Her body heat turned up a notch again when she wondered if he could see her lace bra underneath the blouse. Maybe not. The lobby wasn't brightly illuminated like most. She glanced up at the light fixtures. Flames wavered in gas lanterns.

The old world ambience invited the viewer to step back in time, although her thoughts returned to the plight of her bag.

When the clerk didn't reappear at the counter, she tapped on the elaborately detailed brass bell sitting on the corner. The bell jangled, echoing across the high-ceilinged lobby. She only meant to give it a nudge, but it sounded like it could rouse the fire department. Still, no one responded.

She called out, "Excuse me!"

The young man hurried out of the office, his face red, his lips pursed. "Yes, Miss, may I help you?"

No, she just liked to bang the tar out of brass ringers and hang around the check-in counter for the heck of it.

"I'm in room number three and my tapestry bag is missing from it. Did I leave it here last night by accident when I checked in?" She kept her voice calm and sweet, the same tone she used when conducting audits, hoping to get better cooperation.

The man turned to an old-time register and considered the open page. "And your name is Miss Josephine Rogers?" He glanced up at her, a strange expression on his face. "But I…I thought you'd…well, checked out."

"No, it's Lisa Welsh." She pulled the register closer, then ran her finger along the penned-in names. "I don't understand. The page is dated October 29, 1870. Is this some kind of centennial celebration or historical reenactment day?"

"The town's not old enough to be celebrating the centennial, Miss," he said with a sniff, his stubby chin raised a bit. "I'm not sure what a historical reen...what did you call it?"

Lisa folded her arms. "I know Salado's at least one hundred years old, *for your information*. I'm not sure when it was established exactly, but certainly..." She paused, considering the age of the town. "Well, it's probably closer to one hundred and fifty years old. I guess a centennial celebration wouldn't be the word for it."

The clerk pulled at his black-corded bolo tie. "Folks around these parts would be amused to hear you say so. The village was established eleven years ago. Of course, a few settlers arrived in the area before that." His gaze drifted to her blouse and locked on. "You must not be from these parts." His eyes shifted back to hers. "An easterner?"

Lisa raised her leather purse and held it over her chest. She'd never thought the blouse was *that* risqué. Though the v dipped down, the large lace trimmed collar didn't reveal any cleavage, unless she leaned way over. She straightened a bit. The fabric wasn't *that* sheer. A hint of the lace bra would show if the viewer stared hard enough. Like the clerk had been doing. Now she really wanted to find her bag and a change of clothes.

"You *must* be having a reenactment, like the

Renaissance fairs that celebrate medieval times or the Civil War Reenactment they hold in Texas every—"

The clerk shook his head. "I don't know what you're talking about, Miss. I can't imagine anyone wanting to relive the War. Most of us would prefer to forget it ever happened. Those of us who survived it, I should say."

His voice was so gruff she was taken aback. Then she rethought the situation. "Oh, I understand. Everyone's required to stick to the storyline." *Good for them.* "I need to find my bag. Can you help me?"

"I really can't help you, Miss, if you're not Josephine Rogers."

Okay, she could play the game. "Very well, I'm Josephine Rogers. *Now* can you find my bag?"

"But you said—"

"I *know* what I said." *Breathe in, breathe out.* She'd had enough aggravation over Barry during divorce court. She wouldn't contend with anymore. Heck, she had clerked when she was in college and high school. At least when *she* did it, she had been taught to accommodate the customer—in other words— he or she was always right. Didn't they teach that here? "I *am* staying in room three, therefore, I must be Miss Rogers, right?" *Clown.* There should be a law against aggravating guests.

The clerk gave her a steely-eyed look. "Well, the manager's not in at the minute. I'll have someone look into the matter in the meantime. It'll be a while though since I'm the only one here right now. You might enjoy breakfast down the street at the new restaurant while you're waiting."

Now *that* was a twist. "You don't even recommend

your own restaurant?"

He fiddled with the pocket of his vest, then pulled out a watch. "I'm sorry, Miss, we don't have one yet. The new hotel owner might put one in, I wouldn't know. I'm just the new day clerk."

This was going too far. When the hotel hired new clerks, the ownership should make sure they know they have a restaurant. Wouldn't the management like to know he was sending patrons to other places to eat?

All conversation had died behind her, and Lisa glanced back at the lobby. Two men and three ladies watched her, including the western stud, whose gaze was fixed on her. She narrowed her eyes at him, perturbed that she would serve to entertain him. He raised his brows and shifted in his stance, his mouth turning up again just a hair at the corners. Amused to find that she wanted to see if he was still there? She hadn't. Not really. Well, just a little.

Her blood heated to volcanic proportions, and she faced the clerk. "I ate at *your* restaurant here last night when I first arrived. I had roast beef, mashed potatoes, a salad, and a pecan pie, *your* specialty." At least she seemed pretty sure she'd eaten that before she took a room. Every time she visited Salado to shop, she ate here, and she ordered the same thing. Her mother had forever and a day teased her when she was little that she was a stick-in-the-mud for not trying different dishes. Why experiment with something new if the tried and true was what she liked?

"You must be mistaken. We have no restaurant, I assure you, Miss," the clerk insisted.

Clenching her teeth, she shook her head. "I've been to the Stagecoach Inn's—"

"Stagecoach Inn? Ahh, well perhaps *that's* the problem. You're thinking of another town. This here place is called the Shady Villa Inn." He pointed to a sign hanging on the wall behind him.

Lisa stared at the sign situated above a rack of shiny new brass keys, but antique in design, filigreed bows with long round blades designed to unlock a door in olden times. Above the keys, room numbers were painted. She felt inside her skirt pocket and touched a key, remembering vaguely she'd put it there last night. Pulling it out, she examined the large, flat, square-bow key that looked modern, like hotels use that hadn't converted to computerized keycards. Hadn't this been what she used to get into her room last night? Maybe the ones hanging on the wall were just for show.

"Why did the new owner change the name? It's been the Stagecoach Inn forever." The clerk eyed her inquisitively, and she shook her head. "I'll check back in a little while." Maybe a good decaf would clear the cobwebs from her brain. She was definitely eating at the restaurant at *this* hotel, whether the clerk knew about it or not. Their homemade cinnamon rolls were to die for.

Although she told herself not to look, she had to glance back in the direction of the western guy. Yep, he was still watching her, curiosity and concern etched in his expression.

Lisa turned and stalked across the lobby.

Something she couldn't pinpoint about him intrigued her...maybe that he showed an unwavering fascination in her, when her ex-husband had lost that interest overnight. Heck, this guy could have a heart as black as his clothes. Yet, she didn't think he did. For one thing, he didn't approach her and mention anything about what had happened between them.

Speaking of last night, when he realized she wasn't Charlotte, he seemed disconcerted and hadn't pressed his advantage. He seemed intrigued but reserved. She liked that. She knew then she was nuts.

When she reached a carved door that led to the outside, she tried to tug it open, but it seemed to weigh a ton. Before she tried again, the gambler dude leaned around her, brushing her shoulder with his firm chest. He took a deep breath, as if enjoying the perfume she was wearing, smiled in a too-sexy way with just a fraction of his mouth curving up, his eyes sparkling with interest, and, his brows raised slightly, as he pulled the door open for her.

"Door's heavy, but the Texas wind blowing against it, doesn't help much either." His voice was the richest baritone she'd ever heard, which made Barry's seem squeakily high-pitched in comparison. The guy's eyes held hers captive, and she felt like melting into the wooden floor like a vat of heated wax.

He tipped his hat. "Name is Jack...Jack Stanton. And *you* are?"

Totally in awe.

"Lisa Welsh," she finally managed to get out.

He paused before he spoke, his dark eyes taking every bit of her in. "Not Josephine Rogers?"

The way he said the name sent a chill up Lisa's spine—like he knew Josephine Rogers, like she resembled her in some way, like she was caught in a very real nightmare.

CHAPTER 3

Jack Stanton studied the striking woman who called herself Lisa Welsh and wondered how she could think she wasn't Josephine Rogers. Her brows pinched together in a tight little frown, and she stared at the elms and giant oaks casting shadows that stretched over the acreage between the Shady Villa Inn and Main Street.

With every intention of getting on with his life, he'd thought he could start over again. At least that's why he'd come into town.

He lifted his Stetson and ran his hand through his hair, then replaced his hat on his head. *Two years*. It had been two dreadfully long years on a fall morning like this that he'd lost Charlotte, his beloved fiance.

You'll find a new lady to love today. One that will need you as much as Charlotte had, his housekeeper had said before he'd left the ranch.

No matter how many times her predictions came true, he didn't believe in Esmeralda's premonitions. He took a deep breath as the woman who looked like Josephine brushed a wayward blond curl behind her ear, her gaze taking in every bit of the area.

Hell, five years ago, everyone had known his parents were dying. No mystery there. When Charlotte succumbed to cholera, everyone knew she'd never make it as weak as she'd grown. So certainly, Esmeralda's predictions had come true.

He glanced back at the inn. Another hour and the stagecoach would arrive, carrying three women bound for Salado College, the first marriageable women in six months to come here where men were in the vast majority. He had no intention of going to one of the bigger cities, looking for an unmarried maid who might hate the small town life, if she even agreed to come here initially.

He assumed Esmeralda also had heard the rumors the women would be arriving, and that's why she was adamant he'd find a wife at the inn today. Well, in fact, most everyone in town would know. Every bachelor would be here, clamoring to get a chance at catching the young ladies' attentions. The last two who had arrived in Salado were wed within the week. No unattached woman stayed that way long. Except for Josephine, but that had been her choice.

The woman wrung her hands, glanced down at the dirt road, shook her head, and walked north. Torn between waiting at the inn to see if Esmeralda's prediction for him would come true, or following the confused young woman to ensure she wasn't accosted, Jack stood anchored in place, momentarily undecided.

Smiling his teeth, he cursed inwardly. He didn't know what was wrong with the woman, but she had to be Josephine. She'd come out of room three, and the clerk verified Josephine was registered in that room. He still couldn't believe he'd almost made love to her, and she'd encouraged it.

He watched her retreating backside, didn't see any sign of her usual beau, Bill McCrory, but he knew he'd be around after the last cattle drive brought him home. Jack spied a fellow he didn't recognize across the street, puffing away on a cigar, taking too long a gander at the lone filly. Ah, hell.

Jack stalked after her.

With every intention of taking her to the restaurant and making sure she got back to the inn safely afterward, he caught up to her. Bill would have a fit if he learned Jack ate breakfast with her, but Bill should have kept better track of her.

Jack would confer with the doctor even, if he thought that might help.

She glanced over her shoulder at Jack but didn't appear surprised. He gave her a small smile, intending to put her at ease in the event she began to fear his intentions. She definitely didn't show any signs she recognized him, or else she would have brushed him off. Seeming somewhat upset, though, she didn't smile back, but continued to consider the surrounding buildings.

"If you don't mind, Miss, I was headed to the restaurant myself and thought I might walk you there."

She didn't say a word, just stared at the Salado Saloon when they passed it by, her jade eyes round. He glanced at her boots, the darnedest things he'd ever seen. No bootlaces, no buttons, and they showed off a lot of leg on account of her denim skirt rested several inches higher than her ankle. The soft leather rose up her calves, showing the curvature of her shapely legs. The boots disappeared beneath the skirt, and his thoughts shifted to when he'd run his hands up her naked thighs. No pantaloons.

He'd never seen Josephine wear clothes like these. Hell, he'd never seen anything like it, period. He stared at the blouse and glimpsed a hint of lace hugging her rounded breasts, highlighting their sensuous form.

He took a ragged breath.

Ever since he'd held her tight, ready to ravish her, she'd triggered a craving in him he couldn't deny. Her alluring floral scent, the feel of her soft body beneath his, the way she'd kissed him more passionately than Charlotte ever had triggered his drawers to tighten, nearly strangling him. *Again.* If he didn't quit thinking about her in those terms…he'd get himself in trouble.

Her clothes were downright distracting, and he wanted to take her back to her room and make her stay there until she was properly dressed. His gaze drifted to her hair. Wisps of sun-kissed gold curls tugged loose from the strange blue contraption that tied her hair back. The fact it was down and not up for a young lady her age furthered his disquiet. She was just asking for trouble.

"Are you from here, Jack?" Her voice was as soft and sweet as Charlotte's had been, her eyes wide and questioning.

"Austin." He knew very well she was aware of this. "I was born and raised there," he said, playing along. He wanted to ask her where she was from, but then quashed that notion. He knew she was from Belton, although her two uncles and an aunt lived in Waco.

"Austin," she said, her voice quiet and demure, unlike when she'd spoken with the clerk at the inn, when she had become somewhat high-spirited.

She didn't sound like Josephine in the least. Not now and not at the inn. She had a strange accent that made him think of honeyed milk, but at times he had to concentrate on what she said to understand her.

"How long have you been here? I mean, are you staying at the inn for a couple of days?"

Only long enough to meet the stagecoach and the ladies it would bring. "I have a ranch outside of town. Horse went lame yesterday, so I got a room for the night."

"Oh."

Josephine knew he had a ranch. He couldn't figure her out. She looked like Josephine, same expressive jade-colored eyes, the pretty smile that stirred him up no matter how much he chided himself for it, and her hair the color as golden as tassels of summer-ripened corn. She was the same petite size and had silky, peach skin like Josephine's. How could she think she was someone named Lisa Welsh?

Hell, half of the bachelors in town were interested in Josephine. Not him. She was too fickle as far as he was concerned, not that she had ever shown any interest in him anyway.

He motioned to the two-story, boarding house that served meals most of the day when she hesitated to approach it. Opening the door to the clapboard house, he took his hat off and waited on her. Josephine remained at the bottom of the steps.

"This is it." For an instant, he was afraid she would back away and leave. Even though he had it in mind to return to the inn as soon as he could, he hoped maybe a meal would help settle her confusion. "Miss?" He couldn't call her Lisa. Not when he knew better. He couldn't call her Josephine either and upset her if she thought she was someone named Lisa.

"I…I've never seen this place before."

She must have eaten here a dozen times in the past year, at least. Every time he'd seen her here, a bunch of bachelors looking for a bride always made fools of themselves over her. The woman was too attractive for her own good, but it was her teasing personality that kept him at bay. No matter how much she played her suitors off each other, she had a real hankering for Bill McCrory, even if she could never say yes to his numerous proposals of marriage.

"Harriet and Jonathon Johnson serve the best vittles for miles around." Jack waved his hat toward the boarding house.

Josephine looked down the street toward the inn.

"Miss?"

She took a deep breath, climbed the steps, and entered the restaurant. "Thank you, Jack, for walking with me."

"My pleasure, ma'am."

Letting out his breath, he led her to the only empty table in the crowded place, full of widowers and bachelors eating breakfast, all who shifted their attention to the newcomers. Several of the men were sure to ask Jack later if he was making a move on Bill's girl.

Jack pulled out her chair, and when she sat, he pushed it in. The noisy chatter stopped closest to Jack and Josephine, then spread throughout the place until the only sound was Fredericka's boots tapping on the wooden floor. The restaurant owners' daughter set coffee mugs on the table and gave Jack a special smile, lowering her eyelashes when he caught her expression. She'd had a crush on him since she was ten, and four years later, he figured she was still hopeful he'd show some interest in her. Wouldn't be long and all the footloose gentlemen in the area would be calling on her.

He took his seat while Josephine glanced at the attention she'd aroused. Several men smiled appreciably, or tilted their heads down in silent greeting. Her cheeks flushed beautifully, but he'd never seen her embarrassed when men made fools of themselves over her, quite the opposite. He couldn't fathom the change in her. It was as if she'd had a powerful change in her life that had altered her whole personality. Kind of like when the saloonkeeper's wife died and he swore off liquor and took up preaching.

She swallowed hard and focused on Fredericka. "Do you have ice tea?"

Jack had never heard of such a thing. "I think coffee is all they serve."

"Decaf?" she asked, her voice growing smaller.

He sure didn't know what to make of it. He waved at the coffee pot. "Two coffees." Directing his question to Josephine, he asked, "What will you have to eat?"

She spoke low. "Do you have cinnamon rolls?"

Fredericka frowned. "Eggs, bacon, sausage, grits, and corn bread. That's what we have."

Josephine opened her mouth to speak. She took a deep breath, then snapped her mouth closed, and shook her head.

"Are you sure?" He couldn't believe a body could

get through a day without having the most important meal.

Josephine ran her slender finger over a crack in the tabletop and didn't say a word.

"Bring me the works," he told Fredericka.

"Yes, Mr. Stanton." She poured coffee in his mug, but when she started to fill Josephine's, her eyes shifted to her blouse, and she overfilled the mug. The coffee spilled on the table, but before Fredericka could wipe it up with her apron, the hot coffee ran off the table and onto Josephine's skirt. She jumped back, knocking over her chair, and almost fell.

"I'm...I'm so sorry," Fredericka said, tears gathering in her eyes.

"I'm okay." Josephine's voice shook while she held her skirt away from her body.

Fredericka's mother, Harriet, her face flushed from the heat of the kitchen, rushed into the dining area and helped her clean the table. Jack held Josephine's arm, and another man righted her chair.

"Here you go, Miss." The cowhand leered at her.

Jack wanted to floor the guy for leering at her.

"Where's the restroom?" Josephine whispered the question.

"Restroom?" he asked, puzzled.

"Bathroom. You know, where I can wash."

"You want to take a bath?" Jack couldn't imagine why. She smelled like a floral garden in springtime and even now, standing close to her, he couldn't get enough of her womanly fragrance.

"My skirt." She shook it pointedly.

"Come with me, honey," Harriet said. "I've got a bucket of water, and I'll just wash out the coffee before it stains."

"I...I can do it." Josephine waited for Jack to let go of her arm.

Usually not wanting any part of her, Jack had to force himself to leave her in the kitchen with Harriet and the other cooks. He'd never seen this side of Josephine, a sweet vulnerability that tugged at his heartstrings. Her helplessness brought memories of Charlotte's weakness and his inability to help her, crashing back to him.

Fredericka set the plate of steaming eggs, sausage, cornbread muffins, and bacon on the table.

Now he wasn't hungry. He glanced in the direction of the kitchen, worried about Josephine's fragile state of mind.

Fredericka refilled his mug. "I didn't think you were interested in Josephine."

"The lady's name is Lisa Welsh." He really wished she was someone else.

Fredericka raised her brows. "Is she a cousin of Josephine's?"

"Don't know." As far as Jack knew, she only had an aunt and two uncles—that was it. Maybe Lisa was a cousin. Her aunt had been childless, but her uncles might have raised some children. That would explain why she and Josephine looked so much alike but why Josephine had such different speech, clothes, and mannerisms.

"She sure is wearing strange clothes."

"New riding habit," he explained and looked back at the kitchen.

Her face flushed, Harriet dashed out of the kitchen and hurried to his table. The conversation in the room died again. "The young lady washed the coffee out of her skirt with a rag, then she said she had to leave. She told me not to bother you, but she appeared confused as to who she is. She shouldn't parade down Main Street alone the way she's dressed. Most of our men are decent folk, but some of the cowboys who just came through on the last cattle drive—"

Jack jerked a bill out of his wallet, dropped it on the table, and dashed out the door, his heart slamming against his ribs. He had no business feeling anything for Josephine, not the way she was, but damn, the lady was bound to get herself in a heap of trouble. Looking south, he figured she would be returning to the inn, but he saw no sign of her. Jerking his head north, he spied her stalking along the road, her arms swinging at her side, determination in her frantic pace.

He tore after her. "Josephine! Wait up!"

She quickened her pace and didn't look back.

Despite her head-start and hurried step, he quickly caught up to her, grabbed her arm, and pulled her to a stop. "Where do you think you're going?"

He couldn't help the anger in his voice. Wearing the clothes she was and without an escort...he shook his head.

She jerked her arm away. "Listen, Jack, my name is Lisa Welsh. I have no idea what's going on, but I'm walking up the street to locate an antique store. That's the last thing I remember vividly last night. Even if I can't recall that I'd been there, I bought this." She slipped her hand into her blouse and his eyes riveted to the spot.

The woman was hotter than a freshly fired pistol, and he couldn't contain the illicit thoughts he had about seeing more of the lace undergarment she wore, screened by the cotton blouse. She pulled out an amethyst necklace. *Josephine's* amethyst necklace. The one her mother had given to her on her deathbed when Josephine was thirteen. As much as Josephine had loved her mother, she would never have given up the necklace willingly to anyone, not even a look-a-like cousin.

Which meant Lisa Welsh truly was Josephine Rogers.

And he needed to get her back to the inn safely, return her to her room, speak to the doc about checking her out, and welcome the women coming in on the stagecoach before he lost the opportunity.

"I'm escorting you back to the inn, Josephine," Jack said.

Her expression turned from upset to angry as quick as a flash of lightning speared a cornfield on a stormy day. He knew if he insisted the lady return to the inn, he'd have a battle of major proportions on his hands.

She looked down at the road, and her anger seemed to dissolve into something else. Sadness? Defeat? He wasn't certain.

Her eyes pleaded with his for understanding when she spoke again. "They're not filming a western here, are they, Jack? There's no centennial going on, no move to return the town to a quieter existence by tearing down the new buildings and keeping the old ones—the ones that are no longer old but new again. Where's the little red, wrought iron stagecoach that the kids used to play on in front of the Stagecoach Inn? Someone got sued because a kid was hurt? No. It hasn't been built yet, has it, Jack? It won't be—not for a long time."

He didn't understand anything she was saying, but when she headed north, he trailed alongside her, unsure what to do next.

"No cars, a dirt road, no electric wires, or telephone wires. Were the wires all buried underground for aesthetic purposes? Maybe. I never noticed before." She crouched down and dug her hands in the dirt road. "No asphalt underneath the dirt." Brushing off her hands, she headed north again.

A few homes spread out farther from each other in this direction, but nothing else.

"No grocery store, post office, bank."

"Bank's back that way." Jack pointed south.

She gave a slightly hysterical laugh. "My dad was a bank auditor. Guess that's why I took up auditing, too. Except I didn't want to travel all the time like he did. He said every small Texas town had a church, a cemetery, and a bank, if nothing else. Guess even in the old days it was true."

She wrung her hands and stared straight ahead. "My mother hated that my father was gone so much of the time. He was going to make it up to her and take her on a trip to Cozumel."

"Cozumel?"

"The plane crashed, killing everyone on board. I was thirteen."

"Plane?" Josephine's parents had died in a carriage accident when she was thirteen. That much he knew. Her father had been a bank president in Belton. None of the rest made any sense.

"I thought living in the past would be interesting. Ever since I was a kid, I loved hooking rugs, making quilts, embroidering, cross-stitching, even pleated. Although I never could master knitting or crocheting."

He *knew* Josephine had no interest in sewing or cooking.

She stopped when the last house came into sight. After that, mesquite trees and oaks stretched as far as the eye could see.

"There's no antique store, is there, Jack?' Her voice wavered.

He reached for her to comfort her, but thinking better of it, he shoved his hands into his pockets. He didn't want to get tangled up with Josephine and care for her the way he wanted to right this instant. Not when she'd act in her usual manner and cast him aside for the attentions of another man once she was in her right mind.

Tears streaked down her cheeks. He gritted his teeth and tried not to look at her, but when she sniffled, he touched her arm, his mind playing tug-of-war with his conscience. She sobbed and that was it. The woeful sound pierced his heart. The same sound Charlotte had made when she knew she wasn't going to live.

He knew he'd be damned if he did it, but he couldn't stand to see Josephine so distraught when she had no family here to comfort her. Taking her wrist, he eased her into his arms, half expecting her to tell him off the way she would if she'd been acting her normal self. Instead, she melted in his embrace, her head resting against his chest, the sobs increasing, and the feel of her soft and defenseless.

He struggled to keep his thoughts pure and clean, the notion he was only providing solace to the confused young woman. But his body reacted quickly to the way she pressed against him and sent his senses reeling. Just like when he held her in his embrace in the middle of the night. He should have maintained more distance between them, and when her sobs died down, he should have pulled away. But she didn't move, and he waited for her to send a signal she wanted to be released.

She reached up to wipe her cheek, but didn't pull away. When *he* did, she leaned against him as though she was ready to collapse. He knew beyond a doubt she needed the kind of help he couldn't provide that a doctor might.

The notion crossed his mind that the stagecoach was due in another forty minutes. If he didn't hurry Josephine back to the inn, he'd miss his opportunity to meet the women. Who knew when more young ladies would arrive?

If he had to guess whether Esmerelda's prediction concerning his finding a wife today would come true, he'd say it wouldn't.

"I'm…sorry." Josephine's face was still planted against his chest. "I'm in a real quandary, and I don't know how to get out of it."

"What's happened, Josephine?" He worried someone had done something untoward to her, which had caused her behavior to change so drastically.

"I'm…I'm from Sacramento." She looked up at him. "In case you're wondering. You didn't ask, but I thought you might like to know."

"The Sacramento Valley? Your father had the gold fever?" He didn't think her family had ever been that far west. Maybe she'd been born there and her dad had moved them to Belton afterwards.

"We panned for gold, a time or two." She still

leaned into him, and he couldn't help craving more of her touch, as much as he knew even the most casual of relationships wasn't a good idea.

Hell, he'd gone way beyond that last night. In fact, if he'd been more of a gentleman, he'd have offered his hand in marriage. For propriety sake. She'd be scandalized if anyone knew they'd been together alone last night. Who was he kidding? If she was Josephine, she'd never consent to marry him. If he forced the issue, she'd be a hellcat to live with.

She took a deep breath and parted from him, but her gaze focused on the ground. As soon as she moved away, the chilly air blew between them, and he missed her warmth.

"Listen, Jack, thanks for being so nice to me. I'll be fine. I'm just going to walk a little longer. Maybe I'll see you later." She headed north again, and he grasped her arm.

"I'll escort you back to the inn. We'll take it from there." He had to get word to her aunt. She needed to be with her family.

"I...I don't belong here. I want to go home, but I don't know how to get back." Josephine rubbed her temple and stared northward.

"Is your aunt in Waco still? Or has she returned to Belton?"

Josephine rubbed her arms, her whole body trembling. He realized her blouse couldn't be warm enough to keep out the chill. "How did I end up here? How do I get home?"

He pulled off his jacket and wrapped it around her shoulders, but couldn't offer her any answers. Best to look after her until he could locate the doctor.

The sight of the posse caught their attention. Six men rode toward them into town with another three whose hands were tied in front of them. Thank God they'd caught some of the vermin.

Riding close, the men considered Jack and Josephine, while Deputy Severson tipped his hat, "Miss Rogers, Jack."

"I see you got some of them," Jack said, hoping they'd catch the rest of the gang before long. They'd stolen two of his best horses, killed one of his ranch hands in the process, and he'd provide the rope to hang the polecats.

The deputy twisted in his saddle and smiled at the bandits. "Yep. Caught them red-handed. They won't be causing no more trouble."

One of the robbers leered at Josephine. "Josephine Rogers? You wouldn't be any relation to Trevor Rogers of Belton, now would you?"

"Shut your yap, Caruthers." The deputized man tipped his hat to Josephine. "Miss." He gave her a wink and a smile, then he and the other men continued into town.

"Come on," Jack said brusquely to Josephine, annoyed with the usual attention she garnered from other men. "I'm taking you back to the inn, then getting word to Doc Weston to come see you."

"I'm not sick." Her voice sounded unsure while she walked with him without further resistance.

He still held her arm and he told himself it wasn't proper when the lady wasn't his. He shook his head. The woman needed help and at the moment, he was the only one offering who wouldn't take advantage of her in her current condition.

A crowd gathered near the jail, when the deputy and his men made ready to dismount. Some of the town's men waved their fists and shouted, "Hand over Dempsey and his men!" The rest watched in silence, their faces red and scowling.

Josephine faltered in her step, and Jack glanced down at her. She drew closer to him, and he realized the frenzy at the jail was making her nervous. He put his arm around her shoulders when she tried to distance herself from the ruckus, but they were halfway to the inn and this was the most direct route. At this rate, he could still make it in time for the stagecoach's arrival.

Then he saw Bill McCrory speaking to the deputized man who had recognized Josephine on the road. The deputy motioned north in her direction. Bill's head whipped around. He glanced from Josephine to Jack.

The look in Bill's narrowed eyes meant he was ready for one thing—a fight.

CHAPTER 4

God, Jack Stanton was gorgeous, gallant, and a true gentleman. Long ebony lashes framed his dark chocolate-colored eyes. His gaze slipped Lisa's way, worried, anxious. His masculine lips looked sinfully seductive, perfectly kissable. Remembering how they felt against hers in heated passion late last night made her cheeks flush. With his arm wrapped around her shoulder, pulling her closer, she felt a little warmer and not so lost—but she wanted him to kiss her, to chase the nightmare away. She assumed he was already overstepping his bounds being this close in this day and age, and he wouldn't go any further, but she didn't care.

Worse, she knew his helping her couldn't last. As soon as he dumped her at the inn, she was on her own. Then what?

She swallowed hard, trying to keep from crying again. Resilient, independent, used to being on her own, she didn't see herself as a wilting flower, but being in a world she didn't understand, a place where she knew no one…

Squeezing her eyes shut, she held back the tears and stumbled.

Jack kept her upright, moving forward, ready to get rid of her at his earliest convenience. She didn't blame him. If she told him she was from the future, he'd have her locked away.

How in the world had she ended up in the past? Could she ever return to her world? She wished it was all just a horrible dream, but she knew it wasn't. Everything was too real, and unreal.

She stared at the men shouting at the deputy and the robbers they'd caught. Any minute the angry mob could overwhelm the deputy and his men and lynch the thieves. Her stomach clenched, and she moved closer to the buildings away from that side of the street, pulling Jack with her.

The deputy fired a gun in the air, and Lisa's knees buckled.

Jack rubbed her shoulder and kept her on her feet. "Are you all right?"

No, she wasn't all right. The longer she was stuck in this time, the more *not* all right she was.

A man headed in her direction, sandy-haired, his face as red as the bandana circling his neck. Wearing a bright blue woolen hunting shirt, jeans, and a six-shooter nestled in its holster while a bowie knife fit snugly in his belt, he looked like the rest of the men dressed for Western Day in Salado. He dashed across the road in front of a horse-drawn wagon, his spurs jangling on his high-heeled boots. "Josephine, wait up!"

Jack pulled his arm free from her, but she continued walking at a fast pace toward the hotel, not liking where this was leading. Jack was distancing himself from her, and the rejection hurt, although she hated admitting it. Hadn't she sworn she didn't want anybody else in her life right now? Under the circumstances, she'd make an exception in Jack's case.

The cowboy seized her arm, and her blood instantly sizzled. "I said, wait up. Didn't you hear me?"

"Hey! Watch it!" Lisa jerked her arm free. No cowboy, whether he was from the past or living in the present, was going to manhandle her. *The nerve of the guy.*

He glanced at Jack who tipped his hat in greeting.

Why didn't Jack stick up for her? He seemed the heroic type, but maybe when the cards were down, he was the kind of guy who wouldn't stick his neck out for someone he barely knew.

"What's up, Josephine?" the cowboy asked. "I heard you died while I was outta town, but I didn't believe a word of it. Someone trying to pull a fast one over me?"

"My name's not Josephine, and I don't know you from Adam."

He scratched scruffy chin whiskers. "Adam? Who's he? It's Bill. Bill McCrory, and I don't know what you're trying to pull, but it ain't gonna work. What's the matter with you, anyhow? Got some other fellar? It's Jacob, ain't it? I knew he took a fancy to you at the spring dance." He glanced at Jack and glowered.

"Listen, you..." Lisa narrowed her eyes.

"Bill's the name. Don't tell me after that cattle drive, you've plum forgot all about me...those nights under the moonlight..." He looked up at the sky and put his hands over his heart. "Why I carved our names on

Table Rock. Don't you remember?"

Lisa shook her head. "You've got the wrong girl." She was beginning to feel really queasy about this. It was bad enough to be stuck in the past, but worse when everyone thought she was someone else. Even more aggravating, the lady caught every guy's eye. No way did Lisa want them to think she was an easy pick up.

"Sure you remember, honey. Come on. We can take a stroll up there now...refresh your memory a bit." Bill smiled and grabbed for Lisa's arm, but she moved out of his reach.

Jack raised his eyebrows a little and gave her a coy smile.

Lisa scowled at him and turned to Bill. "I don't know you mister, Bill, whatever—"

"See your memory's coming back already. Oh." Bill frowned and tipped his hat back. "Maybe it was the fever. I'm sorry, Josephine. You just sorta got me all shook up, saying you didn't remember me nor nothing. Kinda gets a fellar right here." He pounded his fist to his heart with a thump.

She skirted around him and started walking back to the inn. The men's footfalls crunched on the ground behind her as they caught up to her. "I'm sorry, Bill. You seem like an awfully nice guy." *Not.* "I'm sure Josephine loves you very much, but..."

Her hand brushed against her skirt pocket and the letter inside crinkled. Her heart nearly stopped dead. The letter. *If not in this lifetime, we will surely be together in the next. Our love for one another can never die.*

Bill and Jack watched her, expecting her to say something more. "Oh." She clasped her hand to her head and her knees weakened. Bill grabbed her arm and Jack seized her other.

Bill and Josephine. Josephine and Bill. Her vision blurred. No way in hell was...was... She stared at the changed buildings and stifled a sickly sob. She couldn't be Josephine. And Bill was the guy she loved? What the hell had happened?

The fever...the chills, the suffocation. Ohmigod, Josephine couldn't be...dead. The men, their threat...it had to have been a nightmare. A horribly vivid nightmare.

Lisa pulled her arms free from Bill and Jack. "I'm not her." Deep inside, her stomach wouldn't quit spinning like she was being flung around on the Mad Hatter teacup ride at Disney Land. She wasn't Josephine...she just couldn't be. No...no, she was Lisa Welsh, an auditor in Waco, Texas. *This* was all an unreal, hellish, night terror.

Bill grabbed her hand and pulled her to his chest. Squeezing the breath from her, he pressed his dry lips hard against her mouth. Her heartbeat quickened while she struggled to free herself from the lunatic's grasp. "Let me go, you...you, idiot!"

Jack grabbed Bill's arm, forcing him to release her. "The lady doesn't seem to know you. Maybe you ought to move along."

Bill stepped back and glared at Jack. He reached for his revolver, but Jack palmed his colt in his hand in the next instant.

Lisa gasped, then she took a deep breath to steady her rapid pulse. Jack *was* going to protect her, but at what cost? She blurted out, "They're not real."

Whatever made her say that? Of course they were

real. This whole place was real. And she was in a whole lot of trouble.

Bill studied Jack's gun. "What do you mean, Josephine? It's as real as any I've ever seen."

"So are the bullets." Not backing down, Jack held his weapon at the ready.

"Do you have a license to carry those guns?"

"What?" Jack asked, while Bill's brows arched in confusion.

"A license. Oh, honestly, you two can play this silly game all you want, but I'm going back to the inn," she said, trying to get them to give up shooting each other, her heart beating so hard she was sure she'd have an early heart attack.

Maybe if she lay down for a bit and slept, she would wake to find herself back home.

Bill took a step toward her, but Jack blocked his way. Why couldn't anyone be heroic for her like that in her world? She scoffed at herself. If she didn't find a way to undo things, this *was* going to be her world.

"All right, Josephine. That's not the last you've heard from me. As for you..." Bill scowled at Jack. "I'll deal with you later." He turned on his heels and stormed down the road, stirring up the dust with his boots.

Jack holstered his gun, took her by the elbow, and ushered her the rest of the way to the hotel while she searched for signs of her car. She knew it wouldn't be here. She knew, but she couldn't help looking.

Jack seemed to be searching for something, too.

"Are you expecting someone?"

He glanced at her, his expression surprised, but he didn't answer her.

When she reached for the brass doorknob at the hotel, Jack opened the door to the lobby. "Allow me."

"Thank you for the rescue, by the way, but I could have managed on my own." She was still perturbed he let Bill kiss her before he finally stepped in.

"I could see you were nearly out of the grasp of the octopus's tentacles."

"I didn't know you knew of topics such as that way back when." Lisa folded her arms.

"What...of octopus? Do you imagine we are less educated than those of you in Waco with its Baylor College? After all, ours is one of the first colleges in the state. Just last year they added a two-story building. And we have around two-hundred and fifty students."

"Oh?" *No* colleges were located in Salado. She'd found the first mistake he'd made in this whole mixed-up business.

"Salado College, founded in 1859."

"Never heard of it."

"Never heard..." He shook his head. "Never mind. Texans from all over the state come here to our fine school." He escorted Lisa into the lobby. "I need to get word to Doc Weston." He motioned to the sitting area. "Would you care to have a seat, or do you want to wait for him in your room?"

"Thank you for worrying about me, but I don't need a doctor." She needed to take care of other business though, pronto, like find a way to get out of this nightmare.

"Bill sure seemed to think you are Josephine. You do look quite a bit like her—same complexion, height, same lovely eyes. You seem to have her temperament somewhat also. Then again, you're different."

"I'm not her." She knew she wasn't because she knew nothing about...about this time period. So that meant she was either going mad, dreaming, or...she'd somehow been thrown into the past. How could she be locked in the eighteen hundreds? She didn't believe stuff like that, not in reincarnation, or aliens, or ghosts, or anything that couldn't be proven by hard scientific evidence. Like her auditing work. If numbers didn't justify the findings, it wasn't real.

"If you say so," Jack said.

She gave a heavy sigh. "You said you knew her, so you must know I'm not her."

"I waltzed with her at the dances a couple of times, but nothing more. Too many others stood in line. I don't care for that much competition."

"Oh? I would think you'd beat out the opposition." Certainly, Jack impressed her much more than Bill.

Jack didn't comment, but instead gave her a reserved smile as if something darker bothered him.

Exasperated with herself, she wished she had stayed in Waco and tied one on instead of getting into the mess she was in now. What was she supposed to do?

"I have to go and—" What? She wasn't sure what she should do. "I...I need to return to Waco."

"To Waco? To stay with your aunt?" His expression brightened, then it darkened again. "Not unaccompanied."

"Don't tell me...wild Indians are on the loose out there." Lisa waved her arm to emphasize the point. Although half joking, she feared it might be true now. "So what are you...my guardian angel?" If she had been thrown back into the past, shouldn't she have a guardian angel? Jack seemed right for the job, if she discounted the way he didn't stick up for her in front of Bill to begin with.

Jack gave her a Rhett Butler kind of smile, one part totally sexy, and one part rogue. "Nobody's ever called me anything nearly as nice. I'm not as concerned about the Indians as I am with the outlaws plaguing the citizens around these parts. Not that the Comanche haven't been causing trouble, but that's been around the western part of the state in the Panhandle and the Red River north of here."

Outlaws? Raiding Comanche?

Her heart began to thump at a faster beat, her skin prickling with renewed concern.

She had to get home. Somehow.

Folding her arms to keep from showing her upset and trying to think of something else other than the dire circumstances she was in, she considered Jack from head to toe. "I see you're dressed as a gambler...tough-guy type." The elicit dream she had of him winning her in a hand of keno was still fresh on her mind.

"You can tell from looking at the clothing I wear?"

"Yes." Lisa touched his vest. "Silk, isn't it?"

Jack's eyes sparkled as he nodded.

Lisa pointed to his holster. "Gamblers always carry guns. Southern gentlemen don't. At least that's what they tell you at those old-time photo places." She had one hanging in her living room from the time she, her girlfriend Pauline, and Pauline's husband had gone to Six Flags. She and Pauline had worn scarlet dresses, showing off a lot of leg, pretending to be saloon girls while Pauline's husband played the role of a gambler, poker cards in one hand, his other on the grip of his pistol.

But none of it was genuine. Not like this. The real old west was giving her heart palpitations.

"Gentlemen who don't protect themselves," Jack said easily, patting his revolver, "don't live long around these parts."

Lisa furrowed her brow. "The bad guys wore all black, at least in most of the Westerns I've watched."

"Westerns? They sure have an odd way of speaking in the Sacramento Valley. West of the Mississippi you mean...westerners? We wear all kinds of different clothes. We're not quite as fashion conscious as those back east, I've heard tell. Never been there myself. I've never heard anyone say the outlaws wore only black. Easton James and his gang wore light-colored dusters and Sam Bass and Bill Langley, well...I don't know that any of them wore black. Saw John Wesley Hardin once. He wore a white hat that I recall. Where do you come up with such funny notions?"

"Maybe that's Hollywood. You've never been east before? Don't tell me you're one of those people born and raised in one place and never stepped foot out of it."

"I said I'd never been east. Now farther west, that's a different story."

"Oh? So did you check out the California gold rush?"

"In 1849? Are you serious? How old do you think I am?" Jack glanced in the direction of the door.

She cleared her throat, wishing she knew her history better. "What about the Civil War. Didn't you fight in that?"

"Like every young man here in the region did."

"But you never ventured past the Mississippi River?"

"No, not with the cavalry unit I was with. There was plenty of fighting to be done around here."

"I guess I don't know enough about the local history to trip you up." Although she'd hoped she'd have been able to shed some light on the strange set of circumstances. She definitely had fallen into Alice's rabbit hole.

"Josephine!" a redheaded man yelled from the entrance to the building, making her heart lurch. The broad-shouldered man strode across the lobby to join her. "I heard you were back, but I thought you had died."

Not another one. Lisa looked the man squarely in the eye. "I'm *not* Josephine."

"Ahhh, come on. Quit funning."

Her throat felt parched and a trickle of spine-tingling discomfort set her nerves on edge. "I don't know any Josephine." She had to make everyone understand she wasn't this woman that some thought had died. Why hadn't Jack?

"That's what Bill said, and he poked me in the eye saying I had a hankering for his girl, and you were pretending not to know him. I told him it wasn't so."

She considered the man's reddened eye. The swelling and circular blue color were just making their appearance. "And you are?"

"Jacob. Surely you remember me?"

"At the spring dance."

Jacob smiled. "So you *do* remember me."

"No, Bill said you danced with me...I mean, with

Josephine." Jack's eyes darkened, and Lisa made a disagreeable face at him. "I'm sorry, Jacob. I don't know you. I don't know Josephine either, but according to Jack, I look like her, and therein lies the confusion."

Jacob stroked his red beard. "Bill said he thought it might've been the yellow fever. You'll be your old self before long." Jacob kissed her hand, then waved at her while he walked toward the door. "See you later."

"Certainly appears everyone knows you as Josephine, but you. Maybe..." Jack moved in close to her and pushed her bangs aside. His action startled her and she took a step back. "Maybe, you were hit on the head and suffered a concussion, resulting in a form of amnesia." He touched her forehead. "Doesn't look like a mark one, however."

Even his light touch sent a pang of longing through her. She had to be nuts. "Sorry to disappoint you."

"Not disappointed, wouldn't want to see a big lump on that pretty forehead of yours. Just would help to explain a lot of things."

Instantly annoyed, her voice rose slightly. "I've *already* explained everything."

"Yes, I know and none of it makes any sense."

"You really don't think I'm Josephine, do you?"

"Whosoever you say you are is fine with me."

"There was no funeral for her," Lisa said under her breath, staring at the floor, deep in thought. "But she died." *In the dream.* She looked up at Jack. *My God, Josephine hadn't died of natural causes due to the fever. She was murdered. Someone murdered her in the inn.* "I'm *not* Josephine." But she had to get out of here as quickly as she could.

Without another word, she strode off to the

reception desk, leaving Jack standing alone in the sitting area.

The clerk busied himself with the register and avoided looking at her. She tapped her fingers on the counter. "Did anyone locate my bag?"

The young man's eyes grew larger. "I think maybe you need to talk to the manager, Miss." He scurried away and returned forthright with a taller, gray-haired man sporting a beard.

He limped out to the counter. "I'm Mr. Daemon. May I help you, Miss?" His beady steel gray eyes instantly widened with recognition.

"I'm missing my tapestry bag. Maybe you can help me?"

"And you are?"

She glanced down at the register, then looked up at Mr. Daemon. "The occupant of room three."

His eyes and voice darkening, Mr. Daemon cleared his throat. "That doesn't seem likely."

"I have the key."

"And your name is?"

Not intending to lie and say she was Josephine, she stiffened her spine and said nothing.

The man frowned at her. "We've searched everywhere for your bag and haven't found anything matching the description you've given."

"Maybe we need to check with the police."

"Police?"

Exasperated, she said, "The law, sheriff, whatever."

"The sheriff's out of town on business, and the deputy's busy."

Lisa twisted her mouth in annoyance. "How am I

supposed to return to Waco?" she said to herself, but the manager answered her anyway.

"The stagecoach leaves soon."

Lisa glanced around the lobby. Jack watched her curiously. Did he think she was as crazy as she felt?

The manager lowered his head to the clerk and spoke in a hushed voice. Turning to Lisa, he said, "Would you like to purchase a stagecoach ticket, Miss?"

"The stagecoach?" She chuckled, albeit slightly hysterically. What if she could ride out of this nightmare? "I need a one-way stagecoach ticket to Waco, Texas. You do go that far, don't you? You used to only run the coach around Salado—"

"Yes, Miss, the stage goes to Waco. It'll be five dollars for the trip."

Lisa pulled out her credit card, the habit so ingrained it took her a minute to realize her mistake. "I'm sure you don't accept credit cards," she muttered to herself. She didn't have cash either, but she figured as strange as the currency would look to him, she'd never be able to use it.

For having a cane and gray hair, Mr. Daemon had the hearing of a wolf. "No. The local grocer accepts credit now, but we don't. Money has to be paid up front. I'm sorry." He didn't sound like it.

Lisa dug through her bag. "I don't have even a nickel in here. I never carry cash." Although she knew her attempts to find anything that would work were futile.

Jack moved in next to her, his arm brushing hers, as if he was trying to get her attention. He got it all right. No matter how much she didn't want to be attracted to him, the guy was just too seductive for his own good…or rather, hers.

"This is Josephine Rogers," Jack said, ignoring Lisa's glower.

"Oh?" The manager's eyes bugged out. "I don't believe that's possible. Besides, I thought she told my clerk her name was Lisa Welsh."

Lisa opened her mouth to speak, but Jack said, "Yes, well, she's been trying to avoid a couple of fellows in town who've been pestering her all day."

"I see." Mr. Daemon's wrinkled fingers stroked his long beard.

"I'll pay for the ticket." Jack handed the money to him.

The manager accepted the cash. "Here's the ticket, Miss. I'm sorry for inconveniencing you. The stage will be on its way…" He pulled his watch out of his pocket, then snapped the gold cover open. "…in a quarter of an hour. It leaves promptly on the hour, so don't delay because it waits for no one."

"Thank you." Tears filling her eyes, Lisa took the ticket. "And thank you, Jack, for paying." Just when he'd annoy her most, he'd do something nice. Five dollars had to cost him a fortune, yet he was willing to throw it away on a woman he didn't know? She wished she could pay him back.

They moved away from the counter, and she whispered, "I can't believe I've lied about my name."

"What lie? Everybody thinks you're Josephine, only some think she's—"

"Please, don't say it." Lisa glanced back at the desk. "The manager doesn't seem to think I'm Josephine."

"He's the only one. I have to check on my horse. They'll be boarding the stagecoach soon, so stay here. All right?"

Her lower lip dropped slightly. "You're not leaving, are you?" The only one who'd helped her in this upside down town, and he was leaving? She should have known.

The sparkle returned to his eyes. "I do believe you'll miss me."

Smug man. "I don't know anyone here and everything seems so strange." She believed he'd take care of her if she needed him to. Shades of Barry all over again. Men were all the same no matter the century.

"I have some business to take care of, so stay here," Jack reiterated, and kissed her hand.

Heat sparked along her nerve endings, and she chided herself for feeling anything for a stranger. She pulled his jacket off and handed it to him.

His dark eyes twinkled with the devil. Slipping his jacket back on, he tipped his hat in farewell and left her standing alone in the lobby.

What if she couldn't ride out of this nightmare? What if... She shook her head. She'd return to Waco...to her home and find it was just as she'd left it.

The clerk busied himself with the arrival of a new guest, while the manager eyed her with suspicion, then departed the room. Trying to settle a case of nerves, she took a seat in one of the Queen Anne chairs situated in the lobby. A small man sitting on one of the sofas nodded off while another conversed with an older woman nearby. Three more men stood talking in another corner of the lobby about the last cattle drive.

She shook her head inadvertently, then glanced at her gold watch. The time was still twelve. After winding the stem, she listened, but it made no sound. She took a deep breath. She'd had vivid night terrors before, even envisioned her parents had come home after they'd died, and it had been so real, she'd wanted to leave her foster parents and return home. And she did. The police gave her back to her foster parents, stating she'd run away. But she hadn't. She'd returned to be with her real family. Even to this day, it seemed so real. Was that what was happening? In a few hours, the night terror would go away, and she'd be home again?

"They'll announce when the stage is ready to be boarded," a man said, breaking into her thoughts, his voice deep and persuasive. Tall and auburn haired, he twisted his handlebar mustache between his fingers. "Are you leaving town already? You just got here. You didn't even let me know you were back. I had to hear it from Bill and Jacob."

A bubble of hysterical laughter caught in her throat. The list of Josephine's admirers was endless.

The man scanned Lisa's blouse. "They said you suffered from a memory loss, but I didn't think it would be possible when you laid eyes on me." He glanced back at the door and waved his hand in that direction. "I can understand you wouldn't remember the other fellas."

Now, she knew she had to get out of this town, if only for her own sanity. "I'm not Josephine."

"They said you'd say that, too. Who are you supposed to be?"

"Lisa...Lisa Welsh. You haven't told me your name

yet."

"All right, fair enough. Maybe you *do* have a form of amnesia. It's Jack Stanton." Lisa's eyes widened, and he laughed. "Guess I didn't fool you none. Bill said Jack's been hanging around you all morning. Sure got Bill all riled up. I guess you know he punched poor Jacob in the eye for it."

"Then maybe you better stay clear of me."

"Nah, I'm not afraid of Bill. Jacob's always been a little slow on his feet. You must have noticed when you danced with him last spring."

"I'm *not* Josephine."

"Ah, yes. It's a pity really." He sauntered off and the slight relief that ran through her faded when he picked up a chair and carried it next to where she was seated. "But we could get a fresh start this way." He sat down and ran his gaze over her blouse and skirt. "What kind of clothes are those? New women's riding outfit?" He shook his head. "I don't care for it. The cowboys wear overalls, not the ladies. I suppose for traveling they might be all right, but for town, it's just not dressy enough."

"I *am* traveling."

"If Jack locates Doc Weston, you won't be going anywhere."

Ohmigod, *that's* where Jack was going. To get her a shrink, the traitor. The doctor would have her committed. She rose from the chair, but so did Josephine's suitor.

"Can't I persuade you to stay longer?"

"I don't even know *who* you are." She wasn't usually so rude to anyone, but jeez. She wasn't used to guys hitting on her every second of the day—or rather, hitting on a woman they thought she was, which was even worse. The biggest nightmare was what she was going to say to the doctor. Already her skin prickled, and her heart began to race.

The man reached for Lisa's hand, and she jumped back. She knocked her chair over, and the snoring man on the couch shouted, "What?"

The auburn-haired man laughed and righted the chair. "My, you're jumpy. I promise I won't bite. I can't believe you don't know who I am. It's me, Frank Collins." He watched her closely for any sign of recognition.

"Are you sure that's your name?"

He cast her an amused look. "Come and sit with me, Josephine. Yes, it's Frank. I was just funning with you over Jack. I didn't think you were interested in him, by the way."

"Why not?"

Frank raised his brows. "Is there something here I should know about?" He smoothed his gray jacket. "You always said Jack was too serious to be much fun."

"Oh." She didn't think he was too serious. Just about right, really. If it wasn't for the fact he was looking for a doctor who would probably try to commit her.

"Well, that's so, isn't it?"

She scowled at him. "How would I know?"

"That's right. You don't know him either. Is that why you ate breakfast with him this morning?"

"I didn't eat. What am I telling you this for? It's none of your business anyway." She folded her arms, wishing he'd go away. If it wasn't for her trying to catch the stage, she'd leave. But where would she go?

"I love it when you get your feathers ruffled, Josephine."

"I really don't see how she could have liked you."

"Do you want to go up to Table Rock, and I'll show you?"

"What is this Table Rock everybody keeps talking about?" Although she suspected it was some kind of lover's tryst.

Frank gave a sheepish smile. "If you don't remember the place, this isn't the time to mention it." He glanced at his pocket watch. "I can get a refund for your ticket." Frank held out his hand. "We have enough time to get a cup of coffee up the street. Stage won't leave for another forty minutes."

"Stage boards in five minutes!" the clerk called out.

Frank smiled. "Well you can't blame me for trying." He glanced at the clerk, then said to Lisa, "I'll be right back."

"Take your time."

"I don't know," Frank said, winking, "I think I'm kind of getting to like the new you."

Frank walked over to the reception desk and leaned on the countertop. While he waited for the clerk to wait on him, he smiled at Lisa.

Five minutes. Would she be out of here before Jack returned with the doctor? She prayed to God she would.

She headed out of the hotel lobby and into the clear, crisp air, wanting to leave this world behind and get on with her life, despite the shambles it was in.

The Overland Stagecoach stood in front of the inn where four men, an elderly woman, and three pretty young women unloaded. Several men crowded around the coach, vying to get a word with the young ladies. The way the men went after them, they acted like the women were movie stars or famous singers.

A man was loading sacks of mail into the coach while two others were changing the horses. She approached the dusty conveyance, running her hands over her soft leather purse. A wisp of hair pulled loose from her scrunchy and tickled her cheek. The choking dust blown askance by the breeze, the birds chirping in the live oaks nearby, it was all so real, yet everything was horribly unreal.

When she boarded the scarlet red coach, it would take the usual trip up the street, circle around town, and return here within the hour. *If*—and that was one hell of a big if—the stagecoach did travel to Waco, the city just had to be the same as she left it last night.

It just had to be.

CHAPTER 5

With haste, Jack paid to board his horse at the livery for another day and sent a messenger to his ranch to let his brother know he would be gone longer than they had expected. He cast a glance in the direction of the Doc's office. Wouldn't you know he *had* to be out of town delivering a baby the one day Jack needed him for the first time in a year. Next best plan was to reunite Josephine with her kinfolk in Waco.

He stalked back to the Shady Villa Inn, bought a stagecoach ticket, and found Josephine waiting to board. Small and demure, she stood so close to the coach; it looked as though she was ready to jump on, afraid they'd leave her behind. Her back stiff, she held her leather satchel tight against her chest. She concentrated on the driver and his assistant still loading the mailbags, which looked to take up a goodly sum of the boot and part of the interior of the coach. He would never believe in this century or the next he would be escorting Josephine to Waco to keep her safe.

The women bound for Salado College were nowhere to be seen, but when he spied a crowd of men nearby, he figured the girls were in the midst of it. Esmeralda was sure to think he'd struck gold with one of the college-bound ladies when he didn't return home. He *knew* her prediction wouldn't come true.

He wasn't sure what to make of Josephine though. She glanced back at the inn where the manager, Mr. Daemon, and a shorter, fat-faced man watched her. The breeze tugged at the golden strands of her hair freed from the strange looking tie confining the rest of it.

Mr. Daemon spoke to the runt of a man, his face ruddy and pockmarked. Jack thought he was the out-of-town owner, a Mr. Worthington. He nodded and walked back inside with Mr. Daemon.

"Do you have any bags, Miss?" the stationmaster asked Josephine, and she jumped.

She frowned at him. "No. I should have, but everything I owned has disappeared."

No matter how bewildered she appeared, she had real sand. Jack couldn't help admiring her for it.

"Yes, ma'am." The stationmaster weighed another passenger's bag. "That's under the twenty-five pound limit. You won't be owing any more for your bag, sir."

Before Josephine entered the coach, Jack moved in close to her. "Be sure to sit on the bench nearest the driver's side," he whispered over her shoulder, watching her shudder. He smiled at her when she turned to face him.

So she *had* missed him. The look on her face was one of relief and happiness. There wasn't any way he would allow her to return to Waco without his accompanying her. In her current state of mind, there was no telling who might attempt to take advantage of her. Although he'd really hoped to have the doctor take a look at her.

"Don't tell me you're going to Waco, too?" She sounded so hopeful, it struck a chord.

"You said it. I'm your guardian angel." He fought wanting to get to know her better. The nagging voice in the back of his head told him any minute she would turn into the real Josephine and shun his attention.

Trying to focus on her sparkling eyes and not on the dip in her blouse or the lace undergarment covering her breasts, he was having a devil of a time. The clothes she wore were provocative enough to tempt a preacher.

Josephine shook her head and climbed into the coach. "Where did you go?"

"Did you miss me?" His innards were on fire. A hint of the most heavenly scent drifted about her like an invisible mist of flowers, and her cheeks blushed whenever he drew near. She didn't react to him like Josephine would, which made him begin to doubt she *was* Josephine. He couldn't deny she was the prettiest, unattached filly in Salado at the moment. Here he hadn't even once looked at another woman since his girl died, but he'd finally vowed to give up the ghost and what does he do? Hooks up with a look-alike Josephine who heats his blood to high heaven when the other made it run ice cold.

Maybe she wasn't Josephine Rogers. She remained aloof with the other fellows, unlike Josephine, but he could tell she liked him. Josephine would never have breakfasted with him. When Bill had barged in on them, if she'd been Josephine, she'd have never spoken another word to Jack. He glanced at the gold chain around her neck. But the necklace was Josephine's. He was certain.

She poked a loose curl behind her ear. "I was just curious about where you went."

"You missed me." Jack wanted to get her to speak her real meaning. "I had to stable my horse and send a message home to let my brother know I wasn't returning for a while."

His gaze drifted to her lace-covered breasts. He couldn't help himself. The fabric tantalized him, his eyes straining to see more.

She cleared her throat, and he looked up to see her eyebrows arched.

He played with the brim of his Stetson. "I haven't seen the new suspension bridge in Waco. I was interested in joining the historic opening in January, but fences desperately needed mending. It's hard to believe it's the longest in the United States and the second largest in the world."

"It *is*?"

His jaw dropped. He couldn't imagine anyone wouldn't have known, particularly someone who was from Waco. Was she befuddled about that also?

"Didn't you go to the grand opening? I heard Kate Ross led the parade. Surely, you would've known, living in Waco as you do. Travel across the Bosque River is much easier now than taking the ferry. But you'd know that."

"A ferry," she said under her breath.

He leaned back against the seat, wondering what else she must have forgotten. "Since Waco sits on a spur of the Chisholm Trail, the number of cattle driven to market has increased tenfold because of the bridge.

Aren't they planning on incorporating the town into a city next year?"

"City? Uhm, oh, yeah. It was a town first, probably."

He didn't know what to make of her confusion. Even if she wasn't Josephine, if she was from Waco, she should have known these things. "Just think, the Waco and Northwest Railroad are coming next year also. This place will be a real boomtown."

"Yeah," she said softly. "That's progress. I was telling my friend how easy life would have been in the past, compared to now, with all of our complicated technology. My year-old car's transmission went out on me, then the flasher, the dishwasher's been on the blink and oh well, you name it. All this modern machinery doesn't hold up well. When you try to have it fixed, either the servicemen can't figure out what's wrong with it or they fix it and they charge you an arm and a leg."

"That much, eh?" She sure had a funny way of talking and not a lick of it made any sense, but it made her more charming and less like Josephine. Yet, the way she wrinkled her brow, like she did at him now, looked just like Josephine when she was perturbed with a fellow.

"I'm serious. I thought living in the past would have been simpler, but now I'm not so sure."

"Living in the past was simpler, but harder, too. Folks had to carry water from the creek instead of having it pumped to their homes. Fireplaces provided warmth and a place to cook the meals, now we have stoves. Indians were a constant threat—"

"Wait up!" Frank Collins called to the coach when

they were about to shut the door.

"Oh, no," she said.

"Do you know him?" If she knew him and he knew her—

"Just met him in the lobby."

"Oh." A modicum of relief washed over Jack.

Frank grabbed the last seat on the other side of the coach between two burly cowpokes and frowned when he saw Jack seated next to her. She gave him a smug smile.

Since the mail took up so much of the coach, everyone's boots rested on the mounds of sacked letters. A portly gentleman Jack didn't recognize sat on the middle seat, his knees pressed against one of the cowboys. He took up way more than his allotted fifteen inches of seating space so it was a good thing they didn't have any more passengers than that.

"Giddy-up," the driver yelled and cracked the whip over the horses' heads. The carriage jolted. The six horses lunged forward, and Lisa fell from her seat onto the mailbags. Horrified he hadn't been quicker, Jack grabbed her arm and helped her back to the bench. "You have to brace yourself. Haven't you ever ridden on a stagecoach before?"

"No." Her cheeks wore a full blush. "They need to have seatbelts."

"Seatbelts?" Now that was a strange notion. "How did you get to Salado if you didn't come by coach?"

"By car," she said, under her breath.

No trains ran through the area. "Who escorted you here?"

"I came alone. Why did you say to take *these* seats?"

"The backseat old Frank is sitting on," Jack said, pointing to him, "has the bumpiest ride. Ours has more of a backrest than the middle. The best seat in the house is next to the driver."

"Poor Frank." She gave him an impish smile. Lifting the leather flap over her window, she peered out while they left the outskirts of town.

"The carriage wheels and horses stir up too much dirt along the Chisholm Trail to look at the scenery," Jack warned, as the coach filled with dust, making the passengers cough and cover their faces.

She quickly dropped the flap.

"Besides, there's not much to look at between here and Waco, believe me."

"I wanted to see if we were really leaving Salado. Why aren't there more passengers?"

Why wouldn't they be leaving Salado? He caught himself before he shook his head. "Mail gets priority." Which he assumed she would have known also.

"Really? How long does it take to get to Waco by stagecoach?"

"Five hours if we have no trouble along the way."

"You're kidding? Forty-five minutes by car and I would have been home." She stared at the floor, her brows pinched together in a deep frown. "I should never have left Waco last night."

Probably would have been best for all concerned, as much as he hated admitting it. Jack glared at Frank, wishing he'd never come along for the ride and knowing full well, he had no business going to Waco today. He thought about the three girls arriving on the coach and guessed Frank lost out on catching their interest, too.

Lisa shook her head. "Poor ol' Jacob looked like he was going to have quite a shiner over me."

His worst fear realized, Jack stared at her.

Seeing his expression, she quickly amended her words, her cheeks crimson, her eyes narrowed. "I *meant* he was going to have a black eye over Josephine."

***

Later that afternoon, after a long, dusty, bumpy ride, the stagecoach arrived in Waco. As soon as it stopped, Lisa's heartbeat quickened. She stared at the leather flap, willing herself to lift it, to look at the city and see if it was an 1870 version like Salado. Taking a deep breath, she pushed aside the leather flap and gaped at the sight. She felt like she'd stepped into one of the old-time sepia pictures she'd seen of Waco—only everything was in vivid, living color.

"What in the world..."

Jack leaned over her and looked out the window. "What? What do you see?"

She put her hand to her mouth and her eyes watered. Her stomach grew queasy, and if she hadn't been sitting, her legs would have given out.

She'd hoped with all her heart returning to Waco would have brought her home. The bone-jolting, five-hour ride wasn't the worst of it. Somehow, she really was stuck in the past, and her stomach knotted with the realization it wasn't just a night terror that wouldn't go away.

"What's wrong, Lisa? I thought a tornado had hit town." Jack reached over and touched her arm. "You're shaking."

Tears welled up in her throat, and she couldn't say anything. God, how had she ended up in the past? She wasn't equipped for this.

The stagecoach driver began helping passengers out, but Lisa didn't want to leave. In a weird way, the coach was the only connection she had with Salado and the last known link to her world.

The assistant unloaded the bags and dropped them on a wooden walkway. Frank and Jack waited for Lisa. She wasn't leaving. She didn't belong here, and she wanted to go home.

"Ma'am." The driver offered his hand, a curious expression on his face when she didn't move.

Jack touched her shoulder. "Where to now?"

"We need to get on our way, sir," the driver insisted.

Jack took Lisa's arm and before she could object, he helped her out. She felt disconnected—in a world so different.

"Are you all right?" Jack asked.

Frank hurried to join them. "Why did you want to come here, Josephine?"

Jack scowled at him. "Do you mind? I was having a private conversation with the lady and nobody asked you to come along."

Lisa stared at the brick buildings, the buggies, wagons, and horses filling the street. "It's just like Salado."

Jack glanced around at the city street, bustling with carriages and horse traffic. "Waco's much different from Salado. The town''s larger and it has more—"

"I can't stay here." She had no money, no clothes, no home, no family, or friends. How could she hope to survive? What would become of her? She couldn't stay. She had to find her way home.

Frank offered her his arm. "I'll take you back to Salado. I never did like this wild place with its gambling and saloons. It isn't the place for a lady like yourself. Why the town is known as Six Shooter Junction."

"She knows that, Frank. She lives here." Jack glowered at him, then turned his attention to Lisa. "We just got here. I thought you had to return to Waco, your hometown, right?"

"Not this Waco." Tears collected in her eyes, and a colossal headache pooled in her temple. Not that she was happy in her Waco, but she was certain she'd never be able to manage here without a support system.

"There's another? No, this is it all right. What's the matter, Lisa? Is it the fever?" Jack asked.

Her legs failed, and she grabbed a hitching post to steady herself. Jack grasped her arm and guided her to a wrought iron bench next to a dress shop storefront.

Chill bumps coated her arms, and her stomach churned with nausea

"Sit here, Lisa." Jack felt her forehead. "Your temperature feels normal. What's wrong?"

Frank sat on the bench next to Lisa and studied her.

How had it happened? She stared at the boardwalk, trying to recollect the events of last night that might have sent her here. "I'd—I'd fought with—"

"With Bill?" Jack asked, his voice harsh.

When he interrupted her, she stared at him. "I didn't know about that," Frank said. "What was it about? Was it Bill?"

"I'm talking to myself, Jack, trying to make sense of what happened to me last night." Lisa ignored Frank.

"Sorry, go ahead, and I'll be quiet." Jack folded his

arms.

"I went to Salado, checked into the hotel—"

"Purchased the necklace first, remember?" Jack offered.

Lisa touched the amethyst at her throat. The necklace. Ohmigod, *the necklace.* "I'd—I'd had an obsessive compulsion to shop at an antique store despite that it was closing time. I wanted something to—to appease myself because of Barry."

"Who's Barry?" Frank asked.

Jack's brows furrowed deeply.

Closing her eyes, Lisa envisioned the white stone façade of the store, the metal roof extended over a boardwalk. The building had been designed to give the appearance of an old western Salado, but now that she had seen the original version of the town, she realized how fake everything had been.

"The—the fading sun streamed through a big picture window and shined like a spotlight on an amethyst necklace inside a glass case. The purple gem is my birthstone, and anytime I see one, I'm drawn to it. The crystal beckoned me to touch it. In the next instant, I was handing the clerk my credit card."

Frank looked puzzled. "Credit...card?"

"I—I..." Lisa rubbed her temple and tried to recall what happened next. "I had dinner and—"

"Yes, roast beef, mashed potatoes, salad, and pecan pie," Jack added.

Lisa frowned at him.

"I overhead you tell the clerk."

She took a deep breath, but it didn't settle her nerves. "I checked into the hotel and retired to bed. In the morning my bag was missing, everything had changed, and—"

"You ran into me."

Yeah, of all places—in bed. Her body heated. Had he rented the room like he said, and she paid for the same room, popped in from the future, climbed onto the mattress, and joined him? But *Josephine* was registered to the room. Which meant someone had disposed of her before Jack settled there for the night.

"What's happened to me?" She bit down on her lip to keep it from quivering.

Taking her hand, Jack crouched in front of her. "We're in Waco. Remember? Don't you recall this place at all?"

"How come you let him hold your hand, Josephine?" Frank asked.

A surrey rolled by, its black fringe jiggling from its flat top, similar to the restored horse-drawn buggy she'd seen in a vintage carriage show in Waco, with its black leather padded seats for three passengers in front and back, and wooden spoke wheels. "How could I have gotten here?" she asked.

Jack frowned. "Don't you remember the stagecoach ride?"

"Of course, Jack." She wasn't *that* out of it. She stared at his clothes and glanced at the shop window behind her. "I've got to go back to Salado."

"What? Now? We just got here. Wouldn't you like to eat first? Maybe you can show me the shop where they have the clothes you're wearing."

"I'll take you back, Josephine." Frank stood up from the bench.

"We have to return. I have to find out what happened. I'm not supposed to be here."

Jack frowned at her. "The next stage doesn't leave until tomorrow. I've heard of women changing their minds, but—"

"Tomorrow? Why didn't you tell me?"

He cleared his throat. "I figured you'd already know. Listen, we'll eat. You'll feel better. We can take a look around. Afterward we can…" He paused, his brow furrowed as if deep in thought, and then he glanced away. "We can head back to Salado tomorrow, if that's what you've a mind to do." There was something about the way he wouldn't look at her that made her think he wasn't being totally honest. He turned and reached out to touch her cheek. "You're feeling all right, aren't you? You look peeked."

No, she wasn't feeling all right. She touched the necklace. What if she took it off? Try as she might, she couldn't remember when she'd put it on—after buying it? Before dinner? After she got a room? If she took it off now, and that's what had brought her into the past, her car would be stuck forty-five miles away in Salado. And she'd be on foot in a part of downtown Waco that wouldn't be safe for a woman alone in her time period. As much as she hated riding that rocking coach back to Salado or spending another minute worrying she couldn't get back to her time, her options were dismal.

With the best cheerful face she could muster, she hoped she wasn't stuck here for good and would try to see this as an adventure until she could return to Salado. She let out a heavy sigh. "Thank you, Jack. What would I have done without you?"

"What about me?" Frank asked, looking annoyed.

Jack offered her his arm. She glanced at the window of the dressmaker's shop again and admired the robin's egg blue dress in the storefront.

"Would you like to try it on?"

"Oh, no. I don't have any money. At least, not the kind they use here."

"I do. I'd love to see you wearing the dress."

"I would also." Frank glanced at the gown.

Lisa's brows furrowed while she considered the garment further. If they couldn't return to Salado for another day, she wouldn't mind trying on a genuine dress from the nineteenth century. She'd never have another opportunity, hopefully. "If you're sure we can't return to Salado, I guess I could try it on."

Jack opened the door for her. The bell jingled overhead, announcing their arrival.

Lisa took a deep breath of the fragrance of violets scenting the air and glanced back at the dress in the storefront window.

Frank walked up to the door, but Jack let it slam in his face.

"Hey." Frank pushed the door open.

The clerk smiled at Lisa and brought the gown off the display. "It's the latest fashion, Miss, from back east. This pale blue will look beautiful with your coloring."

Jack and Frank sat down in the waiting area, while the woman escorted Lisa back to the fitting room.

Glad Josephine was feeling a little better, Jack thumbed through the newspaper. "Would you look at this. Texas Rangers arrested John Wesley Hardin for murdering a man in Waco. The wily seventeen year old bought a Colt .45 and an overcoat off a prisoner in the log jail at Marshall before he was brought back here for trial. Ever see that jail?" Jack asked Frank. "Pretty crude."

"Why in the world would the sheriff put an armed prisoner in a jail cell?" Frank shook his head. "How many people they say that kid's killed now?"

"Not sure, but he added another to his list. Says here while they were on the trail headed for Waco, Texas Ranger Captain Stokes left a guard, Dallas Smolly, in charge of Hardin while he rustled up fodder for the horses. Hardin slipped the gun out from underneath his overcoat and shot Smolly dead, stole a horse, and ran."

"Guess he won't be tried in Waco anytime soon. I've heard he's got kinfolk all over the state, and they'll make sure he doesn't get caught again. Can you believe his father's a Methodist minister? Wonder what he thinks of all this."

"I heard he told his son to run."

A shadow drew over the newspaper, and Jack looked up. The clerk wrung her hands and cleared her throat. "The young lady needs some—uhm—other items, sir."

Jack raised his eyebrows. "Other things?"

The woman's face flushed. She looked back at the dressing room and whispered, "Yes, some..." She paused when another customer entered the shop.

"Yes?" Jack asked, his curiosity piqued.

The clerk nodded to the other lady. "I'll be with you in a minute, Ma'am." She said to Jack in a hushed voice, "The lady needs proper undergarments."

The image of Josephine in bed with him and her legs bare underneath the skirt flashed through his mind. He'd thought she'd removed the garments for the night. Apparently not. The lacy item she wore under her blouse was just as intriguing. He glanced at the dressing room, not believing all the time he'd been with her she was half naked. "Get her whatever she needs, Miss."

The flustered clerk nodded, grabbed a few articles of clothing from the store, and returned to help Josephine dress.

"What did she mean by that?" Frank asked.

"Don't you have business in Waco, other than bothering us?" It wasn't that Jack didn't like Frank, or Bill for that matter, but until the woman knew who she was, he was not about to allow any of them to confuse her further. Yet, he couldn't believe how much she intrigued him.

For an instant, guilt washed over him when he thought of his cherished Charlotte, although he reminded himself it had been two years since he'd buried her, and she wouldn't have wished him to mourn her the rest of his life. Besides, he was here to protect Josephine from the unwanted attentions of other men, and return her to her family so *they* could take care of her until she was less—bewildered.

Frank scowled. "You have no business here either. Wait 'til Bill gets word of this."

"I don't imagine he'll be none too happy you tagged along, either."

Josephine cried out, "That's too tight!"

Jack chuckled.

When Josephine joined them in the waiting area, both Jack and Frank jumped from their chairs and gawked at her. She smiled and the expression was pure joy. She turned around and showed off the bustle of the blue gown.

"You look stunning," Jack and Frank said at the

same time.

The clerk smiled at them and waited for one of them to purchase the garments. Jack took the woman aside and paid for the items.

"Yes," Frank said, "now that's how you should look."

"I didn't mean for you to buy the gown, Jack. I was only going to try it on since we're stuck here for so long." She admired herself in the gold-gilt, oval mirror.

The clerk handed Josephine her original clothes bundled, which Jack took hold of. "Here, let me carry that. Let's see what else we can find."

"But, Jack—"

He led her outside, silencing her objection.

"We'd better stick to lunch, or we'll never be able to afford the stage back home." She touched the folds in her skirt.

"Home? I thought this was your home." At least it had been, except for the time when Josephine lived with another family in Salado the previous year when her aunt had been so sick. Once she'd moved into town, the fellows had fallen all over themselves trying to get her to commit to marriage, especially Bill.

Jack studied her expression and worried about how she seemed so thoroughly confused. He was torn between helping her remember and losing her to the old Josephine, if that's who she truly was. Heck, now he was not so sure. Lisa Welsh. He liked the sound of the name she'd given herself.

"I mean, we should return to your home, Salado," she said, her voice soft. She seemed so unsure of herself at times, like now, that he wanted to take her into his arms and shield her from whatever ailed her.

He pointed to a restaurant. "How about we eat there?"

She gave a slight nod. He wished the spirit she'd exhibited earlier in the day would return. He didn't know how to take her current mood.

When they passed the millinery shop, a blue hat decorated with ostrich plumes displayed in the window caught his eye. "Let's stop in this one." Her hair should have been off her shoulders for a young lady her age. Only young girls left their hair hanging past their hips. Maybe a hat would make her appear less conspicuous. More than once, his gaze had drifted to her ponytail swaying slightly with the movement of her narrow hips. She drew way too much attention from the male passersby on the street.

"You've spent enough on me, Jack. You don't even know me."

"I haven't had this much fun in a long time. Please allow me—"

"Bill's going to be furious," Frank said.

Ignoring Frank, Jack opened the door for her. Frank hurried to grab the door before it slammed in his face a second time.

Before long, Josephine was modeling the newest fashions in hat designs, her brilliant smiles cheering Jack on.

He shook his head at the first, laughed at another, and nodded at the third. "That'll do." He paid the lady and escorted Josephine to the hotel restaurant next door.

"I know I don't belong here, but at least I feel I fit in somewhat, now. Thank you," she said to Jack when the three of them took their seats.

"You fit in just fine, wherever you are. But what do

you mean by you don't belong here?"

"It's hard to explain. I don't really understand what's happened myself."

He hoped she'd elaborate, but when she didn't, Frank filled the silence, talking about himself the whole time between mouthfuls of food. He didn't even seem to notice she wore a faraway expression, and Jack bet his last dollar she hadn't heard a word Frank said.

After lunch, Jack escorted her outside while Frank tagged along like their pet retriever. Jack eyed the portrait studio across the street and steered Josephine that way. He wasn't sure what had gotten into him to want a portrait, but something compelled him to do it. "William Jackson is a friend of mine and does portraits for a reasonable price. Let's get one while we're here."

She balked when they reached the door. "This isn't a good idea, Jack." She studied the grim-faced family portraits on display in the front window.

"Humor me, if you would." He *had* to get a photo of her, maybe to prove she wasn't Josephine in the event she was telling the truth.

The three of them entered the shop, and the photographer greeted Jack warmly. He acknowledged Josephine with eyebrows arched while a smile stretched across his face. "Seems you've been busy, Jack."

"I want a portrait of the young lady." Jack took her arm and led her farther into the studio.

"With you also, Jack, surely," William said.

"What about me?" Frank asked.

Jack took a deep breath. *You can get lost.* "You can have one taken of yourself after we're through, Frank."

"Bill isn't going to like this one bit." Frank tapped his foot on the wooden floor.

William motioned for Jack and Josephine to sit together while Frank sat nearby to watch. He chuckled when she smiled at the camera. "It takes a long time for the photographer to get set up. You ought to relax a bit."

She continued to smile. Jack smiled at her. "I've never seen anyone smiling in a photograph before."

William cleared his throat to get his attention.

"Sorry." Jack looked back at the camera.

Josephine took Jack's hand in hers and squeezed. "Smile," she whispered to him.

Amused by her comment, Jack smiled and the light flashed.

Frank shook his head. "Bill's *really* not going to like this."

After Jack paid for the photo, William led them to the door. "I'll have your portrait sent to you in Salado when it's finished. Good seeing you again."

"You, too, William."

"We fought together in the War. We kept each other's spirits up during the worst of it," Jack said, escorting Josephine outside, knowing it was now or never to propose what he had to, but he wasn't taking no for an answer. He glanced at his pocket watch. "Let's locate the post office, Frank."

Frank gave him a puzzled look.

Jack hadn't wanted to be this obvious in case she threw a fit. "You know, locate Polly Rogers. Maybe she could help us with—"

Josephine frowned at him. "I don't have any family."

She seemed so sure of her words, but Jack knew for a fact Josephine had relatives. Although even if she wasn't Josephine, someone had to be caring for her.

Frank intervened. "Now, that's not so, Josephine, why—"

"My parents died in a tragic airplane..." She paused. "I mean, a bad accident a couple of years ago. I was an only child and—"

Frank softened his approach. "We know you're an only child, but you have—"

"My mother had no siblings and my father's sister died at an early age. So I'm alone in the world," she insisted, her expression changing from being reasonable to perturbed with Frank.

"What about Aunt Polly?" Frank asked.

"I have no Aunt Polly or any other aunt or uncle. I told you my mother was an only child and my father's sister died at a young age. Weren't you listening?"

"I met her at a picnic. She's really a remarkable lady. You favor her, too," Frank said.

"You mean, Josephine favored her aunt. I'm *not* Josephine."

Frank looked at Jack. "Miss Rogers had a house both here and in Belton. Josephine has a couple of uncles who live here, too."

And a cousin named Trevor Rogers if the outlaw they had brought into Salado was right about that. If Jack could help sort out the dilemma about her, he was willing to try. She seemed so adamant she wasn't Josephine, he hoped this would prove she wasn't. The other fellows would leave her alone, and he'd have a chance at the whole deck of cards. "Sounds like a good idea."

Her eyes widened. "I'll stay here, thank you very much, while you wander around the city looking for someone I don't know."

"You said this was your home. We'll talk to Polly Rogers. Put Frank's mind to rest."

She glowered at Jack. "What about you?"

Jack took her arm and walked her toward the post office down the street. "I believe you." As much as he could. Certainly, his heart desired to learn beyond a doubt she wasn't Josephine, but his mind had serious reservations.

***

"Excuse me," Jack said to the window clerk who nodded to the three of them when they entered the post office. Except for the postal clerk, the place was deserted. "We're trying to locate the home of Miss Polly Rogers. Could you tell us where it's located, sir?"

The clerk frowned. "Miss Rogers is deceased, mister."

A queer look crossed Josephine's face.

"Deceased? Are you certain?" Jack asked.

"Yes, we have only one Polly Rogers in Waco." The clerk studied Josephine who considered the oak mailboxes stacked in neat little rows. She ran her fingers over the brass plates etched with numbers. The clerk turned to Jack. "She has a couple of brothers and a niece who survived her."

"How did she die?"

"She died of yellow fever from what I heard."

Josephine's face turned white as a sheet of colorless parchment.

The clerk threw his hands up in the air and exclaimed, "Your missus!"

Jack caught her before she crumpled to the wooden floor in a heap of blue gown and petticoats.

CHAPTER 6

"Josephine." The dark-haired cowboy's expression seemed stricken while he fanned her with his Stetson. Disoriented, she stared at him—unsure as to where she was or who he was—until her head began to clear. Offering his strength, Jack Stanton helped her to her feet. "I'm sorry. The news must have come to you as a shock." His voice expressed profound regret.

She couldn't believe this could be happening to her.

The clerk brought her a glass of water. "You're her niece, aren't you, Miss? I remember you coming in here with Miss Rogers quite often." Lisa stared at the man, unable to croak a response as he quickly added, "I've got some mail for Miss Rogers. She mentioned you'd been ill, too, but I guess you got over the sickness. Her brothers were here looking for the mail, but I wanted to make certain you got it. It was a shame she had to go like that. She was a kind soul...brought me cookies every Christmas."

Tears streamed down Lisa's cheeks, and she choked on the words. "I don't know any Polly Rogers."

Had Josephine given her aunt the dreaded yellow fever and Polly died? And poor Josephine was recuperating when the men must have killed her at the hotel in the room where Lisa spent the night. *It had to be*. Josephine had tons of suitors in Salado, and not one of them knew what had become of her. But some of them had thought she'd died. From the yellow fever?

The worried clerk looked at Jack.

"It's the fever," Jack said. "She's not been herself of late."

The man nodded and handed the mail to Lisa, but when she refused to take it, Frank grabbed the letters for her.

It wasn't hers. She had no right to take them. And neither did Frank. But if she made a fuss, would they arrest Frank for stealing the mail?

"Would you happen to know where Miss Rogers' brothers live?" Jack asked.

The clerk frowned. "You wouldn't want to take the young lady there."

Frank shoved the mail into his coat pocket. "Where?"

"They're probably down by the waterfront. Several saloons and houses of...*ahem*, they refer to it as the Reservation, Two Street, all legal and licensed," the clerk said, then glanced at Lisa. "It's no place for the young lady."

Great. Just great. They thought she was Josephine, and the woman couldn't even have a decent family to prove Lisa wasn't her.

"What about any relations for a Lisa Welsh?" Jack

asked the clerk.

He shook his head. "No one by the name of Welsh gets mail here."

Of course not! She could have told him that.

Jack said to Frank, "You can take Josephine to look at more of the town while I check on this other business." After Jack thanked the clerk, he guided Lisa out of the post office.

Frank fumbled with his hat. "I'm sorry about your Aunt Polly. I had no idea."

"We've covered this ground before, Frank," Lisa said, scowling. "You, too, Jack. I'm not Josephine, and I have no living relatives whatsoever."

Jack handed her his handkerchief, and she wiped the tears from her face. The scary part was she had to get home before whoever murdered Josephine tried to kill her, too. What if they thought she could identify them?

Frank shook his head. "I know Polly Rogers never married and that your father and mother died a couple of years ago in a carriage mishap. Your father did have two brothers besides his sister Polly."

Lisa's mind shifted between worries. What if she stayed here too long? Would she get stuck in this time period? She laughed a bit hysterically, and Jack and Frank shared a worried look.

Hell, she *was* stuck in this time period. Whatever made her think she was going anywhere? Her body chilled.

Jack rubbed his chin. "What upset you at the post office, if Polly wasn't a relation?"

Feeling the letter in her pocket, Lisa took a deep breath. "Josephine must have given the fever to her aunt while she cared for her at the inn. Her aunt never returned for her, and someone at the inn killed her niece."

Frank and Jack exchanged furtive glances. Jack slipped his hand around her arm and led her down to the main street. His touch was comforting, but she couldn't bite back the annoyance running rampant through her that he didn't believe her.

Yet, even though Aunt Polly was dead, Josephine's uncles could clarify she wasn't Josephine. For her own sanity, Lisa needed Jack to believe her. "I'll go to the waterfront with you."

Jack's eyes widened, and he shook his head. "No."

Frank chimed in, "Jack's right, Josephine. It wouldn't be a good idea."

"I'll go by myself. I'm *not* Josephine, and they'll vouch for that." She headed for the riverfront.

"Wait up!" Frank hollered, and he and Jack jogged to catch up.

"You can be just as stubborn as Josephine, that's for certain." Jack's brow furrowed in annoyance while he walked beside her.

Frank pleaded with her, "You can't go there, Josephine. It's not the kind of place a proper young lady belongs."

"It can't be that bad, and *quit* calling me Josephine." Because of all the racy stuff she'd seen in the movies, she didn't imagine much could shock her.

Scowling, Frank shrugged. "I've tried to talk sense into her. What about you, Jack?"

Jack reached for her arm and pulled her to a halt. She glared at him. "You don't have to prove anything by me. You *are* Lisa, as far as I'm concerned."

"You don't really believe me. I want to see Josephine's uncles, now. Either you come with me or you don't, but I'm going." She shook loose of him and continued to walk toward the river while Jack and Frank stalked alongside her.

When they approached the two and three-story wooden buildings squashed along the waterfront, she saw women hanging out of windows, their corsets barely covering their milky white breasts. They waved at potential customers and one woman shouted, "Ask for Lilly, boys. Leave her kind outside. Unless she's looking for work."

Seeing the real thing wasn't what Lisa thought it would be. Most of the women were harder looking. Certainly not like the movies portrayed them. Some appeared to be in their teens and some approached their sixties. Most looked to be in their twenties.

Frank's face reddened. "Haven't you seen enough, Josephine? I'll find out if your uncles are here. No need you coming in."

Curious as to what a house of ill repute really looked like in the old days, Lisa shook her head. "I'll go in." She hoped she wouldn't regret it.

Jack cast her an aggravated look and pushed the door aside. The situation was his fault. If he had believed her, she *wouldn't* have to do this.

They entered the smoke-filled room, the player piano rolling out tinny tunes. The smoke burned her eyes and lungs, and Lisa coughed. Boy, was she glad Waco had passed a city ordinance banning smoking in restaurants. Right, like that would matter any longer unless she lived another one-hundred-and-forty years.

She stared through the haze at the tables where

men wearing suits or suede chaps edged in fringe played keno and poker. The men shifted their attention to the new arrivals, and one of the rugged-looking characters whistled at her. She stiffened her back and was glad she had Jack and Frank to protect her.

Jack took her arm and held her close, giving her a boost of courage while they walked deeper into the room. The men leered at her, and her resolve faded.

Frank walked over to one of the tables. "Do you know the Rogers' brothers?"

A bearded gambler with narrowed eyes shifted his attention from Lisa to Frank. "Who wants to know?"

Another lifted a whiskey glass to his ruddy lips. "Can't you see we're playing a game? Get lost."

"We're looking for this young lady's relations," Frank persisted.

"She's related to Clyde and Melvin?" the first gambler asked, raising his black bushy brows. "Who would have ever thought..." He stood and offered his chair to Lisa. "Here, Miss, have a seat."

Lisa shook her head.

The other said, "They could have thrown her into the pot when they were divvying up their cash." He smiled and looked Lisa over. "She'd have been a darn good trade."

Frank stepped toward the man, but Jack took hold of his arm. "Easy, Frank. We didn't come here to fight. We just want to see Josephine's uncles."

"Probably can't even cook," the other man said.

"Something's wrong with you, Isaac," the first gambler said, giving his head a shake.

Her face brightly colored and with her breasts nearly bare, one of the women working in the saloon sashayed up to Jack and put her hands on his chest. "Hey, fellas, want a drink?" She ran her fingers over his vest. "Maybe you want to come upstairs with me, big boy." She pointed at the sign on the stairs that read: *Satisfaction Guaranteed or Your Money Back.*

Not believing the same message was used back in the nineteenth century in a house in the red light district, Lisa laughed. Both Frank and Jack glanced at her, their jaws dropping.

"No," Jack said to the bawdy woman, his deep voice shaded with annoyance.

She considered Frank next. "Maybe *you* got what it takes, mister."

Frank shook his head.

She switched her attention to Lisa. "Did you bring her in here for the trade, or what?"

"We're looking for her uncles." Frank pushed the groping woman's fingers from his jacket.

She nodded and touched Lisa's hair. Lisa gave her the evil eye but stood her ground.

Lisa's response brought a touch of a smile to the woman's lips. "What do you think, Missy? Have you got what it takes to work here? I'm Rose, and I own the joint. Your uncles aren't here. I've given them enough credit they'll owe me their next month of wages. Maybe you could pay off their debt, being you're a relative of theirs."

Lisa glared at the woman. "I wouldn't be related to anyone like that." Not that she'd ever admit to it.

Frank shoved his hat back on his head. "Where are they?"

The woman motioned with her head at the building next door. "I hear they're trying their luck at Josie's, but I doubt their game will be much better."

Jack escorted Lisa to the door. She assured herself Josephine's uncles wouldn't recognize her, but she was beginning to think this might be a mistake.

"If you change your mind, honey, ask for Rose. We could sure use your kind." Rose smiled and winked at Lisa, then puckered her red lips and made a kissing motion at Jack.

***

Jack hadn't wanted her to see the darker side of Waco, and now he wished he hadn't mentioned looking for Josephine's relatives. He wasn't certain what he was going to do with her next though. The three walked to the saloon next door, and Jack said to her, "Stay outside on this one. If I find the men, I'll bring them to you."

"No, you insisted we track down Josephine's relatives. So let's get it over with." Her voice sounded not half as sure as before, and her stiff demeanor was melting.

Jack took a deep breath and pushed the door open. She was definitely as stubborn as Josephine, but she was a lot more vulnerable, which made him take his guardian angel role seriously. "This way."

They all squinted to adjust to the hazy light in a scene similar to the other saloon. The house was not as elegantly furnished—no player piano, only spare furnishings, no paintings on the walls. The men were dressed in cowpoke attire, a mix of black or brown vests, leather chaps, white shirts, patched Levis, their garments wearing a coat of dust.

Lisa glowered at the men who ogled her, but her arm trembled. She wasn't as certain of herself as she led them to believe, and Jack admired her for her courage.

A man glanced up from his cards, and his eyes instantly reflected recognition when his gaze lit on her. He pushed his chair aside and strolled over to her. This wasn't good.

"What are *you* doing here?" He reached for her hair.

She slapped his hand away and moved closer to Jack. He knew they were in trouble now.

"We're looking for the Rogers' brothers," Jack said, hoping the woman pressing herself against him was *not* Josephine.

"What fer?" The man's green eyes speared Jack with a look of contempt.

"To clear up a matter for us," Frank responded.

"Hey, Melvin, come here and have a word with our niece."

The sickening realization Lisa *was* Josephine slugged Jack in the gut. He'd heard of amnesia cases before, but hadn't a notion how to help someone with that condition. Even so, he wasn't about to leave her in the hands of these vile polecats.

Melvin jeered at her.

Josephine backed away.

Clyde glanced at his brother. "Come on, *Melvin*, welcome your niece."

Josephine shut her eyes and took a deep breath. When she opened them, she turned to Jack. "I don't know these men."

Clyde smiled. "Sure you do, honey. Come on over and sit with us a spell. I want to thank you gentlemen for finding our niece. We didn't know where she'd disappeared to. When her Aunt Polly died and we'd no word of where she'd gone, we were beside ourselves with worry."

Clyde grabbed Josephine's arm and tried to pull her to the table, but she jerked free and narrowed her eyes. "I don't know you, Mister."

She turned to Jack. "I'm ready to leave."

Wishing he'd never suggested seeking her uncles, he took her arm and turned to depart.

"Wait a minute, Josephine," Clyde said, his brother joining him. "You'll stay here. No more running off to God knows where. We're your kinfolk...guardians now. You come on over and wait with us while we play out our hand."

Melvin stroked his beard and gave her a sinister look. "You ought not to have run off. Aunt Polly wouldn't tell us where you'd disappeared to even when she was taking her last breath."

"Why?" Josephine's voice was filled with tears, but her tone was edgy. "What made Josephine so afraid of you she had to leave town?"

"What are you trying to pull?" Melvin seized her arm. "You're going to learn some manners. After your folks died, our sister never had a tight enough rope on you. You're coming with us."

Jack grabbed Melvin's arm, and then jerked it away from the steel grip he had on Josephine's. "We'll be going."

"You can't take her with you, whoever you are. She's our responsibility, and we'll have you hand her over to us now if you know what's good for you."

Clyde studied Jack's features. "You must be that Bill character Josephine was hung up on."

Jack glowered at the man. "Jack Stanton's the

name."

Clyde smiled at Josephine. "You already got two more fellers on the string, eh? You'll fit in here just fine."

"You two have no claim to the girl, so beat it," Melvin growled.

"This was a mistake, Frank." Jack pulled his coat aside and rested his hand on his revolver.

Frank nodded and did the same. He pushed Josephine behind him and backed toward the double-swinging doors with Jack. Melvin and Clyde kept their eyes on them, but didn't make a move to follow.

When the bartender brought out his rifle, Josephine turned and ran for the doors. "Y'all take it outside!" the bartender said, cradling the weapon across his chest.

One of the sage hens sidled up to Melvin and looped her arm around his. "Come on, Mel, I'll give you a free one if you come upstairs with me."

Melvin looked down at her and smiled. "I thought you'd never offer."

Clyde hit his brother on the shoulder. "Knock it off, Melvin. We gotta get the girl."

"What difference does it make? Who cares what she does?"

"She might come in handy, right, boys?" Clyde said to the other men sitting at the card table. They all smiled and nodded. "Besides she sort a complicates things, Mel," Clyde said under his breath. "We ain't got the title to Polly's house yet."

Hearing Clyde's words, Jack tensed. Josephine didn't belong with the likes of these men.

Melvin eyed Jack's and Frank's guns. "Nothing doing. I've had too much to drink to be much good with my trigger finger. Besides, I ain't had an offer this good in a long time. Come on, Sadie, let's see what you got for me."

Clyde glowered at Jack and Frank while Melvin headed upstairs with the woman. Josephine screamed outside. His heart thundering, Jack dashed out of the saloon with Frank on his heels.

Josephine struggled to free herself from the clutches of a drunken cowboy, but before Frank could react, Jack punched the man in the jaw. The drunk stumbled to his knees, and Jack guided Josephine away from the building. "Let's get out of here before we have any more trouble."

Josephine tugged at Jack's jacket sleeve. "I...I don't belong here. I have to get home."

"Tomorrow. We'll get the stagecoach back to Salado in the morning." But Jack began looking for the nearest doctor's office.

They crossed the busy street, dodging horse-drawn carts and buggies. Gunfire rang out nearby. A small pitiful cry escaped Josephine's lips. Jack grabbed her before she sank to her knees. Her blond lashes fluttered shut. *Hell.*

Lifting her, Jack said, "Let's get her a room at the hotel across the street, Frank. We need to find a doctor." Cradled like a rag doll in Jack's arms, he carried her down the street, her body soft, vulnerable, her mind fragile like a precious porcelain vase.

"Do you still have doubts she's Josephine?"

A wagonload of winter squash passed in front of them. Jack sighed deeply. "She doesn't seem like Josephine. I can't believe it's her. On the other hand, everyone else thinks she is, including her family, so who am I to say she isn't? I didn't know her that well."

"Come on," Frank said, when the road cleared. They hurried across the street, and he glanced at Lisa. "Besides Aunt Polly, probably Bill knew her best. He's convinced she's Josephine."

A young man hastened to open the ornately carved oak doors at the hotel entrance for Jack and Frank. Guests talking in the lobby observed them. Whispered voices ensued, while Jack carried Josephine to a sofa. "Pay for the rooms, Frank. I'll reimburse you later. And inquire about a doctor."

"Sure thing." Frank strode over to the reception desk.

Jack sat beside her and rubbed her hand, calling to her in a coaxing voice. Rapid steps clicking on the wooden floor headed in his direction. The young man had something clutched in his fist. He was one of the hotel staff, Jack presumed.

"Do you need smelling salts, sir?" he asked, motioning to her.

"Yes, do you have any?"

"The hotel carries them in good supply for the ladies who become indisposed like your missus, here." He handed the bottle to Jack. "Happens all the time."

"Oh." She gave a start and waved the bottle out of her face. "Where are we?" She glanced around at the lobby's furnishings. Turning to Jack, she stared at his clothes. "Ohhhh," she moaned and closed her eyes again. "I thought it was a bad dream."

He wrinkled his brow. She was as confused as ever. He helped her to sit. "We're getting you a room. Frank and I'll share another for the night. We'll have supper here at the hotel later."

"No, no, I've got to go home."

"You need to rest. As soon as Frank has your room key we'll take you up, and you can lie down before supper."

"Oh, Jack, whatever am I going to do? What if I can't get back?"

Frank returned with the room keys and interrupted them. "Are you ready to go to your room, Josephine?"

She glared at him. Jack wrapped his arm around her waist and eased her up from the sofa. "Let's take you upstairs."

They walked up the wooden stairs creaking with their footfall. When they reached her room, Frank opened the door. "Here you go." She hesitated and stared at the patchwork quilt covering the bed. "Get some rest and we'll call on you in a while." He handed her the brass key. "Lock the door after us."

Concerned by her frail appearance, Jack was reticent to leave her. "Do you need anything more before we go?"

Shaking her head, she crossed the floor and sat down on the bed.

"We'll be next door if you need us. Get some rest, and we'll see you in a little bit." Jack shut the door and took a deep breath. "What do you want to do?"

"I thought of running to the drugstore for a couple of necessities before it closes." Frank rubbed his face. "I can't stand an evening shadow."

"Me either."

"Well, what are we waiting for?" Frank asked.

The door lock clicked.

"I guess she'll be all right."

"Sure, she'll get some sleep and be her usual self

when we return."

Jack shook his head. "I hope not." He had no desire to see her as Josephine ever again.

***

A rapping...a tapping at the door made Lisa sit up in bed, her mind groggy. "Yes?"

She frowned when there was no response. *Guess I was dreaming.* Though, she could see she was still in the nightmare of the past. She studied the door and listened for further sounds. Feet shuffled in the hallway. Heavier knocking followed. Lisa pushed her unbound hair back away from her face, climbed off the high bed, and crossed the floor.

"Jack?" Her voice was soft with sleep.

"Yes." The man's words were gruff and muffled.

Not recognizing the voice, Lisa paused. "Jack?"

"Yes."

Taking a deep breath, she twisted the long brass key into the keyhole. The lock clicked. Before she could turn the knob, the solid oak door hit her. Throwing her against the wall, it knocked the breath out of her.

Sharp pain shot through her spine, and Josephine's Uncle Clyde lunged into the room. Her heart nearly stopped. Before she could scream, his roughly calloused hand clamped over her mouth. He slammed the door behind them as she grappled with his steely fingers.

"Blasted, Josephine! Behave!" he growled.

He shoved her against the door and wrenched the key from her. Her eyes watered from the pain. With his left hand blocking her cries, he locked the door with his other.

"Now," Clyde said, his heavy breath reeking of whiskey, "you're coming with me whether it's to your likin' or not."

Terror filled her, but she wouldn't go without a fight. Crumbs of cornbread clung to his blond beard, streaked with wiry gray hairs. Dirt piled up in the creases of his tanned skin, while his thin lips turned down in a scowl. Her eyes met his. Cold, calculating.

She dug her fingernails into his hand, but he acted as if it didn't bother him. Her heart pounded so hard she was certain Jack would hear her fear.

Clyde dragged her to the bed. Twisting her body, she kicked him with the toes of her boots. Nothing she did fazed him, and her resolve faltered. He threw her on the bed, and she sank onto the mattress. Before she bolted from the bed, he crushed her with his weight, pinning her down. The air fouled with his ripe body odor, and she wrinkled her nose in disgust. Squirming with renewed gusto, she tried to unsettle him from his pose.

"You listen to me, young'un. I won't have any more trouble from the likes a you." He glanced at the window.

When she struggled to remove his hand from her mouth, he glowered at her with bloodshot eyes.

Muffled protests escaped her lips. He grabbed his sweaty neckerchief with his right hand, and her eyes widened. God, no. After he untangled the knot from the stained cloth, he yanked it from his neck. Shaking her head, she fought having the grimy blue-and-white scarf tied against her mouth.

He slipped it around her head, pulled the cloth hard, and knotted it tight. She managed to strike him in the side of his temple with her fist as forcefully as she could. Immediately, he locked her wrists in his vice-like grip. His thick body pressed against hers, and she sensed the same suffocation she'd had earlier that morning before she had fully awakened from her nightmare.

Reflecting the identical green coloration, her eyes studied his bloodshot ones while she tried to calm herself. *Think, Lisa, think. Panicking won't help.* Her mind clouded over. *The tightness of the corset...the weight of his body...keep a clear head, Lisa. Think.*

"Can't sees how you can deny we're kin, seeing's how much we look alike," he muttered. He grabbed a fistful of her hair and lifted it to his nose. "Smells a might fine."

Scanning the room, he said, "What can I tie ya up with?" He unbuckled his belt while one hand held her wrists. Lisa's eyes widened. He laughed. "Other gals are one thing, but I ain't into that sort of thing with my own kin."

The rattlesnake leather encircled her wrists. She flailed her hands to fight the confinement. The mottled brown leather grew taut, and her struggles grew.

"Be still. You're wearing me out, girl." With a tug, he tied a knot into the belt.

Her heart raced hard, the blood pounding in her ears.

He glanced out the window, rolled off her, and sat up. She breathed in a deeper breath and lay quiet. His noxious odor still permeated her surroundings, and she turned her head away from him, seeking fresher air.

"We'll have to wait until it gets dark. I suspect those two you was with is really the gentlemanly sort and won't be bothering you none tonight."

Lisa squirmed to sit up on the bed while Clyde watched her.

"Nah, I think it'd be a safer bet if you just lie down there." He shoved her back. "Where'd you go for all this time? We looked all o'er Waco, but couldn't find no sign of you. Went searching for you in Belton, too."

He stood, stretched his arms above his head, and walked over to the window. Pulling the velvet curtain aside, he peeked out the bottled-glass.

She glanced at the door, wondering if she ran for it...

Clyde was still staring out the window. His body tensed. She sat up on the bed and scooted to the edge of the mattress, continuing to watch him. After one more push, she jumped down. Her boots smacked the floor, and she cursed the noise she'd made. Clyde swung around.

Her heartbeat accelerating, she dashed for the door. He grabbed her arm. She gave a swift backward kick to his shin. Cursing up a storm, he released her.

"Blue blazes, if I have to, I'll knock you out. I ain't above slappin' a woman around. So mind what I've to say." He grabbed her arm again and yanked her to the bed. When he shoved her down, she sat back up. He glowered at her. "When we're at our place, you'll be mindin' me good, or you'll be feelin' the back of my hand. You're lucky I can't do much here for fear of bein' heard."

To think she'd always wished she'd had relatives. She looked at the door, listening for Frank's and Jack's voices or footsteps in the hall.

"Don't you get no ideas about warnin' your

friends, Missy. I'll kill 'em tombstone dead and claim they was tryin' to harm you. Melvin will back me up, and everyone knows how wayward girls can be."

Boots clicked on the wooden floor in the hallway, and she scarcely breathed. Clyde walked over to the bed and sat next to her. He wrapped his arms around her and squeezed hard. "Just be quiet," he whispered. His warm, whiskey breath on her neck sent chills down her spine.

"Yes, that was something at the spring dance last year. What do you think about the one we're having for the fall fling?"

Jack.

"Plum forgot all about it. It's in a couple of weeks, isn't it?"

"Sure thing."

"You're not thinking of asking Josephine to the affair, are you, Jack? Bill would be furious."

"Not as incensed as he'd be if he learns we stayed with her at the hotel overnight."

Frank laughed. "Guess we'd better not let the word get out. Shall we check and see how she's doing?"

"She's probably still sleeping." They stood silent at her door for a minute. "We'll call on her in another twenty minutes or so when the dining room opens."

Footfalls echoed down the hall. A door opened and closed.

And Lisa's saviors were gone.

Clyde gave a tight smile. "Now, Missy, before they come to check on you, we're goin' to head out that window o'er yonder. It'll be getting' dark soon. We won't have much time, but..." He paused. "Should be enough to make a getaway."

CHAPTER 7

No matter what, Lisa couldn't allow Josephine's uncle to take her away, but she still hadn't come up with a plan. When it grew darker, Clyde unlocked the window sash with a squeak. A glass lantern on the bedside table inches away caught Lisa's notice. Clyde struggled to open the stuck window, and she edged closer to the lamp. The creaking of the bed frame made her heart race with renewed panic. The door slammed next to theirs, and Lisa and Clyde jumped. Clyde shifted his attention back to the window. He worked harder to open it, all the while cursing under his breath.

Footsteps approached her room, and a firm hand knocked on the door. Lisa held her breath.

"Lisa, are you awake?" Jack called out.

Lunging for the lamp, she hit it with her shoulder and sent it crashing to the wooden floor. The cobalt blue glass and floral porcelain shattered.

"No!" Clyde shouted and slapped her cheek, knocking her down on the floor.

"Lisa!" Jack banged on the door. "I heard a man's voice in there and something broke."

"Should I get a key for the room?" Frank asked.

"There's no time."

"Lisa!"

Two sets of fists pounded the door.

"It won't give, Jack. The doors are solid oak." Footsteps ran off.

No, no, no, don't leave me.

Clyde fought again with the stuck window.

Her cheek stinging where he had slapped her, Lisa managed to get to her knees. Desperate, she maneuvered to stand in her long skirt. She whipped around and dashed for the door, her boots making a racket. Before she reached the door, the sinking realization struck her—she didn't have the key.

Clyde bolted after her. He jerked her off the floor, carried her back to the bed, and threw her down. The look in his eyes reflected murder in his heart. He raised his fist threatening her and growled, "Don't move."

She nodded, hoping Jack would bust through the door any minute as the sound of someone's body kept slamming into it. Clyde worked his knife on the rusted latch. The window gave, and Clyde shoved it up.

God, no.

When he grabbed her arm, Lisa jabbed her pointed boots at him, kicking and flailing. Ignoring her futile attempts, he dragged her from the bed and tried to shove her through the window frame. She grappled for it and held on for dear life.

A shot rang out in the hallway. The door handle jiggled and another shot echoed through the hotel.

"Come on, you." Clyde wrenched her loose from

the frame and shoved her onto the wrought iron fire escape. She fell to her knees in the long skirt. He gripped her arms and yanked her up, but she pushed against him, trying to thwart him. "You're worse than that blasted mule I owned. You don't want to know what become of him."

A bullet ricocheted off the knob with a metallic clunk. Clyde pushed her down the stairs, and the fear of falling made her heart jump in her throat. "Hurry it up, girl!" he growled.

"Hey!" Melvin called to them, seated on his mount below the fire escape. "I wondered what become of you. One of them fellars said you'd gone into town to search for Josephine. I saw your horse—"

"Yeah, yeah, help me get Josephine down from here before them fellars catch up to us."

"Sure, thing." Melvin jumped on the step and hauled Lisa onto his horse.

Her heart sank when she realized they could actually get away with her. She was doomed.

***

Jack and Frank burst into Lisa's room. The curtains fluttered in the breeze, beckoning them to the window. They dashed across the room, their boots crunching on the shattered glass. Her hat lay on the side of the bed where the covers had not been disturbed.

He poked his head out the window. "Lisa!"

She struggled with Melvin, her eyes wild with panic. Clyde rode close behind.

Jack shoved his legs through the window frame. "Come on, Frank. We've got to get some mounts and catch up to them."

Frank followed him down the fire escape. "Maybe

we don't have any right interfering because they *are* her relatives and—"

"If you feel that way, fine. I'm going after her. They can't be up to any good. Besides, the doctor's coming to check on her within the hour. You think those men would let her see him?" Jack sprinted for the livery stable.

Frank chased after him. "Can't argue with you there."

When they reached the stable, Jack shouted to the man in charge, "Need to rent a couple of horses, now!" He shoved bills into the livery owner's outstretched hand, while the boy raking the hay in the stalls helped Frank saddle two horses.

Jack had to catch up to the men before they got away. No telling what they'd do to her once they spirited her to their place. Like when Charlotte slipped away from him in death, the notion of losing his charge terrified him. Charlotte had been weak and defenseless, yet he could do nothing to save her. At least with this woman, he had a fighting chance. Someone had to look out for her. It wasn't going to be two whiskey-guzzling, gambling, whoremongers either.

As soon as the horses were ready, Jack jumped into the leather, and kicked the palomino to a gallop. Frank and he guided the animals down the main street.

Frank shook his head. "I haven't seen this much excitement since the War."

"I could do with a lot less of this where she's concerned."

They soon caught sight of Josephine's uncles, turning their horses in front of a wagon filled with hay crossing the road. Maneuvering the rig sharply to avoid hitting the brothers, the driver of the wagon plowed the vehicle into a hitching post. The rear axle cracked and sank to the ground. Hay scattered about the street, and the man shook his fist at them, cursing a blue streak.

Jack pointed to the sheriff walking out of a mercantile to see the commotion. The Rogers brothers skirted around the wagon and headed out of town. The sheriff ran for his horse. When he poked his boot into the stirrup, Frank and Jack galloped past, leaving him choking in a cloud of dust. "Hey!"

Jack yelled over his shoulder, "Those men took my wife!"

Frank raised his brows, his eyes sparkling with humor. "Wife? That's news to me, Jack. When did this happen?"

"When we're chasing two men who bound and gagged their niece, and we're no relation. The law wouldn't be on our side." Jack couldn't get his mind off what he'd nearly done with her in the Shady Villa Inn. He'd compromised her for certain, and if the word ever leaked out, her reputation would be ruined. Hell, even the clerk knew of the mix-up and had to have guessed Jack had been alone in the room with her for a couple of hours. Unless the man was tight-lipped about it...

Now Jack claimed to have married her, and if they managed to free her from Clyde and Melvin Rogers, he couldn't risk her being alone in a hotel room again. Which meant only one thing. He had to propose marriage.

On the other hand, how could he, when the lady didn't know who she was? Or rather, he didn't know who she really was?

"What if Josephine doesn't go along with you on

the ruse?" Frank asked.

"She'll have to stay with her uncles. I'm sure she wouldn't want that. Watch what you say. The sheriff's catching up."

Frank waved his arm. "Josephine's uncles have switched off to a side road."

The sheriff pulled up alongside them and shouted, "What in thunder's going on?"

"Those two men kidnapped my bride," Jack said, hoping he could pull this off. Frank looked wary.

"Weren't those the Rogers brothers?"

Jack looked the sheriff straight in the eye. "Yes, sir, and she's their niece, but they didn't like the idea we got hitched, and they've forced her to go with them."

The sheriff eyed them, and asked Frank, "Who are you?"

"Best man at the wedding." Frank tipped his hat and looked like he struggled to keep a straight face.

***

Melvin twisted in his saddle and glanced back at the riders following them. Lisa hoped Jack and Frank would catch up and free her. "I thought you said there was only two of 'em."

Clyde looked back. "Hell, looks like we done got the sheriff on our backs now."

Lisa's hope soared.

"Yeah, but them two don't have any claim to Josephine," Melvin said.

But she wasn't Josephine. Trying to get loose, Lisa squirmed in the saddle. Melvin gripped her tighter.

"Maybe so, but we've had our passel of trouble with the law, and they may not look none too good on our actions."

"You wanna dump her and—"

Yes, please.

Clyde ran his hand over his whiskered cheek. "Nah, seeing's we come this far we might as well play our cards and see what's dealt us."

How could she have been so stupid to insist she see Josephine's uncles? Well, how did she know they'd be such rotten characters? She should have realized the way others thought she was Josephine, the woman's uncles would also. Yet, she kept thinking if they were her relatives, they had to know Lisa wasn't her.

"Wanna stop?" Melvin squeezed Lisa hard when she tried to slip from the horse. She could barely breathe as tight as the corset was, and her head was fogging again.

"What for?"

"We can say we was runnin' from them men who was after our poor lil' niece to do her harm. When we eyeballed the sheriff, we aimed to straighten the matter out," Melvin explained.

"I guess it wouldn't look none too good to be runnin' from the sheriff if we was in the right. What about Josephine?"

"What about her?"

"Should we untie her? Don't you think it looks odd she's bound and gagged?" Clyde asked.

Yes!

Melvin looked befuddled.

"She'll talk. Hell, I've changed my mind," Clyde said. "Let's head to the cabin like we planned and settle it there. We can kill them men and explain it to the sheriff afterwards. He won't believe what Josephine has to say anyway. Just don't shoot the sheriff."

Ohmigod, she had to warn them.

They slipped down a trail barely visible because of the overgrown shrubs. The trickling water in a creek flowed nearby, and an old cabin came into view. Trees towered close to the roof, and weeds waist-high poked though the weathered, wooden porch.

Clyde dismounted. He grabbed Lisa from Melvin's grasp and dragged her to the house.

Hoping to buy herself more time, she fought him with every ounce of strength she had.

Clyde's face reddened. "Quit kicking me, girl."

She could barely breathe from the dust from the trail and the corset squeezing the breath out of her. She figured if they didn't kill her outright for fighting them, she'd end up dying from all the germs crawling on the dirty rag gagging her. Her vision blurred, and she wished she could wipe the dirt out of her eyes. If she survived this nightmare, she wanted to bathe for a week.

Melvin joined Clyde in the one-room house, then bolted the door. "Tie her to the bed so she won't be interfering in matters, making things worse for us," Clyde said.

"Which bed, Clyde? Your'n or mine?" Melvin held Lisa's arm with a titan grip while he looked from one of the dusty beds to the other.

Ragged blankets lay on each and dingy flour sacks hung lopsided on the windows. The place was cold, just like the men who owned it. The chilly breeze blew through the rough-hewn planks covering the walls, and Lisa shivered.

"Don't matter." Clyde tugged a length of rope

coiled around a wooden peg on the wall and tossed it to Melvin. He peered out the window while Melvin yanked Lisa to the bed. "Here they come."

Melvin struggled with Lisa. "Hell, Clyde, she won't be still."

"Let me do that." Clyde snatched the rope from his brother. "You go to the door nice and easy, and be real friendly like. We'll shoot them two fellars and say they was reachin' for their guns."

Clyde looped the braided hemp through the belt tied to Lisa's wrists and jerked it up. Her arms were nearly wrenched from the sockets, and she let out a muffled cry. He knotted the rope around the bedpost, but as soon as he turned his back on her to watch his brother, she slipped off the bed. Wrenching at the rope, she twisted and turned, trying to pull herself free.

She couldn't let either of the Rogers brothers shoot Jack or Frank.

***

Melvin opened the door slowly, and Jack was ready to shoot the bastard. Hoping they could resolve this without a fight, Jack and Frank sat stiffly in their saddles while the sheriff dismounted.

"Melvin," he said, tipping his hat, "what seems to be the trouble?"

"Why them, varmints," Melvin said, then spit on the ground, "took our lil' niece and were tryin' to have their way with her. You know she's our charge since her ma and pa and our dear sister died."

"What of your wives?"

"Run off. They ain't blood relatives anyway. Now Josephine, she's our kin and got no one to look after her. These varmints were tryin' to take advantage of her at the hotel."

"Let me see Josephine."

Clyde poked his head out the door. "She's tied up at the minute. Besides, she's just a girl. She'll lie to you."

Itching to dismount, Jack shifted in his saddle.

"This here fella," the sheriff said, pointing to Jack, "said he's married to the girl."

Melvin looked at Clyde.

Clyde scowled. "He's lyin'. He ain't gotten hitched to her." He looked back into the cabin. "She ain't even wearing no weddin' band."

Jack's neck muscles tightened as taut as corded rope. He gripped the reins and pushed his jacket aside. The pearl handle of his revolver glistened in the moonlight, but he kept his eager fingers away from the grip.

The sheriff looked at Jack. "Suppose you boys got another story you'd like to tell?"

Trying to settle his temper, Jack took a deep breath and did some fast thinking. "She was wearing the ring this morning. Maybe she removed it when she was washing her hands. These fellows waylaid her. They've got her tied up and gagged. They've taken her against her will."

"Let me see the girl, Clyde," the sheriff said.

"Just a minute, Sheriff, and you can come in, but not them two."

Melvin stood in the doorway with his hand fiddling with the loop over his holster.

The sheriff rested his hand on his gun. "Hurry up, Clyde. What's taking you so long?"

Jack ground his teeth, ready to take matters into his

own hands.

**

Lisa hoped the sheriff could control the Rogers brothers, but she had her doubts.

Clyde whispered to her, "You're not leavin' with them men. So you'd better tell 'em to go away or we'll shoot 'em. You understand?"

Lisa nodded. She had every intention of doing the opposite. No way was she going to be left to the mercy of Josephine's uncles.

Clyde untied her hands and removed the gag. She quickly wiped her mouth.

"Okay, you can come in."

The sheriff removed his hat and entered the house, and nodded to Lisa. "Miss, what's this all about?"

"Please make them let me go."

"Is it true, you're married to that fella out there?"

Lisa hesitated. "Yes, of course and...," she said, and glared at Clyde, "and he didn't like the idea. But I'm married. He has no right treating me like this. Make him let me go." She figured pleading was the only way to get her out of this mess. She looked over at Melvin. His hand gripped his gun still holstered at his waist. "He's going to shoot—"

The gun cleared the holster, but the sheriff swung around and struck Melvin in the back of the head with the pistol grip. Melvin groaned and dropped to the floor in a dusty heap. The sheriff glanced back at Clyde who waved his hands in the air. "I ain't doin' nothin'."

"Smart man." The sheriff turned to Lisa. "You're free to go, Miss. I'm not sure I believe your story, but this isn't the place for you." He looked at the redness on her cheek. "Did one of your uncles do that?"

Her heart still pounding out of control, Lisa nodded. She didn't feel she would be safe until she left Waco. This period Waco anyway.

"Go on, get out of here. I'll take care of this business."

"Thank you, Sheriff." Without thinking, she hugged him.

He gave her a fatherly smile. "If more people were as thankful as you, I'd find it a might more pleasurable job. Take care of yourself, young lady."

Lisa dashed outside to Jack, and he was already dismounting to get her. His look stern, brows knit into a deep frown, he helped her onto his horse. After he slipped into the saddle behind her, he guided them back up the narrow trail away from the cabin and creek, but her heart still beat out of control.

"Are you all right, Lisa?"

She nodded, but she wasn't. She felt like she was jumping from one hot spot to another.

Frank considered Lisa sitting stiffly in the saddle. "Bill's really not going to like this when he hears you got hitched to his girl."

Lisa shook her head, unable to stop thinking of the danger she could be in by staying here. "I've just got to get back home."

"I don't think she had enough rest," Frank said.

"At least she didn't tell the sheriff those men weren't her uncles. I'm afraid he would have thought she was crazy and left her with them."

"Do you think we could have supper and make an early night of it?" Frank asked.

"Sounds like a plan to me." Jack ran his hand over Lisa's while she held tightly onto the horn of his saddle.

"What do you think?"

"Yes." There wasn't anything else to be done for now. Not until she returned to Salado. She'd remove the necklace and hope like hell that would send her home.

Frank studied her for a minute. "What do you think about having married old Jack?"

Shaken from her thoughts of returning home, she faced Frank. "He'd make any girl proud to be his wife." And she believed it for any girl who lived in this century.

Jack smiled and tilted his head to the side in response to Frank's jeers. He wrapped his arm around her waist. Warming to his embrace, she rested her head against his chest. Taking a deep breath of the light scent of his spicy cologne, she said, "You smell like a bit of heaven."

Jack laughed. "I guess I am your guardian angel."

She nestled her face against his silk vest. Running her hand over the soft fabric, she glanced up and found him watching her. "Feel like one, too."

He lowered his mouth and brushed his lips against hers with the faintest touch that stirred her blood. She wanted more, damn it. Hadn't she suffered enough humiliation to deserve a healthy kiss?

But it wouldn't be proper.

Damn propriety. She leaned into him and kissed him back, his mouth soft and smooth, hot and sensual. For an instant, he didn't respond as the horse's gait rocked them on the rain-rutted road. She figured she'd stunned him into a coma. Then Jack's expression subtly changed. His eyes smoldered with lust, and his lips melded against hers, firmly, possessively, and he gripped her tighter like he never wanted to let her go.

A strange sensation swirled through her, a bit of warmth and comfort, but a whole lot of dread, too. She had the oddest feeling she'd sealed her fate. Surprise reflected in his eyes, too. Probably because she'd so wantonly kissed him back.

She wished he lived in her world.

"You're courting disaster, Jack," Frank warned when they cantered back to town.

Rubbing his chin, Jack ignored him, but his expression seemed thoughtful, and she was dying to know what he was thinking.

"I wonder if they'll let us back into the hotel."

He was thinking about the hotel? Not about her?

"Just because you got trigger happy and shot up the door to Josephine's room?" Frank patted his bay's neck. "At least you didn't get our rented horses shot up none."

Lisa fingered Jack's jacket, her thoughts a million miles away. "How will I ever get home?" she said under her breath, while the horses clopped away on the dirt road and the ancient stars sparkled overhead, one-hundred-and-forty years younger than when she'd seen them the night before.

***

Jack didn't know what had come over him to kiss the woman, but he suspected it had to do with being glad Lisa was safe and the overwhelming desire he felt to confirm she was interested in him. The way she kissed him back told him she was.

Very interested. After all, she said he'd make a girl proud to be his wife. He sighed deeply. He had a sneaking suspicion the doctor wouldn't be able to help

A GHOST OF A CHANCE AT LOVE

her. Which meant he would have to take matters into his own hands.

He still couldn't get her kiss out of his mind, sweet, somewhat reserved, but a hint of passion lurked just beneath the surface. Yet there was more to it than that, as though her reaction to him had sealed a promise, forever she would be his.

He glanced at his pocket watch. They were late. And they still hadn't stabled the horses. "Frank, do you mind returning our mounts? We might have missed Doc King, but if not…"

"I'll take care of them."

As soon as Jack went to help her down from the horse, he noted her mood had changed from grateful to stormy. "Lisa?"

She yanked her arm free of Jack's hand. "I *don't* need to see a doctor."

Frank chuckled as he led the horses away. "Think I've got the easier job."

"We'll just talk to the doctor," Jack coaxed, trying to escort her into the hotel.

She backed away from him, her green eyes blazing with heat. "I won't see him."

"He might have recommendations concerning your condition."

Her eyes filled with tears. "There's nothing wrong with me."

"All right, just humor me, will you?"

"You sure need a lot of humoring, Jack Stanton."

He managed a small smile and escorted her into the hotel, but he wanted to throw her over his shoulder and haul her inside as much as she balked. The worse she acted, the more trouble they'd have.

He spied the doctor speaking to the hotel manager, and a mixture of relief and concern washed over Jack. Relief, because they hadn't missed him, concern because he worried what the doctor might have in mind, and *that* didn't set well with him.

The manager's eyes widened, and he hurried to join them. "You rescued your sister, thank heavens, Mr. Stanton. Frank Collins said a couple of down-on-their-luck gamblers had taken off with her."

"Uh, yes. This is Miss Lisa Stanton."

The bearded doctor observed them. Lisa didn't seem to notice him, or else she might have headed back outside.

"I'll pay for the damages to the door, Sir. And I'll be needing another room for my sister." Hopefully the sheriff wouldn't visit the hotel and discover Jack had "married" his sister. Couldn't Frank have warned him beforehand?

"Mr. Stanton," the doctor said, offering his hand. "You wished to see me concerning the young lady?"

"Yes, Dr. King. I'm sorry we were delayed."

"Quite all right under the circumstances. The manager informed me of the situation. Perhaps we could find a quiet place to talk?"

Lisa's face had grown pale again, and she looked ready to bolt. Jack grabbed her hand.

"I'll get you a key for the room next to yours," the manager said and returned to the registration counter.

"My pleasure to meet you, Miss. I understand you had a bout of yellow fever," the doctor said.

Lisa pursed her lips and shifted her tempestuous gaze to Jack. Before he could confirm her condition, she said, "I'm fine, Doctor. It's so good of you to see me, but Jack was mistaken. I feel great. There's nothing wrong with me."

The manager returned with the key. "Please, if you need anything further, don't hesitate to call on me."

"Thank you kindly, Sir." Jack slipped his hand around Lisa's arm, but when she balked again, he used a little more force. "Everything will be fine."

She *humpfed* under her breath.

Dr. King watched their interaction, and Jack hoped the doc wouldn't recognize he and Lisa were not brother and sister.

They entered the hotel room, and while Lisa sat down on the bed, the doc took Jack aside. "You said she's confused about who she is. When you came to my office, you said she suffered from a case of amnesia, and that she believes herself to be Lisa Welsh, while others think she is Josephine Rogers. Now you say she's your sister Lisa Stanton. Are you certain the young lady is the one who suffers from amnesia, Sir?"

Evidently having heard the gist of the conversation, Lisa smiled.

Jack cleared his throat. He wasn't normally a lying man, and now he knew why. "The truth is she looks like Miss Josephine Rogers who had suffered from yellow fever. Everyone believes her to be this woman except for Lisa."

"And you, apparently, have your doubts," the doctor said.

"She has a curious manner of speaking and doesn't act like Josephine. Not only does she deny she's Josephine, she has difficulty understanding some of our ways."

Dr. King rubbed his chin thoughtfully. "I see." He

considered Lisa. Her face was grim, and she looked like she had been condemned to hang from the gallows. "So, young lady," he said, approaching her in a non-threatening manner, "would you like to tell me who you are and where you're from?"

She gave a short laugh. "Lisa Welsh. I'm from Sacramento originally. That's why I have an unusual speech pattern. And...out there," she said, waving her hand, "...we do things differently."

"Mr. Stanton tells me you're from Waco."

She didn't respond. Though Jack wanted to get to the bottom of her condition, his heart went out to her. Her hair flowed over her shoulders like a golden waterfall, and despite being dusty, tired, and aggravated with him, she looked like a goddess, chin tilted up in defiance, green eyes flashing with pride.

"Can you tell me what day this is, Miss?"

"October 31." A funny look crossed her face, but she didn't say anything more, and Jack wished he could read her mind.

"Day of week?"

She gave the doctor an annoyed look. "Saturday."

"Where do you live?"

"I'm not sick."

"No, you appear to be healthy. If you'll answer the question..."

"You didn't ask me what year it was."

The doctor raised his brows. "All right. What year is it?"

"1870."

"Can you tell me about your family? Where they live now?"

"They're dead. I don't have any living relatives."

The doctor looked at Jack. He shrugged and folded his arms. "Josephine has two uncles and apparently, she had a cousin named Trevor."

"What was your father's occupation?"

"Bank examiner."

"Ah, he must have known Dr. Niles Smith, Texas's first bank examiner. He was a good friend of mine, but couldn't make enough money doctoring patients in Galveston. Not enough of a need. Your father must have known him."

Lisa's cheeks colored. "He might have. I wouldn't know."

The doctor turned to Jack. "What kind of things didn't she know about? Has she forgotten how to eat with forks and knives? Sometimes amnesia victims will forget how to do the simplest of tasks that we take for granted."

"She was surprised about the bridge. If she had been living here, I would have thought she'd know about it."

"I see." The doctor faced Lisa. "You didn't remember about the bridge?"

"Of course, I remembered." She cast Jack an irritated look.

The doctor nodded and said to Jack, "According to the lady, she has no family?"

"Yes, Sir."

"But if she's Josephine, she has two uncles. I recommend that she be sent to the Texas State Lunatic Asylum in Austin for a rest. The surroundings are free from stress. Carriage rides and picnics are held on the landscaped grounds. Dr. Thomas Kirkbride of Philadelphia designed the program and Texas has modeled their facility after his ideas for behavior modification, drug therapy, and an unrestricted environment. The concept is that the patient will get well and return to his or her home, reintegrating once again into society. Normally, a family member would have to sign the papers though. If this facility doesn't suit the family, there's also the Southwestern Insane Asylum in San Antonio, and the North Texas Hospital for the Insane."

"No way, Jose. Josephine's uncles would sign me in just so they could get ahold of Aunt Polly's belongings. No way am I going to any loony bin," Lisa said.

The doctor observed her outburst and took Jack aside. "I see what you mean about her strange language. Again, it's probably a manifestation of her illness. Is she delusional about her uncles?"

"No, not about them."

"All right. I'll make a recommendation for her to go to the asylum. Can you take care of the arrangements to get her there, or do you want me to?"

CHAPTER 8

That was it. Lisa was firing Jack as her guardian angel.

How in the world could she stay out of the asylum? Running for the hills wasn't an option. Not in this time and place.

Lunatic and insane asylums. Didn't these people know how politically incorrect it was to call people that? Even when she mentioned the loony bin, a wave of remorse had washed over her.

She had a thought. If someone married her, he would be responsible for her and somehow, if she couldn't return to her time, she'd learn to cope with this life—in one hell of a hurry. No matter how nice the asylum was made out to be, she wouldn't want to live there, *even* for a short stay.

Frank would probably marry her in a heartbeat. All she had to do was ask him before Jack told him he was making arrangements to have the men in white coats haul her away.

Jack looked a little peeked and shook his head at the doctor. "I'll take care of the preparations."

"Fine. The little lady should be good as new after a rest."

The doctor bid them goodnight, but before he left, Frank knocked on the door. The doctor exited the room and Frank said to Jack, "From the grim expressions on everyone's faces, looks like the doctor's call didn't go well."

Lisa wrung her hands and frowned at Frank. No way did she want to wed him, but the alternative was worse. She fired off her proposal before she lost her nerve. "Did you want to marry me, Frank?"

***

That evening, Lisa poked at her catfish, her expression still mutinous while Jack and Frank chomped on steaks drifting over their plates at the hotel restaurant. Jack still couldn't believe Lisa had proposed marriage to Frank. He shook his head.

Frank sipped some of his wine and set the glass down. "I don't see why you think I can't marry Josephine. Although, a lady doesn't normally ask a gentleman. What is the problem if we are both agreeable?"

Lisa cast Frank a scowl.

Jack nearly laughed. "You're not making any headway by calling her Josephine. Besides, I told you why you can't marry her. Until we know for certain she's Lisa, or she realizes she's really Josephine, no one can." And he knew she wasn't interested in Frank.

"Better than sending her to Austin, Jack." Frank's gaze drifted to the doorway. "Uh-oh, here comes trouble."

Jack and Lisa looked at the doorway, and he cursed inwardly. "You could have mentioned that you told the hotel manager Lisa was my sister. You'd better hope the manager didn't tell the sheriff that."

With a woman on his arm, the sheriff headed straight for their table. "Howdy, folks." He glanced at Lisa's hand, but she wasn't wearing a ring. "I need a word with you gentlemen after supper." He escorted the lady to a table across the crowded dining room.

"Wonder if he spoke to the doctor," Frank said.

"Or the hotel manager." Jack leaned back in his chair and frowned at Lisa. "What made you propose to Frank?"

"*He* wouldn't send me to an insane asylum." She looked at Frank. "Would you?"

"No, ma'am." Frank smiled.

Jack shook his head. "I told the doctor I'd make arrangements, but I had another notion in mind."

"Oh?" Lisa's brows arched, and she sounded like she didn't trust him.

He couldn't blame her. But he hadn't wanted to make the proposal in front of the doctor in case he objected. "You can stay with me. Esmeralda is my housekeeper, and she takes care of the chores around the place. You'd have to put up with my younger brother, Matthew, but he's not too bad. The ranch hands are a good lot. That's what I had in mind."

"Oh." The tension drained from Lisa's stiff posture, and she managed a small smile. "Thank you, Jack."

"I wouldn't have sent you to that facility no matter how nice it might be."

She sighed and tears filled her eyes. Hating that

he'd worried her so, he reached out and gave her hand a gentle squeeze.

"What are you going to tell the sheriff?" Frank asked.

Jack glanced back at the sheriff and found him watching them. "The truth."

***

Luckily, the sheriff's wife sat with Lisa in her room or Jack was afraid she would bolt. As soon as he'd said he would tell the truth, she was upset with him all over again. She was certain the sheriff would lock them all up, or return her to her uncles' place when he heard what Jack had to say.

"I don't appreciate that you boys lied to me about the little lady," the sheriff said to Jack and Frank in a deserted part of the lobby.

"No, sir," Jack said as contritely as he could.

"But I see the dilemma you were in. Thank God I have sons. If I had a daughter, I'd lock her in her room until I had her wed."

"Yes, sir," Jack said.

"I propose you marry her for real, and you can keep her away from the Rogers' brothers," he said.

"She asked *me* to marry her," Frank objected.

The sheriff's eyes widened, and Jack wanted to punch Frank.

"She wants to marry me," Jack said. "I'll take her home and my housekeeper can watch over her in the meantime. When she's feeling better, I aim to propose marriage to her."

The sheriff shook his head. "Like I said, I'm glad I had boys. All right. I don't want any more trouble from the Rogers brothers, so I'll expect you'll be leaving on the morning stage."

"We will, thanks, Sheriff." Jack walked with him up to Lisa's room, while Frank followed.

"Good luck and best wishes." The sheriff collected his wife and left the room.

Now they had a new problem. What if the Rogers brothers came back for Lisa in the middle of the night? Jack could sit at the door, but they could get in through the window.

Gaslights flickered against the floral papered walls and murmured voices in the rooms down the hall drifted to them. Men and women were settling down for the night. Like he wanted to do with Lisa.

"Frank, why don't you ask a maid to fill Lisa's pitcher?"

Frank scowled and skulked off. Jack wouldn't have much time to propose his idea because he knew Frank wouldn't leave them alone together for long. As soon as Frank's footsteps faded down the stairs, Jack cleared his throat. "You shouldn't be alone, but I can't come up with a proper way to handle the matter."

"You really wouldn't have sent me to the asylum?"

"No," he said, taking her hands in his and kissed her cheek. "I wouldn't have done that to you."

"Will you stay with me?"

His heart thundered. Stay with her? He couldn't believe she was making it so easy for him. Did she understand what it meant? That he'd have to marry her?

Josephine was a flirt, but had never been with Bill or any other in an uncompromising situation. The news would have spread around town faster than a blue norther blew in if she had. If she wasn't Josephine, but really a woman named Lisa, she wasn't even a tease.

He couldn't fathom she had been with a man in an intimate way. Though she melted in his arms every time he drew close to her, and he was certain she was interested in him.

"If I stayed, I'd compromise your respectability, but I can't leave you unprotected either."

"Maybe after Frank falls asleep you could stay with me for a while? I'm not sure I can sleep, knowing those men might return. You keep the key and when you can, slip back in. I'll leave the lantern burning for you."

He never thought she'd agree to marry him. Yet, if she'd willingly have him stay with her, that had to be her understanding. He didn't know how to feel about it either. Part of him was downright pleased, but the fear she'd recall she was Josephine and wouldn't take to him dampened his enthusiasm.

He meant to speak to her about the marriage part of the bargain, when Frank's voice reached the room. "We'll need water, too," Frank said to the maid, as the petite woman filled Lisa's pitcher.

"Goodnight, Lisa," Jack said and nudged Frank into the hallway.

Frank smiled at her. "Goodnight."

"Goodnight, and thanks for everything."

Frank hit Jack in the shoulder. "You'd better not have kissed her while I was gone."

Jack closed the door and locked it.

"You're keeping the key?" Frank asked, his brows raised.

"In case she has any trouble. I don't want her to open the door to the Rogers brothers again." Jack vowed to return to her as soon as he could and hoped her uncles wouldn't try to break in again in the meantime.

Now if only Frank would fall asleep quickly.

After he climbed into bed, Jack listened for any sound of trouble in Lisa's room. Close to one in the morning, Frank began to snore, and Jack yanked on his clothes and hastened to Lisa's room.

He hoped he wouldn't wake her when he slipped inside. Twice he fumbled with the key in his haste, dropping it with a clatter. So much for being quiet and cautious. Finally, the lock clicked open, and the door creaked when he pushed it. He closed, locked it, and looked at the bed.

The flickering amber light reflected off Lisa's ivory skin, her sleep-filled features, angelic in the soft glow, the quilt tucked under her chin. He caught sight of her gown and corset folded neatly over the end of the bed frame, the four petticoats stacked beside them, and the lace trimmed drawers on top of these. His mouth dropped. He hadn't considered she'd be naked in bed. But she didn't have a gown to wear for sleeping either.

He eased into the chair, but he couldn't get his mind off what she'd look like under the covers. He pulled off one of his boots, then the other, but as soon as he set the second one on the floor, it knocked the first over. The noise woke Lisa, and she gasped when she saw him sitting in the chair.

He whispered, "I'm sorry. I was trying not to wake you."

"It's all right. I thought Josephine's uncles had gotten in." She frowned at him. "You're not going to sit up all night, are you? There's plenty of room for you to stretch out on the bed, and it won't bother me." Her voice was soft and tantalizingly seductive.

Lying next to a naked woman was not sleep-inducing. Besides, his job was to *protect* her, not get a good night's rest. So why in the hell the next words slipped out of his mouth, he couldn't fathom. "Are you sure I won't disturb you?" He walked slowly over to the other side of the bed, in case she changed her mind.

She shook her head and closed her eyes.

After removing his gun, he laid it on the bedside table and climbed on top of the bedcovers. He had no business desiring to be with her like he did. He didn't really know her. She didn't even know herself. Hell, their relationship was bound to become more and more of a nightmare. Bill would insist she was his. So would half a dozen other guys who wanted Josephine. Yet the longer he was with her, the more Jack wanted to believe she was the Lisa Welsh she thought she was.

"Lisa," he said, breathing in her heady floral fragrance, lying on his back, his head resting on his arms. He wanted to tell her about his fiancé, how broken up he'd been when she'd died. He couldn't help wondering if the same thing was happening all over again. Her parents had died in an Indian raid and her aunt and uncle had taken her in. when he learned her uncle abused both her aunt and Charlotte, he'd vowed to marry her and save her from her uncle's brutality.

Men needed a woman in these rugged parts. Jack didn't think he'd find one he'd feel anything for after Charlotte died, and he didn't believe in love at first sight. But a man often didn't marry for love. He married to have children, a woman to cook for him, clean, and mend his clothes. In turn, he took care of the woman, provided for her, and protected her.

Lisa needed protection, of that Jack had no doubt. But he felt a whole heck of a lot more for her than just wanting to protect her.

"Lisa?" he whispered. He touched her shoulder buried under the quilt. "Lisa?"

"Hmm," she murmured in her sleep and rolled over. Her arm slipped out from under the blanket, and she wrapped it over his chest.

Desire raged through him. He knew he should tuck her arm back under her covers, safe from his view, but what if in doing so he saw more than he ought to? Her breasts were no longer confined in lace and the cover was all that hid them. He longed to run his hands over her skin, to kiss her passionately with the fever that filled every inch of his body.

"Kiss me, Jack," she whispered, her voice intimately arousing.

He traced her silky skin and wanted so much more. But he wouldn't compromise her.

She moved closer, lifted her head and enticed him further with her mesmerizing eyes. "Kiss me, and make the nightmares stay away."

Then his would begin. Even so, his resolve to keep his distance faltered. "Lisa—," he began, hoping to dissuade her.

"I can't sleep. I'm afraid. Kiss me and make all the bad stuff go away."

She wriggled against his body, raised her chin, her eyes and lips begging him to satisfy her. Touching her face, he studied her determined expression, and leaned down to kiss her. He only meant to press his mouth lightly against hers, but she tasted of sweetened wine and smelled like exotic flowers. Before he could stop himself, he was leaning against her, the covers still separating them, her lips—soft velvet, warm and inviting.

Her heart was racing and her whisper-soft breath fanned his mouth before she gave into him—parted her lips and pressed her mouth harder against his. She mewed with pleasure, undoing his determination. He drew his fingers through her satiny hair, his heart thundering. He groaned and pulled away. What was wrong with him? His brain had traveled south, for certain.

"I'm sorry, Lisa. I didn't mean to let my feelings get out of hand." He began to rise, but she grabbed his hand.

She licked her lips and looked as concerned as he felt, almost shaken. She sighed. "Stay, please, Jack. Now I'll have something pleasant to think of if I get caught up in the nightmares again."

"I didn't mean to be so forward."

She tugged him down, then drew close again. "Keep me safe, Jack."

Esmeralda's words came back to him in a flash. *Protect her—keep her safe.* All at once his skin grew chilled. Was Lisa the one Esmeralda had been speaking of? Not one of the college-bound women? He stared at Lisa and couldn't believe it. Esmeralda couldn't have known.

"I'll try not to disturb your sleep too much." Her voice was dreamy as she snuggled up against him.

As if he could sleep after what he had pulled. Not only that, but the lady's naked body pressing against him, would keep him awake all night. He had to remind himself, he was here for her protection. If he had it in mind to sleep.

When her breathing grew shallow, Jack closed his eyes, hoping she wouldn't be screaming her head off when she awoke and found them nestled together.

***

The hotel room grew cooler, and Lisa snuggled next to the warm body beside her when she saw her mother and father staring at her from near the door.

"Momma? Daddy?" She tried to say the words but her lips parted and no sound issued. They didn't look real, like fog filled the room, yet the room wasn't foggy. No, it was her mother and father in misty forms.

"Momma?" Lisa tried to go to her. She wanted desperately to hug her, to tell her she loved her, but she couldn't speak or move. Her foster parents didn't understand her, didn't want to try. She wanted her family back. She wanted to go home.

She blinked and her mother and father faded into the darkness, growing fainter until they were gone. "No!" she cried in a strangled voice, jerking upright.

"Lisa, it's a nightmare," Jack said, his voice soothing while he covered her with the quilt and forced her to lie down. "I'm here. I'm not going anywhere."

"They left me," she sobbed. "They promised they'd be back that weekend, but they didn't show up. I could never go home. I could never return."

Though Lisa slept again, Jack couldn't. He kept his arm around her while she rested her head on his chest, her hand resting against his stomach. Being with her felt right, no matter how wrong it was. If Frank or anyone else caught them, Jack would be honor bound to marry her. Though he intended to. But he wanted to give her more time to feel comfortable in his home before he made the arrangements. He'd never been able to understand how a fellow could get himself into a predicament where he was facing a shotgun wedding—until now.

Lisa again stirred, and he held on tighter. She suffered nightmares twice more, and he wished he knew what was terrifying her. When she was finally sleeping soundly, someone knocked on the door, and his heart nearly stopped dead.

He figured it was Frank looking for him.

Lisa lifted her head and stared at the door, then quickly pulled the covers under her chin. "Who is it?" she whispered to Jack.

"Most likely Frank," Jack whispered back, grateful she hadn't gone into hysterics when she found him lying with her, in the event she'd forgotten about inviting him in last night.

She groaned. "Yes?"

"It's me, Frank. Have you seen Jack?"

He knew it. Now what?

Lisa raised her brows. "Is he not in your room?"

"No, and we've got to hurry and get to the coach."

The coach. Hell, he'd forgotten all about the time.

She jerked upright, exposing her backside to Jack. He looked away, but not before he'd gotten an eyeful of her creamy skin.

"Give me a few minutes to dress," she called out. "I'll meet you in the lobby."

"I'll wait here and walk you down. We don't want any more mishaps."

Jack bolted from the bed, grabbed his boots, then tried the window. The brass lock was frozen in place. He peered at his pocket watch. "We've got to hurry,

Lisa."

"You can't stay here."

"I can't get the window open."

She sighed deeply. "Crawl under the bed."

Ranch owners didn't hide under beds, though to protect Lisa's dignity... He spied the dressing screen and ducked behind it instead, hoping they'd reach the stagecoach in time.

***

Lisa's heart was pumping as if she'd been running in a tournament, and since she wasn't a runner, that was saying a lot. God, she couldn't miss the stage.

Not wanting Jack to see what she was about to do, she grabbed the corset at the end of the bed and stuffed it under the quilt. No way was she going to wear that again. She slipped into the knee-length drawers and pulled the chemise over her head. She tied the bustle around her waist, then yanked the four petticoats over this. Man, if there was a fire, she'd never get out in time. Well, not properly dressed anyway.

The gown was next. She hurried to pull a brush through her tangled hair. After she had doubled up the scrunchy on it, she grabbed her necklace, the purple stone shimmering in the window's light. For a minute, she stared at it. Then her knees gave out.

Jack hurried from behind the screen when she collapsed and grabbed her. "What's wrong, Lisa?" he whispered. "You look as white as the bed sheets."

She wouldn't be going home. She'd removed the necklace sometime in the night without realizing it, and she hadn't returned to her world.

"Lisa, honey, we've got to go." He lifted her from the floor, but she could barely stand.

"I'll—I'll join Frank and keep him occupied outside the hotel. You figure out how you're going to explain your absence," she whispered, her voice wavering and her whole body trembled.

"Are you sure you're able to stand?"

She nodded, though her head swirled with the notion she was stuck here for as long as she lived— which might not be long. She motioned to the bed again.

He shook his head and stepped behind the dressing screen again and waited.

When she opened the door, she held onto the knob with a fierce grip, not wanting to collapse in front of Frank. Her legs were boneless, and her stomach churned with upset. Frank looked behind her, but despite how wobbly she felt, she hurried out of the room and closed the door.

"So you couldn't find Jack? He unlocked the door for me, and said he'd be right back. I'd hate to leave him behind." She hoped to give Jack enough time to make it to the stagecoach station.

The look on Frank's face said it all. The notion of taking her back to Salado without Jack pleased him to no end. He offered his arm and a bright smile, and though she preferred Jack's support to Frank's, she gripped him to keep from collapsing.

His cheerful expression quickly shifted to concern. "Are you all right, Josephine? You look—a bit unwell."

She clutched the necklace in her fist and nodded. No, she wasn't well at all.

In no time, Jack joined them in front of the hotel, looking concerned and a little guilty. She assumed staying with her the night hadn't set well with his 19th

Century conscious.

Frank scowled. "Where have you been?"

"Took a walk. You know how confining stagecoach travel is. Wanted to stretch my legs before we began the long journey back. I stopped by our rooms, saw that you both had left, and found Lisa's hat in the room."

He winked at Lisa and her face heated, but at least he hadn't found the corset, and she was a bit more herself now. Though she felt bad she'd forgotten the hat Jack had bought for her. She wondered what the maid would think when she cleaned the room and found the corset.

When they arrived at the stagecoach station, the driver motioned for the passengers to load up. Lisa touched her dress. "Jack, where are my clothes?"

He stared at her, uncomprehending. When it dawned on him, he grabbed her hand. "Confound it. So much happened yesterday, I must have laid the box down somewhere." He rubbed his chin. "Maybe at the restaurant where we ate lunch earlier in the day."

"Are you going or not?" the driver said to Jack.

She couldn't miss the trip to Salado. No telling if the Rogers brothers might try to kidnap her again. And what if the doctor stopped by to ensure Jack was taking her to the asylum? "Maybe they'll give them to some poor soul in Waco." She desperately wanted her bra back if she was going to be stuck in the past. In the garment she wore, she had no support. Her breasts jiggled way too much with every step she took, which she feared would garner unwanted attention. She pressed her leather purse against her chest, hoping no one would notice.

Jack took her hand and helped her into the coach. When he sat beside her, Frank hurried to sit on the other side of her.

Jack ran his hand over hers. "I'm awfully sorry, Lisa. That was an especially nice riding habit you had. Can I pay you for it?"

"After all you've done for me, Jack? No. I should reimburse you." She could tell from the deep fissures in his brow that having lost her clothes bothered him.

"Whoever heard of such a crazy notion? A woman paying for a man...well, I mean sometimes it's..." Frank said, pausing when Jack frowned at him.

She sure had to learn to watch what she said.

Jack gripped her hand tightly to keep her from slipping from her seat when the stage galloped across the bridge and headed out of Waco.

If the nightmare she'd had at the inn was any indication of what had happened to Josephine... She shuddered. As far as everyone was concerned, *she* was Josephine. If the guys who'd murdered her still wanted to eliminate her, Lisa was walking right into a pit of deadly diamondback rattlers. But she had to retrace her steps and find a way home, if she could.

"I...have to return to the inn," she said.

"I'll need to get my horse. I can take you to your room, and you can freshen up a bit," Jack said.

"That would be fine." The restaurant and antique shop no longer existed. The inn was the only connection to her world. She fingered the necklace. With some apprehension, she pulled it over her head. Nothing happened, just as she suspected.

Maybe it had to do with the room where Josephine was murdered. Maybe it didn't have anything to do with the necklace. Or maybe the combination of the room and the necklace was the key. The long rocking ride back to Salado would be interminable.

She looked over at Jack, his face a mask of uneasiness. The hurt concerning her ex-husband still made her angry, but Jack was definitely the kind of guy a girl could rely on. They didn't make men like him any longer...a perfect gentleman. She'd had that awful nightmare again last night, the chills, the fevers, the suffocation. But when she woke with her head on Jack's chest, she'd felt comforted, and he hadn't tried to take advantage of her.

"Would you like me to help you with your hat?" Jack asked.

"Thanks. I'm so sorry I left it behind."

"We were in a hurry this morning."

The carriage shook violently on the rut-filled road, and she stared at the flap over the window while Jack helped her with her hat. A funny notion occurred to her. How come Jack had hung around the inn? He hadn't intended to take the stage into Waco. "I was curious about something, Jack."

"Yes?" he said, and Frank leaned over to hear their conversation.

"Why were you hanging around the inn yesterday morning?"

His mouth lifted a little. "You said it...I had a mission as your guardian angel."

"Tell her the truth," Frank warned, "or I will."

Lisa smoothed out her skirt, waiting for Jack to say something more. When Jack wouldn't say, Lisa said to Frank, "Since a cat's got Jack's tongue, perhaps you can enlighten me."

"My pleasure. Ol' Jack was waiting for the stagecoach to arrive."

"To go to Waco?" She didn't believe it. He hadn't seemed to have had any business there but taking care of her.

Frank gave a smug smile. "You want to tell her or should I?"

"It's your show." Jack folded his arms and glowered at Frank.

"All right, then. Three young misses were arriving on the morning stage...all bound for the college. We don't get too many unattached young ladies, so there's always a stir among the menfolk when a new gal arrives."

"I see."

Jack's ears turned slightly red.

"Did you get to see the ladies first hand, Jack?"

"Nah," Frank said. "He was too busy occupying his time with *you*, once he got you in his sights. Too bad I missed seeing you first. I was late arriving at the inn."

"What about you, Frank? Why were *you* there?" she asked.

"Why I've had a hankering for you every time you returned to Salado since I was a young'un, Josephine, and no one else."

"Right. That's why you were at the inn."

Jack laughed. "You didn't play your cards right that time, Frank."

Lisa smiled, glancing at the other passengers. Four men of varying ages held onto bags, and she wondered what they did for a living.

"Drummers," Jack told her.

She looked at him. "Drummers?" She couldn't

imagine the four men could be players in a band.

"Traveling salesmen."

"Oh."

An older man, his black hair streaked gray, looked up from the Bible he was reading and gave her a nod. A younger woman sat next to him, her hair grayer, with kind eyes, and a soft smile. Lisa assumed the woman was married to the older gentleman.

Another robust man fidgeted with his watch, and she wanted to tell him to quit pulling it out of his pocket because it was making her more anxious. She didn't realize how much she looked at her own watch until it wasn't working. Every mile added more bruises to her bottom and her back. Every time she drifted off, a bone-jolting jerk would make her eyes pop open. But the nightmares had disturbed her sleep so much she was barely able to stay awake.

"Have you ever been a cowboy?" she asked Jack, figuring if she couldn't sleep, she had to do something to fight the boredom.

He smiled. "Got my first horse when I was six. By seven, I was riding well enough that I worked as a cowhand. Blue up above and green below was where I bunked." She must have looked puzzled because he added, "Slept on a bedroll, covered in a tarpaulin, and rested my head on a saddle for a pillow under the great Texas sky."

"I'm afraid I'm like *The Princess and the Pea.* Every pebble would bruise me for sure."

He raised his brows.

"Oh, I've roughed it. Used to camp out a lot without a tent. Less of a hassle really if it was warm enough." Although it was something she liked doing.

"Ah."

"So, did you eat out of a chuck wagon?" she asked.

"Yup. Beans, sour dough bread, and black coffee. Cut a yearling out of the herd when we wanted meat. Lots of antelope also, more than a hundred at time. Tender meat and tasty, too."

"Antelope?" Wonder where they all went. "Did your cows ever get mixed up with others?"

"Sure. We'd rope a calf and as soon as it went to bawling, the mother would come to it. The mother's brand would tell us which to use on the calf."

"I wondered how you'd ever be able to figure it out. Did you ever have Indian troubles?"

"No, not that they couldn't be a problem in certain areas. One time we were crossing the Red River and a delegation of Indians met us. The women waved red blankets and shawls, and the trail drivers were afraid they'd stampede the herd. We learned the Indians wanted a toll for crossing their reservation. We cut out some of the cattle. As soon as we did, they killed them and didn't even wait to cook 'em. Just cut 'em up and ate the meat raw. We met Comanche, Kiowa, and Cherokees later and gave 'em part of the herd, too. We knew the Comanche were pretty warlike so we didn't want to start any trouble."

"It's sure a good thing someone figured out what they wanted. Did you work as a cowboy also, Frank?"

"My dad owns the bank. I work there."

"Ah." She imagined her expression said she wasn't much impressed with Frank's occupation. Jack relaxed a little.

A popping sound like fireworks exploded outside the stagecoach making everyone sit up straighter, wide-

eyed and mouths agape.
    Not fireworks! Gunfire!

CHAPTER 9

"Robbers?" Lisa asked, scooting tighter against Jack in the already cramped stagecoach.

"This happens so often around here, that most folks feel cheated if they don't get robbed," Frank said, sounding casual about it, but no one else looked like it was no big deal. When the gunfire first sounded, he had looked just as shook up as everyone else. "That's why it pays not to carry much cash."

The drummers exchanged nervous glances.

The driver yelled, "Whoa!"

The coach came to a halt and Jack seized Lisa's arm. She didn't want to show how scared she was, but her body wouldn't quit shaking.

Jack glanced out the window, then squeezed her hand. "They'll take our money and be on their way."

"You...you don't fight them?"

"Eight outlaws against a couple of men with guns? We wouldn't risk the women's lives," Jack said. "This isn't a fight we aim to pick."

She couldn't believe it. Then she reconsidered and figured he was right. Wasn't that what the police said in her time? Better not to resist and let the thieves take the cash and be on their way?

"What are they doing?" Lisa asked, while no one else ventured a word.

"Unhitching the horses, I reckon," Jack said.

"Believe in the Lord and all will be well," the older gentleman said, patting his Bible.

The door to the coach opened and a masked man motioned with a gun for the passengers to get out. Pale blue eyes stared at her, and a shiver crept up her spine.

Because of their proximity to the door, the salesmen got out first, then the older man, who helped his wife from the coach. Frank exited next and offered to help Lisa. She balked. It was one thing to see this at the movies where if any of them were killed in the story, they'd still be eating supper that evening. Not in this scenario.

"Hurry it up, Miss," the thief ordered, waving his gun.

Didn't the idiot know it could go off? Stop pointing that thing.

She climbed out of the coach, clutching her purse. Jack followed. One of the robbers held a gun on the driver. Another watched the passengers while two of the others relieved the salesmen of their cash and coin. Lisa guessed they must always carry a lot of cash. No wonder thieves hit the stagecoaches.

One of the men took Frank's watch and what little money he had. He rifled through Lisa's purse, but a man on his horse said, "We don't rob women. Leave them."

The thief released her bag, but lifted the amethyst necklace. She took a step back. He couldn't have it. What if it could still take her home?

He grabbed her arm, and Jack reached under his coat. Tears filled her eyes. She couldn't give up the necklace. She couldn't allow anyone to kill Jack over it either. She began to pull the chain over her head, and the leader said, "Are you deef? Let her go! I told you, don't mess with the women."

"Don't let him hurt her, Pa," a younger robber said, his blond hair curling down to his shoulders, his eyes a striking blue.

His voice wasn't yet a grown man's, and he hadn't filled out like one either. She thought he looked like he was seventeen or so, and she didn't think he had the killer instinct like the one whose face was in hers. Yet the two looked to be around the same age.

The robber grunted, his steely green eyes boring into hers. He lifted a brow. "I'll remember you, ducky. Some other time."

He moved over to Jack and jerked his coat back. "Cowpoke?"

She thought Jack looked like a gambler type. How did this guy know Jack had been a cowboy?

The robber grabbed Jack's pistol and jabbed his own into Jack's ribs. "Keep your stuff. Ain't no cowboy got a blamed thing worth having."

The young man with the pale blue eyes sneered. "Getting soft, Trevor. Next thing you'll be letting Pinkerton men off."

The leader of the men hollered, "Let's get a move on." He tipped his hat to Lisa and the older woman.

Without another word, he and his gang rode off,

leaving the passengers coughing in the dust.

"Lisa, are you all right?" Jack asked, rubbing her arm.

As if being robbed by armed bandits was something she did on a daily basis. Maybe most stagecoach passengers were used to this, but she couldn't quit shaking. "Yes. No. I'll be fine." She lifted her skirt and climbed into the coach while the men re-hitched the horses.

As soon as the passengers were all aboard, the stage pulled out. Jack patted Lisa's hands folded in her lap. "We should be in Salado in a couple of hours."

"That was John Wesley Hardin," Frank said. "Wasn't it? The one with the narrowed mild blue eyes, slight build, and square jaw who named the other thief?"

Jack cast him an annoyed look.

Frank glanced at Lisa. "Ahem. Maybe it wasn't."

"Yeah, it was him," one of the drummers said. "I heard tell he wasn't hitting any more stages on account of he didn't get enough money. That he was robbing trains next." He stroked his handlebar mustache. "Guess after what Hardin got from us, he'll be sticking to the stages a might while longer."

"Who was that Trevor fella?" the older man asked. "Anyone hear of him?"

"An outlaw by the name of Rogers," the tallest of the drummers said. "He robbed me last year when I was traveling to San Antone."

Both Frank and Jack looked at Lisa, and she frowned at them. "What?" None of this meant anything to...oh, hell, Trevor Rogers? The outlaw who'd been caught and brought to Salado asked if she was related to

Trevor Rogers…a cousin of Josephine's. They waited for her to say something as if she knew the man.

Her face flushed with heat and she closed her eyes, hoping that when she arrived in Salado, she could end this nightmare, once and for all.

**

Later that morning, the stagecoach stopped in front of the Shady Villa Inn, and Jack glanced at his pocket watch. He smiled when Lisa opened her eyes, yet he couldn't shake the worry over her loss of memories. He considered calling on the doc, but dismissed the notion. He'd probably suggest the same as Dr. King had. "I'll take you to your room and get my horse."

She looked at the inn and took a deep breath and shuddered.

"Are you getting chilled?"

"No," she said, shaking her head. "I'm fine."

She didn't appear fine. She had that faraway look again, yet she seemed anxious, too.

He escorted her inside the lobby to the reception counter and to his annoyance, Frank tagged along. Didn't he know when to quit?

**

A new day clerk manned the hotel desk—to Lisa's relief—smiled and asked Jack, "May I help you, sir?"

"We need the key to room three."

The young man looked from Jack to Lisa, then at the register. "Ah, yes, Miss Josephine Rogers. Your room is booked through the end of the month."

"It is?" she asked, frowning. "I mean, yes, may I have the key please?"

"Certainly."

"Are you new here?" she asked.

"Yes, I'm sorry, does it show?" the clerk asked, straightening his bow tie.

"No." Lisa smiled, glad he didn't know who she was, as she feared the man with the gray beard wouldn't have allowed her access to the room again.

"Oh, good." The man let out his breath and handed her the key.

"You don't know me?"

"No, Miss. I just moved here from Belton. In fact, several of the staff are new here from Temple or my hometown. One is from Waco."

"The day clerk from yesterday told me the hotel had changed ownership."

"That's what's supposed to have happened. There's been some kind of a muddle and the old manager and owner are still running things."

"The manager and owner's names?"

"Mister Worthington is the owner and Mister Daemon, the manager."

Lisa thanked him, then noticed Mr. Daemon watched her from the doorway of his office and gave her a cold glare. Lisa shivered.

Jack ran his hand over her arm as he escorted her to the room.

"See, I told you that you were Josephine. It said right there on the register. If you have a room reserved for the month, how come you had to go to Waco?" Frank asked.

"Oh, Frank, some other time. I'm really tired."

"Really? Do you mean it, Josephine?"

"Frank, the lady is trying to politely tell you to get lost."

Frank cut Jack a glower. She turned the key in the

lock. Jack opened the door for her and waited until she was inside while Frank hovered next to him. Jacob might be slow on his feet when dancing with the ladies, but Frank definitely couldn't take a hint when it came to trying to brush him off.

"I'll be back for you in a few minutes," Jack said.

"Thank you, Jack, for everything. I won't ever forget your kindness." She reached up and kissed him on the cheek, and he smiled, his ears tinging red.

"I'll be right back." He closed the door, and she locked it, but fear filled every inch of her. Would removing the necklace allow her to return? It was now or never.

She reached up to remove her hat so she could take off the necklace. When she touched the first of the hatpins, her vision blurred. Stumbling for the corner post of the bed, she grabbed for it. The room swirled in darkness before her knees sank to the floor.

A knocking at the door from far away, a tapping, a banging, then a pounding rattled the floor. Intruding on her nightmare, the impatient trespasser roused her. She narrowed her eyes and focused on the door. Unable to shake loose of the grogginess enveloping her, she watched the handle turn in a sleepy blur.

"I'm sure she's in there," a man's rough voice said.

Her skin chilled. She was certain he was one of the men from her nightmares.

"Use the other key," another man said.

"I can't find it. I don't know where it's gone to."

"Do you think she'll tell the sheriff?"

"What's to tell? She's alive, isn't she?"

Her heartbeat accelerated. These were the men who killed Josephine? She barely breathed.

"Yes, but...I'm not so sure she's Josephine."

"You've got us in a fine pickle, you know."

"Shh, someone's coming."

Footsteps faded down the hall while new ones approached from the other direction. Tapping on the door followed, and Lisa stood. "Jack?" she whispered.

She glanced at the pillow lying on the floor where she'd thrown it the other night and touched her necklace. A light appeared next to the door, and the hair stood on the nape of her neck. The light shifted, reformed, took the shape of an ethereal woman dressed in a long gown, all shimmering white, no colors in her features or gown, no discernable face, only a misty outline. One minute she stood at the door, the next she appeared in front of Lisa, only an arm's length away.

"Josephine," Lisa determined, wanting to help her, but when the spirit reached out to touch her, she took a step back.

The ghostly woman glided forward. Lisa tried to pull the necklace over her head, but the chain tangled in her hat. She moved out of the specter's path, but ran into the bed and fell backward. For an instant, she felt immobilized, though her brain warned her to leave this place if she could, right now. The figure wavered in front of her. A frigid breeze scented with violets touched Lisa's cheek, leaving an icy, burning imprint on her skin. Her breath turned frosty and something tugged at her necklace.

Panicked, Lisa yanked at the ribbons holding her hat in place, the tightness returning to her chest. She couldn't breathe. Icy fingers touched her throat. The ties to the hat slipped away. The ghost's presence chilled her to the bone, and Lisa dropped the bonnet on the bed. Still grasping the necklace in her hand, she jerked it over her head. The light and everything else faded from her vision and the world vanished in the blink of an eye.

A sharp knock at the door brought her to.

Seeing the changed appearance of the room, Lisa rubbed her temple, trying to quell her disorientation. The necklace still clutched in her hand, she sat up and stared at her long blue dress, then glanced at the bedside table. An electric cord snaked its way out of the backside of the porcelain lamp. The pieced quilt was once more a floral one-piece, factory-made bedspread. The washstand...had vanished. And the mirror over the dresser reflected a perfect image.

"Housekeeping?" a woman called from beyond the door.

Lisa closed her eyes to still the spinning sensation in her head. "I'll be out in a little bit. Can you wait?"

"Sure, Miss, I'll work on the next couple of rooms and be back."

"Wait!" Lisa had to know for certain. Slowly rising from the bed until she could regain her equilibrium, she crossed the floor to the door. Peeking out, she stared at the maid dressed in jeans and a T-shirt. "I'll...I'll be out in a little while."

"Of course," the woman said and smiled. "I love your dress." The maid pushed her cart overflowing with clean towels down the hall to the next room and pounded on the door. "Housekeeping!"

Swallowing hard, Lisa shut the door and leaned against it. She touched the bodice of her gown and stared at her tapestry bag sitting beside the bed, just where she'd left it, but her plumed hat was gone.

She should have been ecstatic to be back in her own time, thrilled to be safe from Josephine's uncles and the men who killed Josephine. Away from ghosts and stagecoach robbers, and from a life that was so foreign.

So why were tears rolling down her cheeks, and her heart breaking in two? The sweetest man she'd ever met would come for her, and she'd be gone without a word. She gripped the necklace harder and wanted to go back and tell him goodbye at the very least. That she couldn't remain in his world and why. Another part of her warned her, returning meant she'd be submerged in a world of danger. He'd think she *was* crazy and pack her off to the asylum. What if she couldn't return to her world again? Better that she vanished from Jack's life, than end up incarcerated or murdered.

So why did she already feel half-dead?

CHAPTER 10

Her body and mind numb with all that had happened to her the last couple of days, Lisa returned to her apartment and powered up her computer. She probably couldn't find much online about Jack, if anything—though she couldn't quit thinking about him, about how he must have felt when he returned for her and she'd vanished—but Josephine was a different story. Was she related to Lisa? Determined to sort out the truth, she opened her family tree.

The number of dead relatives Lisa had located topped ten thousand—a *minor* obsession. Since she didn't have living relatives, she had delved into the past with enthusiasm to learn about the lives of those already deceased. Even if she didn't know them, their stories intrigued her—their struggles, successes, the famous, and infamous. A living history connected to her through blood.

Because she'd collected so many names, Josephine's could be there, and Lisa would not have remembered it. She typed in the name and held her breath.

Josephine Rogers's page opened, daughter of Ann Avery and Luke Rogers. Parents died thirteen years after Josephine was born. No reason given, just the dates of death. Lisa clicked on Josephine's father, Luke Rogers. He had two brothers and two sisters: Polly, Melvin, Clyde, Matilda and a half brother, Samuel Thornburg. No wives listed for Melvin and Clyde. But Clyde had a son by the name of Trevor. Josephine's outlaw cousin. Polly was never married and died at forty due to the yellow fever.

Lisa swallowed hard and typed in more details under notes: *Polly gave Christmas cookies to the postmaster and had a home in Waco and Belton. Clyde and Melvin were drunken gamblers, and their wives had run off. Trevor became an outlaw.*

The tension pooling in her temple, Lisa closed her eyes. She still couldn't believe she'd actually visited her ancestors. It put a different perspective on her genealogy research. No longer were they simply names and birth dates with a few interesting notes of intrigue. No matter how much she wanted to disassociate herself from Josephine's uncles, Lisa *was* related.

Wondering why there had been no mention of Josephine's Aunt Matilda, the youngest of the siblings, seven years older than Josephine, Lisa clicked on her name. She'd been married to Jonathon Wentworth, and had died shortly after her son's birth. There was no mention of what had become of her husband.

Lisa didn't see any other information about Samuel Thornburg either, except he had the same mother as the rest of the siblings, but his father had died young. His widowed mother had married Luke Rogers while Samuel was only a baby. So why wouldn't anyone have known him? Unless he moved away and had never been heard of again. Was he an ornery cuss like his younger half brothers, Clyde and Melvin? Or someone decent who couldn't abide them?

Lisa sat back in the suede desk chair and stared at the monitor. She lifted the antique necklace off the desk and held it tight. She set it back on the desk and typed: *Josephine's mother gave her a lovely amethyst necklace before she died. Lisa Ann Welsh discovered it in the Remberances Antique Store in Salado, a hundred and forty years later. Coincidence or fate?*

How closely related was Josephine?

Lisa set the curser on her own name, then poked the button for kinship. She ran her finger down the list until she came to Josephine. *3rd great aunt.* A chill cloaked Lisa. Josephine was a direct relation on Lisa's mother's side.

She took a steadying breath and shut down her computer in the living room. The one-bedroom apartment filled with her grandmother's Queen Anne furniture and porcelain antiques seemed smaller than before. The place was quieter, too. As if Lisa had left the wild world of the past and was suspended in limbo, still separated from the present day.

All the modern conveniences stared back at her, the familiar smell of cinnamon potpourri scenting the air, the gentle hum of the fan circulating in the dining room. The only thing out of place was the amethyst necklace. She tightened her grip on it again. A small nagging voice warned her she should have left it behind. But what if she had, and it found its way to the antique shop again? What if she was compelled to buy it again? She bounced back and forth between believing in fate and believing that everyone had some control over their lives.

A knock on the door caused her heart to skip several beats. A flood of memories filled her with instant dread. The tapping ensued, and Lisa took a deep breath, shaking herself from the ominous feeling. She was home, for heaven's sake...safe and sound.

She opened the door and found her friend Pauline standing in the entryway, wearing a red sweater set and black denims, staring at her, black eyes wide, her red lips parted. "Lisa, I was ready to call the state police to put an all-points bulletin out on you!" She wound an ebony curl around her finger, her brows pinched in a frown.

"What?"

Pauline was not one to jump to crazy conclusions, and Lisa had told her she'd be gone the weekend. Since she didn't have any family, Pauline was it and Lisa always let her know her schedule, or Pauline gave her hell. So what was the problem?

"Can I come in?" Pauline didn't wait for an invitation and stalked into the apartment.

Lisa shook her head. "Sorry. I'm...I'm kind of spaced out."

"A quicky divorce can do that, I suppose. Missing two days of work with no word? I told the boss you were sick with a bout of the flu, but—"

"Two days?" Lisa glanced at the calendar as they walked into the kitchen. She'd left for Salado Friday night after divorce court concluded. She woke the next morning in Salado, different time period. Slept overnight in Waco in same vintage time period. Returned to Waco, this time period. She frowned. How long between passing out in the room and returning to Waco, she wasn't sure.

Pauline climbed onto the barstool at the kitchen island counter. "Don't tell me you don't know what day this is?"

Lisa poked her finger at the square on her garden landscapes calendar where trees' leaves were painted in nature's fall colors of orange and yellow. "Sunday."

"Whoa, you must have really tied one on this weekend."

Uncomprehending, Lisa stared at her. "What do you mean?"

"What's up with you? Today is Tuesday." Pauline breathed a heavy sigh. "You should have come with us to the Starving Artist Show in Austin. We bought two paintings of flowering fields of bluebonnets you'd have died for. And can you believe it? Our favorite restaurant, The Magic Time Machine, had closed down." Pauline tapped her bright red fingernails on the white tile counter.

"The Magic Time Machine," Lisa said softly, staring at the amethyst amulet, trying to figure out how she could have lost a couple of days.

"Oh, now that's beautiful. Where'd you find your birthstone in such an unusual setting?"

Lisa glanced at Pauline. "What?"

Pauline made a face. "Earth to Lisa. I don't think you've heard a word I've spoken. I said where'd you get that necklace?"

"At an antique store in Salado."

"Figures. So, how was your...extended weekend?"

Pauline waited while Lisa studied the engraving on the backside of the necklace, but she couldn't quite make out the name. "Lisa?"

Lisa jerked her head up to consider her friend's dark eyes. "I'm sorry. What did you ask?"

"Ahem. What's up with you tonight? You seem totally distracted. I asked...are you listening, Lisa?"

"Yes." Intending to give her friend her full attention, Lisa placed the necklace on the counter.

"I asked how your weekend was. Did you buy a lot of nick-nacks?"

"No."

"What happened to you? I called and called and you never came home. I thought you'd be gone through Saturday night—Sunday the latest."

"I...uhm...got stuck in Salado."

"Was it car trouble?"

Lisa looked at the necklace. "Sort of."

"Couldn't you have called?"

Lisa shook her head. "No phones. And...I need to replace my cell phone battery because it won't hold a charge."

"All the phones were dead?"

Lisa touched the amethyst stone, wishing she could tell Pauline what had happened to her. Would she think she was as nuts as Lisa felt about the whole bizarre experience? "Something like that."

"What happened, Lisa? You're definitely holding out on me. Oh, no, don't tell me." Pauline sat up taller and gave her an evil smile. "You met a guy and you're feeling guilty because you just divorced Barry. You don't have to go into mourning for a year. Honey, you deserve a fling."

"That's not what happened." Lisa wondered if Pauline could handle it if she told her. They'd been best friends since college, then began working at the same firm. She'd always been able to confide in her. But she'd never had anything this strange to tell her. Lisa ran her fingers over the necklace. She took a deep breath and exhaled. "If I tell you what happened, will you promise not to laugh?"

"Only if it isn't funny."

"It isn't. You know I don't believe in out-of-the-ordinary occurrences."

Pauline nodded. "Most sensible person I know."

"I mean, like, I don't believe in ghosts or anything."

Pauline's eyes widened. "You saw a ghost?"

Shaking her head, Lisa said, "No. Well…yes." She touched the necklace and bit her lip. "Actually, it's worse."

"What's worse than seeing a ghost?" Grabbing her hand, Pauline hopped off the stool and pulled Lisa into the living room. "Don't leave anything out."

They sank onto the floral sofa, and Pauline looked like she was about to open Christmas presents, sitting on the edge of the cushions, her eyes sparkling with intrigue.

Lisa took a minute to think about how she would pose the question. "What would you say if I told you I went to bed in Salado and the next morning, I was living in the year 1870?"

"I guess it would depend on whose bed it was." Pauline waggled her brows, her lips and eyes smiling.

Heat crept through Lisa as she recalled Jack's passionate kisses in that very same bed. She frowned at

Pauline.

"Sorry." Pauline couched her amused expression and tried to look more serious. Her lips formed an "o." Her brows lifted and she smiled. "You're blushing which means you were in some guy's bed. He has to have been cute."

"Are you going to be serious?"

Pauline chuckled. "You bet. But I want to know more about this guy."

"All right. Just listen. I checked into the Stagecoach Inn on Friday night in Salado, but Saturday morning the place was called the Shady Villa Inn and according to everyone there, I was living in the year, 1870."

Her eyes round, Pauline shook her head. "I've never heard of anything so strange. Are you sure you weren't dreaming? I've had the weirdest dreams, and in the morning I think they've really occurred they seem *so* genuine."

"No, Pauline. This *was* real, and I'll prove it to you. Wait here." Lisa retreated to her bedroom and returned with the blue dress, petticoats, and bustle. "Jack purchased these for me."

"Whoa, torture." Pauline touched the wire coils underneath the bustle. She looked over the dress. "He bought it for you in the past?"

"Yes."

"They do make great reproductions for parties and reenactments. Heck, I don't know what a dress would have looked like in the 1800's, let alone a copy. This appears too new to be a dress from that period." She set the garments aside. "Where's the corset? Didn't you wear one of those cute little things?"

"Ugh. Too restricting. Made it difficult to breathe. As for the garments, they *were* new, from a dress store in Waco."

Pauline shifted her attention from the dress to Lisa. "You need to see a spiritualist. Madame Esparazo claims to deal with bizarre things. I'd say this qualifies."

"Have you seen her before?"

"No, but a couple of my girlfriends have. She was right on the money with her predictions concerning them—boyfriends, jobs."

Except for talking to Pauline, which was hard enough, Lisa didn't want to mention this to a woman who was probably a charlatan. Yet, she'd love to have some closure. "I don't believe in spiritual hocus-pocus."

"From what you've told me, *I'd* talk to her. What have you got to lose?"

"What do you think, Pauline? Do you think I'm losing my mind?"

"Did you have a lot to drink while you were down there...or up here?"

Lisa made a face.

"You were upset about the divorce and the fight in court when Barry tried to get half of your inheritance. *The creep.* I thought maybe you'd tied one on."

"You know me better."

"That's true, but the end of a relationship can lead you to do some strange things you normally wouldn't. You were totally hooked on the worm."

Lisa frowned at her.

"Sorry. You look exhausted. Didn't you get any sleep this weekend?"

"Nightmares have been keeping me awake." Lisa picked up the necklace and gazed at it.

"Gotta watch what you eat or see on television before you go to bed. They say milk can help you sleep. We've got a hectic schedule Tomorrow, the audit of a century. I guess I'll head home." Pauline stood to leave and spied the hooked rug on the dining room table. "Oh, oh, Lisa, you've finished the rug." Running her hand over the colorful wool strands, she examined the detail. "Is this the one you said I could have?"

Lisa nodded, her thoughts already back on Jack. She envisioned him being frantic. He'd lost his ward, a woman who was strange as all get out who didn't know a lot about the time period and could have been Josephine with a case of amnesia.

Pauline hugged the rug to her chest. "Oh, thank you. It's beautiful. You're so talented that you can design your own rugs. Of course, the quilts, the needlepoint pictures, ribbon-embroidered pillows...how do you ever find the time?"

Lisa raised her brows. "Time?"

"Yes, how do you find the time to do these wonderful projects?"

"No kids, no boyfriend, no life, I guess."

"Would you like to have supper with us tonight? You seem a little down. Maybe—"

"No, thank you, Pauline. I'll call the spiritualist and try to see her tonight. I have to find out what happened to me this weekend. There has to be a reasonable explanation."

Spiritualists. She didn't believe in them. A strange sense of dissociation tugged at her, as if she didn't quite belong here. Which was totally crazy. She *really* didn't belong in Jack's time.

"If you do find some answers, please let me know. I'm always up late, so call any time." Pauline gave Lisa a hug. "The bluebonnets on the rug look so real. Thanks again for the lovely gift."

"I'll…I'll call you."

After Pauline left, Lisa located the spiritualist's address and hoped she wouldn't regret forking over a bunch of money to a possible fraud. But like Pauline said, what did she have to lose?

***

An hour later, Lisa arrived at Madam Esparazo's Victorian home, not looking forward to baring her soul to a complete stranger. Intricate scalloped-siding dipped in pink dressed the upper edge, while the lower half of the home wore white, making it looked like the gingerbread house in Hansel and Gretel—which meant the evil witch lurked inside. Candlelight, flickering next to the windows, twinkled through lacy curtains, adding to the cheerful mood. Yet Lisa's mission was anything but festive.

She hurried up the path before she changed her mind, glancing down at the old recycled bricks wearing the Texas star, dated 1865. Interesting that the brick maker put his mark on the pavers. She paused at the burgundy-colored door where a small stained-glass window cheered the solid wood. Before she pushed the doorbell, Madame Esparazo opened the door.

The slightly built woman's black hair and eyes and brown-sugar skin sparkled in the candlelight, her gaze taking in every inch of Lisa.

Her skin crawled under the woman's scrutiny, and Lisa asked, "Is there something the matter?"

The medium's eyes widened. "You're one of them."

"Pardon me?"

The woman wasn't lessening Lisa's discomfort.

"Excuse me. Where are my manners? Come in, Josephine."

Lisa's heart nearly stopped, and her feet remained cemented to the porch. She hadn't told Pauline Josephine's name, only Jack's, in the event Pauline had called Esmeralda and let it slip.

"Please have a seat." The woman motioned to one of the soft-cushioned chairs of burgundies and forest green filling the dark parlor.

The sweet fragrance of watermelon floated in the air. A whispered melody of pipe and whistle flutes and harps drifted to her ear, but Lisa couldn't take a step into the house. "You called me Josephine."

"Did I, dear?"

Lisa stood firm. No way was she going to make her life any spookier than it already was.

"All right," the woman said, sighing deeply. "There is an aura about you—a ghostly aura. The name it gives you is Josephine—Josephine Rogers."

Lisa's knees buckled, and Esparazo grabbed her arm to steady her. She guided her to a chair in the parlor and sat Lisa down. Pouring a cup of tea for her, she said, "You have unfinished business to conduct elsewhere." She wrinkled her brow. "Not here though. Somewhere far away."

"Salado."

Esparazo's expression was kindly and thoughtful. "Yes." She motioned to Lisa's tea. "Drink, before it gets cold."

Lifting the porcelain cup to her lips, Lisa breathed in the minty flavor. She drank some of the hot tea. The scent in the room changed to violets, and she nearly dropped the cup. Esparazo grabbed it from her, and her smile zigzagged across her face. Lisa reached her hand to her forehead. Her vision blurred, and her thoughts spun out of control. The medium's smile distorted and faded as she whispered, "He needs you. Don't delay. Go to him."

***

"Lisa, Lisa, are you there?"

"Jack?" Lisa would recognize his deep voice anywhere but it sounded muffled and distant, and she couldn't see anything. Just a black void as if she were adrift in a space capsule between her world and his.

The space filled with shadows, and the scent of roses permeated the air. The hint of violets touched her upturned nose. Her cheeks grew icy cold, and her chest tightened.

"The necklace," a voice whispered in her ear. "Use the necklace."

Lisa touched her purse where the necklace securely rested. No way would she wear the necklace again.

"Lisa, where are you?"

"Jack?"

The shadows shifted, and she saw the lobby at the Shady Villa Inn. Jack paced across it. He looked both agitated and worried sick. She reached her hand out to him, tears dribbling down her cheeks. But she wasn't there. Where was she?

An overwhelming need rushed through her. She had to return to him—to comfort his aching heart, to explain...how could she explain who she was and where she was from? But she had to let him know she was all right, and that she couldn't see him again.

"Jack?" she whispered. The notion she could fall in love with anyone in two days' time was preposterous...just plain nuts, yet, she'd been heartsick ever since she'd left his world. Like she was connected to him despite the time and distance between them.

Was she mad? Before she could think further, she slipped the necklace over her head.

***

Knocking at the apartment door roused Lisa from sleep as she lay in her bed. She stared at the four walls and wondered when she'd returned home.

She jumped out of bed and hurried to open the door.

Her arms folded, Pauline stood in the entryway. "How did you sneak past me? I was putting away the dishes and happened to see your car parked out front again. Did Madame Esparazo give you any answers?"

"I have to go back," Lisa muttered, touching her necklace. "I have to." She walked into the kitchen and pulled out the jar of ice tea mix.

"Back to Salado?"

"Do you want to come with me?"

"Are you kidding? It'd be bad enough for me to leave my poor husband alone overnight, but to return to the past more than a hundred and thirty years? I don't think so." Pauline brought out a jar of fudge sticks. "Did she confirm what happened to you? That you weren't imagining things?"

"She..." Lisa rubbed her temple, trying to recall what had happened. "She said I have a ghostly aura."

"Whoa, that's sooo cool. What about the time

travel stuff? Did she mention the dangers of using the amulet?"

"No, she didn't." In fact, Lisa couldn't recall having spoken with the woman much.

"In one movie, the lady couldn't go back in time after a while, like it could only work for so long."

"Like the genie's lamp, you have three wishes and that's it?" Lisa stirred sugar into their tea, twice as much for Pauline to satisfy her sweet tooth.

"Yeah, only you could be trapped in the wrong time if you're not careful. Also you know what they say about altering the future."

Lisa handed the glass of tea to Pauline. "I have no intention of—"

"That's the problem. You don't intend to change anything, but already several people in Salado are upset about seeing you in town." She took a sip of her tea. "Will Michael let you leave again this weekend? He said that audit had to be done this week. Which means we'll be working overtime."

"It'll be done. Why does he keep pestering me and not you?"

"He prefers blondes. Besides, he's a coward. He leaves the married women alone because he's afraid a jealous husband's going to shoot him."

"He's such a slime. I have higher qualifications than most of the staff, and he still won't promote me."

"You know how it goes...it's a boy's club there. You're to outperform most of the men, but when it comes to the bucks, it still goes to them. Now if you were to put out a bit more—"

"That's what *he* keeps saying." God, how she hated the creep. But she liked the work, and she didn't want to abandon Pauline.

"He does?"

"Not right out, but he's always touching my cheek or hair or...well, he's just repulsive."

"Oh, now he's really adorable," Pauline said in a mocking way.

"Yeah, right. A strawberry-blond, freckled cutie, *married,* and such a creep!"

"That he is. What are you going to do if he wants you to work this weekend again?"

"I'm *not* going to stay late."

"But your promotion?"

"It's never coming, Pauline. The carrot is dangled before me, but just as I snatch at it, it's yanked out of reach."

Pauline stretched her arms. "I know what you mean." She finished the rest of her tea and grabbed a cookie to go. "I'll see you at work tomorrow. I had to know what happened with you and Madame Esparazo. Remember what I said about tampering with the past."

"You know, Pauline..." Lisa's voice deepened. "I found some discrepancies in the books concerning Michael's brother-in-law. I've been afraid to mention it to anyone because over half-a-million dollars appear to be missing."

Pauline sat back down on the kitchen stool. "Whoa, and you've said nothing to Michael?"

"To no one but you, now. I didn't know how he'd respond. He can get pretty sore."

"I don't know, Lisa. Michael and his extended family are pretty thick. Do you think he already knows?"

"Maybe. Anyway, I dread going to work. I can't

quit the job, it pays well even without the promotion, but I hate working for that family any further."

"I'm glad I didn't have that account."

"Thanks, Pauline."

"Sorry, I didn't mean that the way it sounded. It's too bad they hadn't given it to one of the guys."

"Maybe they thought I wouldn't catch the discrepancies."

"No, he knows you're good. Maybe, he wanted his brother-in-law caught. Get him out of the business altogether so he could have free reign."

"Oh, I never thought of that." Lisa took a deep breath and exhaled. "Now, I really don't want to go to work Tomorrow."

Pauline's expression turned gloomy. "Me either."

CHAPTER 11

Jack ran his hand through his hair, rested his Stetson on his head, and left the house. This one last time, he was going to look for Lisa at the inn. Hearing his housekeeper and brother talking in the garden, he stalked in the direction of their voices.

Jack came around the path when Matthew asked, "What are we going to do with Jack? I think he's fallen head over heels for someone new."

Esmeralda pulled weeds from underneath a wrought-iron bench while Matthew raked leaves off the brickwork in front of it.

Esmeralda smiled. "It would do him good to find someone to love again."

Jack cleared his throat. Matthew dropped the rake and Esmeralda stood. "Oh, how long have you been there, Jack?" Matthew asked.

"Long enough. I'm going into town. Does anybody need anything?"

"Again?" Matthew asked. "You've ridden into town every day this week. What's going on?"

"I think you know I've met someone."

"Yes, the lady who was supposed to come to stay with us but vanished. I think I'd go for someone a little more reliable than that."

Jack shook his head. "I'm worried sick something might have happened to her."

"They say she's Josephine. Is it true?" Matthew asked.

"Who's they?" He furrowed his brow at his younger brother. Though he was a good ranch hand,

Matthew could be more than annoying when it came to Jack's personal life.

"You know...Jacob, Bill, even Frank said she's returned to town. Bill, in particular, is pretty shook up you've been seeing her. Have you been seeing her?"

"Her name is Lisa. She's not Josephine."

Matthew pulled off his Stetson and scratched his head, his dark brown hair showing a slight red cast. The brothers were often mistaken for twins, which had gotten them into trouble when they were in school and with the girls. Usually they were as close as kernels of corn, but this matter with Lisa had Jack's stomach in a stew, and any mention of her twisted him further into a knot.

Esmeralda's ebony eyes considered Jack, and she frowned.

"What's wrong? I know when you have that look, you're having one of your premonitions."

"No, nothing."

Jack rose from the bench. "I'm going."

"Be careful." Esmeralda tucked her black curls into a net. "I feel something's wrong concerning the lady."

"Yes." Matthew returned to his raking. "She evaporates like the morning dew in the hot Texas sun."

"I'm serious," Esmeralda said. "She needs your protection, Jack, but...I can't see any visions of her now, as if she was swallowed up by an endless void."

Jack shook his head. "I don't want to hear it. I have to see her and make sure she's all right."

Esmeralda nodded. "I know. It's inevitable." She stooped down to pull another weed. "Just use caution, Jack."

The clippity-clop of horse's hooves announced a

rider's approach, and they looked at the gate. Hell, it was Bill.

"Now you've gone and done it," Matthew said to Jack.

Bill looked down from his vantage point, sitting tall in his saddle, his blue eyes sharp and wary. "Where's Josephine?"

"She's not here." Jack walked past him to the stable.

Bill followed, leaning down. "I heard you took her shoppin' in Waco and bought her a new hat and dress. Do you reckon your money will buy my Josephine?"

"She's not Josephine." Jack threw his saddle over his horse's back, while Matthew joined them.

"Hey, Bill, how's it going?" Matthew asked.

"Fine, if your blamed brother would stop interferin' in my business."

Jack mounted, then rode toward the gate while Bill followed after him. "You leave my girl alone." Bill narrowed his eyes into slits. "I mean it. You never took any interest in her before. Why now?"

"She's not Josephine. She's Lisa. Can't you see the difference? I don't have any idea where Josephine's gone. She came back to town for a while, but as far as I know, she returned to Waco."

"I heard her Aunt Polly died. Are either of her uncles goin' to take her in? She always said they was lookin' to get her aunt's money, and she wouldn't have nothin' to do with them. Said her mother was terrified of Clyde before she died."

"You'd know more about that than I would. I never took any interest in Josephine, just as you said. I have business to take care of in town."

"You're waitin' for her to return, ain't you? Well, you'd better forget seein' her again. I'll be watchin' you." Bill turned his horse toward the bridge over the creek while Jack headed for the inn, hoping with all his heart Lisa had returned.

He had it in mind to ask her to marry him, on account he'd stayed with her alone in the hotel room. Anything to make sure he could keep her safe. He feared somehow her uncles had managed to get ahold of her, though no one had seen any sign of them.

Where was she?

***

After a hectic day at the office on Thursday, Pauline dropped by Lisa's apartment, and she knew what her friend wanted to know. "Did you tell Michael about the missing funds? I've been dying to ask, but I've been so busy with my own audits I didn't have a chance."

"I'm still reviewing my figures to make sure I haven't made any errors." Lisa rubbed the antique necklace. No matter how hard she tried not to worry about Jack, her thoughts were drawn to him.

Pauline sat down at the kitchen counter and looked at the amethyst. "You're not still thinking about Salado, are you?"

"I can hardly concentrate on anything else."

"What's to consider? All the antiques you have would be brand new in old Salado and the roads are dusty and dirty instead of paved. I imagine there are no quaint gift shops. What's the attraction?"

Pauline wouldn't understand. She had a loving husband of five years and a neat little apartment, perfectly happy with their two-income, childless family.

Lisa wanted the home, the husband, the children. She had no family at all, and the thought she could have her very own with someone like Jack—Pauline wouldn't understand.

Lisa opened the cupboard. "Would you like some ice tea?"

"That would be nice. So what goes through your mind, Lisa, when you think of that old place?"

"I'm drawn to Salado. I keep wondering..." Lisa hesitated, stirred the glasses of tea, and took a deep breath. Whenever she closed her eyes at night, she could see Jack's warm smile when her words tickled him. His dark eyes studied her with an intensity she wasn't used to, and though he'd tried to be a gentleman, she sensed his interest in her went deeper. Lisa sat at the island counter and rested her chin on her hands. "Jack's warm and caring and handsome. Definitely handsome."

"You can't get involved with this guy from the past. You're meddling with things you shouldn't. Do you want me to get rid of that necklace for you? Maybe that's what has the hold over you."

"No, Pauline. I've got to see him again." *And say goodbye.* "He reminds me of Rhett Butler, in *Gone with the Wind*...charming, attractive, a bit of a rogue."

"A bit of a rogue? You didn't tell me this side of him."

"He was waiting for three women to arrive in town, bound for the college there."

"There was a college in Salado?"

"Yeah, and Frank said once Jack caught sight of me, he didn't look any further."

Pauline's eyes widened. "Who's Frank?"

"Another of Josephine's beaus."

"Gee whiz, how many did she have?"

"She seemed to be the life of the party."

Pauline shook her head. "You're playing with fire. If I were you, I wouldn't go back."

"I thought you were into this stuff."

"Sure. But not to participate. I'd rather watch it on TV."

Not willing to change her mind, Lisa sipped her tea. "I researched Salado and learned the Robertson family started the town. I couldn't find anything about Jack and his family, or Josephine. I'm sure if I went through county court records for Salado, I'd find some information on them. Did you know the area lies on the Balcone's Fault, and underground springs feed the creek? Also the Chisholm Trail ran straight down the main street. The citizens had to build stone walls to keep cattle from the drives from muddying up too much of the creek because that's where the townspeople got their drinking water."

"Sounds fascinating." Pauline made a face.

"Yes, and caves exist all over the area. Indians used to take shelter in them, and outlaws holed up in them, too. Gold's supposed to be hidden in one at the fork of three rivers somewhere nearby."

"Now that's more interesting. Maybe in your travels to the past, you'll find the gold. You can share it with me, then we could quit our crummy jobs at the firm and retire in the grand manor we shall quickly become accustomed to."

Lisa smiled. "Maybe I should take a shovel and pickaxe with me when I return so I can dig for the stolen gold."

"I'm kidding. You shouldn't go."

"I have no choice. An awful nightmare where a man tries to smother me with a pillow keeps plaguing me. When I can't breathe any more, I wake up in a cold sweat."

"I thought you looked tired. You need to meet a new guy who hasn't been dead for over a century. In fact, Dave Henderson's nice and looking for a girlfriend. I thought it was too soon, but if you're getting involved with some Jack from the past, maybe you need someone from the here and now to raise your spirits. If nothing else, he's making good money in real estate, and he can take you to nice places. Do you want me to have him call you?"

As much as she didn't want to give up Jack, Lisa agreed Pauline was probably right. Going back to the past was a bad idea. All she had to remind herself was that whoever killed Josephine would most likely want her dead. *And* she didn't belong there.

"Good. Give me your phone."

"Right now?" Lisa's words rose in a squeak.

"Yes, before you change your mind." Pauline punched in a number. "Hi, Dave, this is Pauline. If you want to call my friend Lisa, she's ready to go on a date. You're welcome. Bye." She hung up and smiled.

Lisa *really* didn't want to do this. "Well?"

"He'll contact you in a little while." The phone rang, and she winked. "See you later."

Her nerves on edge, Lisa grabbed the phone and waved at Pauline as she headed out of the apartment. "Hello?"

"Hi, Lisa, my name is Dave Henderson, a friend of Pauline's from high school. Would you like to go to dinner with me tonight at six?"

"Tonight?" She could do this. She had to give it a try. "All right. At six." She gave him directions to her apartment and said goodbye. Twisting the amethyst between her fingers, she hung up. She knew in her heart she needed to break the spell Salado...that Jack, rather, had over her.

A lump formed in her throat, and she fought tears. "Sorry, Jack. It's time for me to get back to reality." She needed to start over.

***

Both angry and concerned, Jack exited the inn. No one had any idea where Lisa had disappeared. All he had to show for his trouble was the hat he'd bought for her that she'd left behind.

Frank caught up with him and seized his arm, his face madder than Jack had ever seen it. "What did you do to Josephine to make her go away?"

Jack yanked his arm free. "Her name is Lisa, and I didn't get a chance to see her after we returned."

Frank eyed him with suspicion. "She wouldn't have left Salado because of me. It had to have been something you said or did. I thought you were taking her to your home."

Jack turned away and headed for his horse.

"Hey," Frank said, following him. "You had dinner with her, didn't you?"

"No." Fuming, Jack mounted his horse.

"No?" Frank shook his head. "Maybe Bill slipped in and saw her first. Maybe that's why she hasn't been around."

But she hadn't been with him, because Bill was just as sore that she was missing. Jack headed his horse in the direction of his home.

Frank grabbed hold of the reins. "You shouldn't have left her alone."

Jack jerked his horse's reins away. Jack had been hating himself for making the mistake. He didn't need Frank or anyone else riding him about it.

"You need to find someone else more suited to your disposition. Maybe that new maid over at the inn. I hear she's looking for a fella," Frank said.

Jack spurred his horse and galloped away.

Frank hollered after him, "Heck, the maid's not that bad looking!"

With every passing day, Jack feared he might never see Lisa again. The torment that had filled his soul when Charlotte had died, twisted his heart again. He couldn't let Lisa go, not yet. Would she find her back to Waco? Or maybe her aunt's home in Belton?

Call it stubborn pride, but he wasn't giving up.

***

At work on Friday, Lisa copied *the* documents, trying not to get caught by her boss before she spilled the story about the embezzlement.

"Well?" Pauline asked, raising the goose bumps on Lisa's arms.

Dropping several slips of paper on the floor, Lisa's heart nearly stopped. If it had been her boss, she'd have some explaining to do. She reached down to scoop up the papers. "Do you have to sneak up on me like that? You almost gave me a heart attack."

"Sorry. Did you go out with Dave?"

Lisa tilted her head to the side. "You said he was a nice guy. We went to Le Creperie for dinner, but before the food was served he asked me how I liked it. You know, whether I liked it on top or underneath."

"What?"

Lisa rolled her eyes and tapped her foot on the floor.

Pauline's eyes widened. "You mean...sex?" Her face turned three shades of scarlet. "I'm sorry, Lisa. I had no idea. So what did you say?"

"What do you think? I told him I don't discuss topics like that with men, period. I don't even talk about things like that with you!"

"The nerve of the guy." Pauline glanced at the papers. "Are you—"

"Yes, I'm copying the documents just in case."

"Did you tell Michael yet what you found concerning his brother-in-law's handling of the accounts?"

"No, I'm making these first. I've got to figure out a safe place to keep the originals."

"Don't look at me," Pauline said, raising her hands.

"No, Pauline, that's the second place they'd look."

They walked to Lisa's desk, and she slid the original documents into a black leather case. She placed it on her desktop that once sported pictures of Barry and now looked barren, which made her think again of Jack and the picture they had taken. "As soon as the boss is out of his meeting, I'm going to waltz in there and tell him about the discrepancies on the books."

Pauline tapped the case, her voice low and worried. "You'd better secure that now because here comes trouble. I'll see you later."

Michael joined Lisa at her desk, a smug smile curving his lips. "We need to talk."

If he was finally offering her the promotion, then

what? She still had to tell him about the embezzlement.

"Yes, sir." She grabbed the copy of the documents and followed him into his office.

"Close the door and have a seat."

Reluctantly, she did, then sat in the chair in front of Michael's desk.

He steepled his hands under his chin and studied her with his electric blue eyes as if he was trying to seduce her. "I'm afraid you won't be making the promotion."

If she had another job lined up, she'd quit.

"You do a great job and you certainly deserve the promotion. But..." Michael tapped his fingers on the desk, and gave a conceited smile. "If you were more amenable to—well, more sociable...let's not be coy. You know what I mean."

Lisa narrowed her eyes. "You're married."

He shrugged, clasped his hands behind his head and leaned back in his leather chair. "What difference does that make?"

"All the difference in the world to me."

"That's your problem, not mine. I guess that's all, unless you have something else you'd like to say."

Inside, Lisa was seething, so angry she could smack him upside the head with one of his brass dollar sign bookends. It didn't matter that she'd earned her master's in accounting just to help get the promotion, or that she worked extra hours to placate the boss. No, all that mattered was she wouldn't accommodate his sexual prowess.

Lisa looked at the papers she held in her hands, placed them on the desk, and stood to leave. "You might want to take a look at these. Half-a-million-dollars' worth of missing funds may interest you." Giving him the report on the financial scandal helped to alleviate the sting of not getting the promotion, a *little*.

Michael stared at her, his eyes widened and his mouth slightly agape. For once, he was speechless. She fought giving him a catty smile, turned, and stalked out of the office.

When she returned to her desk, Pauline strolled over with a cup of coffee for her. "Okay, so what happened?"

Lisa swallowed the tears wanting to surface. "I didn't get the promotion, and I dropped the half-a-million-dollar bombshell on Michael's desk."

"I'm so sorry about the promotion, but we figured he wouldn't give it to you. What did he say about the money discrepancies?"

"I didn't hang around to find out." She shut off her computer.

"I don't blame you. I think I'd drop the ball and run, too."

"I'm going to revisit old Salado." Lisa pulled the black leather satchel off her desk and headed for the front door.

Pauline hurried after her. "We have another hour left on the clock, and Michael said you *have* to work this weekend."

"I have to go to Salado. I can hardly eat or sleep. All I've thought of is returning." Lisa touched the amethyst. "Don't let Michael work you too hard." She hurried outside to her SUV.

"Lisa!" Pauline called after her.

Lisa looked back. "Yes?"

"Be careful."

***

Not sure she would be able to return to the past, Lisa parked at the Stagecoach Inn and grabbed the satchel and her tapestry bag. When she looked at the inn, her skin prickled with fresh anxiety. Returning to the room wasn't a cheerful prospect, but she had to see Jack one last time. After all he'd done for her, all the money he'd spent on her, she had to let him know she was all right, but that she could never return to Salado after this.

At the check-in counter, she asked for the key to room three, ready for whatever would happen next.

The male clerk's face turned from cheerful to solemn. He wore a black suit and somber expression, which made him look like he had attended his best friend's funeral. "Room number three is booked through the month."

Her jaw dropped. She hadn't expected a glitch like this and couldn't contain the frustration in her voice. "I specifically asked for that room when I called Wednesday. They said it wouldn't be any problem and reserved it." Of course she hadn't remembered to bring the confirmation number and she didn't think to give them her email address either.

He leaned over the counter and whispered, "The owner said the room's been booked since Tuesday after you checked out, and a soul hasn't come for the key since." The man straightened. "You can have the room next door, if you'd like." Under her scrutiny, he smoothed his black tie. Finally, he whispered, "If you must know, strange happenings have occurred in room number three."

Her skin chilled with awareness. "What *kind* of

strange happenings?"

The clerk glanced around the lobby and seeing no one within earshot said, "The cleaning staff said it's haunted."

"You don't believe that, do you?" Yet goose bumps erupted down her arms.

"I don't know what to think, but the maid cleaned the room after you left and was scared out of her wits. She quit her job within the hour. Three other employees, two other ladies from our housekeeping staff, and a maintenance man checked the room out. They've since found other employment."

Ohmigod, somehow Josephine's ghost was trapped in that room for all time. Why had Lisa thought she'd only be there in the past? No way had she considered that anyone else would experience any ghostly phenomenon. "Are you sure I can't have that room? It won't bother me to stay there for the weekend."

"No, I'm sorry, Miss. I can't afford to lose my job."

"I understand. I'll take the one next door. Thank you." Lisa took the key and walked toward the hallway, her feelings in turmoil. She had to return to Jack, if it was at all possible, and she was certain she had to be in Josephine's room.

Inside room number two, she laid the blue gown, petticoats, and bustle on the bed and changed into them. She sat on the mattress and fingered the necklace. Taking a deep breath, she shoved the chain over her head before she changed her mind.

The room remained the same. She let out her breath, partly relieved, partly perturbed. She grabbed her black satchel, tied a beaded bag over her wrist, and left the room. Walking around to the outside of the building, she peered through the window of room number three and didn't see anyone. She pulled at the glass pane, but it wouldn't budge.

With growing frustration, she returned to the lobby counter. Seeing no one around, she skirted the front desk and grabbed the key for room number three. Her heart in her throat, she ran to the room, and stood at the door so she could catch her breath and settle her nerves.

After turning the key in the lock, she twisted the doorknob and entered the room. When she shut the door behind her, the darkness surrounded her and a light floated above the bed. Disoriented, Lisa shivered and stared at the strange aberration. Her head spun and the light faded from sight. Reaching for the bed, she collapsed and clutched the satchel to her chest, before she slipped into the black hole of time.

***

Her temple throbbing, Lisa awoke to find the room like she envisioned, in the year 1870. She sighed deeply. *Jack Stanton, how will I find you?* She frowned. What if he had given up on her already? Why hadn't she considered that before now?

Wanting to set things right with Jack, Lisa hurried out of the room. As soon as she reached the unmanned front desk, she rang the bell.

A flushed, round-faced man greeted her with a smile, but when he recognized her, he frowned. "What do you want?" Mr. Worthington, the owner, demanded.

Lisa hesitated. "Can you tell me how to get in touch with Mr. Jack Stanton?"

The man glared at her and muttered under his breath, "You can't have that room, Miss, whoever you are."

"What? I just wanted to find Jack Stanton." She rubbed her forehead. "Besides, the room was paid up through the month. Isn't that so?"

The man fidgeted with the quill pen. "If you're Josephine Rogers—"

Lisa pulled the folded paper that Josephine had written to Bill from her beaded bag and held it up. "I am."

The man stared at the letter, his eyes round. "Oh, uh, we'll refund your money."

"I don't want a refund. I want to keep my room."

"You can't have it. It's booked," the man blustered, flipping through a book, "for the next month and a half. The folks specifically asked for that room."

"But I've paid through the month—"

"Here, take your money." Mr. Worthington fumbled through the cash register and handed her a fistful of bills.

Lisa stared at the cash, then shook her head. "I want what I paid for."

"You can't have the room, and that's the end of it."

How can things get so muddled? I just want to see Jack. But she'd have to return to Waco via the room.

"In fact, the inn is sold out." He smiled, tilting his head back a bit, and jutted his stub of a chin out.

"But..." Lisa said, slipping a key out of her purse and examined it, "I have the key to room three."

"What do you think you're trying to pull?" Mr. Worthington leaned over the counter, his face red. His chubby fingers snatched the key and he examined it. "This isn't ours. Who are you? You're not Josephine Rogers. She's—"

"Dead?"

Mr. Worthington gasped. "How did you…you're not her. You can't be." Lisa seized the cash and shoved it into her beaded bag along with the letter from Josephine, and the key to room three in the future. She glared at the owner when a familiar voice caught her ear. *Jack.*

***

"Lisa!" Jack's heart thundered when he saw her standing in the lobby like a mirage. She couldn't be the genuine deal, but when she swung around and smiled at him, she was as real as ever.

He dashed across the lobby, grabbed her arm and pulled her toward the sitting area. "I've returned to the hotel so many times this past week…" He paused, shook his head and squeezed her hand soundly. "I was afraid they'd charge me for taking up space in the lobby."

Her sweet smile took the edge off all his worrying, though a hint of concern reflected in her green eyes. "I'm glad to see you, too, Jack."

Taking a deep breath, his outlook brightened. He knew he had scared her off with something he had said or done. Now with her cheerful expression brightening her ivory complexion, he was about as elated as when Charlotte agreed to marry him.

"I was afraid you'd be mad at me for leaving. I'm—I'm so sorry."

"I couldn't be angry at you." He touched the sleeve of her gown. He'd been upset all right, but he was so glad to see her the irritation faded. "You're wearing the dress."

"Yes, I love it."

"But not the hat?"

"Oh, I'm so sorry." She touched her hair swirled into a chignon on her head. "I must have left it behind when I returned to Waco last weekend."

Jack wasn't sure what to think of the situation. The stationmaster had said no woman fitting Lisa's description had ridden the stage the rest of the week. She had just vanished. "When I looked for you, they said you'd left the hat in the room, but you had disappeared. They gave it to me for safe-keeping."

"That's wonderful, Jack. I was afraid I wouldn't see it again and you'd never forgive me."

"What happened? You didn't even leave any word for me. Couldn't you have written a note?" He hadn't meant to sound upset with her, but the days of worrying had left him soured. Though he chastised himself for sounding annoyed.

"If I explained what happened, you wouldn't understand. I was here one minute and in Waco the next."

He frowned. "A reoccurring amnesia?" This wasn't good news. He had to discover where she'd been or who she'd been with who took her back to Waco.

"Something like that," she vaguely said.

"So what is it that you do? You said you had to get back to work on Monday in Waco, I overhead you tell the clerk." He had to know everything about her. Maybe, if he could find out her occupation, he could discover where she had disappeared to and who she really was.

"You have such big ears. I'm an auditor for an important firm."

"An auditor?"

"Yes, I review accounting documents to find discrepancies."

"Oh, a bookkeeper. I didn't think they allowed women to handle such matters, unless it was a family-run business."

"Why, Jack, you're a male chauvinist."

"Male what? You mean chauvinism as in fanatical patriotism? What does that have to do with your being a bookkeeper?" He fingered a golden curl dangling over her shoulder, unable to stop his action. He wanted to touch her, to prove to himself she was here, real, his, if he could get her to agree.

Lisa laughed. "I'm not a bookkeeper. So what is it you do?"

"I'm a guardian angel, remember? Only the one I was sent to protect disappeared. I don't think I'll ever earn my full set of wings now."

"I'm certain you'd wear them well." She traced the swirling paisley design on his black silk vest.

He ran his hand over her fingers, soft and delicate. He was having a devil of a time concentrating on the conversation. If only he could get her alone somewhere quiet. "Would you go up to Table Rock with me?"

She gave him a look like she knew better. "I've read about that place."

"Where in the world would they have written about it?" He squeezed her hand and smiled.

"In a couple of books I found in the Waco library." She looked down when his fingers caressed hers.

"What did they say?"

Her eyes met his and her lips curved up. "It was where lovers met."

He laughed. "They still do." The air was nippy, but

he had to get her alone after being apart from her for so long. He stood and offered his arm. "Would you like to see it for yourself?"

CHAPTER 12

Curious about this old-time lover's meeting place, Lisa wanted to see it for herself. Yet she scolded herself too. *Tell him you have to leave for good.* But she couldn't. Not when he was so happy to see her and she could tell from his expression and actions, he'd been beside himself with worry when she'd disappeared without word. For an hour, she would stay with him, explain to him how she couldn't return, then leave.

When he rushed her out of the hotel and hurried to his horse tethered at the hitching post in front, his enthusiasm for taking her to Table Rock made her smile. Yet, her mind nagged at her to end the relationship before she hurt him any further.

After securing a blanket from his horse, he escorted her across the main street. They entered the woods some distance from there. Upon reaching the bottom of a hill, she stopped and looked up to measure the climb and noted several trails left by others who had made their way to the top.

"Are you still game, Lisa?"

"Sure." She wasn't certain how she'd ascend the slope in a long dress. She had a devil of a time avoiding stepping on the hem of the long skirts, while grasshoppers did jumping jacks in her stomach.

As chivalrous as always, Jack took her arm and helped her. If he had been Barry, or most guys she'd dated, he would have let her fend for herself.

As they crested the top of the hill and came to the outcropping of rocks, she stared at the monolithic limestone carved with names, initials, mottos, and verses. A lover's retreat from the eyes of the world. The notion that dozens of men and women had visited the place over the past one-hundred-plus years intrigued her.

She knelt down to examine the writings more closely. "If Bill was correct, my name is encircled with his somewhere."

"Josephine's name, remember?" Jack sounded more than concerned.

She straightened, her skin prickling with heat. "You're right, of course." She hated making the slip. With all her heart, she wanted Jack to believe she wasn't Josephine.

He spread out the blanket, and she walked over to the edge of the rock and looked down.

"Don't get too close to the edge. That's a mighty long drop. It's about twenty-five feet to the bottom."

"Ouch."

Giant pecans, elms, and oaks lined the creek, while perpetual springs rippled over the rocky bottom. "Hmm." She folded her arms and rubbed them, taking a deep breath of the fresh air. "Somehow the air smells better here," she said and shivered. "It's cooler up here, too."

He joined her and rubbed her arms. "Are you too cold?" He kissed her neck, and she tilted her head to the side to encourage his attention.

"You warm me, Jack. Just being near you..." She stopped speaking when he touched her hair still coiled in a bun.

He turned her around and looked down at her with such compassion, it stole her breath. He ran his fingers down her throat with a gentle caress.

"Oh, Jack, how can I..." She sighed.

His lips brushed against her mouth. A curl of heat and need sparked her blood.

Weak-willed was what she was, and she hated herself for it. *Stop this now, before it's too late.* But the situation was already beyond repair. She should have said no to coming up here. She should have told him right off she had to end their relationship now. But she was a coward.

She reached up to touch his hair, but his hat blocked her. He jerked off his Stetson, tossed it to the blanket, and smiled. His mouth looked so seductively kissable. His chocolate eyes—the dark, semi-sweet variety—were clouded with lust, and she was making everything worse.

Still, she couldn't give up the moment and craved knowing what it would feel like to be desired so. She ran her hand through his rich brown waves curling to his collar, some of the strands streaked by the sun, giving them a wistful caramel appearance. His hands held her shoulders, the heat from his palms penetrating her dress, searing her through the fabric. Her silk panties were damp with expectation, and he'd barely kissed her, for heaven's sakes.

All he had to do was look at her, touch her, and she came undone.

How she wished she and Jack were in a hotel room where it was warm and private. But he was too decent for her to propose such a thing again.

He swept his fingers over her cheek and pressed his lips against hers. Like a flame heated a candle, she felt warmed and pliable. She parted her lips slightly, willing him to go further without being too pushy with her own modern way of thinking. With a playful sweep of his tongue, he caressed her mouth.

Caught up in the feel of him, she craved taking their actions further. As if they had a cosmic connection, she couldn't let him go, in this time or her own.

He pushed his advantage. And she allowed it. When she *knew* she should have put the brakes on. She wrapped her arms around his neck, her breasts pressed lovingly against his chest. The contact seemed so natural, as though they belonged together.

His hands rested on her lower back, his fingers dipping dangerously low to the base of her spine. If she'd been a Victorian woman, she would move discretely away from him, wouldn't she? Her mother had once told her about her great-great grandmother and the man she courted were dressed in heavy clothes and a board placed between them in bed. They were to get to know each other, but not have sex. Though truth be known when she became pregnant, they had to move the wedding date forward. Did they still do bundling in this day and age?

Before she could ask, Jack's tongue delved into her willing mouth, exploring with caution at first. Caught up in the heat, hers danced with his, mating, testing, simulating deeper sexual desire. Encouraged, he kissed her with so much passion, her senses reeled.

He groaned and nuzzled his face against hers. His hand trailed down the hollow of her throat, lower, until his fingers brushed over her breast. He paused to look at her with such longing; she knew where he wanted to go next.

She had to ask. "Do people still bundle?"

For a second, he looked startled. A slow smile spread, and his dimples appeared. "We don't have to wait to get married, honey."

Ohmigod, she hadn't thought about that part of the equation. The couple who bundled had to be betrothed. Even her great grandmother "bundled" with her great grandfather on sleigh rides in Canada. The only way to be alone with her fella while they courted. Lisa guessed it was too cold to do much more than fumble under the heavy quilts and blankets, her great grandparents' breaths frosty in the chilly air.

"You stir feelings inside me I never thought I'd have for another," Jack said, his arms hugging her tightly against his hot, firm body.

She loved the hard and protective feel of him—something she couldn't find with a man of her own time.

The bubbling water drifted endlessly downstream, and she sighed, remembering her childhood when her parents were alive. She'd play for hours in the cold water of a California creek, the soft whisper of pine needles whooshing in the breeze, the sweet aroma of pine in the air. "I could stay here with you, forever, listening to the trickling water." She could have, too. Forever and always—give up the ghosts of her past, her awful job, her nothing life. If it wasn't for the men at the inn and Josephine and the worry she'd never be able to adjust to the harsh realities of this life, she do it in a heartbeat.

Jack rested his cheek against her head. "For you, I'd buy Table Rock itself and build a castle on its top."

"Would you?" She looked up at him and believed he would. Yet her sensible mind nagged at her. *End it now.*

He touched her face with a gentle caress. "Yes, for you, I'd do anything."

"You wouldn't grow tired of me, would you?" After Barry and Dave, the so-called "nice" former high school friend of Pauline's, or the other guys in her life, Lisa didn't trust her feelings about most men.

Jack shook his head slowly. "To have you by my side 'til the end of my days would be a dream come true."

She took a deep breath. "If I could only stay here like this forever."

"I've thought of nothing else all week but of seeing you again."

She glanced down at the rock and all the names carved in its ancient surface. "Have there been many ladies you've courted?"

He chuckled.

She pulled free and sat down on the blanket. Running her fingers over the stone, she considered the names. "Maybe I should look for *your* name."

He sat next to her and took her roving hand in his

and kissed it. "I don't think you'd find it."

She studied the impish smile on his face. "Not here? Not even once?" Kneeling down, she examined it closer.

He pulled her back. "Quit looking."

She laughed and ran her hand over the blue blanket, the zigzags of rich browns and burgundies stretching across its length. "So there is."

"Other Jacks have lived in town over the years. Even my paternal grandfather was named Jack. It's a popular name after all."

"Oh, I see." She smiled.

"Besides, none of that matters. I've only known you for a short time, though I feel I've been with you all my life." He touched her cheek, and she nuzzled her face in his hand and kissed it. "I know this is sudden, but I aim to marry you if you'll say yes."

Hating feeling like a sentimental sap, she fought the tears filling her eyes. She wanted to say yes, knowing it was crazy, but would it be so wrong to stay with him?

"I've never met a man who's touched me the way you have." She squeezed his hand. "You've been so kind without expecting anything in return. I want to stay with you more than anything else in the world, but I'm afraid." She stood, and walked to the edge of the rock again, wishing she could explain the bizarre set of circumstances that drew her to his world. What if a doctor heard her bizarre story and sent her to an insane asylum?

She couldn't risk it.

Drawing near, Jack ran his fingers through the curls that had loosened from her bun, and she shivered.

He took her hands in his. "You're ice cold. Do you want to go back to the inn?"

"No. I want to stay here forever. I don't want to ever go back. Being with you makes me feel alive again."

Jack tilted her head back, and she parted her lips and took a deep breath. "You're so beautiful." He kissed her mouth gently and touched her hair, then pressed his lips firmly. Her heartbeat raced, and he returned her to the blanket.

Forget the betrothal. She was all set for bundling. Without the bundling board.

"Oh, Lisa," he whispered, his eyes smoldering with desire. His frame resting next to her, he circled his finger over her throat and kissed her deeply again.

It was now or never. She wanted his body on top of hers, pushing out the chill of the fall air, but he had other notions in mind. His fingers touched her bodice tentatively and when she didn't stop him, he caressed her breast. The nipple drew taut, the nerve endings so sensitive, it screamed for his touch.

She had to know—did he still have reservations about who she was? "Do...do you still think I might be Josephine?"

He lifted his head and shook it. "I don't know how I know, but you're *not* Josephine."

If she'd had any hope to push him away and end this now, she'd lost any sense of reason. She pulled at him to join her, to lie on top of her and heat her to the core.

"We ought to see the judge, honey, before I get too carried away with my feelings for you."

Oh, hell, the judge, the betrothal. He meant to get

married right away. But too much stood between them.

A stirring of leaves nearby startled them. Jack disengaged himself from Lisa, and they sat up quickly. Bill stormed across the rock, his face as red as his bandana, his blue eyes ice daggers.

"Hey!" he yelled. "What's the big idea anyway? Stealing my girl like that."

Lisa nearly died.

Jack jumped from the blanket and pulled her to her feet. "She's not Josephine. She looks like her, but she's *not* her."

"Jack's right, Bill. I'm not Josephine," she tried to persuade Josephine's old beau, but the guy wasn't convinced.

He swung at Jack who dodged the punch. Instantly, he charged Bill and tackled him to the rock face. "Stay down! I don't want to fight you."

"Please, Bill," Lisa pleaded. "I'm not Josephine." She'd never thought the two might hurt each other to win her favor. No way did she want the altercation to continue, but she didn't know what to do.

Bill wriggled free, jumped to his feet, and threw another punch. Jack grabbed his arm and pulled it behind him, yanking it up.

Bill groaned.

"Give it up, Bill! I don't want to have to break it."

"Oh, no, Jack, you can't!" Lisa clasped her hand to her mouth. If Jack broke Bill's arm, it might not set right, and it could be useless.

"You'd better return to the inn, Lisa," Jack warned, his tone gruff.

She assumed he didn't want to upset her. But he wasn't quitting. And she wasn't leaving. God, how could her great-great grandmother have thought her great-great grandfather, wearing his Teddy Roosevelt Rough Rider's uniform, knocking out her beau at the Worlds Trade Fair in Chicago was gallant? Lisa didn't have the stomach for it.

Jack shoved Bill to the ground. "Stay down! You know I'll always whip you whenever you have the urge to fight me."

Bill pushed himself away from the rock and charged at Jack, throwing him toward the edge of the stone.

"Bill, no!" Lisa screamed.

She grabbed Bill's arm, but he tossed her aside. She fell, skinning her hands against the rough surface and tumbled toward the cliff's edge. Her heart in her throat, she went over the ledge and grappled for a branch. She grabbed a limb overhanging the cliff and screamed. Her fingers slipped. Scrambling to get a toehold before her arms gave out, she couldn't find any purchase and dangled precariously from the dizzying height.

"My God, Lisa!" Jack shouted and rushed to her with Bill close on his heels.

"Josephine!" Bill reached for her while she hung on with a fierce grip to a leafless shrub, the torn up skin of her fingers burning.

Jack and Bill pulled her onto the solid rock surface. Jack turned to glare at Bill. "You almost killed her, you idiot."

Bill knelt beside Lisa. Her whole body shook.

"I'm so sorry, Josephine. Will you forgive me?"

"I think you've done enough harm, today. Why don't you make yourself scarce, Bill?" Jack said.

"Josephine?" Bill offered his hand.

Lisa looked away from him and at the branch that saved her life. She wanted to stay with Jack, but this business with Bill was likely to get deadly. Could she ever convince him she wasn't his deceased—*no*, not just deceased—but murdered girlfriend? She could never live with herself if either Bill or Jack died fighting over her.

"I'm not Josephine," she said, her voice on edge.

Bill kicked the rock. "I'm not done with you, Jack. You can't have my girl." He leaned over and kissed the top of Lisa's head. "I'll see you later. I'm so sorry, honey."

Bill retreated down the hill, kicking rocks all the way, while Jack helped Lisa up. He held her in his arms but she couldn't quit trembling. "Lisa honey, I've got to get you to the inn and get you warmed up. Are you going to be all right?"

No. she didn't think she would ever be all right again.

***

Jack escorted Lisa to the lobby of the inn, her body chilled through and through. She'd planned to tell him she had to leave him, despite that she really cared for him, until a chambermaid bustled by, sweeping a feathered duster at a table. Lisa's skin chilled with dread recognition—the maid, black-haired, black eyed, skin as white as ice, the one who'd been in the room with the two men when Josephine had died.

The woman's eyes focused on the amethyst amulet Lisa was wearing. The maid let out an ear-piercing scream, shattering the quietness of the lobby. Grabbing her throat, she collapsed in a dead faint. The night clerk

TERRY SPEAR

ran to the woman's side before Jack could assist, and
Lisa shivered uncontrollably.

When she swayed unsteadily, Jack grabbed her
arm. "What's wrong? You look ill." He helped her to
the nearest sofa.

"She's...she's the one. She was in on the killing."
Lisa clutched the necklace. Her eyes searched Jack's
for understanding, but she knew he wouldn't be able to
accept the trouble she could be in, or that she wasn't
truly from here.

She couldn't stay no matter how much she cared
for Jack. "I have to go home. I can't be here. I'm—I'm
afraid," she said, hating to admit it.

"You want to return to Waco? But you just got
here." The look on his face was of utter disbelief.
"Besides, there are no more stages out tonight."

She tried to stand, but grew dizzy and collapsed on
the sofa.

Her hand in his, he said, "I'll get the management
to give you a room. I'd take you home with me, but you
couldn't ride in the condition you're in."

"It has to be room number three."

His expression concerned, Jack hovered over her
while the staff carried the maid from the lobby. When
Mr. Daemon returned to the reception desk, Jack patted
her hand. "I'll talk to the manager." He headed for the
check-in counter.

"They'll want to kill me, Jack," she said under her
breath. "And you'll never know what became of me."

When Jack reached the check-in counter, he set his
hat down, then pulled out his wallet. "I need a room for
the night, sir."

"For you, sir, we have room six," Mr. Daemon

said.

"Could I possibly have room number three?"

Mr. Daemon's eyes widened, and he glanced at Lisa. "No, that room is...has been booked for several weeks. I don't know when it will be available again."

Jack looked up at the rack of keys. "Room number six will be fine."

Rejoining Lisa, Jack offered his hand. "Let me get you settled into your room."

"Number three?" she asked, though she thought she'd heard the man say he would give Jack another. She hoped she'd heard wrong.

Jack crouched in front of her. "I'm afraid not. But at least you have a room. I'll pick you up tomorrow and bring you home. Salado is having a picnic. If you're well enough, I'd love to take you."

Hadn't she told him she needed to return home? She had to get the key to room number three. She glanced at the floor where the maid had collapsed.

"She's gone. What did you mean by she was in on the killing, by the way?"

"I had a dream. She was the one—"

"A dream? If that's all there is to it. I don't put stock in dreams. You probably saw her tidying your room, and in your dream she appeared sinister. Maybe she didn't clean your room satisfactorily?"

Frowning, Lisa knew Jack wouldn't believe her.

"I'm sorry. I'm trying to make you feel better, but I guess it's not working. Let me escort you to your room."

She took his arm, and he helped her to her feet. Mr. Daemon had vanished while the clerk warily watched them. "They said there were no more rooms."

"Well, they came up with one. It is rather odd. The keys for room number three were hanging on their hook. More may be going on than meets the eye."

"Yes, murder. Josephine's murder."

"You're tired and Bill's confounded actions have, well, upset you." He dismissed her concern, and she knew then he'd never believe her about any of it.

She was out of her element. Always, reasonable paths were available, but not this time. She clenched her teeth, angered she had no control over her fate.

They walked in silence for several minutes, then Jack said, "I can't tell you how much I enjoy being with you. I didn't think I'd ever feel this way again."

When they stood before the door of room number six, Lisa asked, "What was she like, Jack? The lady you loved that you miss so terribly."

At first, he didn't say, then he took a deep breath. "Charlotte was a lot like you. Just as petite, blonde, and spunky. She was sweet, too. She wouldn't have hurt a living soul. A month before the scheduled wedding she collapsed with cholera. The epidemic swept through the village and killed several, including my sweet Charlotte. I felt I should have died with her."

Lisa would hurt him, too, and leave him behind just like Charlotte had done. Her heart ached for him because she was betraying him, like when her parents promised to return home and never came back.

"I'm so sorry, Jack."

He pulled her close, her heart beating rapidly against his. He ran his hand over her hair. "Please don't leave me, again."

She nestled her head against his shoulder and sighed. *Why can't you be in my world, Jack?* If she could, she'd take him with her in a heartbeat. "Thank you for everything."

He studied her for a minute, then kissed her cheek. "Get a good night's sleep. In the morning, I'll come by to check on you first thing."

Her heart in her throat, she quashed the tears trying to form. "I really care for you. I just come from a different world, yet I wish with all my soul I could take you with me."

His expression brightened. "That's certainly good to hear." He kissed her hand and brushed her cheek with his fingers. "Oh, Lisa." He pressed his lips against hers and her heart beat erratically. She tilted her head back, encouraging his kiss, desiring so much more. "You mustn't leave again," he whispered.

"Jack," she said with shortness of breath, wanting him to show her how much he loved her, but she knew she'd be getting in deeper when nothing could come of their relationship, "your pistol is jabbing me."

He touched his colt holstered at his hip, shook his head, and smiled. "My feelings for you have grown out-of-bounds. As much as I don't want to leave, I must or I'll get us both into trouble. Until tomorrow." He kissed her hand again.

Secretly, she wanted him to get them both into trouble. But if Jack got the wrong impression about her, she'd ruin things with him. Despite the desire to feel his warm body tackling hers further, she had to call it a night. Then she had to leave here for good.

This time she'd write Jack a note, for all the good that would do. How could she explain how they couldn't be meant for each other? She watched him walk down the hallway, her thoughts in turmoil. She wasn't even sure she could steal the key to Josephine's room. Later tonight, maybe, when everyone was asleep.

When Jack disappeared from view, she felt adrift, her anchor in this world gone, and her heart sank with the notion. Without him, she didn't belong in this time, in this place. She truly didn't belong here.

She opened the door to her room and stared into the darkness. A sense of dread filled her. *Get a grip,* she told herself. *The boogieman doesn't exist. I watch too many horror flicks.*

She listened for any sound of movement in the room, then a man opened his door down the hall. Lisa took a deep breath and walked inside. No soft candlelight glowed here like at the spiritualist's home, no sweet instrumental music, no melon scent to chase away the empty void, only blackness.

Chastising herself for not asking Jack to light the lamp, she reached for the glass sphere, but her fingertips touched a man's woolen vest instead.

Her mouth dropped open, and she took in a breath to scream.

CHAPTER 13

When Jack returned to his ranch, his brother met him at the stable, and Matthew's brow arched in good humor. At the moment, Jack didn't need his ribbing. "I want you to come with me to town later and sign a bonding agreement, and I'll pick up a marriage license."

Matthew's eyes rounded. "Hell, you're getting married? To Josephine? Bill's likely to pop you one. You know he socked Jacob over her."

"She's not Josephine, and I'm not worried about Bill." Jack removed his horse's saddle.

"Are you really going to marry the lady?"

"She's agreed. Anyway, I want to get it in writing that I'm not married, underage, or too close a familial relationship to Lisa."

Matthew shook his head. "I'll sign for you. I hope you know what you're getting into. So where is the blushing bride-to-be?"

"Staying at the Shady Villa Inn. Something's odd

211

there though."

"Why, because it's changing hands?"

"No, they told Lisa there were no rooms available, but several keys were hanging on the board."

"Maybe folks were coming in later this evening."

"Maybe."

"Have you heard about the haunted room?"

"What?"

"Rumors abound that two couples and a visiting bank president left one of the rooms in the middle of the night when strange moans and groans and a woman crying disturbed their sleep. One of the women claimed she saw a ghostly aberration floating above the bed."

Jack stared at his brother. "Sounds like a lot of foolishness to me."

"Yeah, well, it's all true. We better get inside. Esmeralda cooked us one of her famous Mexican dishes, only if we let it get cold, she'll make us wear it."

Entering the house, Jack couldn't get his thoughts off Lisa, the way she'd kissed him and melted to his touch. She didn't seem able to resist him any more than he could her. And all her talk about bundling... He smiled. He had no intention of bundling with her in some drawn-out courtship process. As long as she was agreeable, he was marrying her.

"What do you see in Josephine that you didn't before?" Matthew asked, ditching his hat on the rack as they walked into the dining room. "You told me she was fickle and had too many suitors to please you."

The aroma of spicy Mexican beans and tamales filled the air, making Jack's stomach grumble in anticipation. "She's *not* Josephine."

Matthew took a seat at the long wooden table and made a face. "So who *is* this woman who looks like Josephine, but isn't?"

Esmeralda placed the porcelain dishes on the table. "She's a good soul," she interjected. "She'll put the restless spirit to peace, if she lives long enough."

Jack shook his head. "Now you've got her started again. We ought to call you Madame Esparazo, the fortuneteller."

"You joke, but I tell you, there's wrong-doings at the inn, even tonight. I feel it in my bones. That young lady you have longings for is in grave trouble."

The ranch hands all hurried into the house, their boots stomping on the wooden floor like a herd of horses. They ditched their hats, then they hurried to pull out their chairs. Twenty-year old Hank Anderson, looking a little ragged, his long blond hair needing a cut, his blue eyes smiling, as he tossed a napkin on his lap. "Sorry we're late, ma'am, boss. We heard Bill's in a furor over Josephine." He raised his brows and waited for Jack's response.

He didn't offer one.

The oldest hand at thirty, his black hair streaked with a smattering of gray, Tommy Thompson chuckled. "Hear the boss is getting purdy serious about the young woman. When's the weddin'?"

"I heard the lady's not sure who she is. Is it true, boss?" Andy McNeil asked, the youngest at fifteen, been riding since he was five, bright, hard working. Jack figured if he saved up enough of his money, he'd have a ranch of his own someday.

"When do we get to meet her?" Reb asked. He was Hank's older brother, and he'd been asking the question ever since he'd first heard Jack had been seeing her.

Rory Campbell leaned back in his chair, a tortilla in his hand. "Need another woman around the place to cheer us up after a hard day working the ranch. So when you tying the knot?"

Jack tried to couch appearing downright annoyed. "Does everyone know about this?"

"It's a small town," Matthew said. "What do you expect? Remember when I stole a kiss from Mary Lou down at the creek, and she pushed me in? The whole town knew about it by suppertime. At school the next day, I couldn't live it down."

"I would have liked to have seen that," Andy said.

Jack snorted. "That wasn't so bad until she did it again ten years later."

"Ah, heck, Jack, I told you my foot slipped."

Everyone laughed.

"Did you break those feral mustangs?" Jack asked Reb, wanting to get the conversation off his personal life. Reb and Hank had saddle broke horses during the War and were the best he'd ever seen at the job.

"Two of 'em, boss," Reb said, winking at his brother.

Hank smiled and rubbed his own back, mock pain showing on his face. "The last one is a might cantankerous, and I've got the bruises to prove it. Easy does it, and he'll be eating out of our hands."

"Yeah, but will anyone be able to ride him?" Andy asked, dishing up another mess of beans. The kid could eat twice as much as a grown man, Jack swore.

"By the end of the week," Reb promised.

Esmeralda was quieter than usual, which meant something was brewing in that mind of hers. Probably not good. Everyone noticed, too, as they cast glances in her direction while she filled up another bowl of beans.

She carried two more serving dishes to the table filled with beans and tortillas. "I have to warn you, Jack, something evil has happened in room number three at the inn."

Jack stopped eating and stared at her. "Room three?" He glanced at Matthew. "Don't tell me, that's the one that's supposed to be haunted."

"Yes, Jack, something that involved Josephine. I've had premonitions about it all morning." Esmeralda started to take her seat, but Andy jumped from his to pull her chair out for her.

If Lisa hadn't already warned Jack that Josephine had been murdered, he wouldn't have believed Esmeralda, figuring it was one of her crazy notions. He couldn't settle the worry something could be wrong. He set his napkin on the table. "What about Josephine?"

Esmeralda wiped flour off her cheek and shook her head. "I don't know exactly. Only that she's no longer among the living, and Lisa is in terrible trouble."

"I left her at her room and everything was fine."

"Something's happened, I know it," Esmeralda insisted.

"Did she stay in the haunted room?" Matthew asked.

"No, she wanted to stay in room three, though, didn't she, Jack?" Esmeralda asked. "Josephine is connected to her in some way. Maybe she's a distant relation—I don't know. She's reaching out to Lisa to help her find rest. Whoever has caused Josephine harm is still at large. They mean to do Lisa the same kind of injury, I fear, because she's bound to stir up questions.

Since she looks so much like Josephine, they think she might even *be* her."

Jack frowned at Esmeralda. "Lisa was afraid of the chambermaid, and she wanted to go home. She said she had to be in room number three. I don't understand."

Esmeralda placed her hand on Jack's arm. "She needs to leave there, if it's not already too late."

***

Lisa lay on a rock floor, the smell of the damp, chilly earth lingering in the air. A spring bubbled nearby in the darkness, and she sat up. Her head clouded over again, and she held her temple until her thoughts cleared. A bump on the side of her head throbbed with gusto. Then she recalled being hit right after she touched the man's vest while he stood in the darkened room.

"Where am I?" She touched her neck...the amulet had vanished. A twinge of fear snaked up her spine. "Oh, no," she groaned, then groped around the floor, searching for the gold chain. Instead, her fingers ran across a long, thin, smooth object. She examined her find and gasped, then dropped it with a clatter to the floor. "Bones," she whispered, bile rising into her throat at once.

Whose bones?

She stood up, fearing her bones would be resting with the others if she didn't get away now. Swaying unsteadily on her feet, so dizzy, she felt she'd collapse.

"Oh, my head." She put her hand to her forehead to still the pounding sensation. The amulet was gone. Even if she was able to find her way to Josephine's room now that she wasn't wearing the necklace, she might be able to go back to the present, but she'd never be able to return to Jack's world again. What about Jack? Josephine's restless spirit? The murderers who got away with the deed?

She shivered, the cold clinging to her like wet sheets on a windy, winter's day. In her heart, she knew she had to leave, but she wanted the option of returning to Jack. Then again, if he attempted to protect her, would the ones who wanted her dead, kill him, too? She hadn't considered that. Her emotions grew more jumbled, and all hope seemed lost.

In the gloom, the flicker of a light illuminated the cave in a wash of warmth. A drop of groundwater trickled down her cheek, and a streak of panic shot through her. She looked up. Bats hugged stalactites poking down from the ceiling. She turned her attention to the light again.

With hands outstretched, she felt her way through the cave toward the illumination and hit her shin on a rock rising from the floor. "Ow," she moaned and rubbed her leg. *Bruised for sure.* She crept and stumbled over the rough, rocky floor. The light disappeared and blackness enveloped her. "No, come back," she said under her breath. "Please, come back."

Her boot brushed against an object and it crinkled. Reaching down, she touched the package and frowned. The light appeared farther away, and she saw wrapped meat stacked neatly against the wall of the limestone cave, preserving it in the naturally cool place. She headed for the light again. It vanished at the cave entrance. *Josephine?*

Shadows of tree branches stretched across the acreage in the moonlight near the Shady Villa Inn. She wasn't in the wilderness as she'd feared.

When men's voices reached her, Lisa bolted for the forest, her nerves raw. She crouched low behind a juniper and stayed still, afraid to move an inch and alert them while she watched the men's ghostly silhouettes in the misty lantern light. Her skin chilled even more, and she shuddered.

"I don't know. I swear we killed her the first time."

"God, almighty, you didn't have to do a thing to her. She was nearly dead already."

"You know as well as I how that would have looked to the new owners, having a guest with yellow fever staying in one of our rooms. We had to burn the mattress and the bed linens as it was. Besides, her aunt stopped coming to care for her. What was I supposed to do? We would've lost the sale," Mr. Daemon said.

"Now the place is haunted, and the new owners have backed out of the deal anyway," the owner growled.

Mr. Daemon shook his head. "What was that silly maid ranting about?"

"She said Josephine had taken the amethyst necklace from her from out of the grave." Mr. Worthington tipped his hat back and wiped his brow.

"What amethyst?"

"Josephine was wearing the necklace the night she died. The chambermaid lifted it. When the woman calling herself Lisa Welsh arrived, she was wearing the necklace, sending the maid into hysterics."

Mr. Daemon shook his head. "I told that stupid woman not to touch anything of Josephine Rogers'. If anyone saw Lillian with it, they'd suspect foul play. How did this other woman get ahold of it?"

"Lillian didn't know. She said she'd misplaced the

amulet and fainted when she saw the woman wearing it."

Stumbling over a rock, Mr. Daemon cursed out loud. "Who *is* this woman anyway? Surely it can't be Josephine, though she looks a hell of a lot like her."

"The maid says she's Josephine reincarnated come back from the dead to get us for what we did."

"Nonsense. Besides, I didn't do anything," Mr. Daemon said.

"You were there when the deed was done and helped us hide the body. As soon as we can find the time, we've got to get rid of it."

"I told you nothing good would come of this," Mr. Daemon warned.

"Come on. Let's get rid of the other one, whoever she is, before she comes to."

Mr. Daemon shook his head and entered the cave.

When the owner and manager disappeared from sight, Lisa slipped deeper into the forest. She had no idea what to do now. She hadn't a clue where Jack lived. Getting as far away from the inn was her only chance for survival.

***

Jack arrived at the Shady Villa Inn at a gallop, sending a cloud of dust flying. The place was deadly quiet, but even he felt a sense of malice, when he wouldn't normally admit to anything of the kind. He figured it had to do with Esmeralda's message of doom.

He rushed to Lisa's room, but it was empty. His heart pounding, he observed the shattered lamp and overturned desk chair. Someone must have taken Lisa by force.

He dashed to the lobby and finding the reception

desk unmanned, he skirted the counter. Grabbing the room number three key, he strode there. After unlocking the door, he pushed it open slowly and walked inside. His eyes adjusted to the darkened room, but nothing was amiss, and he hadn't a clue where to look for her next. Just as he began to shut the door behind him, footsteps approached. He slipped back inside and closed the door. With his ear against it, he heard two men conversing.

"I told you we should have done the job when we first dumped her in the cave and not waited until it was too late. You have no backbone."

"I'm not a killer like you."

"You wanted to save your investment as much as I did. Get another lantern, and we'll search for her. We'll have some time finding her now."

The two men shuffled off.

His temple pounding with anger, Jack couldn't believe what he was hearing. He was certain they, whoever they were, were talking about Lisa.

He exited the room and locked the door. Repocketing the key, he made a dash out the side door of the inn. After sprinting to the cave closest to the hotel, he circled around it first. Then he headed into the woods, searching for any sign of Lisa. Whispering loudly, he called, "Lisa, it's me, Jack. Lisa."

He wished he'd brought his brother and men with him, every one of them willing. But he hadn't believed Lisa was in real danger, and his ranch hands could ill afford going without a decent supper after working hard all day and having another early day of it tomorrow. Now he wished he'd allowed them to come.

Dry leaves stirred in the breeze and a coyote

howled in the distance. Lantern lights flickered on a path approaching him, and he moved deeper into the shadows of the forest. "Lisa," he continued to call in a hushed voice.

All night he searched for her, as did the two men. He wouldn't give up until he found her, but his fear of losing her unsettled him. If she lost her way in the woods, no telling what would become of her. Wild animals and lawless bands of men roamed the wilderness. He attempted to clear the notion from his mind.

At first light, the two men returned to the hotel empty-handed. "Maybe a cougar got her," the one man said.

The other responded, "We can always hope."

He wished he could see who the men were, but he couldn't let them know he was onto them, and finding Lisa unharmed remained tantamount. Jack headed back to where he'd tied his horse and found the maid near the hotel, fingering the amethyst necklace around her throat. She smiled and entered the inn. Jack's face heated, and he fought the urge to wring the woman's neck. Hell, she was in on the killing of Josephine like Lisa had said? And now apparently Lisa's abduction also.

A twig snapped behind him and caught his attention. When he whirled around, a fist connected with his eye. Pain streaked through his eye, and he took a step backward with the impact.

Bill swung at Jack again, hitting him squarely in the jaw. "You leave my Josephine, alone!" Bill hollered. "I'll whip any man who messes with her."

Relieved it was Bill and not the killers, Jack almost

smiled, making Bill hesitate. "I thought you were somebody else."

"You mean someone else is mad at you? What...over Josephine?"

Jack's face heated. "No, you've got to help me find Lisa."

"Not on your life." Bill folded his arms across his chest.

"Listen. Two men were talking about killing Josephine at the inn."

Bill's eyes narrowed. "You're making that up to save your scrawny hide."

"Damn it, listen to me. Josephine was sick with yellow fever, right?"

Scowling, Bill nodded.

"She disappeared without a trace, and rumors she died started to circulate."

"So then she came back calling herself Lisa," Bill said.

"Except Josephine *did* die, and Lisa is really someone else. Someone who looks a lot like Josephine but isn't her—a distant relation." He had to make Bill understand, Lisa couldn't be Bill's. *Ever*. Jack needed his assistance in finding her immediately.

"Can't prove that by me."

"It doesn't matter. Tonight, they intended to kill Lisa or Josephine, or whoever you want to call her."

"Who tried to kill her?"

"I don't know. I couldn't see them clearly. They left her in the cave, but she managed to escape. They hunted for her, but couldn't find her in the dark. I searched all night long, but couldn't locate her either. Where could she have gone that would be familiar to both Josephine and Lisa? Somewhere she'd feel safe..."

Bill's face lit up and at the same time Jack had the same notion. "Table Rock," they both said.

They ran all the way to the spot, but when they climbed the hill to reach the monolithic stone, they didn't find a soul, only the dappled sunlight shimmering off the rock face. Jack glanced at the creek bed where a diminutive figure wearing a blue gown sipped water, stirring his heart. He turned to see Bill studying him.

Jack moved away from the rock's edge. "I'm heading home to gather my men to help us look for her."

"I'll take a gander south of the cave. Sorry about the eye...and the jaw."

Jack rubbed his sore jaw. "Let me know if you find her."

"Will do," Bill said, though Jack knew he wouldn't if he located her.

Bill climbed down the hill, then ran off in the direction of the forest. As soon as he disappeared, Jack dashed down the slope. He hit the ground running and bolted for her. "Lisa!"

When he reached her, he swept her up in his arms and crushed her against his body. He'd never let her go again.

"Oh, Jack," she said, breathlessly. "I didn't think I'd ever see you again."

He smothered her lips, her cheeks, and her throat with kisses. She reached for her forehead, her brows pinching into a frown. He smoothed back the straggles of her hair curled along her face. "Are you all right, Lisa?"

For a moment, she appeared dizzy and leaned against him for support. Her gaze shifted from his chest. She stared at him, her look puzzled. She tilted her head to the side, her mouth dropping. "Lisa?"

She shoved him away. "What's the matter with you, Jack? I'm Josephine...you know that."

CHAPTER 14

Not only did Josephine have one cursed headache, but her stomach wouldn't stop swirling. Riding with Jack on his horse didn't help. Every bounce was taking its toll.

She didn't know what was the matter with her. Unless she was still afflicted with yellow fever, although she seemed better, and she wasn't feverish. Jack had insisted on taking her to his ranch for a good meal and rest. She figured she might as well take him up on the offer, the way her head was swimming.

She didn't know what was wrong with him either. *Lisa?* Who in the world was he talking about? He wore the most hangdog expression, and she assumed someone he had cared for died. At least the last time he looked this sorrowful, Charlotte had passed away. Of course, the black eye and bruise on his jaw didn't help his appearance. She'd never seen him brawling with guys, so she wondered what that was all about.

"Have you seen Bill?" she asked casually. She was

dying to see him and wondered if he'd gotten back from the cattle drive yet.

Jack didn't reply. Several strands that had come loose from her chignon swept across her face in the chilly breeze, and she really needed to fix it. She must have looked a sight. Reaching up to touch her hair, she found it coiled in a strange manner. Her fingertips grazed something thin and hard, and she pulled it out. Examining the item, she wondered where it had come from. She'd never seen a hairpin so diminutive and unadorned. She poked around her hair and felt several more of the skinny little pins, but left them in. "Do you know where my bonnet is?"

"At..." Jack cleared his throat. "No."

"What about my hair pins? I don't remember putting my hair up this morning, but even so, I would have used my mother of pearl pins."

Again, he said nothing. What did she expect? He wouldn't know anything about her hair. She touched her gown, soft blue like the sky, but the hem was dirty as if she'd climbed the hill to Table Rock. She hadn't been there in a month of Sundays. Not since she'd been sick, and Bill had been away on a drive.

She stared at the dress. She'd never seen it before in her life. For an instant, a chilling disconnectedness swamped her. Then the strange sensation passed. She glanced down at her boots. Black? Not brown? And...and the top edge seemed to reach just below the knee. She lifted her skirt a tad. No buttons on the shoes? How...where...? She lifted her skirt higher. She should have been able to see her drawers. Which meant she wasn't wearing any? She quickly dropped her skirt.

Jack shifted in the saddle and tightened his hold on

her. She wasn't going to fall. She'd been riding horses since she could walk.

Another stab of pain centered at the side of her temple. She reached up to inspect it, but noticed her palms were skinned. What...? She gingerly touched her scalp and found a lump the size of an egg. "What in the world happened to me?" she finally voiced aloud.

Either Jack didn't know, or he wasn't saying.

Then again, she never talked to him much. And he hadn't anything to say to her. Not when Bill was around. She'd danced a time or two with Jack. He'd be a decent marriage prospect for most any woman, she figured, but he wasn't her type. Too sophisticated, too serious for her liking.

She took a deep breath, enjoying the smell of the clean air, glad to get away from the stuffy inn. Wood smoke drifted on the breeze, and she smiled. Hearth and home. She couldn't wait to see Aunt Polly and tell her she was fine. When had she seen her last?

She took another large breath and realized she wasn't wearing the restrictive corset. But something was holding her up. Trying to be inconspicuous, she touched under her breasts. A hard, rigid wire cupped each. What in the world?

"Jack...?" She dismissed the question before she even proposed it. He wouldn't know why she was at the creek any more than he'd know about her clothes or anything else.

Her hair kept tickling her face, and it was driving her crazy. And so was Jack's silence. For some reason, the fact he wouldn't talk to her bothered her. Though she wasn't sure why. Maybe because she'd been cooped up in the room at the inn for so long. While

Aunt Polly had come to see her, in between the times Josephine slept, she'd been fine. But then...

Josephine examined her skinned up palms. She'd been feeling better, but she'd had no one to talk to for some time. Just a dark room, not even a lighted lantern to chase away the gloom. Sometimes footfalls echoed in the hallway outside her door. After a while, not even Aunt Polly had come to see her.

Jack turned off the main road onto a side trail. Here, the trees closed in, and she smelled smoke again. She tucked a loose curl behind her ear and caught a whiff of something else. She smelled her wrist. Something sweet, like an exotic flower she'd never encountered before.

"We're almost there." Jack sounded defeated as if he'd fought a major battle and lost.

His parents had hosted a dance in their barn five years ago when she was thirteen, and for the first time ever, she got to dance with the older boys. The gaiety, the music, the fun she'd had...and then her mother died a month later, exactly a year after her Aunt Matilda and her baby had died. Her world had shattered once again. Thank heavens for Aunt Polly though. She was so much like her mother in temperament, just as caring and easy-going.

Josephine reached up to touch her necklace as Jack cantered up to the house. Not feeling the amulet about her neck, her heart raced. "Jack! Where's my necklace?" she shrieked.

***

With a gnawing grief tugging at him, Jack held onto Lisa as she tried to jump off his horse. He had no idea what to do with her now and hoped Esmeralda had a clue.

Matthew stepped onto the wraparound porch and smiled. "What in the world happened to you, Jack?"

"Bill—"

"Bill?" Lisa quit struggling with Jack and touched his face. "He did that to you? For what? Talking to me?" She smiled and the look was purely mischievous, nothing like the way Lisa would have acted.

He frowned at her.

She clutched at her throat again where the necklace had been, then turned to his brother. "Well, hello, Matthew."

He helped her down and Jack dismounted.

"You know my brother?" Jack asked, disappointment threading his words. She was Josephine, sure enough.

"Why not? You sure are acting strange. Why do you keep calling me Lisa?"

Matthew gave Jack an all-knowing look.

Jack grimaced. He could sock his brother. He couldn't believe he'd rescued Lisa only to discover she thought she was Josephine. Sickened by the notion, there wasn't any way he was interested in Josephine. For all he cared, Bill could have her. He couldn't understand how she could be one woman one minute, then a totally different one the next.

Matthew escorted Lisa into the parlor while Esmeralda joined Jack on the porch. "She thinks she's Josephine now. What in the world is going on?"

"I didn't think this could happen. She needs to return to room number three at the inn."

"I have the key, but I don't understand."

"I can't explain it, but something else seems to be

missing." Esmeralda sighed. "Lisa's not wearing the necklace."

"No, one of the chambermaids at the inn had it this morning."

"You must get it for Lisa. But be careful."

Before he could say a word, Lisa joined Jack and Esmeralda at the front door, her arm interlocked with his brother's. It didn't matter that the woman thought she was Josephine now. His blood turned green when he saw her holding onto Matthew in an intimate pose.

His brother offered a silly smirk.

"Matthew told me about the picnic. Are we really going?" Lisa asked, her expression bubbly.

When Jack looked at the new woman standing before him, or rather the old Josephine, his heart turned to stone. "I've got to take care of business." He took her hand and pressed it gently. "Stay here with Esmeralda and my brother."

"Sure, Jack, whatever you say." She turned to Matthew. "Why don't you show me your spread, cowboy, while Jack takes care of business? You two sure look alike, but Jack's way too serious."

Lisa and Matthew strolled out into the gardens. "I must have left my necklace at the inn. You could take me by there later, and I'll pick it up."

Jack couldn't believe how much Lisa appeared to be Josephine, the mannerisms, the way she walked, her speech. Even that she knew his brother when Lisa had never met him. He frowned at Esmeralda. "I want to know what's going on. You seem to recognize Lisa's not Josephine, despite appearances."

"I told you, Jack. They must be distantly related, and that's why she looks so much like her.

But…Josephine's dead. I sense it."

"Murdered?"

"I believe so."

He took a settling breath. "If Lisa isn't Josephine, why does she seem to think she is? How can she be one woman and act like another in the blink of an eye?"

Esmeralda assured him, "You wouldn't believe me if I told you."

"Try me."

"I believe Josephine's possessed her so that she can live again."

"You're right. I don't believe you."

Esmeralda sighed. "Get the necklace and send Lisa home. You're doing the right thing."

Was he? Sending her away didn't seem right either. He swung his leg over the saddle. "Watch them. Don't let her get away."

Her face solemn, Esmeralda nodded.

Jack spurred his horse toward town, his stomach agitated, his thoughts in turmoil. He didn't trust in ghosts or possessions or most of what Esmeralda believed in. Yet a niggling in the back of his mind made him rethink his viewpoint when he considered how easily it would explain Lisa's behavior. Then another concern took hold. Why would Lisa have Josephine's necklace? If she was related, maybe she did know something about Josephine's death.

He let out his breath in exasperation.

Before long, he reached the inn and waited in the shadows of an evergreen oak while he watched the comings and goings of the stagecoach passengers.

After several minutes, the maid exited the building. He dismounted, then approached the woman, his hands fisted, trying to control his anger. "Excuse me, Miss," he said, tipping his hat to her.

Wearing a pale yellow dress, she appeared faded, unnoticeable. Except for her eyes. Black coals of sin. Fathomless. Soulless. Black hair to match bound in a net. She beamed and reached up to twist the necklace, the purple gemstone sparkling in the soft morning light.

He fought the urge to wrench the necklace from the woman's scrawny neck. "I know you, don't I?"

The woman shook her head. "Don't know if I know you. Just started working here a few weeks back. They keep me busy cleaning the inn."

"You're related to Mr. Worthington, aren't you?"

The woman laughed. "No. What would a relative of his be doing working as a maid here?"

He attempted a smile. "You're the prettiest one I've ever seen." When she blushed, he assumed his tale passed, but as hard as it was for him to say the words, he figured she wouldn't fall for it. "Would you be going to the picnic down by the creek this afternoon?"

"Are you asking me to go with you?" She fluttered her eyelashes.

He tried to cool his heated blood. "Certainly. That's a beautiful amulet you're wearing. May I see it?"

The woman showed the necklace to him, but wouldn't remove it. He reached down to take ahold of it. The gold chain was long enough if he could just pull it over her—

A man shouted from the hotel, "Stop flirting with the guests and get back to work, Lillian Piggerston, or you'll be finding yourself another job!"

"Oh." The maid curtsied. "Pick me up at noon. I'll be free then."

Gnashing his teeth, Jack released the necklace. "'Til then." He remounted his horse and headed home. To think the woman stole Lisa's necklace and had been in on the murder of Josephine. Hell, he was already believing Lisa's story. So how did she come by the necklace?

"I can't believe I had it in my grasp," he muttered under his breath.

When he reached home, Esmeralda stood on the porch, wringing her hands. "You didn't get it, did you?"

"No, but I asked the maid who has it to accompany me to the picnic. Where's Lisa?"

"She's sleeping. She was so worn out from her experience last night I fed her breakfast and put her in the guest room."

He envisioned she would look as sweet and innocent as the night he watched over her at the Waco hotel. "Good, keep her here while I go to the picnic this afternoon, and I'll retrieve the necklace as soon as possible."

"I think that's wise. She doesn't seem to remember her real life any more. I think she's really become Josephine."

Hating that he was in the dark about Lisa, Jack grunted his disapproval. "Tell me what's going on."

Esmeralda gave him a disapproving look. "Will you keep an open mind?"

"As open as I can."

"Lisa isn't from here, not from this time that we know. She has a connection to Josephine, and I sense it's familial. Someone's murdered Josephine, and she's reached Lisa through both the room where she died and the necklace that her momma gave her. Josephine wants to find solace, but her restless spirit doesn't want to leave. If she can use Lisa as her vessel to continue to live her life as before, she's going to."

Jack couldn't believe all that Esmeralda said—that Josephine was taking Lisa's body for her own? That Lisa wasn't even from this time? Yet he couldn't explain any better what was happening to her.

"Jack?" Esmeralda asked, touching his arm. "Do you understand what I'm saying?"

He combed his fingers through his hair. "I don't know." If she was Josephine, and men wanted her dead, he had to send her away, even if it meant losing her forever. Though the notion made his heart shrivel, but what was the matter with him anyway? He hadn't any choice.

Matthew sauntered into the room. "Josephine's as fickle as ever. Did you take care of business?"

"Things didn't work out. I'll take care of it at the picnic this afternoon."

"Why don't we all go? Esmeralda said she'd bring some cold, boiled ham and tea. She even made some fried potatoes and a cake. She's got the tin plates and cups packed already. I thought I'd wander over to Mary Lou's place and see if she wanted to go with me."

"No. You need to keep Lisa...Josephine here for her own protection."

Matthew snorted. "You mean for your protection, not hers. If Bill saw you with her again—"

"I'm serious. She needs to stay here. You watch over her." As soon as he returned Lisa to the room at the inn, he was checking into Josephine's disappearance. If she'd been murdered, where had they disposed of her body? And who had done the deed?

That's what he had to discover.

***

That afternoon Jack picked up the maid at the inn after she finished her chores, but the only thought on his mind: how would he get the necklace from her without creating a scene?

The maid strolled next to him toward the field where the gathering would be held while he tried to keep his dark mood in check. "That's an amethyst, isn't it?"

"Yes, don't you love it?"

He stopped and frowned. "Is it your birth stone?"

"What?" She looked at him, her cheerful expression turning ominous.

"The stone associated with your birth month. The Polish were thought to have started the tradition a hundred years ago," Jack said, frowning. "Then again theologians of both the Jewish and Christian faith believe that Moses commanded Aaron to build a breastplate of twelve gems, which signified the months of the year thirty-five hundred years ago." Jack scratched his chin and acted like he was pondering a weighty concern. "Have you had it long?"

"Not very."

"Have you had any trouble?"

Lillian's eyes widened. "What do you mean?"

"Wearing the stone is supposed to bring bad luck if amethyst isn't your birth stone." He hoped she wouldn't know the truth.

"Rubbish." She managed a small smile, but a frown marred her temple.

He straightened his shoulders. "Really. I'm curious—have you had any bad experiences?"

"Well, yes, but...no, I don't believe in such a thing."

Attempting to look worried, he narrowed his eyes. "You have seen some strange occurrences, haven't you?"

"Yes, but—"

"The ghost in room number three, for instance?"

"Oh, well...everyone's...how did you know about that?"

"It's a small town."

The maid started to walk again while Jack stayed beside her. "I have been breaking more things lately, but I'm under a lot of strain."

"Whatever for?"

"It wouldn't interest you."

Jack looked at the gathering crowd, families setting colorful quilts down in the field, kids chasing each other, a group of men getting ready to race horses down the main street. God, how he hated this charade. He wanted to rip the necklace from her neck and spirit it straight back to Lisa. "Everything about you interests me."

"Really?"

He tried to offer his most charming smile. "But of course."

"The necklace isn't doing me any harm. Besides, I think it makes my eyes sparkle even more. Don't you think?"

Black and chilling. Jack nodded and turned his head away so she wouldn't see the contemptuous way he was feeling.

They strolled up a grassy knoll, and he saw Lisa standing beside Matthew and Jack. His jaw dropped. He could thrash his brother for bringing her.

"Let's spread our blanket here," Jack said to Lillian. He laid the blanket behind an oak, obscuring his view of Lisa.

The maid sat on the blanket, and he joined her. "Can I see the necklace?" he asked again, hoping she'd give it to him.

"Why certainly." Again the woman offered it to him without removing it from around her neck.

"Hey, Jack," Frank said, approaching them from behind. "I see you took my advice." He winked at Jack who made a face at him.

Lisa's voice caught them by surprise. "Well, Jack, I didn't know you'd be here, too. I thought you said you were taking care of—who's this?" She pointed to Lillian, then her eyes widened. "Why," she said, her voice growing high pitched, "you've got my necklace, you thief!" She yanked the chain from Jack's grasp and jerked it over the maid's head.

Jack jumped from the blanket and wanted to grab Lisa and rush her to the inn.

"Hey, that's *my* necklace!" The maid seized Lisa's hands, but Jack captured the woman's arm.

The women's voices caught Bill's attention, and he interceded. "Let me see it. Here on the back, it's engraved right here to Josie, the nickname your mother went by." Bill gave Josephine a smile. "See, I told you so," Lisa said to the maid. "I ought to turn you into the sheriff, you common pickpocket!"

Lisa pulled the necklace over her head, and Jack nearly had a seizure, assuming if Esmeralda was right, Josephine would turn into Lisa, or vanish, or something.

But nothing happened.

Taking ahold of Lisa's arm, Bill said, "Come on, honey, let's take a stroll. It's gettin' crowded around here."

Jack's disposition soured, and he took a step toward Lisa, but Matthew grabbed his arm. "I told you she was fickle."

Frank laughed. "I guess neither one of us have much of a chance with Josephine when Bill's around."

But Bill couldn't have her. She wasn't Josephine.

"Where are you going?" the maid asked, when Jack started to walk away with Matthew.

He ignored her, but he couldn't tamp down the anger he felt for his brother. "What were you thinking when you brought Lisa here? Didn't I tell you to keep her safe at home?"

Matthew frowned. "You can't be serious. That woman has a mind of her own. Once she found out you were going to the picnic without her, she threw a fit and told me I'd either drive her here or she'd walk all the way. That wouldn't have been safe, so I brought her."

"You should have made her walk," Jack growled.

Matthew raised his brows. "I thought you liked the woman."

"Not this one."

"Surely not that one," he said, pointing to the scowling maid.

"Absolutely not."

"Good. You had me worried, Jack. I thought you were falling for her."

"I was trying to get Josephine's necklace back."

Matthew chuckled. "If Bill hadn't stepped in, I think Josephine would have clobbered that woman. Can you imagine the cheekiness, stealing Josephine's amethyst? She must have lifted it from her room at the inn when she was cleaning it. Are you listening to me, Jack? You seem a million miles away."

His blood sizzling, Jack watched Lisa slip away with Bill toward Table Rock.

CHAPTER 15

Josephine felt as giddy as the first time she'd seen Bill. Bubbling with excitement, she climbed the hill with him up to Table Rock. When they reached the stone, she took a breath of the chilly air. "Oh, Bill, where have you been? I thought you hadn't returned from the cattle drive."

The breeze whipped his blond curls around his face and his bandana fluttered at his throat. Eyes as blue as a cloudless sky watched her with a hint of hesitation. "What do you mean where have I been? I've been here all along. You're the one who keeps disappearing. And what's this business with Jack?"

Trying to settle her uneasiness, Josephine took a deep breath. She couldn't remember what had happened to her over the past few days. Even worse, she felt disconnected, strange. And her clothes—she'd never seen the likes of them. After retiring to the guestroom at Jack's house, she'd lifted her skirt to see the strange undergarments. A red, lace-trimmed, silky scrap of garment that wasn't even crotchless. Where in the world had they come from? How could she use the outhouse when necessary? With her luck, she'd fall in the honey hole.

"I have no earthly idea what's going on with Jack."

"When are you and me going to settle down? I want you for my wife." He placed his hands on her shoulders and held tight, possessively.

Part of her needed him to hold her tight. Part of her balked. Josephine sashayed away. "I'm not ready for any old commitment." Glancing over her shoulder to see Bill's forlorn face, she couldn't help it. Fear kept her from saying yes, yet something in the back of her mind told her she had to marry him now or never.

"I can't wait forever." He walked over to her, pulled her close, and kissed her forehead. "You know how much I love you. Just say yes."

Josephine couldn't, no matter how much her heart was warning her to take the plunge.

"I've got a fair piece saved from the last cattle drive. It's not much, but it'll start us out with a nice little place on the other side of the creek. I already done some checking, if you'll say yes."

"Let me think on it a while longer. Don't be in a rush."

"I can't get you out of my mind. The other guys, well, shucks, I don't want them thinking they got a chance with you. Don't make me wait, darlin'."

She wanted him, loved him, too. She'd known it since the first time she'd seen him at the dance when she was thirteen, then again when he strutted into town after a cattle drive, and he'd caught her eye.

But…her thoughts shifted to Aunt Matilda, her

face drawn, beaded with perspiration, her blond hair matted against her head, her eyes filled with suffering. She'd been like an older sister to Josephine, had confided in her about how wonderful having a man in her life had been and shared her deepest desires. How she'd wanted to be a teacher—how she'd loved children. Yet she'd already had three miscarriages.

Blocking the tears that always came when she thought of her beloved aunt, Josephine took a steadying breath. The bleeding...it wouldn't stop. The womenfolk kept bringing in clean rags to mop up the blood. Their expressions fearful. They knew what was coming although she prayed it wouldn't prove true. Matilda's face distorted in pain, the color draining from it. When the baby came... Josephine blinked away the tears. He was dead. Purple, lifeless. *Dead.*

Despite the pain, her weakness, the heartbreaking realization the baby was deceased, Matilda wanted to hold him. She spoke softly to her son, held him tight to her chest, prayed over him.

Josephine closed her eyes.

Two days later, she had stood beside her mother at the funeral for Aunt Matilda and the baby, and Josephine vowed never to marry. She didn't want to die like that.

Breaking into the memory, Bill pulled her down with him and sat on the rock. Leaning over, he pressed his mouth against hers, his kiss as unassuming as ever. She loved him. She really did. But making a commitment...

She nestled her head against his neck and wrapped her arms around him. "When we're like this I have no doubts, but then I think of cooking and cleaning, and having babies." She let out her breath. "Aunt Matilda died giving birth to her firstborn son." She couldn't shake loose of the fear she'd die in childbirth, too. "I just don't want to end my life that soon."

"I'd make you happy, Josephine. Don't you worry none about that."

"I know you'd try."

A strange clicking sound on the rock behind Bill made her look up. Mr. Daemon was poised to strike Bill with his cane. The Shady Villa manager's face was filled with hate, his eyes narrowed, his lips turned down, his brows deeply furrowed.

She opened her mouth to scream. Before she could warn Bill, Mr. Daemon hit him in the head with a loud thwack.

Bill collapsed against the rock and Josephine screamed. She jumped up and backed away from Mr. Daemon, his steel gray eyes hard and cold. She screamed again. Her heart thundering, she feared he intended to kill her. Why?

She didn't have anything to fight him with. As soon as he swung his cane at her, she intended to grab hold and hope she could thwart him.

The edge of the rock fell away to the stones below, bouncing all the way until it hit the bottom, and her heart fell with it.

"I don't know who you are, lady, but it's going to end here and now. Just another step, and we'll have this whole mess taken care of."

He had...he had hurt her. *Somehow.* Her temple pounded with pain, and try as she might, she couldn't recall what had happened. A vision of the room at the inn appeared in her mind's eye, the darkness, the fever, the chills, the whispered voices, and suffocation.

With a distinctive limp, he moved toward her, his cane aimed at her like a spear.

Bill was sprawled out on the limestone a few paces away, blood trickling down his face, his skin colorless. "Bill!" she cried, trying to rouse him.

Bill stirred and groaned, and Mr. Daemon turned his back on her to look at him.

To save Bill, she ran from the rock screaming, stumbling and falling down the hill, snagging her hair on shrubs and branches, hoping someone would come to their rescue.

***

Jack and Matthew and several others ran to where they heard a woman's screams and when he saw it was Lisa, her hair undone, wild and tangled about her shoulders, her skirt smudged with dirt, he grabbed ahold of her. "Find Bill," he ordered his brother, though he'd kill the son-of-a-gun if he'd done this to her.

Matthew charged up the hill to see to Bill, while Jack hurried her to the inn.

"What happened?" Jack asked.

"He struck Bill with his cane, then he came after me only Bill's groaning distracted him. I ran away screaming to attract attention. Hey, where are you taking me?" She tried to squirm loose. "I want to see Bill."

"You need to come with me. They'll bring him to you, shortly. Who was it who struck Bill, and why would he want to harm you?" He had it in mind to return her to the inn where she could go home— according to Esmeralda. Once she was safely away, he'd find out all he could about Josephine. At least that's what he had intended.

"You're hurting my arm, Jack. Where are you taking me?"

"I'm sorry." He loosened his grip, and she tried to wriggle free. "No, you don't." He tightened his hold. "You've got to come with me for your own protection."

When they approached the inn, Lisa dug her heels into the road and pulled away from him. "I'm not going back there."

"What happened, Josephine? What happened at the inn that frightens you so?" She shook her head and her eyes grew terrified while she fought to free herself from him. "I can't go back there!"

Barely able to make any headway because she was fighting him so hard, Jack grabbed her around the waist and lifted her over his shoulder. He hated treating her like this, but damn it. He didn't have any choice.

"No, no!" she yelled and kicked her legs. "Let me go, I won't go back!"

Thankful everyone was at the picnic and no one heard her screams, he would have a hell of a time explaining his uncivilized behavior toward the lady if he got caught.

At the room, he fumbled with the key in the lock while she kicked and hit him. Finally managing to unlock the door, he shoved it open.

He stormed inside and dumped her on the bed. She glowered at him. He watched for some change in her, but instead she bolted for the exit. Outpacing her, he slammed the door shut and locked it. She dashed for the window, and he seized her around the waist again. "You can't leave here, Lisa," he said, trying to reason with her. Yet, he couldn't understand why Esmeralda's words didn't come true.

"Lisa? Why do you keep calling me by that name? Are you mad? You can't keep me hostage here!"

She was right. Once the picnic was over, he was bound to get into hot water over this. He scratched his head and stared at her. "Why isn't anything happening?" The sunlight glinted off the amethyst, catching his eye. "The necklace!"

She grasped it and shook her head. "No, no, you can't have it."

He tried to pry her fingers from it, but he finally slipped the chain over her head. "No!" she wailed.

Her cry sliced through him, instantly filling him with regret.

The room darkened and his head spun. He attempted to keep an eye on her. But he couldn't see her any longer in the blackness, and the amethyst stone slipped from his fingers.

The next thing he knew, he was lying on the floor in the dark. His legs shaking and his stomach queasy, he managed to stumble to his feet. Stretching his hands out, he ran his hands over the rumpled bedcover pulled halfway onto the floor, then touched Lisa's still body.

"Lisa!" He felt her wrist. Her pulse was steady, but she didn't stir. "Lisa! Are you all right?"

She moaned something inaudible, and his heart surged. "Honey, are you okay?" He wanted to light the lantern, but didn't want to move away from her in the darkness, fearing she'd vanish.

"Jack?" she whispered.

He helped her to sit, breathing in the sweet fragrance that was Lisa, hoping she was herself again. "Are you all right?"

"What—what happened?"

"I'm not certain. Let me light the lamp." Despite wanting to see her, he couldn't force himself to release her hand.

"I'm—I'm all right," she said, but she sounded shaken.

Wanting to comfort her, Jack finally struck a match. In the soft glow, she blinked. He was sure she was Lisa again. "I'll light the lantern, then we need to talk." He reached over to it and stared at the porcelain base wearing a strange cloth-covered hat with a hole in its top.

Lisa gasped, the match's flame bit his fingers, and he shook it out, immersing them in blackness again.

"Ohmigod," she whispered, then the bed jiggled and before he could grab her, she vanished.

"Lisa!" Angry at the world, he gripped the cotton fabric, fighting the urge to rip the quilt to shreds. If Esmeralda was right, Lisa had left him in some way he couldn't begin to imagine, and Josephine was truly dead. He would kill Josephine's murderers himself if he found out who they were, but he wasn't sure doing so would free Lisa from Josephine's power either.

Aching with grief, he rose from the floor and walked toward the door with shoulders stooped as if he'd just laid his Charlotte to rest all over again. Like with her, there was no bringing the woman he loved back. Dear God, what had he done?

Light suddenly illuminated the room, and Lisa leaned against the wall, her face ash-colored and her expression concerned. "Somehow I brought you to my world, Jack."

He hurried to take her in his arms before she

collapsed, though his stomach and head hadn't quit spinning.

She leaned against his strength and looked up at him and took a deep breath. "This is difficult to explain." She closed her eyes and passed out in his arms.

***

"I'm from the twenty-first century, Jack," Lisa said some time later, her head resting on his chest, his arms wrapped securely around her as they reclined on the bed. She was so beautiful when she was Lisa, but not making a lick of sense.

Neither was anything else. The bed no longer wore a pieced-quilt, but a gaudy, floral spread. The lamp had a strange-looking black rope snaking out from the backside, and the mirror hanging over the dresser was crystal clear. Even the windows were transparent glass panels.

"Do...do you want to go back?" she asked, her green eyes studying him, watching him closely for his reaction. "I've been talking for a while, but I don't think you've heard a word I've said."

Jack stared at her, realizing he'd been so absorbed in the new surroundings, he hadn't heard her speaking, but he had no intention of going home just yet. "I want to see where you live, where you work. I want to know all about your world. And no, I don't want to go back right away." He didn't want to lose her again.

"All right, Jack." She let out her breath in a heavy sigh, her fingers caressing his shirt.

At some time or another, he'd divested himself of his vest and jacket, but the way she was touching his chest was driving him to want to remove a whole lot more.

She sighed. "Don't tell me I didn't warn you, but you're bound to be in for a big shock."

He'd fought in the War, even been bitten by a rattler and survived, seen enough death and dying that he figured he could handle about anything. "I'm ready."

She smiled at him and the look was more vixen than sweet. All at once, he wondered if he really knew Lisa at all, but he sure was intrigued.

"Uhm, what about your family? If you don't let them know where you are, won't they be worried?"

"Matthew will take care of my horse and won't send out a search party right away."

"All right. We'll have to sneak out of the room because I didn't pay for it. The management wouldn't let anyone rent it because Josephine's spirit is haunting it."

"In the twenty-first century?" Jack pulled on his vest and glanced up to see Lisa slipping pins out of her hair, frowning at her image in the mirror.

"For all time, it seems."

After he'd refastened his holster and pulled his jacket on, he glanced around the room. No Lisa. His heart jumped. "Lisa?"

"In here," she said. "Just washing up."

"Washing?" He envisioned a washbasin, but the strange shlushing sound got his attention. He pushed open a door that led to small, brightly lit room. Steam poured out of a porcelain tub, but instead of having clawed feet, it fit squarely on the floor and was pinned between two walls. In front of it, a curtain of floral material clung to metal rings looped around a white rod. A mirror obscured by fog, hung over a porcelain basin and a matching bowl filled with water sat next to the cabinet.

A waterfall gushed behind the curtain, and curiosity about the strange contraption got the better of him. He peeked around the fabric. And froze.

Her eyes closed, Lisa ran soap over her face, her wet curls drifting over her ivory skin, water sluicing down her full breasts, the nipples—pert red blossoms. Golden curls nestled between the apex of her thighs, wet like the rest of her. God, she was beautiful. And naked. And he had no business seeing her like this. Yet, he couldn't move as if Medusa had turned him to stone, only his heart beat too hard for that.

Lisa sighed and tilted her head back, letting the water run down her face, her hands moving to her breasts, and lower, washing the soap away. "Jack!" she hollered. "Maybe you ought to wash up a bit, too."

They shared baths in her time? To save water. Sure. He ditched his jacket and began removing his vest when she opened her eyes, blinked, and gasped.

She covered her breasts with one arm, though she was too voluptuous to hide much. Her free hand covered her curls lower, and he realized his mistake.

"Sorry, I…" His face heated as if he'd been out in the Texas sun without a hat, and he quickly grabbed his jacket and exited the room.

The running water stopped. Metal rings made a scraping sound. Lisa stepped out of the room, holding a towel around her torso, way too small to hide enough of her. He lifted his gaze from her bare legs and was relieved to see her smiling.

"I didn't mean to use all the hot water. Though there's still probably plenty. The complimentary shampoo is sitting on the tub along with a bar of soap. I've got some clean clothes for myself in the room next door. If I'd been thinking more clearly, we could have showered over there. Not sure what we'll do for you. But when we get home, I can wash your clothes."

"I'm sorry," he said again, motioning to the room with the tub, unable to get the image of her nude body out of his mind. The fact she was naked under the towel didn't help.

She smiled again. "It's okay. No harm done. I'll get my clothes, and then you can take a shower."

He took a deep breath of her fragrance. She smelled like a bouquet of fresh flowers, and every inch of her was clean. Whereas, he was covered in several layers of dust and must have smelled like his horse.

Lisa ducked back into the washroom and returned with an armload of clothes. He wondered why he hadn't noticed them.

"If you need help with the shower, just holler. It has one knob, and you twist it to the left to make the water hotter, to the right to cool it down."

"I'll be just a minute."

She smiled again. "Take your time. Enjoy it."

He walked back into the steamy room, ditched his clothes, and struggled with the knob. It turned left and right, but the water still didn't come out. "I think you used up all the water," he hollered.

"The *hot* water, maybe, but not *all* the water." Still wearing only a towel, she walked in and stopped.

He thought she'd yell directions to him, so he wasn't prepared for her to see *him* naked.

Averting her gaze, she chuckled, then reached in and pushed the knob up and to the left. Water gushed out from a nozzle above.

She smiled again and hurried out of the bathroom. "Need anything else, just ask."

"A good back scrub," he said, climbing into the tub.

"We'd have to get married."

"I thought that was the idea, honey." He ran the bar of soap over his skin, scrubbing away the dirt. She didn't say anything for a few minutes, and he cleared his throat. "I want to marry you. Nothing's changed."

"Even though we're from two different worlds?" she asked, her voice whisper soft. From the projection of her voice, she was standing next to the tub.

He stilled his soap-covered hand on his chest. "Maybe *because* we are from different worlds. I've never met anyone like you, and I'm drawn to you, as if we were meant to be together. I'm not giving you up."

"I feel the same about you." She pulled the curtain back a tad, the towel gone, and stepped into the tub. "Ready for your backrub?"

CHAPTER 16

Lisa knew she was nuts. But what did she have to lose? She wanted Jack, and he wanted her. For a moment in time, all that mattered was how they felt about each other. She just hoped the hot water would last.

After she squeezed soap from the shampoo bottle, she ran the satiny peach-scented cleanser through his hair, the strands silky. He leaned down and kissed her lips while he rubbed his soapy fingers over her breasts. His touch was like heaven, large calloused hands caressing her nipples, causing them to tingle and tighten. He weighed her breasts, making her wet in anticipation.

"I sure could get used to this," he murmured against her mouth. He wrapped his arms around her and pulled her tight.

His rigid arousal poked against her waist. "Hmm." She slid her hands down his back, raking her nails lightly across his hard muscles. "You're in great shape."

"I'd say the same about you, miss."

She smiled, loving how he could feel that way when that dolt of an ex couldn't say one nice thing about her. "Do you need me to wash anywhere else?" She peered up at him, his look a mixture of surprise and intrigue.

"What had you in mind?"

She reached between them and trailed her fingers down his firm stomach, lower until she touched his erection. It jumped. She smiled. "Your pistol's ready." She ran her hand along his thickened length, and she swore he was twice the size of Barry.

Jack groaned and placed his hand on hers. "I won't last if you keep that up."

"Hmm. What are you going to do about it, Cowboy?" She wrapped her arms around his neck and rubbed her leg against the back of his.

"Take you to bed, ma'am, and pleasure you right fine."

"I can't wait that long."

He kissed her mouth, his hands sliding down her wet back until he reached her bottom. "What did you want to do?"

"Get wet and wild."

"I aim to please, though I had no idea..." He tackled her lips with enthusiasm, nipping, thrusting his tongue in her mouth, squeezing her buttocks.

She ran her hand over his, but he was a lot firmer, and she wished she was, too. He seemed to take pleasure in feeling her up just the same. His dark eyes were clouded with desire, and his rod was poking hard into her stomach. Her inner core already sparked and ready, she was long past wanting him to bury himself deep inside her.

He broke the kiss and smoothed out her hair. "I don't want to hurt you."

"I've been married before," she offered, so that he didn't get the wrong idea when he learned she wasn't a virgin.

"Widowed?" he asked, frowning, his eyes fixed on hers.

"Divorced. He left me for another woman." *Kid.* But she wasn't telling Jack that. She thought she was okay with it, but her voice broke. Not wanting Jack to see her like this, she brushed errant tears off her cheeks.

Jack cupped her face and kissed her lips. "I'm not leaving you. This is for good."

That's what she needed to hear. Nothing was ever permanent, but she craved having someone she could count on like who she felt wouldn't leave her except because he had no other choice.

"Make love to me, Jack," she said. "Here, now, without reservation."

She didn't have to beg. Lifting her off her feet, he leaned her back against the steamy shower stall, his hands around her waist, her legs around his. Her tongue and his executed a mating dance, teasing and tasting.

Then he centered her and plunged slowly at first, stretching her tightness over his erection. Either he was a lot bigger than she'd expected, or her lack of sex life had made her shrink to virgin level. She tightened her legs around him and moaned with exquisite ecstasy.

He slowed his approach, and she worried he'd stop and had changed his mind. "Are you a virgin?" he asked, his brows furrowing.

TERRY SPEAR

"It's been a long while," she hated to admit.

Jack grunted. "He must have been an idiot," he muttered, then kissed her mouth again and penetrated her to the hilt.

She rode him like she'd never done before with even her husband, and never had she done it in the shower. Too good to be true. Afraid Jack would think her too unconventional, she couldn't have been happier he would go along with it. Every thrust sent her hormones spiraling higher, catapulting her to the brink of desire. The water was beginning to cool, but he kept the fire burning and with a final thrust, her composure shattered. She cried out with joy, but Jack muffled her elation with another kiss and smiled.

He set her down, they quickly rinsed off, and he turned off the now cold water. She was still thrumming with ripples of orgasm, the first she'd ever had with a man. It felt damn—*sigh*—good.

She grabbed a fresh towel and handed him another. Before she could dry herself, he was running his towel over her breasts. She laughed and dried off his chest. "When you nearly made love to me that first night, I regretted that you weren't my husband. Well, not my husband, but another who would love me the way you seemed to care for me."

He kissed the shower water off her cheeks. "Have I earned my wings yet?"

She laughed. "My God, yes. You took me to the sun and back. I was afraid your wings would singe, and that would be the end of us. Dying in such a way would be worth it."

"Not until we're old and gray, honey, and have a passel of kids grown and gone."

She could handle that.

They finished drying, and he lifted her and carried her to bed. She wanted him for all time, but still, she worried about returning to his world. "We have to prove who killed Josephine. Or they'll want us both dead," she warned, snuggling up to Jack on the mattress.

"Are you sure you don't want to stay here?" He pulled the covers over them to keep out the chill.

Was he already changing his mind? Or trying to change hers? "My heart is with you. I think some part of me knew that from the beginning."

"You won't pine away for your life here?"

"Oh, I won't deny I'll miss the luxuries. Living in your age will take getting used to."

He caressed her arm, his touch sensitive. "I have to return. A lot of folks depend on me, the ranch, their livelihoods. Matthew's a terrific ranch hand, but not a manager. Andy's parents died, and I took him in. The others have been with me since the end of the War. Esmeralda, she's been like an over-protective mother since my own died."

Lisa leaned her head against Jack's chest. He didn't seem to mind that her hair was still damp. Barry would have had a fit. "I wouldn't think of making you stay here. It'll be hard enough for me to adjust, but for a man to have to go forward over a hundred years and try to start over..." She shook her head. "Besides, you have family. I don't."

His hand moved under the covers and stroked her hip, sending ripples of need coursing through her. "After I see your place, we'll return to mine, and I'll get the marriage license."

"No courtship phase?" In a way, she was teasing, but another part of her was scared. What if after the "honeymoon" period, Jack didn't adore her any longer? It wasn't like it hadn't happened before when she was married to Barry. She traced Jack's nipple with her fingertip and raised her brows.

He took her hand and kissed it. "I'm not risking losing you to some other yahoo."

Footfalls drew close to the room and paused outside of it. Jack's stomach muscles tightened, and he quietly climbed out of bed and began to dress. Lisa hurried to pull her gown over her head.

A woman began talking. "I don't hear anything now, but I swear the shower was running earlier and…well, it sounded like a man and woman making out. No one's supposed to be here."

"Maybe our ghost is really a vagrant," an older, gruff man said. "Have you got the key?"

"No. Both are missing, and I haven't found either of our housekeepers."

"I'll call the locksmith."

They walked down the hall.

Lisa took a deep breath. "If they replace the doorknob, we're sunk."

Jack went to the window and unlocked the sash. "We can get back in through here later, if they don't discover it."

She peered out the door. "The hall is clear." She rushed out, and Jack shut and locked the door behind him.

After using the key, they entered the room next to it.

In disbelief, Jack considered the room's

furnishings. Everything, the bedcover, the paintings, lamps, furniture, curtains, all looked identical to the other room.

Lisa dumped the petticoats on the bed and slipped out of her dress. He drew in a sharp breath at the sight of her naked again and watched in fascination. Creamy skin from top to bottom, every inch begging to be kissed. Damp straggles of silky strands of hair caressed her full breasts, the rosy buds peeking out. Lower still, short golden curls hid her womanhood, and shapely legs seemed to go on forever. Curvy and soft all over, she was a dream come true.

She pulled silky white garments from her tapestry bag, and looked up, her gaze meeting his. Her skin blushed from her cheeks and trailed down to her toes. His face heated, too. He felt like a peeping tom, though she would soon be his. He had figured his wife would be hidden from view, bundled in a sleeping gown when he made love to her at night, fully dressed when he saw her during the day. He never expected this.

"Sorry," she said. "I should have changed in the bathroom. Between having been married and being comfortable around you, I didn't give it a second thought."

He closed the distance between them and tilted her face up to his. "I've always been an early riser, but you're going to make it awfully hard for me to get out of bed mornings."

She curved her arms around his neck, dangling the silk and lace scraps of fabric over his back. "You know just the right things to say to me. I think I might keep you."

He kissed her firmly on the mouth, his palms

shifting to lift her buttocks as he pressed her hard against his agonizingly aroused body. "You're mine, Miss Welsh. No doubt about it."

Except for Charlotte, he'd never felt this possessive in his life. If even another man looked crossways at Lisa, he was ready to knock 'em out.

They were in the bed before she realized what was happening, and this time, he pleasured her a lot slower, probing the sweet spot between her legs, smiling as she sank her nails into his shoulders, wringing the pleasure out of her until she was crying out his name. Then he drove into her with single-minded purpose, deeper and deeper, but it wasn't enough, and she raised her hips to take in all of him, moving with him, anticipating his thrusts and exalting in their joining until he found release.

"I would never have thought..." he said, then let whatever else he was going to say trail off, his hands touching her face, her hair, his mouth kissing hers. "I can't lose you again."

"I don't...don't want to lose you either." With that, they snuggled together for a while, drifted off to sleep, and a couple of hours later, Lisa stirred, and sighed.

"If we don't get going, we'll never accomplish anything," she said.

He didn't want to move from the bed, ever. She smelled like flowers, her skin velvet to his touch, her voice sweet and soft.

Like a siren, she ensnared him in her spell, and he could barely think straight. She was right of course, but all he could think of was trying out this bed again, cradling her petite form while he leaned against her in the throes of passion.

"Jack, we need to go."

He groaned and gave her one last bear hug, then released her. Watching her dress was even more painful.

"Panties," she said, as she drew the tiny piece of fabric up her legs. It barely covered her womanly treasures. "Bra," she explained, fastening it in front.

"That's what you wore under your clothes?" He touched her breasts covered in lace, the darkened nubs poking at the garment, visible to the eye. He was thinking how easy it would be to unfasten.

"Yes, this is what I wore underneath." She hurried to pull on a "cashmere sweater," she called it, made of the softest fabric he'd ever touched.

He ran his hands over her breasts again, the garment sliding over the mounds. She was a tactile delight. He frowned when her nipples protruded through the sweater. "You can't be seen like this."

"If you'd leave them alone, they'd settle down and no one would see anything."

He didn't believe that for a minute.

She pulled on men's breeches. Except they had a strange fastener. "Jeans, zipper."

He pulled it down and up and down. He liked the zipper. Running his hands over her butt, he said, "You can't mean to show this off." His fingers went lower, down her thighs. "How can a man get anything done if a woman wears clothes that reveal so much of her attributes? Nothing's left to the imagination." He leaned over and nuzzled her face, pressing his erection against her waist.

"You haven't seen nothing like what some women wear. Men are used to it." She rubbed against him, stirring him up even further.

He slid his hands around to her crotch and stroked. "I'm not sure I'd ever get used to seeing you wear clothes like this unless it's in our bedroom, and then you wouldn't be wearing them for long."

"Promises, promises." She took his hands and moved them to her breasts, then leaned against him. "Hmm, we really need to go."

He kissed her ear and whispered, "I won't ever get enough of you."

"Good. I don't want to be a cast off again."

He hugged her tighter. "Your husband had to have been crazy."

"He is. And I was nuts to marry him. Are you hungry? I want to take you to the restaurant I ate at before I dropped into your world." Lisa wound her hair into a braid.

"Yeah, since we missed eating at the picnic." Oh, hell, Jack hadn't intended to bring that up.

"Picnic? The one you were supposed to take me to? I guess we didn't get to go. I remember stumbling through the cave after whoever murdered Josephine left me there. She guided me out of it to save my life, I'm sure. After that…I remember drinking water from the creek, and then we were here."

He didn't say anything, but an awful dread overwhelmed him. What if when they returned, Josephine took over Lisa's body again? Had she helped Lisa only so she could use her? He was still thinking on it when they walked out of the room, and a woman came around the corner with a big metal cart filled with white linens. Like Lisa, she was wearing men's breeches.

"The maid," Lisa whispered.

"She's dressed like a ranch hand, too."

"Just about all the women today wear jeans or slacks when it's cold."

The dining room was huge, surrounded by clear panes of glass. Women were dressed in breeches, "sweatshirts," or sweaters, and wore their hair either hanging long or cut off. One even had hers sticking out like a porcupine's.

"Spiked," Lisa explained, when he gave her a questioning glance.

When he and Lisa took their seats, he attempted not to stare at the women. Instead, he concentrated on the menu. Or at least tried. The prices were so high he didn't notice much else. "We can't eat here," he said, unable to curb the disappointment in his voice.

Lisa ran her hand over his. "I'll use my credit card."

He didn't believe in credit. Pay the bills up front. That was his way of conducting business. He'd seen a few poor souls become so indebted they were in peril of losing their farms. "A gentleman doesn't allow a lady—"

"My world, Jack. Let me do it my way. Okay? Your money would actually be very valuable today, but we'd have to sell it to an antique store first."

That didn't make any sense. How could his money be worth more when the prices were so much higher? "Antique store...like where you picked up Josephine's necklace?"

"Do you want to see it? Most guys I know wouldn't be caught dead wandering through a shop full of old stuff."

"I want to know everything there is about you." He had no intention of letting her go and that meant getting to really know her. "Food's good," Jack said, mopping up the rest of his gravy with a roll. If nothing else, the meal was a darn sight better than he'd expected.

A couple of cowboys walked into the place, and glad to see someone who looked normal, Jack's spirits rose. "Howdy."

They greeted him in the same manner and took their seats across the dining room.

"Some of the men still dress regular," Jack said to Lisa.

"You'd be right at home at a rodeo here. Just about everyone wears western clothes to those. Ready to go?"

He finished his fourth cup of coffee. "Sure is good."

Outside, children climbed on top of a metal frame of a pretend stagecoach. The oaks that shaded the inn were still there, only much taller and fuller. The sign outside the building said, *The Stagecoach Inn.*

A stagecoach headed down the street at a leisurely pace, and Lisa took Jack's hand. "Tourists pay to ride around town in it."

He couldn't imagine wasting good money to take a jaunt around the place. "Tourists?"

"Out-of-towners." She walked him to an area covered in black tar. Only it was solid like seamless brick pavers stuck together.

"Cars, trucks, all kinds of vehicles," she said, pointing to the horseless, colorful carriages, their wheels covered in rubber. Shiny metal took the place of spokes.

He crouched down and touched one of the wheels.

"Do they break down very often?"

"When they get a nail in them."

"Ah. Cars…you said you rode in one here. One of these?" His gaze lighted on a bright red vehicle.

"That's a Mustang. This one's mine. It's an SUV, or Sports Utility Vehicle." She pressed something in her hand and pulled a door open. "This is your seat."

He climbed into the plush conveyance, the seats covered in red velvet. He ran his hand over the material and marveled at the interior. He'd envisioned the car was run on coal like a train, but now he couldn't fathom what made it go. "You must have paid a fortune for this."

"Cars *are* expensive." She climbed into the other seat, reached over Jack, and pulled a strap across his chest. "Seatbelt. You have to wear one because it's the law. They save lives."

"Save lives?"

"We drive fast. If it makes you queasy, close your eyes, or I'll stop."

As soon as they pulled out of the parking lot, three cars with lights flashing on top drove into the area. The men wore light colored uniforms and Stetsons and hurried into the hotel.

"The army?" Jack asked, wondering if they were at war again.

"Police. Deputies. Looks like someone's in trouble."

As soon as she reached the road, Jack tried to see all the changes, but he couldn't believe it. A few of the buildings were still standing, but many had new facades and were no longer private family dwellings. Dozens of new buildings made of stone, brick, or wood filled much of the space in between. Many had metal roofs and long covered porches.

"The creek's still here," he remarked, glad to see something familiar.

"I know it's all changed. You can see why when I first went back to your time, I was so confused."

She showed him the antique store where she purchased Josephine's necklace. He was awed at how items that were new in his world were displayed as valuable antiques. Hell, even he was an antique if he got right down to it.

"Do you still want to go to Waco?" she asked, getting back in the car.

"Yeah, Lisa. I do."

"I have to warn you. The speed limit is thirty miles per hour in town. When we get on the interstate, it's seventy."

"Seventy?" He couldn't even fathom how fast that would be. "I'm ready."

She glanced at his jacket. "You don't have your gun with you, do you?"

"I always carry it. Why?"

"Uhm, you need a license to carry a gun in Texas."

"You said that to Bill and me when we first brought out our guns."

"Yeah. You can get arrested. And they'll take it away. Is it loaded?"

"What good would an unloaded revolver do me?"

"The police don't like loaded guns. Stick it in the glove box, okay?"

He shook his head. "I hope you know what you're doing." He placed it in the compartment she pointed to. While she drove, he looked out the side window and it made him dizzy. Everything whipped past the windows in a blur. Watching out the front window was just as heart stopping. "Why are you going so slow? Others are passing you." He thought maybe she worried about him not being able to handle the speed she normally traveled, but he didn't want her to make allowances on his account.

"I'm going the posted speed limit. They're speeding. If the police catch them, they'll pay a fine."

"Lawbreakers. How long will it take us to get to Waco?"

"Forty minutes. Tops. Smoother ride. No dust. Heating and cooling. Much quicker trip."

Jack didn't like the sounds of it. How would he be able to convince Lisa she had to stay with him in the past if she had to leave behind her valuable car?

"So what was he like?" Jack asked, wanting to know about her prior husband. He couldn't help wondering what had gone wrong. Although the man had to be a lunatic not to want to make love to his wife.

"Who? My ex-husband?"

Jack nodded.

"A real jerk."

"It must have been an arranged marriage."

"No. Today, most of us marry for love. At least, I did. I found out quickly he didn't want children, and he had a roving eye. Among other things."

"Other things?"

"Affairs."

"I'm sorry, Lisa. Adultery should be a hanging offense." He *was* sorry as far as not liking that she'd had a miserable marriage. But he was glad it was over so he'd had a chance to be the one for her.

On the trip to Waco, Lisa had to brake the car to prevent colliding with different vehicles five times. Her jaw tightened and her hands gripped the wheel, making her knuckles grow white. He couldn't see how she could travel like this on a regular basis. It might be faster, but it would take a toll on one's sanity and heart.

Twenty minutes later, she jerked the car off the interstate and parked. Eighteen-wheelers and smaller trucks and cars roared by in a never-ending stream, shaking hers. "SUV died," she explained. She punched some numbers into a tiny, pink box she called a cell phone and talked to a man about towing the car. She poked at the phone again and raised it to her ear. "Pauline? Thank God, I got you. I think my transmission went out again. I can't get hold of a tow-truck service. Well, one said they'd be here in two hours, but maybe you could…" She stared at the phone, her face red. She shut it with a snap and threw it in the car. "Battery died."

A truck hauling a horse wagon blasted a horn, pulled in front of her vehicle, and stopped. A crusty old cowboy got out of his pickup and tipped his Stetson in greeting. "Howdy, folks. What seems to be the trouble?"

"I've called for a tow truck, but it won't be here for another couple of hours. I just had my transmission replaced, so I don't know what's wrong," Lisa said.

The man nodded. "Wanna pop the hood, and I'll take a look?"

As soon as she did, the cowboy fiddled with something inside. "Try starting your engine," he hollered, while Jack peered inside.

The car roared to life. "Ohmigosh, thanks so

much." Lisa said.

"Mighty obliged." Jack shook the man's hand.

"Don't usually stop for stranded motorists," the man said, jabbing his thumb at the horse wagon, "on account of it's hard stopping with the trailer in tow. But I had a hunch I could help. Take care, folks." He waved and headed back to his pickup.

Jack shook his head when he got into the car. "He said it was a loose electrical connection." He wished he could have been the one to fix her problem. He imagined that if he lived in her world even for a lifetime, he'd never learn enough to be useful.

"Thank God. Just another twenty minutes until we arrive, unless we get stuck again." She called and cancelled the tow truck service, but Jack wished she'd keep both hands on the wheel.

As soon as they reached her apartment complex, he gave the two-story brick building a long look. "I wouldn't want to live on top of people like this."

"As a single woman, it's easier for me than maintaining a large yard."

"You don't have to worry about either any longer." He carried her bag up to her apartment, curious as to how Lisa lived and wanted to see more of her clothes, especially the kind she wore underneath the rest of her garments.

***

They'd barely walked in the door when the phone rang, and Lisa rushed to get it. She figured Pauline had seen her arrive. But did she also get a glimpse of Jack? She probably wouldn't approve.

Jack caught sight of the picture of Pauline and Lisa wearing satin dresses and petticoats, showing off garters. They stood next to Pauline's hubby, dressed as a gambler, at Six Flags.

"Old-time photo shop. We could have worn medieval clothes, but Pauline's husband, Kenneth, insisted on the old west. Why don't you strip out of your clothes so I can wash them?"

Jack raised his brows and peeled off his jacket. "I never knew a woman who wanted me out of my duds so much."

She smiled. "You never knew *me* before."

He chuckled and kept stripping.

She yanked the phone off the hook. "Hello?"

"Ohmigod, what's happened to you?"

"Pauline. We were so lucky. A good Samaritan helped fix my car." Lisa shoved her blue gown and petticoats in the wash, then added Jack's clothes, giving him an appreciative smile. Other than wearing his Stetson, he was the proverbial sight for sore eyes—a real live cowboy pinup in the raw if she ever saw one. He headed into the kitchen, and she poked the gentle cycle button in case the stitches of the garments couldn't handle anything harsher.

With a bath towel in hand, she joined Jack in the kitchen. He'd ditched his hat on the counter and was exploring her fridge. God, he looked good nude. Or dressed. And like he belonged. But in his heart, he didn't. She could tell from the expression on his face he appreciated some of the novelties, the hot shower, the refrigerator, but he didn't like the crowds, the way women dressed, the traffic.

"Listen, I tried to warn you but our connection cut off and when I called back, there wasn't any answer," Pauline said over the phone.

"My cell phone battery died. I've been having trouble with it. Now I've got an electrical problem with the SUV. You know how it is with me. I get one thing fixed and three more mechanical items won't work."

Jack stuck his hand into the freezer.

"Lisa, listen. The boss is furious. He's trumped up charges against you... and said you embezzled all kinds of money. The sheriff's been to your place. In your absence, they've searched your apartment for any evidence they could find. The police have a warrant out for your arrest."

CHAPTER 17

Lisa handed Jack a large blue towel, but her eyes widened and her face lost all its color as she listened to her friend Pauline on the phone.

Jack slipped the soft material around his waist. When he closed the icebox, he caught Lisa's eye, but she quickly averted her gaze. "This can't be happening."

Immediately, he lost interest in all of the wonders of her time. He tried to take her hand, but she shook her head.

Grabbing the suitcase, she hurried out of the kitchen and down the hall. "Do you think they're watching my place?" She paused.

Jack nearly collided with her. *Hell, what was going on?*

Her expression anxious, she looked at Jack and rubbed her forehead. "You told them I went out of town? *Great,* so they assume I really did take off with the money."

Stolen money?

"The original documents? Oh, oh, where did I put the satchel? Wait. Let me think." Her eyes grew round again. "I...I took them to Salado. I've got to get them."

"Lisa, what's wrong?" Jack asked.

She ignored him. He bristled.

"Yes, the documents are the only evidence I have, Pauline. If Michael doctored the copies and is accusing me of embezzling, he must have been the one stealing it and not his brother-in-law. I've got to make this right."

Whoever this Michael was, Jack was ready to call him out.

He followed Lisa into the bedroom, noticing the paintings of blue flowers on the walls, the big brass bed clothed in white eyelet, and the hand embroidered doilies covering a cedar chest. What garnered his attention most was Lisa, filling her tapestry bag with colorful silk panties, more bras, and short satiny gowns barely long enough to cover a body.

Jack raised his brows. She couldn't mean to take them back to the past. Though the notion of seeing her wear them intrigued him.

She moved to the washroom and dumped different shaped and brightly colored bottles into the suitcase. He wondered what miracles they contained.

She lifted her gaze to him, her eyes wide. "Ohmigod, Pauline. Do you think they tapped the phone?"

Tapped? Whatever it was, her expression revealed it wasn't good.

"Gotta go. Uhm, the cowboy?" She gave his nearly nude body an appraising look, offered a wistful smile, and gave his hand a squeeze. "It's Jack from the past.

I'll talk to you later."

She clicked off the phone.

"What's going on?" Jack asked, glad she wasn't talking any longer into that annoying tiny black box.

"My boss has accused me of stealing money from the company. *He* probably embezzled it. The original documents will prove it, but they're at the Salado inn. I think I hid the satchel under the bed in room number two."

"I can't risk you being arrested."

"I have to do this. Michael's *not* getting away with it."

Jack motioned to his state of undress.

"Uhm, yeah." She rushed to the washer and pulled the sopping wet clothes out, then dumped them in another machine. "Dryer." She turned them on high. "I'll call Pauline back."

He glanced at the contraption as the clothes thumped inside. How long would the machine take to dry his clothes? Maybe not long, considering the way cars drove so fast.

She punched in a number and strode to the parlor. "Pauline, I'm washing Jack's clothing, but if we have to leave in a hurry, can we borrow a set of your husband's western duds? Thanks."

Her gaze lit on a colorful photograph of a couple. The woman looked astonishingly like Lisa, her clear green eyes and lips smiling. The gentleman was blond, too, wearing as big a smile. "My parents," she explained, as she tucked the gold framed photo in her bag.

"Lisa, how can I help? I can wear my clothes wet if we need to make haste."

"No, Pauline will be right over."

"I don't want you coming back here. I won't risk losing you," he reiterated, wanting her to agree with him, though his bride-to-be appeared to have a real stubborn streak. He could be mule-headed as well, particularly when it came to her safety.

A knocking on the door sounded. Lisa looked through a tiny glass hole. "Pauline." She motioned to Jack. "Wait in my bedroom. I'll bring the clothes to you."

He didn't like this one bit. He didn't care what evidence she had against her boss. Situations had a way of unraveling.

***

"I can't believe you brought Jack here," Pauline scolded, her brows knit in a deep frown, but then she gave Lisa a warm hug. "I was so worried about you."

Lisa sighed. "I missed you, too. We didn't plan for Jack coming with me. We both had hold of the amulet and voila. He was here."

Pauline turned her head toward the sound of the dryer. "He's naked?"

"Uhm, yeah. Thanks for loaning Kenneth's things." Lisa hurried to the bedroom with the jeans and shirt. Though she imagined Jack probably wouldn't feel properly dressed without his vest and jacket.

When she opened the door, Jack was standing next to it and took a step back.

"They're not quite what you're used to, but hopefully they'll do." She gave him a half smile.

He looked over the jeans and western shirt. "Tell your friend thanks."

She glanced at his towel, then looked up. His

mouth curved at the corners. She smiled. Yeah, he knew just what she was thinking. Trying out her bed. If she wasn't in so much trouble, she'd be all for it. "I'll tell her." She shut the door and returned to the kitchen. "I can't believe that bastard's done this."

"Michael said you were so upset over the divorce with Barry, that when you failed to earn a promotion, you decided to take the money and run."

"The police believe this?"

Pauline glanced out the window. "You're the only one who vanished, along with the money."

"Great."

The bedroom door opened, and both Lisa and Pauline looked toward the hallway. Jack stalked into the kitchen, but his eyes widened when he saw Pauline.

Lisa wasn't sure what shook him up—maybe her revealing clothes that showed off her curves—but he finally asked, "How do you do, Ma'am?"

"Ohmigosh, he's adorable," Pauline said, her brows raised, but they quickly knit together again in a frown. "But you can't keep him."

"We aim to get married as soon as we return to Salado," Jack said, sounding determined.

"After I return the documents," Lisa said, but Jack's eyes had turned nearly black as if a storm was brewing. "I'll bring the clothes back then, too."

"Keep them. Kenneth's put on weight, and they don't fit any more." Pauline gave her another disapproving look. "You can't really mean to stay with Jack." Her face brightened. "Or is he staying here with you?"

Lisa pulled a plastic sack from a cabinet and headed for the dryer. "We're going to stay in Jack's time."

"Are you sure it's a good idea? How could you give up all this?" Pauline motioned to her apartment. "You'll work yourself to death, and if you get pregnant…" She shuddered.

"Life is a chance. I could die in a car accident or any number of ways. I know it'll be hard work, but if I can share my life with Jack, it'll be well worth the sacrifices. Can you do one other thing for me? Take the money I have in my savings and checking accounts and buy old money, anything printed before 1871. Since you're listed on my accounts, you shouldn't have any trouble."

Pauline said to Jack, "You can see what she has here. If you love her, you wouldn't do this to her. She really doesn't know how hard her life will be."

Jack shoved his hand in his pockets. "It's Lisa's choice. I'm not pushing her into this." Yet he looked remorseful, like Pauline had uncovered feelings he didn't want to acknowledge.

Lisa rolled her suitcase to the door before Pauline changed Jack's mind about wanting her for his wife. "I'll call you as soon as I return."

Pauline handed Lisa a cell phone. "They won't be tracing it. And the battery works fine."

Lisa blinked away tears and hugged her. "I'll be back in a couple of hours."

"Be careful."

"I will."

"Ma'am, thanks for the duds." Jack grabbed the bag.

Pauline wiped away tears and gave him a hard look. "Keep her safe. She's the only real friend I've got."

Lisa was certain she needed a real guardian angel if she was going to keep out of all the trouble she was bound to get into.

***

His expression somber, Jack remained silent on the drive back to Salado. Lisa was afraid to ask him what he was thinking, though her thoughts were centered on her boss. Michael *had* to be the one who stole the money and now was covering his sorry ass. She'd fix him.

Forty-five minutes later, she pulled off the highway onto the access road to downtown Salado. Out of nowhere, a police car appeared and began to follow her. He's just a regular cop looking for speeders, she told herself. But she couldn't help worry that the whole state was looking for her, and she would soon be on America's Most Wanted list.

Jack glanced at the side mirror, then removed his gun from the glove box and stuck it in its holster.

"Don't let anyone see you've got that," she warned, her skin chilling. She planned to go directly to room number two and grab the satchel, then return to Waco, hand over the documents, and that would be the end of Michael's scheme. At least that's what she intended to do.

If the police caught Jack with a gun and found her suitcase in the back of the vehicle, she was certain they'd believe he was her accomplice and both were criminals on the run.

Upon entering the city limits, Lisa lifted her foot off the gas pedal, slowing down to the posted speed. The cop was still following her. When she reached the parking lot at the Stagecoach Inn, the patrol car pulled in behind her. Her heart beat so hard she was afraid she'd have a heart attack. "He's going to try and arrest me. Don't pull out your gun, or he can shoot to kill. We'll try to make it to the room before he can nab us."

To her surprise, Jack seized the suitcase and bag of damp clothes. She figured at this point it was better leaving them behind. She grabbed the necklace and dashed for the building while the policeman spoke on his radio. "Stop, Miss!" he shouted.

She ran inside and headed for room number three and their passport to the past. Scrap the room where she'd hidden her satchel. Escaping the police was their priority. Though going back in time at this point wasn't what she had in mind. If she tried to unlock the room she'd paid for, the police would catch her and what if the satchel wasn't there? She couldn't risk it.

When she didn't hear Jack behind her, she looked over her shoulder. *No Jack.* Her heart did a tumble. Where'd he disappear to?

The policeman opened the door to the hallway, huffing and puffing, looking like he'd been eating way too many donuts and wasn't used to chasing criminals on foot. *Thank God.*

Her hands clammy, she struggled with the key in the door.

He pulled out his revolver. "Turn around and put your hands where I can see them, and you won't get hurt."

She tried again to unlock the room. A click sounded and the door opened by itself. Before she could react, Jack pulled her into the room, slammed the door, and locked it. He pointed to the open window, then with suitcase and sack of wet clothes in hand, he wrapped his free arm around her.

"Don't let go of me, Jack. Don't ever let go."

"Not on your life."

The officer banged at the door and shouted, "Open up, Lisa Welsh! You're under arrest!"

* **

Lisa woke on the bed, and the room was dark and still. A strange fragrance wafted through the air. "Violets." She rubbed her arms as the air chilled. The old gas lamp reflected a light above the winged chair. She sat up in bed. "Josephine?" Her skin tingled with apprehension.

Lisa quickly looked around for Jack. "Jack?" She couldn't believe she'd left him behind.

He'd had a tight grip on her. The suitcase and bag were on the floor, but somehow she'd lost Jack. They'd arrest him and find he was packing. She slipped the necklace over her head, praying Jack was still in the room, that the cops weren't there, and she could snatch Jack away to the past. When she returned to the present and her head cleared, she found the room was empty.

Men talked beyond the door. Police car lights flashed outside. Her heart sank. She had to sneak into the room next door, get the documents, and free Jack.

One of the men outside the room said, "The two of them went out the window and disappeared, but they left her vehicle behind. They can't be far from here."

Ohmigod, Jack hadn't been caught? A modicum of relief washed over her.

"Did you find any evidence in the room?"

"Nothing but you can take a look and see if I've missed anything."

The doorknob twisted and with her heart in her throat, Lisa placed the necklace back over her head and returned to the past.

For a while, Lisa couldn't think clearly, but the aroma of violets wafted in the air, stirring her. A light hovered by the door and glided toward the bed.

Someone spoke outside the room, gaining her attention. The light moved outside.

"You want me to follow you, don't you?" Lisa whispered.

"I know I've heard voices in there again," a woman said, jiggling the door handle.

Lisa glanced at the doorknob twisting back and forth.

"I don't know where the confound key has gone to. We'll have to get the locksmith to open it in the morning."

Lisa hated that she couldn't go back for Jack yet and hoped he was safe. Until the police left the hotel, she couldn't return there. What if she could locate Josephine's body and report it to the authorities? The sheriff could arrest the men who'd committed the crime, and she would be safe in this time. And Josephine's body would be put to rest. Well, not all right away, but if she could find Josephine's body, it would be a start.

Then, she could return to her world. The police probably would have vacated the inn. She could grab her satchel and find Jack.

Glancing at her clothes, she realized she couldn't wear jeans, yet the damp gowns would feel clammy and awful. Without a choice, she slipped into the clinging, wet garments and shivered.

After climbing out the window, she followed the wavering small light. The chill in the air nearly froze her. The scant illumination disappeared. "Where are you, Josephine?" she whispered. "Please, show me how to help you."

A dog's barking sent a jolt of panic through her, and she turned to look in the direction of the noise. The orb beckoned her again. Hoping she could locate Josephine's body, Lisa followed the wavering light across the main road and through the woods where the outcropping of rocks led to Table Rock. She raised her skirts and stumbled on the climb as the moon's orange sphere illuminated her way.

When she reached the top of Table Rock, the light wavered over a spot. Her heart pounding, Lisa knelt and touched the heart engraved in the stone that encircled Bill's and Josephine's names. "I'm so sorry. I know you loved him, and he felt the same for you."

The aberration moved back down the cliff. Lisa scrambled after, trying not to break her neck, then headed down a narrow footpath in unfamiliar woods. In the distance, she spied a cemetery filled with several graves. Lisa paused and took a deep breath. She was glad her parents wanted their ashes scattered over the Gulf of Mexico. Visiting a cemetery, *especially* in the dark, made her skin crawl.

She reached the picket gate and pushed it aside. The rusted hinges creaked loud enough to wake the dead. She cringed and headed to where the entity hovered over a couple of headstones. Lisa ran her hands over the cold marble faces and traced the Rogers's names on two. "You wish to be buried here? Where did they take you?"

When the light vanished, the hair on Lisa's arms prickled. "Wait! Where did they hide your body?"

A man chuckled, his voice cracked with age, making Lisa gasp, and she turned. A scraggly, bearded figure—just a shadowy skeleton of a man. Sunken black eyes stared back at her. He smiled. "Seeing things in here, are we? I see things all the time what people say don't exist, but that's 'cuz they say I'm old and crazy. Now, you, you is young and crazy, eh?"

Ignoring him, she rubbed her arms and looked for Josephine's spirit. There was no sign of her. Lisa turned to speak to the old man, but he'd vanished. Chill bumps erupted on her arms and legs. She closed her eyes and took a deep, settling breath. Helping Josephine would have to wait if she wouldn't cooperate. Had enough time passed? Lisa hoped the police were gone by now, and Jack hadn't strayed too far or gotten caught.

The breeze stiffened, sending another chill through her. Lisa moved quickly through the woods toward the road when horses galloped in her direction, filling her with trepidation.

"John Harden told me he left the outfit because he wanted to rob trains. I don't know why we can't. There ain't no money in robbing stagecoaches less'n drummers are ridin' the coach," a redhead said to three other men.

John Wesley Harden? The man who robbed their stagecoach? Which meant the rest of these men had probably been with him. A new shiver trailed up Lisa's spine, and she hurried away from the road.

***

Not wanting to leave Lisa behind in the room for long, Jack hurried to pay for his horse's boarding.

Damned if he could rouse her to come with him. No matter what, he wasn't letting her return to her world so the police could arrest her.

He handed the cash in payment to the livery owner. "Thanks, Mr. Holt."

"My pleasure. Your brother was a might worried about you. Said when you returned he wanted word right away."

Jack tipped his hat to Tucker. "I'm headed there momentarily." *After* he picked up his precious package, hoping she was awake by now.

He tied Spirit to the tree outside room number three's window. Making sure no one noticed him, he sneaked in through the window. Lisa was gone. His heart thundered as he tried to keep his wits.

Her unopened suitcase still sat beside the bed. He searched through the bag of wet clothes, but all that was left was his. Her breeches and sweater lay on the mattress, which had to mean she hadn't returned to her time yet. No sign of a struggle either. He tried the door. Locked. She had to have left through the window. Where would she have gone?

Looking for him, damn it.
Where are you, Lisa?

***

When the dust cleared, Lisa spied the four cowboys riding her way. Not just cowboys. *Outlaws.* Her heart pounding, she ducked into the woods alongside the road.

"Hey!" one of the men shouted. "Did you see that?"

She dove into thick underbrush, then crouched low like a hunted rabbit. The men galloped toward the spot where she had stood beside the road and peered into the forest.

"There she is," one said, pointing at the thicket. Her heart skipping beats and her blood pounding furiously, she felt she nearly had a stroke and ran through the tangled underbrush, heading away from the road. Looking back, she saw the men dismount and pull their horses into the woods, then tie them to trees.

Really not good.

Whooping and hollering, the men crashed through the dried branches and leaves, sending her into a panic. She bolted for an outcropping of rocks. Around these, she spied a cave and stopped briefly.

The Salado inn? The cave where the murderers had dumped her? An irritating shiver shook her. Josephine's murderers were the least of her worries right now. The inn was nowhere in sight. This was a different cave, and she bolted for the entrance.

"Over there," one of the men said, "she's headed for that hole in the hillside."

"Yeehaw!" another shouted.

She'd barely made it inside when the first bearded man grabbed her wrist. She screamed. The redhead chuckled and his gaze shifted from her face to the necklace. "Looky, what have we here."

This close up, she could tell he was older than she first assumed, wisps of gray hair intermingled with the red strands, and wrinkles lined his face. The missing teeth and beard made him seem older, too. His fearsome grip on her wrist proved he wasn't feeble.

He touched the amethyst. "That's mighty pretty, little lady. I think my girly would like to have such a pretty thing."

She tried to back up, to jerk away.

"You don't have a girl, Dallas, you old goat." A younger man shoved him aside. "Let me see that." He examined the necklace. "Yes, that'll do."

"No! You can't have it! I need it."

Dallas sneered. "Don't think she wants to give it up to the likes of you, Easton."

"Oh, I'm sure you want to keep it, but you can see we need it even more than you do. You wouldn't deny us that, would you, miss?" Easton's black eyes sparkled with cold calculation.

"Unless, you have something else that's better you'd like to give us." Dallas leered at her. He pulled at her skirt, and she slapped his hand away.

The others laughed.

Dallas's dingy red hair hadn't been washed in weeks, and his stench made her queasy. His green eyes narrowed, and his yellowed teeth, minus the front upper two, smiled back at her.

"Don't think she wants you either." Easton offered Dallas an evil smile.

"What are you doing out here by your lonesome anyway? Running away from someone or something? You'll join our gang," the gray-haired man said, and Lisa remembered he was the leader when they robbed the stagecoach. "There's no more than fifteen of us at a time, and we could sure use a woman's cooking. Better than you running away from home and getting yourself in real trouble. You do cook, don't you?"

"Yeah, Pa, let's take her back with us. She's awful purty," the youngest man said.

He was the one she recognized as being about the same age as John Wesley Harden, blond, blue-eyed, but he didn't seem the killer type like the rest.

"Hey, Clayton, she'll keep us entertained," Dallas said.

Clayton motioned to her necklace. "We'll let you keep your trinket for a while longer. You just come along with us."

"No!" Lisa screamed and jerked her arm free. She shoved Dallas against Easton and ran down toward the creek. Her heart tripped as she stumbled over loose chunks of rocks. If she'd been wearing jeans, she could've gotten away. Her long skirts snagged on gnarly shrubs, and she faltered on the uneven ground.

How could she have gotten herself in such a predicament? She was angry at herself on the one hand and scared witless on the other.

"Grab her, boys!"

She reached the creek, but the youngest outlaw caught up with her and seized her arm. She twisted free. He reached for her again, and she pushed him hard.

He fell into the creek while the others laughed out loud.

Dallas grabbed her arm. "You're coming with us whether you want to or not."

Easton seized her free arm. He looked like a real charmer, probably bedded whores when he wasn't robbing and killing—handsome, but deadly.

"You only steal from people." She tried to wrench her arms away from the two men. "You don't kidnap anyone."

"Kidnap? You ain't making any sense, woman," Dallas said.

Her mind raced while she tried to think of another argument to win her freedom.

"Is she too much for even a young whipper-snapper, like you, Billy?" Clayton asked when the young man climbed out of the water.

He smiled and pulled at his lightly-whiskered chin. "There's never been a woman who got away from me like that, Pa. Course, they usually don't want to."

The men all laughed.

"Do any of you have rope?" Dallas asked, while Billy removed his shirt and wrung it out, his chest—bare, pale, and scrawny.

They exchanged glances and shook their heads.

"I have some on my saddle," Easton said.

Dallas snorted. "We all do, but that won't do us no good here."

"Somebody get ahold of her good. I'm too old to be running in these woods any longer," Clayton grumbled.

She hit and kicked while Dallas and Easton half-dragged her to their horses. "Please, you don't want to do this."

Billy smiled. "Whatever gave you that idea? I mean to make you my wife."

The others laughed.

Dale yanked rope from his saddle and tied her wrists. The sound of a rider alerted them to trouble and everyone crouched down.

"Someone's coming. We'd better skedaddle, men," Clayton warned.

Lisa screamed to get the rider's attention.

"Keep her quiet, Son."

The outlaws pulled their horses farther into the woods, and Billy clamped his hand tight over her mouth.

Her only hope for escape came into view. *Jack.*

She squirmed and tried to cry out. When the outlaws pulled their revolvers from their holsters, she quieted, her heart thudding hard against her ribs.

Jack stopped his horse and looked into the woods. She barely breathed.

Then he rode off again, and Lisa's heart plummeted.

"That's more like it." Billy took his hand away from her mouth. Tears rolled down her cheeks while the dust and all hope of a rescue faded. Billy pulled her toward his horse.

Lisa balked. "I can't cook."

The men all smiled and shared knowing looks.

"Nobody cares if you can. It's your looks that count." Dallas grabbed a handful of her hair fanned out over her shoulders and held it up to his scruffy face. "Smells like lavender."

"You're going to end up just like those other men in the Salado jail." Lisa twisted her head away from him, trying to jerk her hair free.

"What are you talking about?" Dallas wrenched her arm back and stared at her.

The pain radiated through her arm, and she glared back at him.

"I asked you a question, girly."

"A posse caught the men a while back." She hoped telling them would make them quake in their boots, and they'd let her go. As murderous as their expressions were, she considered it might not have been the best idea she'd had.

Billy spoke up, "We ain't heard from Hanson and his bunch for a couple of weeks, Pa. Maybe she's telling the truth."

"What do you think, boys? Should we scout out the town and find out what we can?" Clayton asked.

Lisa wasn't expecting a democratic leader amongst a bunch of cutthroats.

Dallas kicked the dirt with the tip of his boot. "I'd sure want some of the guys to come get us out if they knew we was in the jailhouse."

Easton nodded, but his eyes remained focused on Lisa, and she didn't have to guess what his intentions concerning her amounted to.

"Two of us will go then, so as not to stir up any suspicions. The other two, stay here with the girl," Clayton said.

Dallas grasped Lisa's chin in his calloused hand. "You'd better be telling the truth, miss, or you'll be wishing you had."

She glowered at him, and his lips curved in an evil smile.

"Pa, don't let him treat her that way."

"Come on, Dallas. You and me'll go on into town. Son, you and Easton stay here. Keep low 'til we return."

The boy led his horse and Lisa back into the woods while she tried to figure out how to escape. Easton's boots clomped on the dried leaves close behind. Her skin crawled.

When the older men left, Easton drew closer. "You know she's not just yours, Billy. When we get back to camp—"

Lisa rotated her arms and tried to free her wrists from the rope while the strands of hemp dug into her skin. "Please, let me go. I'm of no use to you. Besides,

I've got friends who'll come after you, and the sheriff—"

"The sheriff's no threat to us. He'd never find us anyway. As for your friends, I suspect they don't exist." Easton's soulless black eyes pinned her as he reached for her tattered skirt. She backed away. "What were you doing alone in the woods? Running away?" He squinted, his bushy brows knitted together in a scowl. "It's going to take your pa and old Dallas a while, Billy. Why don't we make the most of our time with the girl? When we get back to camp there's so many of us, we'll never have a chance like this again."

Billy considered her hair, then ran his hand over her tresses. His grimy hands made her flinch. His gaze shifted toward town. She had a chance with Billy, maybe. She couldn't be certain, but he wasn't as hardened as the other men.

"I ain't scared, even if you are, Billy. Watch if you like. I'll show you how a real man does it." Easton took a menacing step toward her.

She threw her tied hands into the air to block his advance. With a scream, she stepped back. Her heart was ready to leap out of her chest. He snatched her hands. Turning them, she couldn't free herself. She kicked at him instead.

Easton dodged her kick and laughed. "Feisty, ain't you?"

"You can't do it, Easton." Billy ran his horse's reins through his fingers.

"What? You gonna stop me?" Easton put his hand to his revolver.

"Please, don't." As soon as she said it, she chastised herself. If one killed the other that would be a good thing, wouldn't it? But what if Easton killed the boy? He seemed her only hope of escape.

Easton laughed. "I think she's got a hankering for you. Too bad."

"I won't let him touch you, miss." Billy stepped in front of her and faced Easton.

"Hell, what's the matter with you? What did you expect would happen to her when we got back to camp, eh?"

Billy stood his ground and Easton's face darkened. "You ain't nothing but a scared pup. If your pa and the others wouldn't have me run through I'd just as soon kill you here and now. But you ain't stopping me from getting my pleasure with the girl so step aside, or I'll wallop you good."

Billy swung at Easton. The bigger man blocked the blow and punched Billy in the stomach. Lisa gasped. Billy grabbed his waist and groaned in pain.

She backed away.

Easton glanced at her and sneered. "Your turn's next, Missy, only it'll be a might more pleasurable."

Billy recovered and charged Easton like a runaway bull, ramming him in the chest with the full force of his skull. Easton grunted and gasped for air. Stumbling backwards, he fell on his butt.

Lisa sprinted for the road.

CHAPTER 18

The branches slapped at Lisa's face as she made a desperate dash through the woods. Stumbling over an exposed tree root, she cried out and fell to the mossy forest floor. The leaves rustled behind her, putting the fear of the devil in her again.

Easton shouted, "If she gets away, it'll all be your fault, and your pa will have your scrawny hide!"

She scrambled to her feet and bolted for the road. Her heart was about to give out and shin splints were shooting streaks of pain though her legs. She wasn't going to make it.

"Pa won't like it you were messing with the girl."

Easton gave a dark laugh. "You just don't get it, do you?"

Once she reached the clearing next to the road, a horse's hooves pounded the road, sending the dirt flying. She hesitated. Thinking she recognized the rider on the paint, she ran into the road and cried, "Jack!"

He smiled and pulled her into his saddle. "Name's

Matthew. Jack's brother. Everyone says there's a family resemblance. You must be Lisa."

He wasn't the knight she'd expected, but he'd do.

The sound of a horse galloping behind them made her cringe with a fresh wave of fear. Matthew glanced over his shoulder. "Jack, it's about time you got here. Someone's sure to be glad to see you."

Jack aimed his gun at the woods where Easton and Billy dropped to the ground and grabbed their revolvers. Gunshots exploded and Lisa instinctively ducked.

Jack pulled in alongside his brother. "Are you all right, Lisa?"

"Yes." As all right as she could be, but she couldn't quit shaking.

After another twenty minutes, they rode in through a gate and headed for a two-story ranch home shaded by live oaks. A sweeping veranda and rockers dancing in the breeze made her at once feel welcome.

Matthew reigned his horse in at the porch. Before he could dismount, Jack joined them and lifted Lisa from his brother's saddle.

"What in the blazes happened?" Jack asked, crushing her to his chest.

His embrace comforted her, and she ignored the harshness of his words, knowing he'd probably been scared witless about her safety. Secure in his heat, she felt the shivers wracking her body quieting.

She opened her mouth to speak, but he raved on. "I couldn't wake you at the inn so I got my horse, and when I returned, you were gone."

"Josephine led me to the cemetery. She was trying to tell me something."

His face dark, he shook his head. "You can't be wandering these parts alone. It's too dangerous."

"I wanted to help Josephine. I couldn't find you. What was I supposed to do?" Before he could answer, she asked, "Why are we here? I need to return to the inn and get my satchel so I can clear my name."

"Later. We've got another problem we have to deal with." Jack's expression was so foreboding, she wondered what else could be the matter.

A woman walked out of the house, and Lisa stared in disbelief. "Esmeralda," she whispered. The woman looked just like the medium she'd visited.

Jack's grip tightened around Lisa's waist. "You know Esmeralda?"

Matthew removed his hat and scratched his head. "Josephine?"

Lisa said, "I...I met a woman named Esmeralda Esperazo in my time who was a spiritualist."

Jack finally released his breath.

Esmeralda smiled. "A descendent of mine, no doubt. Come." She motioned to the house. "We eat. I have a dress you can change into."

Lisa considered her tattered gown and tangled hair. She had to look a sight.

Before they could move from the veranda, five cowboys headed in their direction. She wanted to vanish before they could get close enough to see how awful she looked. A flood of heat swept through her as the new arrivals smiled and tipped their hats in greeting with a chorus of "Ma'ams."

The men clustered around, and then Jack said, "Lisa, these are my ranch hands. Hank and Reb Anderson are brothers and do a prime job at breaking new horses. Tommy Thompson overseas the men when Matthew and I aren't around. Rory Campbell repairs anything that needs fixing. And Andy McNeil's a natural at driving cattle. Gentlemen, this is my fiance, Lisa Welsh."

More smiles and "How do you dos."

Thankfully, Esmeralda took Lisa's arm and guided her into the house. "You can use one of our guestrooms to get cleaned up. I'll bring you a gown."

A washing machine and hot shower was what Lisa really wanted.

Matthew steered the men into the dining room, but Jack seemed to want to join Lisa. He looked so worried, she wondered what the matter was. Now that the cowboys were here, who looked like they could handle any menace, she figured she was safe.

After she changed into a blue gingham dress and joined everyone in the dining room, she meant to help Esmeralda serve the food. But she wouldn't hear of it. Jack pulled a chair out for Lisa, although Andy had hurried to do it.

Never had so many males acted this intrigued with her, and heat filled every pore again. Maybe their interest was because Jack was marrying her, he was their boss, and she would become the lady of the house. The reason didn't matter. Feeling self-conscious, she avoided looking in their direction.

Tommy snatched a muffin from a platter and passed the silver tray down the table. "When's the weddin', boss?"

Jack had been eying her—making Lisa even more ill at ease—but he finally gave Tommy his attention. "As soon as supper's done, I want you to fetch the reverend."

That brought a fresh rash of smiles to the table.

"We thought the boss was keeping you secret, Ma'am," Reb said, and offered his brother Hank a conspirator's wink.

Rory chuckled, then coughed when Jack gave him a hard look.

"They've been asking about you since they first learned Jack was seeing you," Matthew explained.

"Ah." Lisa didn't know what to say. Overwhelmed by all the male interest, she was immensely relieved when the men started talking about their next cattle drive, and she began to relax.

That's when she noticed the rack of rifles hanging on a wall, dishes on shelves, Stetsons propped on pegs. Everything was very utilitarian. They didn't have much of anything frivolous—not like what she had filling her apartment.

Her gaze caught Jack's. Frowning, he took her hand. "Is everything all right, Lisa?"

She managed a smile, though his anxiousness was adding to her own. "Yes."

The conversation died and everyone watched their interaction. Again, the smiles. She imagined they must not have seen Jack show a woman any attention. Although he had been engaged before. Maybe they had acted the same way with her.

Lisa's skin heated, and she concentrated on her meal.

Not long after, the men thanked Esmeralda and said goodnight to Lisa. She could just imagine what they'd say back in the bunkhouse.

"Lisa, we've got to talk before…" Jack quit

speaking, looking as uncomfortable as before.

Matthew grabbed his hat. "I'll take care of our horses."

Lisa carried two of the empty platters into the kitchen. "I should help Esmeralda with the dishes."

Esmeralda shook her head. "You and Jack need to talk."

She sounded as worried as Jack looked. If it was about returning to Lisa's time so she could clear her name, she wasn't about to change her mind.

Jack took her arm and led her into a parlor. The couch was a Queen Victorian style with clawed feet just like the one in her apartment, only the fabric was a burgundy instead of blue and the cushions didn't look half as comfortable as the new ones she'd made for hers.

The photograph of her and Jack sat on the mantle, and she smiled at the way he was smiling in the photo. Over the fireplace, a portrait of a man and woman hung, their expressions somber, but the father looked very much like Jack and Matthew, only sterner.

Shattering her perusal of the room, Jack pulled her to the couch, made her sit, and began to pace. Whatever was the matter was making her even more nervous than the interest she'd garnered from his ranch hands.

"What's wrong, Jack? If it's about my going back—"

"It's about staying here."

She opened her mouth to speak, then clamped her lips shut. He'd changed his mind about her? Maybe because his men were making such a big deal of their relationship and Jack didn't like it?

Jack stared out the window.

Her skin chilled in anticipation.

He faced her, his expression haunted. "Do you remember when I talked about the picnic?"

"Yes. You were going to take me there, but then... I was at the cave, and somehow found my way to the creek. We never made it to the picnic."

Jack sat next to her and took her hand. "Lisa, I didn't want to mention this. I'd hoped, well, prayed it wouldn't happen again. I can't help worrying..." He leaned over and kissed her cheek. "I love you with all my heart. I don't want to ever lose you."

"But?" Lisa had the sickening feeling Jack had decided for whatever reason, he didn't want her any more, despite what he said. She clenched her teeth and waited for the bad news.

"You weren't yourself."

She frowned. "What?"

He tightened his hold on her hand. "Blame it all, Lisa. You weren't you. I mean to say you were Josephine."

"Oh now, don't you start saying I'm Josephine all over again. After everything that has happened between us?" She broke his grip on her hand and stood. "How can you think I'm her, when—"

"No, Lisa. Her spirit. Dash it all, she became you. You became her. She...well, hell, she possessed you."

Lisa stared at Jack, his expression sincere but anxious. He couldn't mean what he was saying. He was mistaken. "That's not possible."

"You said she helped you find your way out of the cave."

"Yes, she did. So she aided me."

"To make sure you didn't end up dead."

"When you left me at the room, she led me to Table Rock to show me, I guess in the event I didn't know, who she was and who she loved. She took me to the cemetery where I assumed she wanted to be buried. She didn't possess me. Why wouldn't she have if she wants my body? I…I don't believe she wants anything more than to be found and properly buried."

Jack rubbed his chin and stared at the floor for a moment. "After she led you out of the cave, I found you at the creek, and she took control of you."

Lisa's head spun and she sagged. Jack jumped from the couch and helped her sit back down.

"I don't remember. I recall drinking from the cold creek. I saw you and…" She waited for Jack to fill her in.

"You were Josephine. You knew my brother, Esmeralda, the ranch. You went up to Table Rock with Bill. Someone hit Bill up there, but I guess you wouldn't know who."

Her skin prickling with anxiety, she shook her head. "I don't remember."

"I took you back to the inn, and we ended up in your time. It broke Josephine's hold over you."

"She haunts me. Back home, she comes to me in my nightmares. Why didn't you tell me about this?"

"I hoped it wouldn't happen again. I wanted you to be here with me forever. When you recognized Esmeralda, I feared you had become Josephine again."

Matthew cleared his throat at the entryway of the parlor and motioned to Jack. "Reverend's here."

Jack gave her hand another squeeze. "I'll have to sign a couple of papers. I'll be right back."

Matthew gave her a big smile, and then hurried

after his brother.

Lisa rubbed her temple, unable to clear the fogginess filling her thoughts. Still, no matter how much she tried, she couldn't remember what had occurred after she had seen Jack at the creek, or before she ended up back in her time.

A fragrance wafted in the room. *Violets.* She smelled the strong sweet smell, just before the air began to chill.

***

Jack rushed through the papers while his men waited to witness the wedding. "It's not necessary for all of you to be here." He handed the forms to Reverend Cochrane.

None of his ranch hands budged from the dining room.

Matthew gave Jack their mother's ring. "It's now or never."

Mr. Cochrane shook his head. "I'm delighted, of course, that you've decided to marry. But couldn't you have waited to have a church ceremony?"

Reb chuckled.

Jack cut him a glare.

Reb just smiled, not bothering to look the least bit contrite. His brother wore the same sappy expression.

"Let's get this over with, Reverend." Jack led the group into the parlor, but Lisa wasn't there. His heart stumbled, and he headed for the guest room.

Matthew hollered from the parlor, "She's outside, walking toward the gate."

Jack hoped his worst fear hadn't been realized as he rushed out of the house after her.

She swung around and glared at him. His outlook

on life collapsed inward in one big dusty heap.

"What in the world am I doing here again, Jack? Matthew? Where's Bill?"

With his heart in his throat, Jack said, "I'm taking you into town to see him." As much as he didn't want to lose her, he had to return her home, clear her name, and leave her there until he could figure a way to deal with this dilemma with Josephine.

"Where is Bill?"

The notion she wanted to see him, rankled Jack and his gut clenched. "He said he'd meet us at the inn."

"At the inn?" She narrowed her eyes. "What's going on?"

"Nothing. He just said I'm to take you there. Do you remember anything about what occurred earlier today?"

She lowered her gaze to the ground. "No, not a thing, except—"

Hope sprang up in the pit of his stomach. If he could only reach her while she was Josephine...

"I don't remember."

Jack's shoulders slumped and he turned to the reverend. "We'll have to do this some other time. Reb, can you and your brother hook up the buggy? Esmeralda, why don't you fix some coffee and pie for the reverend. Matthew, you come with me while I take Josephine into town."

Matthew saddled his horse while Jack helped Josephine into the buggy, trying to ignore the way that his men hovered about, their expressions puzzled.

"What a beautiful carriage. Bill doesn't have anything half as nice as this." She ran her hand over the black leather seat. "The leather smells like new." She took a deep breath. "Hmm."

Her purring stirred Jack's loins and he longed to pull her close and kiss her, to draw Lisa back to him. But he couldn't. Josephine loved Bill not him. The very notion made him ill.

Matthew rode ahead as Jack guided the buggy into town.

Josephine wrung her hands, but didn't say anything. She kept looking toward the woods, and he wondered if she had any recollection about the outlaws. But he didn't want to pursue it.

When the town came into view, dark curls framing her face, her blue eyes bright with humor, Mary Lou, ran out of the mercantile and grabbed at Matthew's reins. For an instant, Jack just stared at her, realizing what he had thought was the case was really true. Except her hair was shorter and her eyes brown, Lisa's girlfriend, Pauline, resembled Mary Lou.

Matthew stopped, dismounted, and looked at Jack for approval. Since Josephine was behaving, he assumed he didn't need his brother's help. He waved him on.

Matthew tied up his horse and walked down the main street with Mary Lou. They had their ups and downs. But their problems were nothing like Jack's and Lisa's.

Disquieted about what he had to do next, Jack continued to the hotel.

Josephine stretched her arms above her head. "Looks like Matthew finally got Mary Lou's attention."

"Her father's the only thing stopping him from asking her to marry him."

"What's wrong with her father?"

"He's hoping she'll marry the mill owner's son instead."

"Oh. Well, he's rather smitten with someone else I hear."

Lisa wouldn't know the town gossip. That shattered any illusion Jack had that the woman sitting beside him was Lisa.

The inn came into sight and she shouted, "Stop! Stop here!"

He looked at her and stopped the buggy. "What's the matter—"

"I can't go back." She jumped from the carriage and ran off.

"Lisa!" Jack yelled after her. His blood sizzling, he looked for a place to park the rig, jumped down, and tied the horse to the hitching post. A hand grabbed his arm, and he turned with a start to see the maid from the inn.

"It was awfully rude of you to ask me to the picnic, and then leave me alone. But I'm a forgiving sort of soul and if you ask me out, I could show you how nice I could be."

He tried to get around her, but the woman seized his jacket.

"It was a mistake," he growled.

"What?" the maid said, raising her voice.

He jerked her hand from his jacket and sprinted to the last location he'd seen Lisa.

Finding no sign of her, he began to search the side alleys. He had to return her to her time and break Josephine's spell over her.

***

Josephine ran down the alley by the inn, hoping to

evade Jack. Where in the world could she go? The room she'd stayed in seemed menacing, though she couldn't remember why. She just couldn't return there.

Something moved in the dark, a shadow. The figure came into view, a raven-haired man, eyes as black as a moonless night and the sinister look flickering in them warned her he meant business. She whirled around, but before she could get far, his boots pounded the dirt in her direction, and he grabbed her arm. Afraid of giving Jack her position, she gulped a scream.

"My, my, lookee what we have. I've been hanging around here on and off for some time, scouting out the jailhouse and hoping to get you in my sights. What a rewarding day this is to get my hands on you again." Pinning her against his hard body, he tried to kiss her lips.

She quickly turned her head. He kissed her on the cheek, his stickery stubble raking across her skin. He laughed. "You didn't think you'd get away that easy, did you?"

She pried at his firm fingers gripping her arm and glowered at him. First, Jack was giving her orders, now this varmint, whoever he was. His threatening posture scared her some, but her determination to find Bill overwhelmed her fear.

She'd tell him yes, she'd marry him in no uncertain terms. The thought of being saddled with squalling babies didn't appeal. She couldn't help worrying she might suffer her aunt's fate, but a gnawing inside cautioned her she had to make things right with Bill before it was too late.

The man held her tight against his chest. "No

TERRY SPEAR

woman's ever given me the slip before. You won't be
the first. Not only that, but do you see this black eye?"
He pointed to his face. "Billy's pa give it to me. I ain't
none too happy about it. So you're coming back with
me 'cuz we've got some unfinished business to tend to,
Missy."

He dragged her toward his horse tethered in the
alley. Who in the world was this guy?

"Billy will be mighty pleased to see you again.
He's talked of nothing else since we lost you. I've
never seen such a hard case of unrequited love."

"I don't know who you are, mister, but you'd better
let go of me now or— "

"You don't remember me? That's hard to believe.
Easton's the name."

"I still don't—"

The familiar tapping of the hotel manager's cane a
little ways off silenced her. She stopped on her captor's
foot with the heel of her boot.

Easton cried out and yanked her arm behind her.
Her eyes watered.

"You like it rough, eh?" He lifted his hand to slap
her.

She raised her arm to block his blow.

Just then a man snatched his arm and said in a low
growl, "Let the lady go, mister, and you won't get
hurt."

"Bill!" she cried.

"Just you wait here, Missy, while I take care of
your...beau?" Easton jerked free of Bill. Easton
fingered his revolver.

"No!" She turned to Bill and hoped he wouldn't
challenge the lunatic. "He's a killer."

"The lady's right. Easton Wilcox is the name, and I've killed more men than I imagine you ever have, Cowboy."

"I fought in the War like anybody else."

"I'm quaking in my boots." Easton aimed at Bill.

Josephine shoved Easton's arm down and the bullet ricocheted off the ground.

"Get back, Josephine!" Bill shouted, yanking his gun out of the holster and fired.

Grabbing his chest, Easton aimed again, hitting Bill this time. When Easton dropped to the ground in a dead heap, Bill's jaw sagged. He touched the blood seeping from the wound in his chest and looked surprised. He collapsed.

"Oh, God, no!" Her heart breaking, Josephine ran to him and dropped to her knees, lifting his hand to her chest. "You can't die. I won't let you," she sobbed, rocking back and forth, shaking her head. Filled with despair, she couldn't believe she'd lose him now when she was willing to marry him...to love him forever. "Bill, Bill," she moaned. "I've come back for you. You can't leave me now." Tears rolled down her cheeks, and she tried to blink them back, but they blurred her vision, and she could barely see her beloved.

He reached for her. "We'll be together again, Josephine." His calloused fingers touched her lips, his hand dropped to his chest, and he closed his eyes with one last shudder.

**

Gunshots rang out near the inn, and Jack's stomach twisted into knots. He raced down the street and bolted into the alley. Josephine was weeping, hugging Bill's limp body. Jack tried to pull her away, but she clung to

Bill. The notion Bill's death tore her up inside furthered his own disquiet.

She sobbed. "You can't leave me now."

A cane came to rest near Bill's foot. Josephine jumped up and backed away from Mr. Daemon. "You!" She stumbled and tripped over Easton's prone body, falling backward.

Jack reached for her, but she pushed his hands away and glowered at the manager, his look sympathetic, brows marginally pinched, mouth curved slightly down and shook his head as if in disbelief.

Before Jack could react, Josephine dashed off toward Table Rock.

His jaw and fists clenched, Jack bolted after her. "Lisa!" He shook his head. "Damn it," he said under his breath. "Josephine! Come back!"

She clambered up to Table Rock. His heart pulverizing his ribs, Jack reached the top and found her staring down at the rocks below. He knew what she had in mind to do. He'd contemplated the very same thing when he'd lost Charlotte. He inched his way toward her as she wavered at the edge.

"Josephine," he said with a firm but gentle voice. She didn't respond. He extended his hand to her, willing her to come to him.

She turned her head toward him and narrowed her eyes. "I'm not Lisa!" Tears dribbled down her cheeks. "Leave me be!"

"Josephine doesn't belong here. She died, and it's Lisa's turn to live."

As if she was considering his words, she stared at him. "No, I'm Josephine, sure enough. I don't know what's gotten into you." She looked over the cliff.

His heart skipped a beat, and he dove for her.

She reached her arms heavenward and took a step forward, crying out Bill's name.

Rushing forward, Jack grabbed her arm as she slipped over the edge. She screamed and hit her head on the side of the stone.

"Lisa!" he yelled, his throat dry, his head pounding as he held on tight. "Lisa!"

She was unresponsive. With a tentative hold on her, he drew her lifeless form up.

Josephine didn't seem to have a clue that she'd taken Lisa's place. To her, she truly was Josephine, and her body was hers to do with as she pleased. Worse, he didn't know what to do next.

"Need some help?"

Mr. Daemon stood over him, holding the cane in his hand. Jack hadn't even heard him arrive.

Matthew ran up beside the manager, dropped to his stomach, and reached for Lisa.

Between the two of them, they pulled Lisa onto the rock. Calling to her, Jack lifted her from the stone and tried to bring her around. She stirred slightly and his heart elevated.

Jack turned to ask Mr. Daemon if he'd seen the confrontation between Bill and the other man, but the manager was already headed back down the hill. "Dear God, Lisa," Jack said, holding her tightly against his chest.

Matthew helped him to stand. "What now, Jack?"

"I've got to get her back to the inn."

"Somehow I thought you'd say that."

Jack carried Lisa back down the hill as Matthew hurried beside him. When they reached the bottom, Lisa groaned and opened her eyes. "What happened?"

"Lisa?" he asked, his voice an octave higher than normal. She was back, and his heart leaped bounds. "Has this terrible curse been lifted?"

She reached for her temple where the stone had met her forehead and winced.

"We're going to find that satchel and clear your name."

She offered the prettiest smile, and it warmed him all the way through.

"Thank you, Jack." She sighed. "I love you."

Matthew cleared his throat. "What about the reverend?"

"Later," Jack said. "Do you recollect anything at all about Bill?"

"What about Bill?" Lisa asked, her brows knit together.

"Do you remember the gunman?"

"No, my head hurts when I try to think back. What happened to Bill?"

Matthew shrugged. "She'll find out sooner or later."

***

Tension began to fill Lisa with foreboding. She realized then she was missing more of her memories. How had she hurt her head? What had happened now?

Heading in the direction of the hotel, Jack let out his breath. "I was trying to return you to the hotel and a gunman shot Bill near there."

Omigod... She barely breathed. "Shot Bill? He's all right, isn't he?"

"I'm sorry, no. He died right away."

Her eyes watered and her stomach revolted.

Josephine died, now Bill. She choked on a sob. What if…what if now that Bill was dead, Josephine wouldn't have any need to come back. Yet as soon as Lisa considered the possibility, she hated herself for even thinking it. Bill was dead, cut short in the prime of life just like Josephine.

Jack embraced her tighter as he neared the hotel.

She swallowed hard. "What happened to the gunman?"

"Bill shot him and the gunman died. You don't recollect any of this?"

"I was there?"

"We all were."

"But why can't I recall?"

Jack sighed. "You had become Josephine. There's nothing left of you when it happens."

Feeling violated, a shiver skittered across her bones. She couldn't imagine what it must be like for Jack when it happened, but she couldn't understand how she wouldn't sense some of herself during the time either. The notion she was saying and doing things she had no control over made her skin crawl.

"Matthew, watch our backs while we sneak into the room at the inn." Jack set Lisa on her feet, and she felt dizzy.

She clung to him, and his expression turned concerned, but she shook her head slightly. "I'm all right. Now if we can just avoid the police."

"Police?" Matthew asked.

"Deputies," Lisa clarified, "hopefully we can straighten this matter out." She wasn't sure about the situation with Josephine. Maybe she could get in touch with Esmeralda in her time. Would she know how to exorcise a ghost in the past? Though Lisa suspected she had to locate Josephine's body and put it to rest. Yet, she still hoped Bill's death had broken the spell that Josephine could wield over her.

With a heavy sense of foreboding, she and Jack slipped back in through the window in room number three. They waved to Matthew, who looked as anxious as Jack and she felt.

Before she and Jack could prepare themselves to transport across time barriers, the overwhelming fragrance of violets and a chill pervaded the air.

CHAPTER 19

When Lisa woke, Jack was sound asleep, holding her tight in his arms, pinning her against the mattress in present day Salado. She listened for any sign of the police. *Nothing.* Just the whisper of Jack's warm breath tickling her ear and a bird singing outside the window.

She wished she could enjoy his hard body, pressed against hers, but she was afraid the police would catch them. "Jack," she whispered. "Jack, wake up."

His lips curved up a tad, but his eyes remained closed. He slid his hand over her breast, and she groaned. "Not now. We need to get the satchel."

His eyes popped open, he glanced around the room, ran his hand through his hair, and grumbled. "I thought we were home in bed and the reverend already had married us."

"I wish. It looks like that's not happening until we resolve this situation with Josephine. First, we have another problem."

"The satchel."

"Yeah, and while I was lying here trying to remember what had happened, I realized I had taken the satchel with me to this room. I didn't leave it behind in room number two, because someone might have found it. So I kept it with me."

"And put it under the bed."

"I would have, but dizziness overwhelmed me when I went to the past. I collapsed on the bed and wouldn't have had time to do anything with it."

"So where would it be now?"

"With the hotel staff in the past? If they came into the room, they would have taken it."

"And your luggage, my damp clothes in the bag, and your sweater and jeans on the bed. All were gone." He let out his breath. "All right, but I don't want you going back there. Too dangerous. Do you think the necklace will work if I wear it?"

"I don't want us to get separated. What if something happened to you, and you couldn't return? I'd be stuck here and you'd be in the past. We have another problem if I return."

"Josephine." He stroked Lisa's arm and kissed her cheek.

She sighed and snuggled tighter, loving the feel of his hot, hard body. "Yeah. I smelled violets and the air turn frigid right before we came here. The occurrences finally triggered a memory of it happening prior to my losing a sense of place and time. The same thing happened when she approached the other times when she was trying to show me something—a way out of the cave, the carving of Bill's name with hers. I don't know when she wants help, and when she wants much more."

"But you recognized it this time."

"Yes. The problem is that if I'm not in this room, I can't leave to return here and escape her influence. I don't seem to have any power over her."

"I'll see the hotel staff, while you stay here. If Josephine comes for you, return to your world, and come back in a half hour or so. I should have the satchel by then, and we can return to your place, turn it in to whomever needs it, and go from there."

Lisa didn't have a good feeling about this, but she figured Jack was probably right. With her hand in Jack's, they returned to the past and after the disorientation faded, he kissed her like there would be no tomorrow. She wished everything was resolved, that they were married and in his bed back at the ranch.

Jack sighed, released her, and headed for the window when voices approached.

"Where did you get this?" Mr. Worthington asked.

"The maid found it in the room on the bed when Lisa Welsh left," Mr. Daemon said.

"Burn it."

"You should look at it. It's really unusual...has all kinds of figures. I thought maybe it was a document that exposed some of our finagling, but I couldn't make it out. The amounts are so high it doesn't make any sense."

"Leave it in the office, Mr. Daemon. I'll see to it later. We've got a stagecoach load of passengers coming in we need to accommodate. First, I need to ensure the rooms are ready."

"You'll take care of the satchel?"

"Don't I always take care of your messes?"

"The last couple haven't been satisfactorily resolved, Mister Worthington."

"They will be. Just you do your part."

The conversation stopped and the two men continued to walk past the room.

Jack asked Lisa, "What does the satchel look like?"

"Black leather. About so big." She demonstrated with her hands. "Are you sure you don't want me to go with you?"

"No, I won't risk it." He opened the door and peered out. "I'll be right back." Then he shut the door.

She listened for his fading footsteps until she couldn't hear them. Her arms chilled, but not from the cold in the air. She couldn't help feeling something would go wrong.

Sitting on the edge of the bed, she waited, listening for Jack's return, watching for any sign of Josephine's presence. *Nothing.*

Heavy footfalls approached the room. Heavy, multiple, not one pair of footsteps like it should have been. They stopped in front of the door. Lisa grabbed the necklace. The doorknob twisted.

"It's unlocked," Mr. Worthington said.

"Fine, we'll put him in here. We'll take care of him later," Mr. Daemon said.

The door began to open. Lisa yanked the chain over her head. After several minutes, she realized she was in the room in her time, but she had to get back to Jack. But how could she return, if they put some man in the room?

She paced, glanced at her watch, paced some more. She could barely wait five minutes, let alone any longer. Risking it, she put the necklace back over her head.

When Lisa came to, she was lying in the bed of

room three, the satchel at her side, and Jack was trussed up next to her, his eyes closed. She bolted from the bed, her heart racing. Mr. Worthington and Daemon weren't here. She took a settling breath and linked her arm with Jack's, grabbed the satchel, and transported them to her world. Calling to him, she untied the ropes around Jack's wrists, then his ankles. The back of his head had a knot, and she imagined they'd bushwhacked him. *The bastards.*

He groaned and she gathered him in her arms and held on tight. "Jack, can you hear me?"

His eyes opened halfway. "What...what happened?" His eyes widened. "The satchel."

"We've got it. Thanks to you."

He gently rubbed his head. "I saw the satchel on a desk in the office behind the check-in counter, and heard commotion behind me, but I reacted too late."

Lisa hugged him tight and kissed his cheek. "I'm so sorry. Are you okay?"

He swung his legs over the edge of the mattress. "I'll be fine. Who hit me?"

"Probably Daemon or Worthington. They must have been the ones who killed Josephine."

"We'll need evidence when we return."

"Yeah. We'll take care of them, too." No way was she letting them get away with Josephine's murder. Lisa went to the window and peered out, her heart doing a flip. "Oh, just terrific. My car's gone."

Now what? *Pauline.* If anyone could get her out of this trouble, it was her friend. Lisa reached for the phone and called her. A muffled voice responded.

"Pauline? It's me. Can you pick me up in Salado? I need to get..." The line went dead, and she stared at the phone. "Hello?"

Before she could redial, footsteps approached the room. Lisa grabbed Jack's hand, and he snatched up the satchel.

A key twisted in the keyhole, and she glanced at her gingham dress. *It'll have to do.* She climbed out the window, and Jack followed after. He shut it behind him, then they both dashed for the creek.

"What's the plan?" he asked.

She led them to the main road. "Post office. We'll ship the documents to the DA's office. District Attorney's," she clarified. "I really have an awful feeling about this whole situation. The more I stay out of it, the better." Although she wanted to return to her place and pick up the old currency Pauline was to get for her. No sense in leaving all her money behind. She realized with inflation, she'd be rich. Well, she and Jack would be.

"Maybe I should handle it. You stay at the hotel."

"Not on your life. We're in on this together."

"I'd rather we were in on things together that didn't risk your life."

She gave him a half smile. "Either of our lives, Jack."

After walking a mile and a half, she spied the post office and made a dash across the street with Jack. Inside, the clerk considered their clothing and raised a brow. "Festival going on in town?"

"Out of town. I want to buy an envelope to ship this." Lisa set the satchel on the counter.

"Sure thing."

She realized a new problem as she fumbled through her purse and found only the money from years past. She wasn't sure when, but she must have lost her credit card. "I only have this." Lisa handed the crisp new bills minted in 1869 to the postal employee.

He looked at the money, then raised his gaze to her. His expression said it all. She was either playing Halloween a few days late, or she was trying to rip off the U.S. Postal Service.

"It's a joke, right?" he asked.

"The money's valuable, and I've got to mail the package to the District Attorney's Office. It's extremely important."

"Life or death?"

"Maybe."

"We don't ship anything unless we get money up front."

"I gave you the cash, more valuable than today's currency."

Offering his support, Jack rested his hand on the small of her back.

"If it was genuine. Committing a crime here is a federal offense."

"They're real." She frowned at him. "Any dealer could tell you that."

"The bills are too new to be authentic. You should have aged them a bit before you tried to pass them off for the real thing."

"But—"

"If you wish to pursue this, I'll contact the authorities and let them decide."

Lisa dug around in her purse, but still couldn't locate her credit card. *Just great.*

She gave him a small smile. "I'll be back." After grabbing the money and her satchel, she headed for the door with Jack at her side.

"What now?"

"We'll go to the antique store where I bought the necklace. I'll sell the money for today's currency, then we'll return here and ship the documents."

When they neared the shop, a police car drove along the main street. Adrenaline flooding her body, she took a misstep, and Jack tightened his grip on her arm. To her horror, the patrol car slowed and the policeman watched her. Fighting the urge to run, she took great strides to get to the shop.

Did he know who she was? She envisioned wanted posters hanging up all over town. At least fliers weren't in the post office, *yet.*

She jerked the door to the antique shop open. The doorbell jingled and Jack shut the door behind them.

"Are you the owner?" Lisa asked the clerk, an old woman behind the even older wooden counter.

Jack watched out the window.

"No, the manager," the woman said, her dark eyes glancing from Jack to Lisa. "May I help you with something?"

"Yes, I have some old money I'd like to sell."

The woman examined the currency with a magnifying glass. "Dated 1869. Two-dollar legal tender note." She shook her head. "I'm sorry. You'll have to return and show it to the owner. I don't buy the merchandise for the store. She'll be here later this afternoon. She always checks in before closing time."

"Oh, no that'll be too late."

"Too late?" The woman's gray brows rose.

"Yes, I need to get this mailed before the post office closes, but I found I didn't have the money to—"

The lady's gaze shifted to Lisa's necklace. "If you're interested in selling that, I might be willing to buy it, depending on the price."

Lisa touched the amethyst. "I couldn't— "

The doorbell jingled as the policeman entered the store. He removed his hat and smoothed his inky black hair back. "Lisa Welsh?"

Jack looked like he was about to interfere, but Lisa gave him a slight shake of her head, warning him to stay out of it. Her heart pounded, and she couldn't quiet her trembling legs. She touched the necklace and clutched the satchel tightly in her fist.

The officer took hold of her arm and headed out the door. "May I have a word with you?"

Lisa glanced at the street and freedom.

"Do you mind sitting in the squad car for a minute?"

The doorbell jingled, and she looked back. Jack exited the store, but kept his distance. She couldn't help worrying he'd do something foolish. She remembered, belatedly, he carried his gun—*loaded gun*.

"I have to mail this package to the DA's office. Please, it's very important," she said to the officer.

He looked at the satchel and motioned to the vehicle. "Have a seat."

"You have to understand. A man in Waco has embezzled half-a-million dollars in funds from an accounting firm, and they're trying to pin the theft on me."

"You don't say?"

Her heart thundering, she handed the satchel to the policeman. "These are the original documents concerning the accounting scam." There was no way she was going to allow him to lock her away for a crime she didn't commit.

He refused to take the satchel. "I don't know anything about figures, Ma'am. Just sit in the car, and we'll wait for some other folks to arrive."

"Are you arresting me?"

"Arresting you? No, detaining you. My orders are to hold you until the others arrived."

"Others? Please, let me mail the documents. Afterward, you can arrest me or detain me or whatever you like."

"Just sit tight." The policeman assisted Lisa into the front seat of his car and made a call. "Yes, I've got her. All right. She wants to mail a package to the DA. No? Okay." The man leaned into the car. "They don't want you to mail anything. They'll be here any minute."

She touched the necklace. She had done her part, now it was someone else's job to take care of the matter. "You seem decent."

He smiled. "I try to be."

Laying the satchel on the driver's seat, she patted it. "The evidence is in here, and it needs to go to the District Attorney's office." She rubbed the amethyst stone. "I'm sorry to have caused you any inconvenience."

He frowned. "What inconvenience?"

This. She bolted from the car and ran for the inn, hoping Jack would follow somehow and the officer wouldn't shoot them both. She ran down the hill to the creek.

"Halt!" he yelled and slammed the car door shut, then ran after her.

She dashed through the cold creek. Her gown soaked up the water and weighted her down. She slipped on the mossy rocks, falling twice, hands down in the water.

When she stumbled up the other side of the bank, she saw the policemen hesitate, then run through the creek after her. He quickly fell, dousing himself good, and swore.

Four unmarked cars pulled in beside the vacant police car at the antique store. *Ohmigod.* She'd never make it now.

The manager ran out of the store and pointed toward the creek. "They went that way!"

Where is Jack?

The men in suits returned to their cars and drove after her. All hope was lost that she'd make her escape. Before she was halfway to the inn, they jumped out of their cars. Giving her a near heart attack, the soaking wet policeman pursuing her grabbed her arm from behind.

"I'm sorry," she said nearly out of breath, fighting tears of desperation.

"You shouldn't have done that." He brought out his handcuffs.

"That won't be necessary," one of the men in suits said. "Come with us, Miss Welsh. Do you have the satchel?" The man looked from Lisa to the officer.

"No," the policeman said. "She left it in the squad car."

The suited man waved at one of the others, who drove back to the police vehicle.

"Okay, now, young lady. We've got to talk." He seized her arm, put her in one of the SUV's and had the driver take them to the inn. "Room three, is that where you're staying?"

She nodded and couldn't believe he'd take her there. If only Jack had come with her.

"Do you mind if we talk in the room?"

"Who are you?"

"FBI, Ma'am. George Mason." He flashed his badge.

"FBI?"

"We don't want to talk out here."

The driver parked and the man escorted her to the room.

Removing the necklace first, she unlocked the door. After she walked inside, she crossed the floor and sat down on the bed. Gripping the gold chain, she watched two men take up space by the door, while the other two towered over her.

"Okay, the deal is this. We know the firm you were working for has set you up to take the fall for the embezzlement. Since some of the monies were government funds, we became involved. Now, a couple of murders are attached to the case and all hell's broken loose."

"Murders?"

"Yes, we knew you were the key to clearing the matter up, but we've had some time getting ahold of you, for your own protection, mind you."

"Protection?"

"Yes, he's already murdered two people. Since you had the documents that could convict him of the embezzlement and show his motive in killing your friend, Pauline, and—"

Lisa clasped her hand to her mouth and gasped for

air. "Not Pauline." The realization wrenched her gut, and she leaned over the bed and threw up.

One of the agents hurried to get tissues for her while she choked on sobs.

The agent waited a minute, then continued, "The other is the owner's brother-in-law."

"Brother-in-law?" she said hoarsely, her head still reeling from the knowledge her best friend was murdered...all because of her. A new waterfall of tears burst forth, and she couldn't quit crying. Letting Pauline in on what had happened, Lisa had inadvertently signed her death warrant.

"Miss Welsh."

She heard her name called several more times, but the voice seemed a million miles away.

"She's in shock."

"She may need some time, but we don't know if we have much left before he gets away with the murders and embezzlement."

Time. She had to get back to Jack. What was she doing here? Wiping the tears from her eyes, she knew she didn't belong here anymore.

"Michael did the killing and embezzled the funds?" she said, sniffling.

"I'm afraid so, Miss Welsh."

One of the other agents said, "We need your help to convict Michael Stone for the murders. With these documents, we can get him for embezzlement. We don't have a clear case against him for the murders."

"You need my help?"

"Yes, we just need you to—"

"Oh, no, I'm through with this. I...I have to go. You've got the original documents. I can't help."

"You can't go anywhere until you testify, but if you would help us with Mr. Stone—"

"To do what?"

"If we could wire you—"

"So I can be his next victim?" Her voice came out shrilly.

"We'll be there to ensure your safety while he confesses his crime to you. And he will. Everybody said he was interested in you at work."

She shook her head. "No, I can't do it."

"We'll have to keep you in protective custody until we put him away for at least the embezzlement. The trial could take a year or longer to schedule. If he's found guilty, he'll probably only serve a couple of years. Once he gets out of prison, he'll come looking for you."

As if she was planning on sticking around.

"Not only that," another agent added, "you do want to get him for murdering your friend, don't you?"

A fresh set of tears cascaded down her cheeks. She owed it to Pauline. Lisa wrung her hands, then wiped away the tears again. Whatever she could do to help, she had to. She couldn't live with herself if she didn't at least try. Clearing her throat, she asked, "What do I have to do?"

George Mason said, "Well, here's what we want you to do—"

Someone knocked on the door, and Lisa's heart jumped.

Two of the agents pulled guns, and one opened the door.

Jack was standing in the doorway and he tipped his hat to Lisa, then cast a steely-eyed glower at the agents.

"The lady's with me. If you want her to do something that will endanger her life, you're going to have to go through me first, gentlemen."

CHAPTER 20

No matter how much they tried, the FBI agents couldn't convince Jack to stay behind. Lisa had mixed feelings. On the one hand, she agreed with Jack and wanted him by her. On the other hand, she was afraid her boss wouldn't reveal anything if Jack was with her. Still, she agreed with Jack and the two of them settled down to eat a meal at the Stagecoach Inn, while the FBI did their part to set the trap for Michael.

After Lisa read the Stagecoach Inn's menu, she considered two men in suits eating their meal across the spacious glassed in room. Undoubtedly, they were FBI and none too inconspicuous. Jack glanced at the door again. Trying to settle her edgy nerves, she took a deep breath.

The waitress came up behind Lisa and she gave a start, stifling a scream.

"May I help you?" The woman's brightly colored red hair brightened her peach skin. She smiled. "You're getting to be one of our regulars here."

Lisa attempted to smile back, hating that she had to see Michael, knowing what he'd done to Pauline. "I'll have my usual."

Jack said, "I'll have what the lady ordered."

"Coming right up." The waitress tucked her pen into her pocket and walked toward the kitchen.

Lisa didn't figure she could eat a bite, and afterward thought she should have ordered something lots lighter.

"Excuse me." A tawny-haired man in a rumpled suit pulled up a chair next to Lisa's and gave Jack the evil eye.

Staring at his pale beady, brown eyes, made smaller by the fat accumulated in his ruddy cheeks, Lisa stifled a shudder. This was the beginning that could seal Jack's and her fate. Though her skin felt like gnats were crawling over it, she had to make a good show...for Pauline at least. She owed it to her. "Do I know you?" she asked, trying to keep her voice from wavering. God, she wasn't an actress by any means. Jack looked like he was ready to jump out of his seat to pummel the guy.

"No, but I know you." The man cast Jack another disparaging look. "After we share lunch, we're all going to take a stroll to my car parked out back, then take a little drive. Although no one said anything about the cowboy coming along."

"To Waco?"

He snorted. "You catch on real quick. Michael said you were clever."

"Michael." She hoped she sounded a little clueless.

"He said you probably missed him terribly after your long stay away from work. He was concerned you would run away. I've had an awfully hard time catching up with you."

"If I say no? I won't go with you?" She glanced at the dark-suited men. Were they aware this man was one of Michael's cohorts? One looked her way. When he turned to speak with the other man, she chanced another glance at Jack. His jaw was clenched tight, and his eyes had darkened to midnight, making him look positively lethal.

The waitress strode to the table with steaming plates of food, diverting the thug's attention. Seeing Lisa's astonishment when he twisted to face her, he smiled. "I caught the waitress after you ordered. I told her to get me the same as you were having, seeing as how you are a regular here...overheard your conversation."

After the lady deposited the plates on the table, she headed back to the kitchen. When they were alone, the man fluffed out his white table napkin, then rested it on his lap. "You can call me Leonard. I like when I'm on a first-name basis with the people I deal with. Makes me feel warm and fuzzy."

She glared at the heavy-set man twisting in the chair a size too small for his ample body. She wondered if she could be safe anywhere. Certainly not in old Salado where others wanted her dead, too. She shuddered. Then she considered the fact Jack was still wearing his gun. None of the FBI agents had checked him over. Would Michael's cohort?

"You want to know why you're going with me?" Leonard asked.

He slipped his chubby hand into his ill-fitting coat. A leather strap to his holster appeared. The hard cold steel of the revolver poked into Lisa's ribs, and she jumped. Would he kill her right now? In a restaurant full of patrons? Her heart pounded, and she had to steady her nerves.

Jack reached for his jacket, but Lisa slightly shook her head.

Leonard grabbed her arm with a fearsome grip. Her eyes watered when his fingers dug into her skin. "Just sit still and don't alarm the other customers." His eyes narrowed. "I'm not going to use it unless I have to. It's more like protection."

He released her and began shoveling his food down. Once he was done, Leonard eyed her plate. "Don't want all that good meat?" He stabbed her roast beef strip with his fork and transferred it to his plate, dripping brown gravy on the white tablecloth. "Dessert?"

She shook her head.

"No?" His lips curved up, his beady eyes flat. "I've got quite a sweet tooth. I can't pass up an opportunity like this. I hear their homemade pecan pies are absolutely out of this world...to die for."

He wolfed down both pieces of pie. Leaning back in the chair, he rubbed his chest and belched. "A meal like that makes for a great productive day. Don't you think?" He glanced at Jack's untouched meal. "Not hungry either? If I wasn't so full, I'd eat yours, too. Waste not, want not, I always say."

He wiped his face, and the waitress brought the bill to him. "You can pay for this up front, when you're ready."

He looked at the bill, then at Jack. "You're going to pay for the meals, aren't you?"

Lisa took the bill from Leonard and reached into

her purse.

"Boyfriend got no money, eh? Or is this one of those modern arrangements where the woman pays for the man? I like that."

Ignoring him, she and Jack headed to the cashier's counter, while Leonard followed close behind. Her hand shaking, she paid the cashier with the FBI agent's money. Her heart pounded out of control, and she was having second thoughts. "Do you mind if Jack and I grab some things from our room?"

The agents had the evidence to get Michael. They had the motive behind the killings. They didn't need her to get his confession. She wasn't sure they could keep her and Jack safe.

"Yeah, hell, I mind. You don't need anything from there."

"Just for a minute?" She twisted the necklace around her neck. Pauline would understand if she backed out on the deal. She wouldn't have expected her to face Michael like this.

Leonard studied her. "Not on your life. You've given me the slip too many times already."

The two suited men walked up behind them to pay at the cashier's desk. Leonard motioned for Jack to lead and pulled Lisa out the door. "Time's a wasting and Michael will be waiting."

"What do you want with me?"

"It's not what I want that matters. It's what Michael wants. You have important documents he says belong to him. He's not going to like your friend tagging along."

"The documents belong to the DA's office now."

"Oh? Michael won't care for that one bit."

***

On the drive to Waco, Leonard began to fidget in the passenger's seat while Lisa drove. Jack sat in the back seat watching Leonard's antics, figuring he would soon have a showdown with the varmint. Halfway to the city, Leonard looked at the mirrors and glanced at his watch. "Pull the car over."

When Lisa hesitated, Leonard shouted, "Do it!"

Afraid he'd get in trouble for bringing Jack along for the ride? Might as well call his cards.

"He wants to get rid of me," Jack said, matter-of-factly.

Leonard cast him an evil smile. "Yeah, FBI agents are tailing us, and this yahoo might be one, too, despite his attempt to look like a harmless cowboy."

Jack raised a brow. Nobody ever made that mistake with him before.

"In any event, if we drop him off here, they'll have to pick him up, and we can lose our tail. So we can do this easy-like. No bloodshed. Or you fight me on it, and the guy gets a bullet in the temple."

No way was Jack going to let this snake take Lisa with him alone to see his boss.

When Lisa pulled off the road and parked on the side, Leonard rolled out of the car and motioned to Jack. "Get out, cowboy, or I kill the woman now."

Lisa's eyes were filled with tears as she looked over the seat at him. "Go, Jack. I'll be all right."

"Lisa—"

"Go, please."

Leonard reached for his door and threw it open. "Hell, have it your way." He jerked out his gun and motioned to Jack. "Out, or I swear to God, I'll kill you where you're sitting."

When Jack didn't move, Leonard fired into the seat next to him, ripping a hole in the fabric. Lisa squealed. Jack didn't flinch.

"Go, Jack. Please."

Planning on jumping the gunslinger, Jack got out of the vehicle. Before he could make a move, Leonard slipped metal onto his hand and struck Jack hard in the temple. Pain obliterated the light and the day turned to night.

***

"No!" Lisa grabbed her seatbelt to release it, but Leonard clambered into the car and aimed the gun at her.

"Drive."

Her stomach flip-flopping all over the place, she wanted to go to Jack.

"Go! Or I'll shoot him, damn it!" He shoved the brass knuckles into his pocket and reached for his door. "Hell, have it your way."

Torn between leaving Jack on the side of the road half dead, and risking that Leonard might really shoot him, Lisa jerked the car onto the highway without regard to traffic. Nearly colliding with an eighteen-wheeler, she twisted the wheel, skidding the car toward the shoulder, then back into the right lane again. Other vehicles' tires screeched.

The near-collision threw Leonard against the dashboard. "Hell, woman! I want to get there in one piece."

Her skin freckling with perspiration, she tried to see what had happened to Jack. After the near collision, four vehicles had squealed onto the shoulder to avoid hitting the big rig. She saw no sign of Jack.

Maybe one of the vehicles that had burned rubber to brake on the shoulder was an FBI car.

Leonard ran his hands through his windswept hair. "So was he a boyfriend or FBI?"

***

His head pounding like thunder, Jack was glad to find another soul who understood his dilemma and yanked on the seatbelt in the cowboy's truck.

"Hell," Tucker Anderson said, shoving his Stetson back on his head, driving faster than anything else on the road, "you say the FBI's supposed to be protecting your girl? Not that they don't have some good men. My brother-in-law works for them. But I wouldn't trust having my girl in a setup like this. It's a good thing you have a hard head."

"There!" Jack shouted, pointing at the red car several ahead of them in the far right lane.

"Got it. I'll ease over and make sure he doesn't know I'm tailing him. Me and my brothers chased down a couple of hoodlums who'd broken into our sister's home. Didn't know what hit 'em."

"Just as long as he doesn't hurt Lisa," Jack warned.

"Have you got a gun?" Tucker asked.

Jack looked at the grizzled guy, his brows raised in question. Tucker offered an evil smile. "Yeah, you got a gun. I was going to loan you one of mine. Got a license to carry 'em, too. Was on the reserve police force until we got way too busy with ranching and rodeos."

The lights on the back of Leonard's car glowed red and the vehicle began to slow down as it turned off the road.

"They're going into Waco."

"That's where Lisa worked," Jack said.

"Yeah, you said at the accounting firm, but I doubt this scum's taking her there. Probably some out of the way place."

Jack's gut tightened another notch. All along he'd wanted to take out her boss's henchman, but he knew Lisa wanted to put Michael away for killing her friend. Still, he didn't like that Lisa put herself in harm's way. He dabbed his kerchief at the blood dribbling down his cheek.

"Warehouse district," Tucker said. "I've got to back off. I sure don't see anyone else following them down here though."

"Looks like he's pulling in there." Jack's back was stiff with tension, and he was ready to bolt from the truck and rescue his girl.

"Might be a ploy. I'll drive on by. You watch to see if he gets out."

"They're waiting in the vehicle," Jack said, not liking this one bit.

"He probably suspects us. I'll go around the block."

Before Jack could object, Tucker drove down the next street, and when they made the loop around, they found Leonard's car was gone.

***

Praying the FBI had picked up Jack, that he was all right, and they were following a safe distance behind, Lisa parked next to a brick warehouse situated in downtown Waco. Leonard hurried her out of the car and into the warehouse. At least the car parked outside was like a red flag, and the FBI should be able to find it quickly. *If* they were not far behind.

His look smug, Michael sat on the edge of a desk in the corner of the expansive building, drinking from a tall glass. Crates stacked against the walls behind him stretched up to the ceiling like wooden-slatted giants, but seeing no means of escape or a weapon at hand, her attention quickly shifted back to the boyish, freckle-faced monster.

Leonard grabbed her arm and pulled her to the desk.

"I've missed you, Lisa." Michael tugged at her long skirt. "Dressing strangely these days." His words were slurred. A half-finished bottle of whiskey sat on the desk. Beside this, two tall thin glasses and a bottle of champagne rested. Ice blanketed the bottle, tucked in its pewter bed.

Michael rose to his feet and towered over her. His fingers traced the swirls in her hair coiled on top of her head. She held her breath, praying the FBI would rush in with guns drawn and end this nightmare. Forget the confession.

He ran his fingers over her cheek, then grabbed her chin, and tilted her head back. "You know I'm usually patient, but I want those documents. I had a terrible time convincing Pauline to tell me you'd made copies. I really don't believe she knew where you'd hidden the originals, though."

"You bastard!" Lisa's voice cracked with emotion and tears escaped her eyes. She quickly brushed them away and glared at him, not wanting him to see how much his cruelty hurt.

"She wasn't my type and now she's feeding the fish along the Bosque River." He walked around his desk, then pulled a drawer open.

He pulled out a ten-inch blade, and she stepped back, her heart racing. His brows rose. "You'll join her if you don't tell me what you've done with the papers."

A tremor slid through her. Tilting slightly in his stance, Michael rested his hand against the desk for a minute, then laid the knife next to the whiskey bottle. He walked over to her and pulled the pins from her hair. The strands dipped in waves over her shoulders, and he glanced down at the amulet.

"What's this?" He lifted the necklace. "A lucky charm? Don't imagine it'll bring you much luck." He put his hands around her throat and caressed it. "So where are the documents, Lisa? You can tell me, then we can share some good times, and you can run along."

Shivering with disgust inside, she glowered at him. There was no way he was going to let her live. What kind of a fool did he take her for? She just had to get him to confess to the killings, and then she hoped the FBI would rescue her like they said they would.

Michael reached for the champagne and twisted and turned until the plastic top popped off. He poured a glass, and the bubbles exploded over the top like a volcano erupting.

"You're not a drinking man, Michael."

He shook his head. "You're right. Rarely take a drink." Pouring the second glass, he managed to stop the flow just at the rim. He handed a glass to her. "Here's to us. You know you could share in this little venture, too."

Lisa refused the glass.

"I was hoping champagne would make you a little more receptive, but there'll be more for me that way."

Leonard cleared his throat.

Michael motioned to him to leave. "Go."

"You sure, boss?"

"I won't need you back here for another hour or so."

Leonard nodded, headed out of the building, and slammed the metal door shut. Lisa jumped, her nerves shattering.

"If you had some champagne, you wouldn't be so jumpy." Michael placed the chilled glass against her cheek, and she turned her head away. "Nasty bump." He touched her temple. She winced. "Somebody been treating you rough? Not Leonard?" His eyes widened, then he guzzled his champagne.

She glanced back at the knife. Now that she was alone with Michael and he was so inebriated…

He set the glass on the desk. "Personally, I don't think women should be treated rough. Woman deserve a gentle touch. Barry's gone and you're all alone. Don't you feel the need to be loved?"

She folded her arms, trying to look more sure of herself than she felt. "The original papers have gone to the DA's office. You can't squirm your way out of this one. You can't pin the blame on me."

He smiled and poured another glass of champagne. "Are you sure you don't want some?"

"No, let me go, Michael."

"Drink a glass with me, and I'll let you go."

"You won't."

"I will."

She reached for the glass, and he smiled. She took a sip from the dry chilled drink, and the bubbles tickled her nose.

"What do you have against me? I'm charming,

great-looking, intelligent, very intelligent and— "

"Married, Michael, and a murderer."

"Ah, yes. You have scruples. But you see I can't leave my dowdy wife, because she'll have all her daddy's money. Her father thinks I'm divine so I devised this scheme to bilk the company."

He sat down on the desktop and pulled Lisa close. "I'd have my own money and could get a dame like you, only you discovered the fraud." He furrowed his brow. "You weren't supposed to do that. You told Pauline. You shouldn't have done that either. Somehow my brother-in-law found out. The dominoes kept falling. You're the last one, really. Drink up, darling." He raised another glass to her.

Where was the darned FBI? "How could you have hurt Pauline?"

"Why do we have to discuss her? I want to talk about us." He drained the glass.

"And your brother-in-law?"

"Water under the bridge."

"The Bosque River, too?"

"You catch on quick. I always liked that about you." He poured another glass. After he downed that, he reached for Lisa's shoulders and pulled her close. "How do you get out of this contraption?" He yanked at the ribbons on her dress.

She slapped his hand away. "You'll get the death penalty for what you've done."

"Hmm, well, I've planted the evidence so it looks like you've killed your best friend because she knew too much. My poor brother-in-law found out you were embezzling our hard-earned money, and you had to kill him, too."

"How?"

"You really want to know the gory details?" He cast her a sloppy smile. "You're a woman after my own heart. You shot them with a 45-caliber pistol."

"I don't even know how to shoot a gun."

"Nobody will ever check that far. The gun was found in your apartment. That's all that matters."

"I'll tell them..."

He put his hands around her waist and kissed her neck, his breath reeking of alcohol. "You'll tell them what? I don't need the money. I have a wealthy father-in-law who gives me all the money I want. You? You're a sad, lonely young woman who couldn't get a promotion. Angry, you bilked the company. For shame." He crinkled up his face, then laughed.

"But I don't have the money."

"Nope, all in Grand Cayman bank accounts, not traceable."

She glanced at the door. Had the FBI gotten enough information to convict Michael? As far as she was concerned, she'd done enough. It was way past time for the cavalry to arrive.

"Nobody's coming to rescue you, Lisa." He looked at her dress. "How do you get this damn thing off?" He placed his hands on his hips.

Walking around the desk, he grabbed the long sharp blade. Now was her chance before it was too late. She turned and darted for the door.

"Oh no you don't!" Michael bolted for her and grabbed her arm. "I've wanted you since you first came to work for me. We could have had a lot of good times, you and me. Alas, we'll just have this one." He twisted the knife against her cheek.

"Put the knife down, Michael!" she screamed and turned her head toward the door. "You can't kill me, Michael!" Where was the FBI?

"I know. I've had a lot of trouble with the idea, but I knew it would have to come to this." He shook his head.

In disbelief, she stared at him. "You really do feel something for me, don't you? That's why you had to drink so much before you could kill me."

"Why couldn't things have been different between us? You could have been mine." His eyes filled with tears.

"You can't kill me, Michael!" She wrestled her arms from his grip and dashed for the warehouse door again.

"No, Lisa! You can't go!" He ran after her and stumbled over his feet, falling when she grabbed the door handle. With one hand clutching his bloodied breast the other stretched out to her, he groaned piteously. His voice was strained as he called her name. His eyes reflected pain, but after what he'd done to her friend and his brother-in-law, he deserved worse.

Pulling the door open, she ran into the empty road. She glanced up and down the street. Not seeing any sign of the FBI agents, she dashed to the converted warehouse, turned-restaurant next door and meant to call for a taxi when a muddied pickup charged up next to her. Jack jumped out of the passenger's side and her heart surged with relief.

He pulled her into the truck and held her tight as he slammed the door shut. "Lisa, thank God."

A black suburban and ford sedan with government plates pulled in next to the warehouse.

"Can you give us a lift to my apartment at 412 Hanover Street!" she asked the driver of the pickup.

"Absolutely, little lady." He winked at Lisa.

How'd Jack manage to find a cowboy that looked as old as if he'd lived during Jack's time, she didn't know.

They rounded a corner and an ambulance hurried on past them.

"What happened?" Jack asked, his arm wrapped securely around her shoulders.

"I got his confession," she choked out. If the bastard didn't die due to his own self-inflicted wound, hopefully, the state would take care of him.

"What now, darlin'?" Jack asked.

She looked at the driver, not wanting to reveal their plans to a stranger.

"He's one of the good guys," Jack said.

"We're going home." She rested her head against Jack's chest and held on tight. "To your home."

To face a new danger and hopefully right another wrong.

***

When Lisa and Jack drove back to the Stagecoach Inn and parked, Jack grabbed her bag of old cash, and she pulled her necklace from her neck. They sneaked in through the window of the hotel room while men spoke outside the door. "She gave them the slip, and she's still got the tape."

Damn. She forgot all about the recording.

"What about that Michael Stone? Is he going to make it?"

"It's too soon to tell, but the woman needs to testify in any event. They're still searching Waco for her and figure if her past actions are any indication of what she'll be doing next, she'll head this way today."

"Do we really need her?"

The tapping of footsteps approaching the room made her back away from the door. "They've spotted her car here in the parking lot. Are you sure you've been watching the door all along?"

Lisa lifted her long skirts and exposed the wiretap strapped to her leg. She grabbed at the straps, and Jack yanked at the device, trying to remove it.

"Yes, sir. We've been here the entire time," someone said beyond the door.

"Maybe we ought to have a look inside the room anyway."

The agent pushed the key into the lock and Jack twisted the stubborn straps free. As soon as he tossed the wiretap onto the bed, the door opened. Lisa grabbed the money bag and Jack as he slipped the necklace over her head.

"Hey, grab them!" one man said, while he and two others charged into the room.

***

Sometime in the night, a key rattling around in the keyhole awakened Lisa. She sat on the bed and stared at the door. Footsteps grew louder, approaching her room, then the key receded from the door lock. Rapid steps followed when they hurried away from the door.

"I thought I heard someone in the hall," Mr. Daemon said.

"I told you this ghost thing's got you spooked. No one's here."

"We've got to bury the body, now. No more putting it off. Maybe that'll make the ghost go away."

"Do you think the body's still there?"

"What do you mean?"

"Well, that woman— "

"Of course, the body's still in the cave just where we left her. I don't know who that other woman is but—"

"She bears an uncanny resemblance and—"

"She's probably a close relative. We'll bury Josephine's body and be done with it. If we ever get ahold of the other one, we'll bury her with Josephine."

"Are you sure the body's still out there?"

"Yes, and I'll prove it to you. Let's get the shovels."

"What about the other woman? How could she have vanished again?"

"What concerns me is that Jack Stanton. The way he's been hanging around here."

"Yeah to see the maid."

"What?"

"He took her to the Salado picnic."

Lisa frowned. Jack hadn't said anything to her about seeing another woman. That'd be just her luck as far as her dealings with men. Fighting the anger that welled up inside, she didn't know the situation at all, and Jack said there was no other woman he was interested in. Maybe she was a nice widowed lady who had needed an escort. Sure, that was it.

"Just as long as the maid keeps her trap shut."

The footsteps faded away and Lisa took a deep breath. The faint scent of a spicy cologne drifted in the air. "Jack?" she whispered.

She pulled the window up and peered out. "Jack?" she called out in a hushed voice.

Gathering up her long skirts, she boosted herself out the window, but there wasn't any sign of him.

Clanking in the distance made her jerk her head in the direction of the noise. Lanterns wavered near a shed while two men gathered shovels.

"Josephine," she whispered. "Jack, where are you?"

The soft light of their flickering lanterns dimmed when the men headed for the cave. If she was ever to learn where they'd put Josephine's body, she had to follow them. "I can't lose them, Jack." She gripped her skirts in her clenched fists, then hurried after the men, hoping that if she was properly buried, she'd be at rest. Also, Lisa would know where the body was to inform the sheriff.

After twenty minutes of walking through the thick forest, she recognized the area as the place where the outlaws had grabbed her before. Her pulse quickened and the fear returned. She stared at the cave nearby as lights inside cast an eerie silhouette outside. *Josephine's body was in there all along.* A shudder rippled through her.

Hiding behind a fuzzy, moss-blanketed boulder, she waited for a minute, but unable to see or hear anything, she crept closer.

"I told you she'd still be here. "Cold as it's been, she's perfectly preserved, too."

"Take her legs, and I'll take her— "

"Hey!" a woman shouted.

Lisa nearly had a heart attack when she turned and found the maid running up behind her.

"You give me that necklace back!" the maid screamed.

Lisa shoved the maid aside, but when she turned to run, the manager grabbed her arm. "Well, well, look who we have here."

"Now we can wrap this whole affair up in one fell swoop," Mr. Worthington said.

Lisa screamed, twisted away from Mr. Daemon, and stomped his foot. He yelled and lost his grip on her, but the owner grabbed for her. Dodging him, she ran for the road.

She stumbled over a fallen tree limb when the owner's breath huffed and puffed, drawing close. In the distance, the maid shouted, "Come back here, you! Give me that necklace!"

A gunshot exploded and the bullet whizzed near Lisa's shoulder. She ducked, her blood turning to ice. The projectile struck an oak with a resounding crack. Heavy footsteps crushed the leaves close by. Her adrenaline spiked, and she bolted again for the road.

A shot rang out, and she dove for the ground. At this rate she'd never make it. With a panting breath, she took to her feet again.

Riders on horseback galloped along the road and at first her heart surged with encouragement, but immediately sank when a boy shouted, "It's the girl, Pa! And someone's shooting at her."

"Get her, Billy. After we spring the boys, meet us."

"You promise she'll be mine, don't you, Pa?"

"As long as I'm leading the gang, she's all yours."

The outlaws tore off toward the jailhouse while Billy swung his horse into the woods. Lisa darted away from the road. She couldn't believe how badly the day had gone. The manager aimed his Colt at her. She dashed behind an elm. Shots echoed through the woods,

TERRY SPEAR

and the bearded manager crumpled to the ground with a groan. The maid ran screaming toward the inn. Lisa backed away from Billy.

A hand grabbed her wrist, and she cried out. Using her as a shield to protect himself against the outlaw, Mr. Worthington backed her toward the cave.

Billy pointed his rifle at the hotel owner. "Let her go, mister, and I won't have to shoot you, too."

The owner shook his head. "If I let her go, you'll shoot me for sure."

"Blasted man, let her go. I only want the girl." Billy walked his horse toward them, his eyes narrowed at the Mr. Worthington.

He waved a knife. "I'll cut her if you come any closer."

Billy snorted. "You ain't no killer, mister."

The man glanced back at the cave. "I reckon I am, son, just as much as you and that dead fellow over there. I guess I deserve whatever comes to me, but if I die, so does she."

"She's going to be my wife. I don't care nothing about you. Let her go. Then you can go about your business."

The owner continued to back up toward the cave until he reached the entrance.

"Where you think you're going? Is there a secret way out? You ain't gonna to take her with you. She's mine."

The owner pulled her into the cave and shoved her aside. She fell and touched an ice-cold hand and screamed. "Josephine," she choked out. The woman looked eerily like her.

Mr. Worthington grabbed a gun resting next to the

shovels and aimed it at her. Shots echoed off the walls of the cave, and the smell of gunpowder filled the damp air. Mr. Worthington dropped to the ground with a thud. He held his hand up for a minute, staring at her, his look pained. He dropped his head to the rocky floor, his gaze lifeless.

Lisa's eyes clouded with tears, her attention shifted from the dead owner to Josephine. "Oh, Josephine," she whispered. How could they have ended her young life?

Billy's headed for her, bringing her attention to the new crisis.

"You're coming with me."

"No, I can't."

"I'm an outlaw, miss. I can do anything I please. Right now I aim to take you with me." He reached for her arm, but she backed away from him.

She glanced at Josephine, felt the damp chill in the air, and realized if she didn't get her buried, Josephine might come for her again. She hoped the next words out of her mouth wouldn't be a really bad mistake. "If you'll help me to bury her, I'll go with you without a fight."

He studied her. "Promise?"

She felt she had no other choice and hopefully, someone would rescue her. "Help me bury her at the cemetery, and I'll go with you."

"And be my wife?"

She'd agree to anything as long as she could free Josephine's earth-bound soul. Gritting her teeth, she nodded.

"Whooee!" Billy helped her off the floor, then loaded a shovel and Josephine onto his horse. He took Lisa's hand in his and led his horse to the cemetery.

TERRY SPEAR

"I'll make you proud to be my wife. Just you wait and see. I'll bring you all kinds of jewels and trinkets, even better than the one you're wearing now."

She studied the young man's eager face. "And the others?"

"Pa says they'll leave you be."

She shook her head, and they entered the cemetery.

"If my Pa says something will be some way, you better believe it'll be that way."

Leaders could be ousted or killed so she didn't take much stock in Billy's words. She pointed to the spot besides the Rogers' graves, then he dug the shallow hole. When he lifted Josephine from his horse, Lisa said, "Wait."

She placed the necklace around Josephine's neck. "May you rest in peace now, dear Josephine...you and Bill."

"What?" Billy said.

"Bill was the man she loved, but an outlaw killed him."

"Oh, I thought you was talking about me for a minute."

He laid Josephine's body in the grave, and Lisa said a prayer, then Billy covered her up. Shots rang out, making them both jump.

"It's got to be the boys!" Billy grabbed her hand and hurried her to his horse, then hoisted her into the saddle.

With her heart in her throat, she cringed when Billy wrapped his arm around her waist and pulled her close.

"Giddy-up," he said, and tore off after his pa and the others.

More shots reverberated through the area, the posse

firing away in pursuit, and she was afraid they'd kill her, too.

"Hey, Pa!" Billy shouted, pulling up beside his father.

"Was she any trouble?"

"Nah, she agreed to be my wife, Pa!"

The older man's eyes widened a bit. "She did, did she? Come on boys, we'll split into two groups and head toward the hideout once we've lost this bunch of yahoos."

The men took off in separate directions while Billy and his pa and two others headed west.

"How come you changed your mind for Billy?"

Staring at the woods, she remained silent. Her thoughts on how she could escape. Then what? Find her way back to town through the wilderness? Every step the horses took away from Salado made her fear the worst. Being with this bunch was bad enough. No way would Billy always be there to protect her from the others.

"I helped bury her relative who was murdered."

A familiar glowing light in the leafy mesh of woods caught Lisa's eye. Her heart rate quickened. "Josephine?" she said under her breath. She had to have put her spirit to rest. She just had to have. What had she done wrong now?

"Some of our gang killed the woman?"

"No, Pa. The owner of the Shady Villa Inn."

The old man grunted. "Some folks can be just as bad as can be while they pretend to be the good citizens of the town."

"She said she'd be so grateful if I buried the murdered lady, she'd come with me and be my wife."

"She'll make you a mighty fine wife," Billy's pa said.

"They've headed this way!" one of the posse hollered.

The breeze whispered her name, *"Lisa."*

She twisted her head and listened for further words spoken in the distance. "Jack?" she said softly.

The pop like a firecracker shattered the peace, and her nerves skittered. Then she saw a light shimmering through the branches. Omigod, Josephine was coming for her again.

"I thought we'd lost them back there," the old man said.

They dug their spurs into their horses' sides and pulled away from the lawmen again. One of the men halted his horse and aimed his gun at the posse.

No! She wanted to stop him, to—

One of the deputies fell to the ground, and the redheaded outlaw shouted, "Ha!" He rejoined the other gunmen, stroking his grizzled beard. "One down, three more to go."

Her stomach queasy, Lisa felt like throwing up.

"Good shooting, Gabby. I'm afraid it's going to be a long night, boys," Billy's pa said.

They rode for over an hour, then stopped briefly to water their horses at a creek. Lisa slipped her hands in the ice cold water. Crunching on the stones next to her made her turn her head. Billy crouched beside her and ran his hand through her hair dangling over her shoulders. She shuddered. "You sure are beautiful, Miss." He studied her eyes. "I don't even know your name."

She shook the water from her hands. "It's Lisa."

"Lisa. Just like an angel in heaven. My ma used to read to me when I was little. She read to me of angels. You're just like one."

"What happened to her?"

"Comanche killed Ma. We lived on a farm and worked real hard, but after that Pa was so shook up over Ma's death we went to live with these fellars. After several years, he took over the gang. Now they're our family, Lisa. I love that name...Lisa."

He rinsed out his canteen and filled it with fresh water. "Here," he said lifting it to her lips. He stared at her while she drank the cool water, hoping it wasn't contaminated. "You sure are beautiful."

"Do you think he can keep her?" Dallas asked Billy's pa as they watched her, making her feel like a zoo-kept animal.

"She'll do him a world of good. He doesn't need one of those saddle tramps that hang around our camp. His mother was a good woman." The old man sighed. "God rest her soul."

Dallas rubbed his rough hands together. "There'll be trouble when he brings her to camp."

His words sent another chill down Lisa's spine.

"Not while I'm in charge there won't. Someday Billy will take off and start a homestead of his own. I'd always hoped he'd find a good woman."

An old woman farming a scrap of dirt...that's what she'd become...but only after being an outlaw's woman. The notion sickened her, but before she could think further on the matter, a black bear lumbered out on the rocky bank, and she screamed. Dallas and Billy's pa laughed.

"It's just an old black bear," Billy said. "Just thirsty

like the rest of us."

"I didn't know bears lived in Texas."

The bear's tongue snaked out to lap up the water.

"Where are you from?"

"Waco."

"That's not that far from here." Billy knelt down and soaked his neckerchief. "They've got bear around those parts, same as here." He stood back up and wiped his neck, watching her.

She couldn't believe that the beasts living around these parts weren't just the two-legged variety.

"I guess you're one of those fine city ladies. Never been out in the woods much. You'll like it out here under the wide-open skies." He took a deep breath and patted his scrawny chest. "Just the birds singing and coyotes howling at night...wolves too, fills a body with— "

"Wolves?"

"Don't tell me you haven't seen red wolves roaming around these parts." He re-tied his bandana around his neck.

Her heart picked up its pace. She'd considered sneaking away from the men at night when they were sleeping. Now she wondered if she should chance it. "What else?"

Billy laughed. "You're pulling my leg, ain't you?"

"Mount up and head out," Billy's pa said.

Billy took Lisa's arm and boosted her up on his horse. "Well, there's cougars and..."

"Mountain lions?"

"Yeah and buffalo."

"I'm not afraid of them."

"You've got to watch out for them wild hogs

though. One of the fellers tried to catch one for supper one night and got gored right bad." He tightened his hold on her and jumped his horse over a fallen tree. "Once, one of the guys killed a gator. We had quite a feast."

"Alligator?"

"Yeah, tasted pretty good, too."

She shook her head. "I thought they only lived in Florida."

He kissed the back of her head, and she winced.

"Are you sure you're from around here?"

The scent of spice caught her attention, and she glanced back east. *Jack...where are you?* Then the light shimmered in the woods some distance off, and the hair on Lisa's arms stood on end.

Josephine.

CHAPTER 21

Later that evening, Lisa chewed on a tough piece of beef jerky with the band of outlaws, hoping everyone would bed down for the night, and she could sneak away. But rustling in the woods behind them, signaled danger. The men grabbed their guns, Lisa's skin iced with panic, and shots sounded all over the woods.

Billy grabbed Lisa and threw her to the ground. He covered her with his body while more shots were fired into the trees. A man cried out in pain, causing Lisa's stomach to clench into a knot of fear. She had to get away.

"That's two," Dallas said.

"Can you see anything?" the leader asked.

"Nothing but trees, Clayton," Gabby said.

More shots fired and someone cried out.

"Billy!" his father shouted.

"Not me, Pa."

"Don't shoot unless you can see something to shoot at. Billy get away from that clearing, before you get hit."

Another shot was fired from the woods and Dallas fired back. The shot was returned and then Clayton fired at the spot. The sound of a thud sounded when a man fell to the ground.

"That's three," Dallas said.

"How many did you say there was?"

"I counted four that took off after us."

"Maybe the last one will head back to town to return with reinforcements, and we can lose them for good."

"Let's hope," Dallas said.

"Lisa," the breeze whispered. She turned in the direction of the branches stirring where there was only darkness.

Crunching of leaves and the snapping of a twig caused all of the gunmen to turn in the direction of the noise and fire. The lawman dropped and rolled behind a tree and fired a shot.

Billy groaned and collapsed next to her. Lisa stifled a scream. Ohmigod, not Billy. The only one who had really protected her. She scooted over and lifted his head into her lap. Not good. His breathing was erratic and his heart racing.

His father glanced at Billy. "Will you be all right, son?"

His voice strained, he sounded like he knew where this was headed. She'd hoped she was wrong.

"Yah, Pa," Billy said, gritting his teeth.

Lisa took his kerchief and held it to his chest, but she could feel the blood soaking it through the fabric. She swallowed hard and bit back tears. He was an outlaw, she reminded herself. He might have killed any number of men already. Even Jack, if he came for her.

Billy looked up at her and gave her a pained smile. "You're an angel, Lisa, sent from heaven to look after me."

"Get down, woman!" Billy's father shouted.

Lisa couldn't let go of Billy. She brushed the unruly hair away from his eyes. "Billy," she whispered.

He squeezed her hand, his grip fading, and a sharp pain stabbed her heart. He'd helped her bury Josephine when he needn't have, and it could have cost him his freedom. He'd protected her from Easton, too. Now who would save her from the attentions of the others?

The lawman shot in their direction again, and Lisa winced. Dallas and Billy's father both fired back. The lawman fell and groaned.

Clayton ran to his son. Peering down at him, he said, "Son—"

Billy looked up at his father. "She's an angel, Pa."

"That she is."

"An angel..." Billy said. He shuddered and closed his eyes.

Though she fought them, tears trailed down her cheeks. She didn't need to fall apart now. She touched Billy's wrist, but didn't find any pulse and shook her head at the boy's father. Saddened by his death, she feared what would happen next.

Clayton's body sagged, and he seemed at a loss as to what to do.

Dallas grabbed his arm. "We got to go, now before more come."

"Let's get Billy on my horse and..." Clayton said. He looked around. "Gabby? Where are you?"

"He got hit," Dallas said. "He's dead."

Only two left. Maybe she could get away then before—

"You take Billy's horse and head back to town, miss." He turned to Dallas. "Check on Gabby, and we'll take him back, too."

In astonishment, Lisa stared at Billy's pa. She was sure she was going to be passed around the gang for their pleasure.

"I said you're free to go, miss. Now skedaddle before I change my mind."

"We can't take her back with us?" Dallas asked.

The leader glared at him.

"I guess not."

Billy's father carried his son to his horse as Dallas considered Lisa. "It's sure a crying shame." He shook his head, then retrieved Gabby's body and threw him over his saddle.

The men rode past Lisa as she rose shakily to her feet. Billy's father tipped his hat to her. "Thanks for being good to my son, miss. He really was a fine boy and he loved you dearly. He deserved better than to die like this."

The men rode off, and she looked in the direction they had traveled from town. The breeze stirred the leaves, making them rustle in the dark, and a lone coyote howled somewhere in the distance. She shuddered, rubbing her arms. All alone, she was scared to death of the wilderness. Billy was right. A city girl at heart, she grabbed the reins of Billy's horse and stared up at him.

"I've never done this by myself." She glanced at the stirrup and lifted her skirt.

As soon as she poked her toe into the metal rung,

the horse took a step forward. "Hold still, you." She walked over to him again. The horse lifted his head from the grass he was nibbling and watched her. When he grazed again, she tightened her grip on the reins and took a fortifying breath. After sticking her boot into the stirrup again, she bounced on her tiptoe while he sidestepped away from her.

"Stay!" she commanded. She grabbed the saddle, then tried to stick her foot in the stirrup, but he moved again. She studied the saddle for a minute. "Maybe I'm on the wrong side."

After hurrying to the other side, she lifted her skirt, then poked her boot into the stirrup and tried to pull herself up. The horse walked forward. She fell backward and landed in a heap of lilac skirts on her butt with a thump.

"Everyone in the movies makes it look so easy."

Exasperated, she walked around the horse and grabbed the saddle with a fierce grip. "Stay still," she warned. This time she was able to lift herself slightly in the stirrup, but couldn't swing her leg over the saddle because of the long gown and dropped back to the ground. "Fine, I didn't want to ride anyway." She grabbed the horse's reins and pulled him along behind her while she walked through the woods, hoping she was headed in the direction of town.

At least having the beast with her made her feel not quite as insecure. Until she stumbled over a body. She cried out, her hand flying to her mouth. "One of the posse," she whispered, staring at the sprawled-out figure of a man. She leaned down, then touched his neck for a pulse. Finding none, she sank to her knees and looked up at the stars that sparkled overhead. "Jack, where are you? How do I find my way back to you?"

The scent of spices drifted her way again and she jumped up. "Jack!" She grabbed the horse's reins and walked around the area, looking for signs of the other men in the posse who had fallen. Her heart pounding wildly, she spied another figure lying nearby. She ran to the man's location and dropped to her knees. "Not Jack." Barely breathing, she felt for the man's pulse, but couldn't find one.

The chill in the air intensified, and she wiped tears from her cheeks. She was alive, free, and she had to concentrate on that and not lose her head now.

She stood and took a step, but the horse balked. Looking back at the stubborn beast, she said, "Come." She yanked his reins, but he shook his head.

Josephine appeared in a hazy-mist form, and Lisa dropped the horse's reins and stared at the aberration.

"Josephine," she said softly. "Why aren't you at rest?" The figure floated toward Lisa, and she took a step back. Shaking her head, she said, "You...you can't be me...I mean, I can't be you."

Her mind clouded, and she reached up and touched her fingers to her temple. "Think, Lisa, think. Don't let her take hold."

Josephine's misty form reached out to touch Lisa's arm, and she grabbed at the branch of a tree to steady herself.

Waving her free hand behind her, Lisa tried to find the horse's reins while focusing on the ghostly figure's approach. As soon as her fingers grappled the leather straps, she tugged at the horse and turned. Her heart skipping beats, she ran several yards before she saw Jack lying on his stomach, deathly still.

"Jack!" she screamed, forgetting all about Josephine.

Lisa dropped the horse's reins and dashed to him. Seizing his wrist, she felt his slowed pulse. "Ohmigod, Jack, you've got to be all right."

Rolling him over on his back, she ran her hands over his body, trying not to panic as she attempted to find where he'd been wounded.

The horse whinnied and she turned to see Josephine approach. "No," Lisa whispered. "No, Josephine." *Not now!*

The ice-cold breeze scented with violets touched her cheek, and she cried out, her chest tightening. The suffocation, the chills, the pain...

***

Lisa didn't know how much time had passed, but suddenly she was aware her cheek rested against the soft silk of Jack's vest. She sat up quickly. Josephine wasn't there, only Billy's horse nibbling grass nearby. Taking a deep breath, Lisa hoped Josephine's restless spirit wouldn't come for her again, and she renewed her search for Jack's wound.

Finding moisture on Jack's temple, Lisa searched through his pockets and found a handkerchief. She held it against his forehead, then reached down to hold his hand. His fingers were ice cold, and her heart sank.

Spying a blanket rolled up behind the saddle on Billy's horse, she tried to jump up from the ground, but her joints were stiff from the cold. She soon pulled the blanket free from the saddle and hurried back to Jack. Wrapping him in the wool, she tucked it tightly underneath his body, then shivered again. Cold. She was so cold she could barely feel her fingers and toes.

After tearing a strip of cloth from her skirt, she tied this around the handkerchief that covered Jack's wound and secured the knot behind his head. She ran her hand over his cheek. "Jack, you've just got to be all right." She kissed his cheek, then stood.

She rubbed her arms in the stiff cold breeze. "I have to make a fire." She gathered stones, then placed them in a circle a few feet away from Jack. Grabbing sticks and leaves, she hastened to pile them together in the fire circle. "Matches. I don't have any matches." She looked at the horse. "Maybe Billy had some."

She poked her numb fingers into the saddlebags, but couldn't find any matches. Her hand touched the cold steel of a Colt revolver, and she pulled it out. She laid it beside Jack, then walked over to the fire circle.

Picking up two stones, she struck them together like she'd seen in an adventure movie. One of the stones broke, and she cursed under her breath and picked up another. Time after time she struck the rocks, but there wasn't even a spark, and the frigid breeze blew steadily. She dropped the stones and rubbed her arms again. No way could she have been a pioneer in the olden days.

Exasperated with herself, she looked up at the cloudless night and studied the stars sparkling in the evening sky while the moon glowed overhead. At least there was no sign of rain.

Returning to Jack's unconscious form, she lifted the blanket and crawled underneath it. She wrapped her arm around his waist and snuggled her face against his chest, trying to get as close to him as she could. Shivering, she held him securely, his body slowly warming hers. An owl hooted from a gnarled, twisted form of a towering oak nearby. Leaves rustled in the steady breeze. And Billy's horse shuffled its hooves and whinnied in fright when Lisa's eyelids slowly closed.

"Charlotte," Jack groaned.

Lisa opened her eyes. "Jack?" Her heart lifted slightly.

He didn't say anything more, and Lisa felt adrift again. She nestled against his body, breathing in the pleasant aroma of the scent of his spiced cologne, prayed he'd be all right at first light, and drifted off to sleep again.

Later, Billy's horse stomped his feet and tugged at his reins tethered to the tree, snorting and whinnying. The sound came from far, far away while Lisa slept on the cold, rocky soil, hearing the noises in her dreams.

Until something pounced on her—big, heavy, furry.

She screamed as the cougar went for her throat, and threw her arm up in defense. He clawed at her shoulder and arm, sending a biting pain through every nerve ending in the region. Panicked, she managed to grab Billy's gun. Attempting to shoot wild cat she pulled the trigger. It clicked.

Misfire. The cat snarled and tried to sink his canines into her arm, but she struck it in the face with the butt of the pistol. He shook his head as if dazed. A shot fired wide.

The cougar bolted into the woods, and Billy's horse pulled at his reins to free himself from the tree. Her shoulder burned where the beast had clawed her, but she was lucky he hadn't sunk his sharp teeth into her and ripped her to shreds.

Horses' hooves pounded the woodland floor, heading in her direction. "The posse," she whispered. Then she reconsidered. "Or the other outlaws."

The cougar's claws had ripped the sleeve of her dress and blood trickled down her skin. She gripped her injured shoulder, the wound sending shards of pain down her arm all the way to her fingertips. Afraid to alert the wrong men that she was here, she bit back the pain and crept into the brush next to where Billy's horse stood.

After untying the horse's reins, she led him away from Jack. If they were the outlaws, she couldn't let them find him, but the thought of leaving Jack injured and alone in the wilderness filled her with dread.

The clippity-clopping of horses' hooves pounding the earth drew near, and she released the horse's reins and crouched in the shrubs nearby.

"Hey, it's Billy's horse."

Lisa's heart sank when she heard his words.

"I heard a shot fired, but I don't see a soul."

"No bodies neither."

One of the outlaws walked his horse over to the spot and pulled on the reins. "Billy must've got it."

"Yeah," another said. "Looks like we were too late in joining up with the rest of the gang."

Her breathing ragged, she moved farther away when the man's horse nearly stepped on her, and the horse reared up in fright. "Whoa, boy." The man peered at the tangled thicket.

She'd had bad days before, but the last few days were one for the record. Her heart stopped when the man spied her, and she knew it was all over for her now.

"What's wrong, Ned?"

The man smiled. "Why it's Billy's girl! Grab her!"

Lisa ran through the thick trees and snagged her dress on a tree branch. She struggled to free the material when one of the outlaws grabbed her arm and hauled her kicking and screaming back to the others.

"Shut up, woman, or I'll slit your throat. Where's Billy and his pa and the rest?"

Lisa stared at the tanned creased face. "Billy's dead," she choked on the words. "One of the others was hit, too, and Billy's pa and the man named Dallas, took Billy's body and told me to go home on Billy's horse."

The man sneered at her. "Billy's pa's getting soft in his old age. Well, you're coming with us now. Get on the horse and—"

"I don't know how to," Lisa said. "I've never ridden by myself."

"Never ridden..."

The men laughed.

"Must be one of those citified girls. Come on then," Ned said.

"Wait, boss." One of the men touched her shoulder. "What did this to you?"

"A cougar."

"We've got to bind it, Hanlon, before we go any further."

"Do what you have to do, Roger, but make it quick."

Roger removed his neckerchief, poured whisky on it, and tied it around Lisa's shoulder. She moaned when the burning liquid poured onto the claw marks, the pain streaking all the way to the bone. After lifting her onto Billy's horse, Roger grabbed the horse's reins.

"Which way now?" Hanlon asked.

"Billy's pa set me free," Lisa pleaded. "You've got to let me go."

"Billy's pa ain't in charge here. I am and I say you belong to us now, so be quiet, woman, and let me think," Hanlon growled.

"Maybe we ought to head south for the border," Roger suggested.

"Yeah, 'til things blow over a bit. We can rejoin the others later," Ned said.

Lisa started to shiver again.

"Here," one of the men said, tossing her a blanket. "Put that around your shoulders to keep out the chill."

"Yeah, when we have a chance to stop for a bit, we'll warm you up right proper."

The men all laughed.

"You follow her, Ned, make sure she doesn't try to slip away in the dark."

***

Feeling like a stampede of cattle had run over his head, Jack groaned and focused on his brother leaning over him.

"Are you all right?" Matthew asked, helping him to sit up while other members of the posse stood around and watched.

His temple shrieking with pain, Jack touched his forehead. "Guess I got nicked a bit."

"Sort of." One of the men brought a lantern closer to Jack while Matthew inspected the wound. "Bullet just grazed you. Can you stand?"

Grabbing his brother's arm, Jack rose to his feet. "Lisa is out there." He leaned against Matthew.

Matthew poked the cloth that had been tied to his

forehead. "Doesn't look like you need this any further. Looks like a piece of Lisa's dress. There's no sign of her now."

He couldn't believe she'd taken care of him and now was gone. Had she wandered off to find help? Fool thing to do. She'd never find her way. Then he reconsidered. She wouldn't have left him. Unless the outlaws had come for her, she would have done anything to keep him safe. He was certain of it. They had to have her. He groaned with the pain radiating from his temple compounded with the thought of the peril she was in.

One of the posse kicked a stone in the fire circle. "Looks kind of like she might have tried to make a fire. The outlaws wouldn't have done such a thing."

"Can you ride?" Matthew asked his brother.

"We've got to get her, Matthew."

"I aim to take you back to town."

Jack stared at the horses for a minute and counted the number. "You've got a spare mount for me."

Matthew helped him to one of the horses. "Yeah, one of the outlaw's horses."

He helped his brother climb into the saddle as Jack said, "Where are they headed?"

Matthew exhaled his breath. "I take it going to town isn't a notion you'll consider."

Jack shook his head, then rode with the others, heading south.

An hour later, they discovered a body lying on the ground. "Whoa." Jack pulled his horse to a stop. After dismounting he looked over the body. "He's dead, been shot."

"Is he one of ours or one of theirs?"

"Don't know the man."

"What now?"

"If we're finding bodies we may be on the right trail."

Pain tugging at his heart, at least he was a might hopeful. If they hadn't killed her already, he didn't think they would. He remounted his horse while one of the other men loaded the dead man onto his horse, then the posse took off again.

"It's getting cold. Winter's setting in." Matthew looked at his brother. "Do you think she'll be Lisa still?"

"I don't want to think about it. We've just got to get her back." Jack's temple pounded with pain, but all he could think of was how he had to rescue Lisa.

Matthew nodded. "We will, Jack."

A horse crashing through the underbrush caused the posse to turn with their guns raised.

"It's only me," Frank said. "Are you fellas searching for the escaped outlaws and their gang also?"

"Yeah, and we're looking for Lisa, too," Matthew said.

"We heard that Mr. Daemon and Mr. Worthington were shot by the cave near the inn and..." Frank said, "I hadn't heard...just that a woman was with the gang. What's this about Josephine?"

"Nothing," Jack said, irritation coursing through his veins.

Frank raised his brows. "Do you mind if I ride along?"

Jack muttered under his breath, and Frank smiled. "You don't have to worry about me. The new mill owner has a daughter, and we've hit it off nicely."

"That's great, Frank," Jack said, his outlook brightening a tad. Frank wasn't really an obstacle for him, just annoying. Josephine was still the biggest problem he could see as far as making Lisa his wife.

They all prodded their horses south.

From a short distance off gunshots rang out, and the posse stopped to listen. Jack spurred his horse in the direction of the gunfire. If they had Lisa...not one of them was going to be saved for the hanging tree if he had his way.

They came upon the sheriff's posse hunkered down, firing from behind rocks and trees. Their horses whinnied and snorted in terror, straining to loosen their reins tied to tree branches.

"Who are you?" one of the men shouted at Jack and the others as they jumped from their horses and joined the fracas.

"Part of the posse!" Jack shouted back.

"We spotted some of the gang resting on their laurels. Lucky for us, or we'd never caught up with them."

Jack and the others took positions alongside the members of the posse and added to the clatter of the gunfire aimed at the outlaws.

"I think I got one," Matthew said.

One of the posse fell nearby, and Matthew jumped to his aid. "Can you make it, sir?" Matthew tied his neckerchief around the wounded man's arm.

Looked to be three outlaws left, although one appeared to be wounded. What if Lisa's was with this bunch, and they decided to use her as a shield?

"Prop me up and I'll shoot some more," the injured lawman said.

While Matthew leaned him against a tree, Jack rushed into the thick of the shooting, intending to end this now.

Matthew shouted, "Hey, Jack, wait up!" He ran after Jack, firing away at the gunmen, then Jack dove into the hazy smoke.

***

After an hour of riding, Lisa began to nod off under the warmth of the woolen blanket and the rocking motion of the horse. Her shoulder still pained her, but she could barely stay awake. She slumped further in the saddle.

Ned pulled alongside her and shook her. "Wake up, woman, before you fall off that blasted horse."

Lisa fought the urge to close her eyes. Nothing mattered any more. Not Josephine, not...well, Jack mattered, but she didn't have much hope of seeing him alive again. She was too tired to think about it any further. She felt numb all over.

"What's going on?" Orville asked, stopping for Ned and Lisa to catch up.

"Nothing, just the woman's falling asleep in the saddle."

"She can ride with me. She can sleep all she wants in my arms. I'll keep her safe."

"No, she'll ride with me."

Hanlon stopped his horse, rejoined them and snarled, "What's the matter, now?"

"She's falling asleep, Hanlon. She can't stay awake with her injured shoulder and all. She's just a woman," Orville said.

"She'll be a dead one if we have to leave her behind."

"She can ride with me," Ned said.

"No, with me." Orville shoved Ned.

"Either she rides Billy's horse or not at all. She'll slow your horse down with two riders. Either kill her and be done with it or make sure she stays awake." He glared at Lisa.

"You haven't any heart, Hanlon," Orville said.

"Can't afford one in this business. Now get a move on, or the posse will catch up, and if that happens, I'll kill her for sure."

Lisa stared at the leader with glazed eyes. "Kill me. I'd rather be dead than live with the likes of you."

"That can be arranged, Missy." Hanlon scowled and headed his horse south again.

"Gee, whilikers, Ned, what's eating him with the woman?"

"Rose, the sage hen at the Red Horse Saloon in New Orleans, got in the way of a gunfight over a crooked hand at poker. Hanlon's takin' it pretty hard."

Orville frowned and scratched his beard. "He wouldn't really kill the girl, would he?"

"I reckon so," Ned said.

Her mind drifting, Lisa stared at the mane of her horse while they walked their horses through the forest for another hour or so. Ned poked her and Orville glanced back at them with envy.

Finally, Orville stopped his horse and waited for them.

"What's up, Orville?" Ned asked.

"Thought I'd relieve you."

"Nothing doing."

Hanlon, seeing his men haggling over Lisa again, returned. "Now what's the matter?"

"He's watched her long enough, Hanlon. It's my turn."

The quiet man joined the men. Hanlon shifted his eyes to him. "Roger, watch the girl. The rest of you move out or I'll shoot the whole blasted lot of you."

Orville and Ned maneuvered their horses around Roger, glaring at each other. "Now see what you done?"

"You done it by not sharing the girl, Ned."

Roger moved in beside Lisa. She leaned over the horse and grasped the horse's neck, resting her head against him. "Sit up, miss. You'll fall for sure like that."

"I don't care. I can't stay awake. Shoot me, and get it over with."

"We'll be able to stop before long. We've got a hide-out nearby and you can get some rest there."

***

The gunfire stopped and Jack stared at the carnage.

"Are they all dead?" Matthew asked.

"Yeah." Jack kicked the boot of one of the outlaws.

"What did you go and do that for, anyway? Trying to get yourself killed?"

"I couldn't stand not knowing if Lisa was with this bunch." He glanced around the area. "She's not here, though."

The other men joined them while the one assisted the wounded man. "That's some kind of heroics, Jack. Were you trying to get yourself killed, or what?"

"No, he's just plum out of his head over a woman," Matthew said.

"So that's the one we've heard tell is with the outlaws."

One of the men shook his head. "You may not

373

want her back when we finally do find her."

Jack took a step toward the man with every intention of killing him. They couldn't have touched her, not the way this yahoo was insinuating.

Matthew grabbed his arm. "Don't listen to him. She'll be fine. They haven't had time..."

Jack glared at his brother.

"Sorry, Jack." Matthew looked at his feet.

Matthew's thoughts mirrored his own though. They couldn't have had time, but what if they had? Would it make any difference? Maybe not to him, but what if she'd been so hurt by the experience she could never overcome the shame? What if she shunned all men after such an ordeal? His stomach ground with frustration and his temple pounded.

One of the posse said, "I'll take Randolph back to the doctor. If you'll help me get these bodies loaded up on the backs of their horses, I'll return them to town."

The men began to take care of the grim task, and as Jack draped an outlaw's body over a horse, he cleared his thoughts of anything vile concerning Lisa. He would hold her close, smell the sweet scent in her hair and touch his lips to hers, and make her his wife...soon.

***

Lisa gazed in the direction of the distant gunfire where everything was deathly quiet again. Groggy with sleep, she was hopeful her rescue was close at hand. Her shoulder still throbbed and her legs ached from the uncomfortable position of straddling her rocky, swaying mount for an unbearable amount of time. She knew now why some cowboys were bowlegged. She figured she'd never walk normally again. Despite the wool blanket she had wrapped tightly around her body, her feet and fingers were numb with cold.

"They're getting mighty close. Don't you think of doing nothing now, miss," Roger warned.

Hanlon stopped his horse. "Maybe we ought to split up again. We may have a better chance to slip away unnoticed."

Ned and Orville looked at Lisa who yawned back at them. "We're not leaving her with Roger," they both said.

Hanlon glared at Lisa. "I ought to shoot you right now for the trouble you've been."

"Give it up, mister." She twisted a curl of hair with her finger and tossed it aside. "You know they're going to catch you anyway."

Hanlon narrowed his eyes at her. "You wish, Missy, but you ain't getting off that easy. We're heading east now, men, to that cave down yonder." He nodded in the direction. "Holed up there, we can fight off a whole cavalry regiment, if need be."

Roger smiled at Lisa and reached over to pull a twig from her hair. "You can rest there."

She glanced back at the woods. Would they come for her in time?

CHAPTER 22

Jack and Matthew and the posse headed in the direction that more of the outlaws had taken.

"We're getting close now." Matthew pointed at horse hair snagged on a tree branch.

Jack was sure of it, too, from the evidence of the fresh horse droppings along the trail.

"Look." Frank freed the purple fabric from a branch.

Jack examined it, then squeezed it in his hand. "It's Lisa's. She's got to be with this bunch and freezing out here." That wasn't the least of his worries. All he could hope for was that if they had her, they were too busy fleeing from the posse to take advantage of her. At some point they had to rest and...

"They'll have blankets for her, Jack."

"She won't need a blanket," one of the men said.

Jack glared at the man. If he said one more thing...

"Stop riling my brother. Can't you see how he's taking it?"

"Sorry," the man said.

"No harm's been done." But Jack couldn't settle the anxiousness and anger stirring him to do battle.

"There's nothing we can do here, boys. Let's get a move on. Maybe we can soon catch up with the rest of the gang," the sheriff said.

Jack sat straighter in his saddle and peered into the gloom. His waning hope was renewed. "She's really out there, Matthew. Now we know for sure."

"Whatever you do, don't shoot at the woman," Matthew said to the other men.

"Isn't there a cave around here somewhere?" Frank asked.

"Yeah, there is. In fact, during the War we holed up in it when a blue norther hit," Jack said.

"Yeah, that's the one."

The sheriff led the posse in the direction of the cave.

Matthew leaned over to Jack. "No heroics. I'd hate for you to get killed just when we're rescuing your fair damsel."

At least Jack's optimism was returning. But he wasn't playing it safe if it meant getting Lisa out of harm's way as soon as he could.

The sun peeked through the oaks while one of the men waved for the others to halt. He pointed at the cave where they heard men's voices echoing off the walls. The men dismounted.

"What's the plan?" Matthew asked.

"Maybe we can wait them out. They can't have enough provisions among them to keep them going for long," Frank said.

"But Lisa," Jack said. Hell, no way was he waiting

this out.

Matthew looked at him. "We can't be rushing that place. It'd be suicide."

"I can't leave Lisa to those men. Is there another way in?" Jack asked. He couldn't wait a second longer. If they were bedded down for the night...what would keep them from—

"No, not that I recall."

"I'm going to take a look around the backside of the cave." Jack wasn't waiting.

"I'll go with you." Matthew hurried after him.

"We'll sit tight here, boys. Be careful," the sheriff warned.

Matthew and Jack skirted around the back of the cave and started the climb to the top. When they reached the ridge, they began to search every inch for some kind of an opening.

"Here," Matthew whispered, pointing to the earth a few feet away. "This looks like something."

Jack knelt down and dug away at the rock covered dirt. He took a deep breath to smooth his ragged nerves and fought the fear raging in him as his concern for Lisa's welfare grew. Fighting in the War had never been as tough as this. "Looks like a narrow hole."

Matthew examined the opening. "It's not big enough for a man to fit through."

"No, but we may be able to smoke them out." Jack paused as he thought he heard voices. He put his ear to the opening and listened.

"What do you hear, Jack?"

Jack waved his hand at Matthew to be silent. Matthew stood on one foot then the other. "Come on, Jack. Let me hear."

***

The soft glow of a single fire illuminated the dark cave and in the light Lisa stood with Orville, his hand gripping her arm.

Hanlon snapped, "Ned, you take first watch while we get some shut-eye. Orville you're next and Roger's after that."

Orville pushed Lisa deeper into the cave. She fought the urge to slug him back. She was tired and hurt with aching muscles from riding the horse and running through the woods. Her injured shoulder pained her clear through to her heart, and she feared the worst for Jack. Even if the posse freed her, could she help them find Jack? She had no idea where she'd been or where she was now. "You come away from the entrance to the cave, Missy, so you won't get no ideas while we're sleeping. Besides," he said, glancing at Ned, "you won't distract him none that way." He took a rope and tied her wrists.

Lisa struggled with him. "You don't have to do that, mister." She wasn't planning on sleeping. First chance she got, she was making her escape.

Orville smiled. "Maybe not, but I ain't taking any chances. Here you can have my bedroll. It's a might softer than Billy's." He spread the bedding on the floor and laid Billy's bedding next to hers and smiled at her.

"No, ya' don't," Hanlon said. "Everyone needs to get some sleep tonight." He picked up Orville's bedding and tossed it across the cave. "You and Roger sleep over there. I'll stay with the woman to see that no one gets any ideas."

Lisa was relieved in part. She didn't think Hanlon had any interest in her. If he tried anything, he'd have a fight on his hands with his men. She was sure Orville or the others would have sneaked under her skirt in no time in the dark cave if Hanlon hadn't stayed with her. At least for now, no one would mess with her. She hoped.

***

Jack's neck tensed. He didn't want to leave her for even a second. If he could just see where Hanlon had taken her...

"Come on, Jack," Matthew whispered, tugging at his arm. "Let's get some of that kerosene and smoke them out." Matthew dragged him away from the hole. "You won't do her any good just staying here."

Jack stared at the hole and nodded, although his heart wasn't in it. He dropped his jacket next to the opening to mark the place. His brother was right. He had no time to lose in freeing her. The sunlight poked its gentle rays across the rugged landscape as Jack and Matthew crunched through the woods to the posse's location. "Did you find anything?" Frank asked, running to meet them.

"They're in there all right. They've got Lisa. We might be able to smoke 'em out." Jack's voice was a mixture of enthusiasm and anger. He yanked his blanket roll off his horse while Matthew hurried to get his own.

Frank pulled his blanket from his horse and handed it to Jack. "Here, take mine."

"And mine," another of the men said, tugging at his.

After collecting a couple of lamps, Frank held them out to Matthew. "Good luck. We'll be waiting for 'em."

"Be careful about Lisa." Jack turned to Matthew.

380

"Come on. Let's get this over."

Jack and his brother dashed back through the woods to the hill. They struggled up the steep incline with their supplies, their breathing forced. When they reached the top, they searched for the hole.

The sole of Jack's boot touched the softness of his jacket. "Here it is," he whispered. He dropped to his knees and put his ear to the hole while Matthew soaked the first blanket with kerosene.

"What's happening?"

"I don't hear a sound. They must've gone to sleep." Jack was relieved. If someone was messing with her, she would have cried out. Jack yanked his jacket back on.

He lighted his wool blanket and shoved the burning fabric through the opening. The blanket burned unnoticed in the cave, lighting up the cave a speck.

Matthew soaked the second blanket and lighted it. Jack slipped it through the hole and the additional light caught the guard's attention.

"Hey!" the guard shouted. "They're trying to smoke us out!"

The men jumped up and started to cough while they stomped on the burning blankets. "I can't get them out, Ned," another man shouted.

Jack threw the third blanket into the cave hitting the outlaw on the back. "Get it off me!" he screamed, his wool shirt catching fire.

Ned tossed his bedding around the other's shoulders and pulled him to the floor. "You all right, Orville?"

Lisa coughed and ran through the smoke filling the cavern, heading for the cave entrance. Jack's heart plummeted when he saw her. Don't anyone shoot her, he silently pleaded.

Ned grabbed her around the waist when she tried to slip by him. "No, you don't!"

Damnation!

Ned bolted through the opening holding Lisa in front of him. "Don't shoot! I'm coming out, and I've got the girl!"

"Don't shoot, or you'll hit the girl!" one of the members of the posse yelled.

The other outlaws ran out of the smoke-filled cave and fired their guns at random. With the popping and cracking of gunfire filling the air, Ned dragged Lisa to his horse tethered several yards away in the woods near the backside of the cave.

When he reached his mount, he threw her over his saddle like a sack of grain. He climbed into the leather while she wriggled to be free. "Be still!" He kicked his horse to a gallop.

"You can't...get away...with me...like this," Lisa said, coughing, then squinted her eyes as they burned with smoke and the rough ground passed beneath her. "I'll slow you down! Let me go!" Even worse than riding with her legs spread over the saddle of Billy's horse, was having her ribs pummeled. She'd never hurt so bad in her life.

"They won't shoot me if I've got you, Missy. We'll make it."

The posse had come for her...well for the outlaws and she could have kicked herself for letting Ned get ahold of her again. Maybe since he only held her hostage, she still had a chance. He had to sleep some time. At least a small flame of hope sparked deep inside her.

***

Matthew and Jack fired at the scampering villains from their lofty location at the top of the hill. The outlaws dropped behind an outcropping of rocks near the cave entrance. "Jack, one of them is taking off with Lisa!" Matthew shouted and pointed at the rider escaping to the south.

Jack stumbled down the hill, then bolted for his horse.

"Wait up!" Matthew yelled, scrambling down the rocky slope after him.

A shot fired, clipping Jack's hat. He ducked and scooted into the woods. When he reached his horse, he jumped into the saddle, then turned his horse toward the cave. He wasn't waiting for Matthew or any of the others to help. There wasn't any way he was letting the outlaw get very far with Lisa. He kneed his horse and Matthew passed him by, running for his own mount.

"Wait up, Jack!" Matthew shouted again.

Jack galloped straight through the path of the crossfire. He ignored the gunfire. Lisa was all that mattered.

"Crazy fool!" one of the deputies shouted. He fired at one of the outlaws who stood to take better aim at Jack.

The man cried out when the bullet entered his thigh. He fell to the ground. Twisting his body in a crouch, he fired at Jack.

He missed him, and Orville shouted, "I'm out of bullets, Hanlon!"

"Here!" the other man yelled and threw some ammunition to him.

TERRY SPEAR

Hanlon fired again. "If we make it out of here alive, Ned's a dead man."

Good, if the men were running out of ammunition, the posse would have an easy time of it. But for Jack, taking down the outlaw who held Lisa hostage was a might more sensitive situation. He tore around the hill and galloped after the diminishing sight of Ned and Lisa. When he drew closer, he yanked his horse to a stop, then aimed.

The bullet hit him in the shoulder and Ned cried out, "Damnation! I thought the gang would hold them." He pulled his horse to a halt, dragged Lisa off it, and waited for Jack.

"Lisa!" Jack tugged at his horse's reins. He aimed high and fired again.

"Jack!" Lisa screamed and collapsed to her knees. My God, he was alive.

Ned lost his grip on her and aimed at Jack, but Jack fired again and shot him in the chest. She dashed for Jack as Ned dropped to the ground. Leaning on his elbow, Ned steadied his weapon again.

"No, Lisa!" Jack shouted as she ran into his line of sight. "Get down!"

She turned to face Ned, and he smiled smugly at her. "You're mine, Missy." He squeezed the trigger as a shot rang out.

Lisa screamed, but the bullet fired into the ground, and Ned fell over dead. Before she could turn to see Jack, he lifted her off the ground and pulled her into the saddle. He squeezed her tightly and kissed her cheek. She was his and he'd never let her go. He was a mess and so was she, but none of that mattered. Dust caked his tanned cheeks and his smile wrinkled the pancakes.

384

She figured she must have looked a sight. Then she turned her attention to the surrounding land.

"Where did the shot come from, Jack?"

"There." He pointed at the bearded man sitting astride his horse on a grassy knoll a ways off.

"For Billy!" the man shouted, turned and disappeared behind the hill.

"Billy's pa," Lisa said under her breath, recognizing the rugged outlaw, his gray beard making him appear older than he probably was.

Jack looked at her. "Who?"

"It doesn't make any difference." She was with Jack again and nothing else mattered. She held her tied wrists up to him.

He smiled. "Seems you're always tied up, Lisa." He cut the rope that bound her wrists and noticed the bloodied neckerchief tied to her shoulder. "What happened to your shoulder?"

"A cougar scratched me."

"We'll get that tended to." He frowned.

"How's your head?"

"It's been better."

"What's wrong, Jack?"

"It is Lisa, isn't it?"

Lisa squeezed his hands wrapped around her waist. "Yes." She looked back at the grassy knoll. "Hopefully, Josephine is laid to rest now with her family." She touched his bloodied temple. "Are you really all right?"

"Just a scratch. Come on, I've got to help Matthew and the others. I'll leave you off right before we reach the cave. I don't want to take you back into the middle of all the shooting."

Her heart filled with panic. "You can't leave me

alone out here. There may be more of them."

He kissed her lips and squeezed her tightly. His tenderness warmed her all the way through to the bone. After all she'd been through, he sure felt good. But when he kicked his horse to a gallop and drew close to the cave, her body tensed. The gunfire ceased. He held her firmly, slowing to a canter, and she clung to him like moss to a rock. When they reached the site, several of the posse were mounting their horses to come to his aid. At the mouth of the cave lay the dead outlaws, and Lisa looked away, tears filling her eyes.

Jack pressed her close and kissed her cheek.

Matthew rode over to them with his bloodied arm dangling at his side. "I see you got her back," he said beaming. "What happened to you, Josephine? Are you all right?"

"I'll be all right. And the name's Lisa," she said, her voice showing her irritation. If one more person called her Josephine...

Matthew shook his head. "That'll take some getting used to."

"Are you all right, Matthew?" Jack pointed to his brother's arm.

"It's nothing but a scratch. Looks bad though. I'll swing over to Mary Lou's and show her. She'll feel so sorry for me, she'll be sure to marry me."

Jack laughed. "You sure you're all right?"

"Yeah, it doesn't hardly hurt."

One of the posse hollered, "Why don't you fellas take the girl on into town. You can let them know what happened here. We'll clean up this mess."

"I think it's about time to go home now." Jack glanced at Lisa. "What do you think?"

She snuggled tight against him. The scent of his cologne and the warmth of his body intoxicated her. "Yes, now that you're here with me."

"Maybe we can have a double-wedding!" Matthew said smiling.

She raised a brow. "Have you asked the girl if she'll marry you, Matthew?"

"Well, no—"

"I haven't been properly asked."

"Well, if the lady of my dreams wouldn't keep vanishing..." Jack kicked his horse to a canter and followed Matthew. "Are you sure you're going to make it all right, Matthew? We'll follow you into town, but I don't want you passing out."

"Not me. For your information, Lisa, I'm asking Mary Lou to marry me as soon as I get to town."

She smiled and leaned her head against Jack's chest.

"We'll have to get you a new wardrobe, Lisa." Jack glanced down at her torn clothes. "If you're going to be around for a while."

"I'll be around." She looked up at him. His dark brown eyes met her gaze, and he touched his lips to hers. The warmth of his velvety lips sent a tingling of pleasure through her weary body. She was ready for him to take her right here in the woods if he'd wanted to. When his horse paused to nibble grass, Matthew turned back.

Jack kissed Lisa hard against the mouth while she leaned back in his arms and her whole body warmed. She didn't have any need for blankets with him around.

His mouth trailed down her neck and Matthew said, "Hey, you two, that can wait for later."

"Giddy-up," Jack said. "You sure know how to ruin a fella's pleasure, Matthew."

When they approached the outskirts of town, several of the townsfolk ran at them from all directions.

Boys wide-eyed shouted, "Did you get them, mister? Did you get them outlaws? They all dead?"

The blond-bearded owner of the nearest mercantile ran out into the street and shouted, "Matthew, my son!" He helped Matthew down from his horse. "Why don't you come on in and we'll get you fixed right up. Somebody fetch the doctor for this young hero."

A woman dashed out of the store, her blue eyes wide as she shrieked to see Matthew injured. Lisa stared at the woman. "Pauline," she whispered, her eyes welling with tears at seeing the resemblance.

"Mary Lou," Jack said. "I thought the same thing after I had met your friend."

"Oh! Matthew, oh you poor thing. Oh, Daddy, we can't let him die! He's so pale." Mary Lou grabbed Matthew's arm.

Her father took his other, and they helped him to the store. Matthew glanced back at Jack and Lisa and smiled.

Jack shook his head and headed for the ranch. "He sure has them bamboozled."

She sighed. "Do you think Esmeralda will think it's okay? I mean, do you think it's all right for me to stay here?"

"After all you've been through, Lisa, how do you feel?"

"I'd go through it all again to be with you."

He raised his dark brows as they neared the ranch. "You don't want to ever go back?"

"I couldn't even if I wanted to. I buried the amethyst necklace with Josephine to make sure she could rest in peace."

"How did you find—"

"Oh, Jack, it's a long story and—"

Jack rode through the gates, and Esmeralda rushed out of the house to greet them, her brow furrowed. "Where's Matthew?"

"He's getting hitched to Mary Lou, I suspect. Do you think you can make another dress, a hundred dresses, for Lisa?"

Lisa slid off Jack's horse.

"Are you staying for good, dear?" Esmeralda touched Lisa's cheek. "You'll be good for Jack." She put her hand around her shoulder and walked her into the house. "Let's get you taken care of." She touched Lisa's arm. "Cougar, was it?"

Lisa glanced back at Jack, who smiled at her.

"I'll be in the house in a bit after I take care of my horse."

After Lisa washed and changed into a pale ivory gown of Esmeralda's, Jack joined her in the parlor. He wrapped his arms around her, her back to his chest. She touched the photo they had taken in Waco, resting with other photos of Jack's family on the mantle. Jack and her smiling faces tickled her, and she squeezed his arms tighter around her waist. He nuzzled her neck with his face.

He cleared his throat. "Don't let Esmeralda know, but you look even lovelier in that dress than—"

"I heard that!" Esmeralda shouted from the kitchen.

Lisa and Jack laughed.

He turned her and held her hands, kissing them both. "While she's preparing dinner, would you like to take a walk in the gardens?"

"Yes, I'd love to, Jack."

He led her outside and when they arrived at the bench nestled among the rose bushes, Lisa sat. Jack fumbled in his pocket, then knelt before her. "I was afraid I'd lost it in all that riding." He held the gold ring out, the sunlight sparkling off its smooth surface. "Lisa, when I lost Charlotte, I thought she was the only woman for me. I thought how cruel life was when I'd lost my parents when I was young, then again when I lost Charlotte. I never believed I could find anyone else to love, but when I met you, I knew I could love again."

"I felt the same way, Jack. I really loved Barry, but when the relationship ended, I didn't think I'd ever feel that way for anyone else. I realized he wasn't good for me, like you are." She touched Jack's cheek with a gentle caress. "At first, I didn't know how to break the spell Josephine held over me. I assumed I had to find her body and have her buried properly. Billy, one of the outlaws, shot the manager and the owner of the hotel near the cave where they had taken Josephine's body. Billy promised to help me bury Josephine, if..." She looked away from Jack's watchful eyes.

"If you went willingly with him?" He stood.

She looked up at him. "I had to put Josephine to rest or I would have become her. I'd have never seen you again as Lisa. I didn't know what else to do. Billy wouldn't have released me no matter what I did. I had no choice in the matter."

"I know, Lisa." He leaned over and kissed her temple.

"We buried Josephine and the amulet, which seemed to break the spell."

Jack frowned. "The man on the hill who shot the outlaw who tried to shoot you?"

"Billy's pa. He released me after Billy was shot, then I wound up in the hands of some of the rest of his gang." She reached for Jack's hand and held it tight.

Jack pulled Lisa up from her seat and embraced her. "I went to get my horse at the livery. When I returned, you were gone."

He touched her hair draping freely over her shoulders. "Shots rang out, the jailhouse exploded, and all devil broke loose. The sheriff quickly deputized a bunch of us, one said the men had taken you hostage, and we took off after them."

He ran his fingers over her neck. She tilted her head back and parted her lips for him. He pressed his mouth against hers, and she returned the kiss.

"Will you marry me? If you say no, I will surely die."

She kissed him deeply. He pulled her waist in to meet his, pressing her against his body hard.

"Oh, Jack, I can't let you die."

Fast-paced footsteps clapped on the brick path leading to the garden as Jack's housekeeper, her gray-streaked raven curls dangling loose from her bun, ran toward them. "This was sent to you, Lisa, by special messenger." Handing the box to Lisa, Esmeralda was nearly out of breath.

The tension returned to Jack's tired face, and he seemed to dread the delivery as much as Lisa did.

Since she wasn't Josephine and no one in Salado believed she was some other woman named Lisa, receiving a delivery from anyone in town didn't make any sense. Her fingers trembling, she untied the ribbon from the box. When she opened the lid, she gasped, and felt lightheaded and nauseated. The amethyst necklace shimmered in the sunlight.

Bumping heads, Jack and Esmeralda peered into the box.

Lisa swayed unsteadily, and Jack slipped his arm securely about her waist. "My God."

"What does it mean?" she whispered. She envisioned Josephine's bones clawing their way out of the freshly dug earth and coming for her—Josephine's spirit intending to live in Lisa's body for the rest of her life.

Without hesitating, Esmeralda lifted the necklace from the box. "It means Josephine wants you to have the necklace. The amethyst she treasured from her mother was meant to bring her luck. The necklace brought you to her and to Jack. You're meant to have it."

Lisa couldn't shake loose of the worry Josephine would again try to take over her body and soul. "But—"

Esmeralda's eyes sparkled like black quartz, and she tucked a wayward curl behind her ear. "Not accepting her gift would be bad luck."

Apprehensively, Lisa fingered the amethyst stone but couldn't feel anything evil. "All right," she conceded, not wanting to press her luck if Esmeralda was right. Yet the fact remained, Lisa had buried it with Josephine's body. Who had removed it?

A shiver of trepidation ran up her spine.

Jack fastened the necklace around her neck, the gold chain cold against her skin.

Touching it, Lisa felt oddly connected. "I feel like I've found an old lost friend." Still she trembled deep inside. Who had returned it? Someone had to have dug Josephine's body up to retrieve it. Who would have done such a thing?

Another wave of worry swamped her. Was that why Josephine haunted her in the woods? Because Josephine's body had been exhumed for a time? What if she still wasn't at rest?

She would come for Lisa again as sure as the sun would rise tomorrow morning.

"Are you all right?" Jack asked.

"Yes, yes…I'm fine."

He took a deep breath and reached for her hand. "Will you marry me?"

"Yes, Jack. With all my heart, yes, I'll marry you!" Lisa said with so much enthusiasm, Jack smiled and Esmeralda stifled a chuckle.

Never intending to return to her world again, Lisa prayed Josephine couldn't control her any longer. She couldn't face going back to her own world and living without Jack and his family or Pauline. What if her boss, the murdering bastard, wasn't locked away for good? What if the courts, in their infinite wisdom, released him on a technicality, and he came to get her because she'd gotten his confession on tape for the FBI?

He'd murder her just like he did his brother-in-law and Pauline, just like he'd intended to do to her before the accident.

Jack was the best thing that had ever happened to Lisa. She was finally going to have a real family…a loving husband, a brother, and Esmeralda, who treated her like a daughter when she hadn't had a mother or father in so long.

She realized then Jack was kissing her, lifting her off her feet by the waist, and swinging her around, though careful of her injured shoulder, which she'd barely noticed until now with all the excitement. "Thank God, Lisa, you make me proud."

She gave a weary laugh, the time she'd spent in the woods without sleep finally catching up to her. "You're making me dizzy," she said, knowing beyond a doubt Jack was the one for her.

Lowering her back to the ground, he eyed her suspiciously. "Lisa?" He pocketed the ring and reached up to touch her face.

"Yes, oh yes." She pulled him close and held on tight to his hard body, loving him from the minute she'd met him, truly her guardian angel. "For now and always." At least she hoped so, hoped nothing more could go wrong. With Josephine at rest, what *could* go wrong? Unless Josephine's spirit still wasn't at peace.

Taking her hand in his, Jack asked, "Would you consider it too sudden if we wed this evening?"

"Oh no, Jack. Do we have to wait that long? I feel as though we've already waited for years." Lisa would fight Josephine with every ounce of strength she had. She would not leave Jack again.

He shook his head and pushed his Stetson back off his forehead. "I don't want to lose you again." His brow furrowed, he faced Esmeralda. "You don't have any bad premonitions about this, do you?"

"No, Jack. I see only good can come of this union."

"I'm glad you feel that way as nothing will tear me away from Lisa this time. Shall we see to the Reverend

Wilson then?"

Without waiting for Lisa's response, Jack hastened her to the stable where Spirit whinnied in greeting. "Yeah, boy, we've got another mission," he said, running his hand over the horse's muzzle.

Lisa hoped she could learn to ride well and be as comfortable with horses as Jack was. She guessed she was bound to learn one way or another, living in his world.

He bridled Spirit, then slipped his saddle over his back when the sound of a lone horse galloping onto the ranch got her attention.

Jack hurried her outside of the barn and they found Josephine's old beau, Frank, his face as red as his hair, headed for them at breakneck speed.

"He looks as agitated as the time the Union soldiers were hot on our heels when we'd gotten separated from our unit during fighting in Louisiana."

Which didn't bode well. Her skin chilled in eerie anticipation.

"The Rogers brothers are coming, and they're hopping mad!" Frank hollered. "They claim Josephine's got to return with them now or all hell will break loose. I've sent word to the sheriff to have him join us because there's bound to be a heap of trouble."

CHAPTER 23

Later that night while buried under the covers of Jack's bed, he tackled Lisa for the third time, and she squealed out in surprise. "Jack," she whispered and squirmed under his naked body. They'd wake Matthew and Esmeralda for sure at this rate.

She couldn't see a thing as dark as the room was only felt his kisses while he plied his warm lips against her eyelids and her cheeks. Then he pressed firmly against her mouth, and she ran her fingers along the firm contours of his back. His spicy scent and the heaviness of his writhing body on top of her intoxicated her as he plunged deep inside of her, as if to claim her for all the centuries they'd been apart. She hadn't had more than a couple of hours of sleep and every time his hands had tangled in her hair after brief bouts of slumber, he'd pull her underneath him and begin the lovemaking all over again.

And she loved it. Every time he brought her to the top, filling her with the exquisite rush of a climax, she knew just how right being with him was. She could tackle all the challenges in her new life as long as she had Jack to love her like this.

Coming up for air, he nuzzled her face with his whiskery cheek and said, "You're just too delicious to waste much sleep over."

She chuckled. "But we're making entirely too much noise. Poor Esmeralda and Matthew..." He ran his tongue down her neck, tickling her, and she giggled.

"Nothing wakes Matthew before first light. And Esmeralda, nothing could please here more." He licked her ear. "You taste so sweet."

She moaned when he took her nipple in his mouth again, tonguing it, kissing, and licking. She speared her fingers through his hair, and arched her pelvis as he thrust even deeper.

Then he groaned, calling her name softly, "Lisa," and sank down on top of her, her inner muscles clenching with delicious spasms.

He rolled off her and gathered her in his arms and drifted off to sleep. She couldn't, not with still enjoying the afterglow. She stroked his arm, nuzzling her face against his chest, her leg propped possessively over his.

Tomorrow, breakfast was going to be an embarrassing affair, she just knew it. For now, she was going to give into the minute and nibbled on his ear, ran her fingernail lightly over his nipple, and then licked it, intending to wake *him* up this time.

***

When she awoke the next morning, the bed was empty, and Lisa realized at once everyone must have risen early to do chores. She wasn't used to this part of her new life. Of course, Jack's disturbing her sleep so much the night before hadn't helped either. Poor thing. He had to be half worn out also.

She hurried out of bed to dress and laughed when she found her lacy bra hanging off the armoire, probably tossed there when Jack had hurried to unwrap her from her numerous garments after they were hastily married last night. She wondered what he thought of her wearing the bra. There was no way she'd wear the corset any longer.

After dressing, she hastened down the hall while coffee mugs clanked and forks scraped against clay plates. Her cheeks warmed when everyone looked up from the table. Matthew and Esmeralda both grinned at her. Jack who wore the same silly expression. His ranch hands all greeted her with the same smug expressions.

"Sorry." She hurried to take her seat and knew her cheeks had to have been brilliant red as hot as they now felt. "I must have overslept a tad from having had no sleep the night before."

"Or last night either," Matthew said winking.

She could see this wasn't going to be easy. Jack reached over and patted her hand. "Sleep well?"

"When?"

Matthew laughed out loud and Esmeralda shook her head at him and passed a bowl of eggs to Lisa.

"I mean, yes." God, she wasn't handling the situation well at all.

"After Jack got up," Matthew said, "I imagine. I mean, with no one to disturb your sleep."

Jack socked him in the arm. "You'll get your turn. Just remember."

All the men at the table chuckled.

Jack to the rescue only he was adding to the fun. It

wasn't that she minded Matthew's playfulness, only the topic of their circus performances wasn't something she wished to deal with first thing in the morning and certainly not in front of a whole mess of ranch hands, as nice as they were, or Jack's brother and Esmeralda either.

Jack seemed totally content. Macho male, kind of thing.

She served up some eggs, then set the bowl aside. Jack handed her a plate of rolls, his hand brushing hers. Her whole body warmed with his tenderness, but a hint of desire just simmered beneath the surface. After setting her bun on her plate, she scooped up a forkful of eggs. "Please, just wake me when everyone gets up in the morning."

Matthew snickered.

Esmeralda leaned over and took her hand in hers. "You're new to our ways, dear. You've been injured and had a terrible ordeal with the outlaws and the like. Just make Jack happy, and everything else will fall into place."

Jack winked at her. Making Jack happy was sure an easy task. She hadn't seen Matthew so lighthearted in the brief time she'd known him. Esmeralda, too, wore a new aura of warmth as if she'd just taken a daughter under her wing. Even their ranch hands seemed happy with the new arrangements.

Lisa took a deep breath of relief. Getting up at the crack of dawn definitely wasn't her cup of tea. So the notion that nobody minded her casually adjusting to the normal routine cheered her. This was the family she'd only dreamed of having and the notion of living here forever couldn't have worked out better.

"So what is the schedule today?" She buttered a potato roll.

"Mending fences," Jack said. "Matthew and some of our hands will be working the fences today."

"Oh. Well, what did you need me to do?"

"Rest, Lisa. Esmeralda is right. You still look rather peeked from your ordeal. Your shoulder needs to heal and you should get plenty of rest."

"I'll say." Matthew grabbed another roll. "Dark gets here before you know it, and then everyone's tucked under their covers and trying to get a good night's sleep again."

Esmeralda chuckled this time, and Lisa knew Jack's late night maneuvers had kept everyone awake last night, although the ranch hands slept in the bunkhouse. At least they were good-natured enough to just laugh about it.

After breakfast, Jack walked Lisa back into his bedroom. "I'm serious about you getting rest. Esmeralda handles the household chores. When you're feeling better you can look at the books and later we can talk about a store, but for now I want you to return to bed."

His concern and tenderness touched her, but the notion of returning to bed so soon after she had just gotten up was unthinkable. "I'm really not tired. Maybe later."

"All right, but Esmeralda is under strict orders to limit your activities."

"Yes, boss," she teased.

He pulled her close and his dark eyes grew darker. "I didn't hurt you last night, did I?"

If that was hurting, she wanted lots more of it. She

smiled at him. "I never knew having a husband could be so rewarding."

He kissed her mouth with affection, then pulled away, but her whole body was already desirous of fulfilling what he'd begun with his simple kiss, promising much more. His pistol was already willing, and her holster was ready to accommodate.

"Work's got to be done. I've been rather neglecting the place with trying to make you my wife."

"I love you, Jack."

"Love you too, honey." He kissed her passionately this time and moaned when she kissed him back with determination. If he wasn't going to make love to her, she could at least give him something to remember her by while he worked on the fences. "Try that again, tonight," he said, then smiled and hurried off to join his brother.

***

Jack and Matthew inspected the western fences while the rest of his men checked the others for several hours. Just before lunchtime he asked Matthew, "I know you've been avoiding talking to me about this, but what's going on between you and Mary Lou?"

"Well, you know how it goes with us. One day she likes me and the next she's ready to dump me in the creek again."

"What did you say to her this time?"

Matthew shrugged his shoulders. "Just that I wished she was more like Lisa."

"What?"

"You know...the two of you never fight. Lisa just kept vanishing is all. And then there was the problem with Josephine, but the two of you were made for each other like the tip of a boot to a stirrup. Mary Lou and I...why we just clash."

Jack shook his head. "You shouldn't have told Mary Lou you wished she was more like Lisa."

"I like Mary Lou the way she is except I wish we wouldn't fight so much. At this rate, I'll never get her hand in marriage and now there's a new college student who's caught her eye too."

"I don't know what to say." Jack mounted his horse. "I had a devil of a time getting my own filly yoked. I'm afraid this one's your deal."

Matthew jumped into the leather of his saddle. "Yeah, I know. I just thought maybe Lisa might visit with her occasionally and soften her up to liking me better for longer periods of time. I'm really happy for you, so don't get me wrong, but after all that nighttime fun you had with Lisa, I'm ready to have some of that with Mary Lou."

Jack chuckled, then took a deep breath. "I'll speak with Lisa about it. She needs to get to know her cousin and her Uncle Sam better anyway." He wanted his brother to settle down and be happy like he was, and he knew Matthew had his heart set on Mary Lou, but sometimes he just wasn't convinced she was the right girl for him.

They rode back to the house for lunch and Matthew said, "You must be kind of tired too."

Jack raised a brow at his brother. "Just a tad. Thought I might turn in a bit early tonight."

Matthew laughed. "Only way you're going to get any sleep is if you retire to the guest room...alone."

After taking care of their horses, Jack and Matthew hastened to the house. When they found only

Esmeralda in the kitchen, Jack grew concerned. Esmeralda's brown eyes sparkled with humor. "She's resting. She showed me some beautiful stitches to add to that quilt I've been working on for so long. In fact, for several hours, she worked on it herself. Plum tuckered her out. I finally had to insist she lie down before she curled up in the parlor and fell asleep."

He turned on his heels and headed out of the kitchen.

"Let her rest," Esmeralda shouted after him and Matthew's laughter filled the kitchen as his ranch hands entered the dining room to eat.

Jack walked into his bedroom, the velvet curtains drawn, shutting out the light. He pulled them aside so he could observe Lisa, and his heart skipped a beat. Her naked arms folded across the pieced-quilt coverlet while her golden curls stretched down to her blanketed hips. She licked her lips, and before he could think further on the matter he yanked his vest off. Dropping into his chair, he tugged at his boots and hurriedly removed them. Lunch could wait a little longer. Never in his wildest dreams had he thought he'd have neglected his duties over the sight of a woman.

His woman, his love, and his life. Her skin shown like alabaster in the sun-drenched room, and her hidden breasts rose with every gentle sleeping breath she took. She was his to love and to hold.

He tore off his woolen shirt and denim trousers. For a minute, he paused. She was tired and needed her rest...should he wait? Nah. He pulled off his drawers, then slipped under the covers with her, both naked as the day they had arrived into the world. Her murmurs at feeling his hands caressing her breasts excited him further. He ran his hand through her silky strands of hair as her fingers gripped his back, then slipped down to his butt. She pressed him against her with a firm grip sending volumes of desire coursing through him.

This once, his men could get back to mending the fences on their own, and he'd catch up with them.

Lisa's eyes opened dreamily and her lips parted in a smile, then he smothered them with his own. She tasted of the honey she'd coated her rolls with that morning, and her hair was scented with a light fragrance of roses. Never had he expected a woman to stir him so with longings like she did. He'd learned just where to stroke her that had her writhing under his touch, and when she was begging with sweet desire for him to finish her off, he thrust into her as deeply as he could go.

Her body shuddered as she arched her back to meet his thrusts, and he knew he'd satisfied her too. When he filled her with his seed, he gave a self-satisfied groan and held her for a moment more.

He smiled and kissed her cheek, her hair slightly dampened against her face. "It's lunchtime, Lisa," he whispered and nuzzled her cheek.

"Ah, huh." She'd closed her eyes, and he was afraid she was too tired to eat with him.

"Lisa?"

She hummed a satisfied response.

He laughed. "I'm going to get something to eat and have to go back to mending the fences." She ran her hands over his back. "Tonight, we're going to bed as soon as we've had supper."

He rolled off her and she opened her eyes to watch him dress. She inspected every inch of his body and her impish grin made him figure she was well pleased with what she saw. The notion stirred his groin again, and he shook his head. "Everyone has said I'm much too serious a sort."

Lisa laughed. "I never thought you'd make love to me in the middle of the afternoon. I figured the only time you'd do such a thing was at night before you nodded off. Then here you were waking me up all night long and well, if that's being a serious sort...I want all you've got to give. Fact of the matter is I'm rather a serious sort myself. After a night with you...no more serious for me."

Smiling, Jack pulled on his vest and leaned over the bed to kiss her cheek. "I'll tell Esmeralda you're still sleeping."

"Do you think she'll believe us?"

He chuckled. "No. But that's my story."

As soon as Jack left the room, Lisa hurried out of bed. She slipped into her bra and knee length drawers. She'd been afraid to allow Jack to see her dressing as she worried he wouldn't want her to wear her skimpy bra. After pulling on her gown, she sat down on the chair and slipped her boots up her legs. No one had said anything about the fact that her boots had no buttons, but she figured she'd wear them out before long and have to wear what everyone else wore...except for the corset. After she finished dressing, she hurried to the kitchen where not a word was spoken, and she assumed everyone was busy eating.

When she walked into the sunny room, everyone looked at her and smiled. Déjà vu. Her cheeks grew hot just like at breakfast as Jack pulled out her chair and she took a seat. Esmeralda passed her a bowl of potatoes.

Matthew cleared his throat but didn't say anything and the tension killed her. Again, she began the conversation. "Sorry, I'm a bit late for lunch."

Jack chuckled and she could have kicked him under the table. She would have missed lunch entirely if he hadn't awakened her and yet, everyone seemed to know *how* he woke her from her slumber.

Could she ever enjoy being pleasured by her husband without the whole family and his ranch hands knowing? Well, at least she and Jack were enjoying each other's company and everyone seemed pretty pleased.

"Mending more fences this afternoon?" Lisa asked, trying to divert attention away from Jack and her bedroom adventures.

"Yup, but Jack tells me he's rather tired and is hitting the hay right after supper tonight," Matthew said.

She quickly closed her gaping mouth. Her gaze shifted from Matthew to Jack as he scowled at his brother. She assumed Jack had made an offhanded remark to his brother and Matthew was enjoying teasing him over it. Now this was something new she would have to get used to.

Family. She'd never had a real chance at interacting with a family before. Matthew could tease all he wanted, but she was pretty good at the game too. Just wait until he had Mary Lou in wedded bliss. If they needed a little push in that direction, Lisa had an arsenal of feminine notions from the future to share with her newfound cousin that might help the lovebirds tie the knot a little faster.

Then it would be Lisa's turn to tease Matthew.
Just wait. Life couldn't get any better.

ABOUT THE AUTHOR

Bestselling and award-winning author **Terry Spear** has written over sixty paranormal romance novels and seven medieval Highland historical romances. Her first werewolf romance, *Heart of the Wolf,* was named a 2008 *Publishers Weekly*'s Best Book of the Year, and her subsequent titles have garnered high praise and hit the *USA Today* bestseller list. A retired officer of the U.S. Army Reserves, Terry lives in Spring, Texas, where she is working on her next werewolf romance, continuing her new series about shapeshifting jaguars, writing Highland medieval romance, and having fun with her young adult novels. When she's not writing, she's photographing everything that catches her eye, making teddy bears, and playing with her Havanese puppies. For more information, please visit www.terryspear.com, or follow her on Twitter, @TerrySpear. She is also on Facebook at http://www.facebook.com/terry.spear. And on Wordpress at:

Terry Spear's Shifters
http://terryspear.wordpress.com/

ALSO BY TERRY SPEAR

Heart of the Cougar Series:
Cougar's Mate, Book 1
Call of the Cougar, Book 2
Taming the Wild Cougar, Book 3
Covert Cougar Christmas (Novella)
Double Cougar Trouble, Book 4
Cougar Undercover, Book 5
Cougar Magic, Book 6

Heart of the Bear Series
Loving the White Bear, Book 1
Claiming the White Bear, Book 2

The Highlanders Series: Winning the Highlander's Heart, The
Accidental Highland Hero, Highland Rake, Taming the Wild
Highlander, The Highlander, Her Highland Hero, The Viking's
Highland Lass, His Wild Highland Lass (novella), Vexing the
Highlander (novella), My Highlander
Other historical romances: Lady Caroline & the Egotistical Earl, A
Ghost of a Chance at Love

Heart of the Wolf Series: Heart of the Wolf, Destiny of the Wolf,

To Tempt the Wolf, Legend of the White Wolf, Seduced by the Wolf, Wolf Fever, Heart of the Highland Wolf, Dreaming of the Wolf, A SEAL in Wolf's Clothing, A Howl for a Highlander, A Highland Werewolf Wedding, A SEAL Wolf Christmas, Silence of the Wolf, Hero of a Highland Wolf, A Highland Wolf Christmas, A SEAL Wolf Hunting; A Silver Wolf Christmas, A SEAL Wolf in Too Deep, Alpha Wolf Need Not Apply, Billionaire in Wolf's Clothing, Between a Rock and a Hard Place, SEAL Wolf Undercover, Dreaming of a White Wolf Christmas, Flight of the White Wolf, A Billionaire Wolf for Christmas, All's Fair in Love and Wolf, Wolff Brothers: You Had Me at Wolf, Night of the Billionaire Wolf, Red Wolf Christmas

SEAL Wolves: To Tempt the Wolf, A SEAL in Wolf's Clothing, A SEAL Wolf Christmas, A SEAL Wolf Hunting, A SEAL Wolf in Too Deep, SEAL Wolf Undercover, SEAL Wolf Surrender

Silver Town Wolves: Destiny of the Wolf, Wolf Fever, Dreaming of the Wolf, Silence of the Wolf, A Silver Wolf Christmas, Alpha Wolf Need Not Apply, Between a Rock and a Hard Place, All's Fair in Love and Wolf, Silver Town Wolf: Home for the Holidays

Wolff Brothers (New to Silver Town): You Had Me at Wolf

White Wolves: Legend of the White Wolf, Dreaming of a White Wolf Christmas, Flight of the White Wolf

Billionaire Wolves: Billionaire in Wolf's Clothing, A Billionaire Wolf for Christmas, Night of the Billionaire Wolf

Highland Wolves: Heart of the Highland Wolf, A Howl for a Highlander, A Highland Werewolf Wedding, Hero of a Highland Wolf, A Highland Wolf Christmas

Red Wolves: Seduced by the Wolf, Red Wolf Christmas

Heart of the Jaguar Series: Savage Hunger, Jaguar Fever, Jaguar Hunt, Jaguar Pride, A Very Jaguar Christmas, You Had Me at Jaguar

Jaguar Novella: The Witch and the Jaguar

Romantic Suspense: Deadly Fortunes, In the Dead of the Night, Relative Danger, Bound by Danger

Vampire romances: Killing the Bloodlust, Deadly Liaisons, Huntress for Hire, Forbidden Love
Vampire Novellas: Vampiric Calling, The Siren's Lure, Seducing the Huntress

Other Romance: Exchanging Grooms, Marriage, Las Vegas Style

Science Fiction Romance: Galaxy Warrior

Teen/Young Adult/Fantasy Books The World of Fae:
The Dark Fae, Book 1
The Deadly Fae, Book 2
The Winged Fae, Book 3
The Ancient Fae, Book 4
Dragon Fae, Book 5
Hawk Fae, Book 6
Phantom Fae, Book 7
Golden Fae, Book 8
Falcon Fae, Book 9
Woodland Fae, Book 10

The World of Elf:
The Shadow Elf
The Darkland Elf

Blood Moon Series:
Kiss of the Vampire
The Vampire...In My Dreams

Demon Guardian Series:
The Trouble with Demons;
Demon Trouble, Too; Demon Hunter

Non-Series for Now:
Ghostly Liaisons
The Beast Within
Courtly Masquerade Deidre's Secret

The Magic of Inherian:
The Scepter of Salvation
The Mage of Monrovia
Emerald Isle of Mists (TBA)